Davie Mac

Too Young To Die

A BLAKE MORAN NOVEL

Visit the author's website at www.daviemacbooks.com.

Too Young To Die: A Blake Moran Novel

Published by K&D Publishing

Cover and interior design by Nicole Baron Designs

ISBN: 979-8-9855355-0-1 (paperback)
ISBN: 979-8-9855355-1-8 (e-book)
LCCN: 2022901301

Too Young To Die novel word count: 100,761

To my wonderful wife, Kimberly.

I hope this is the start of yet another great adventure for both of us!

DISCLAIMER

This is a work of fiction. Unless otherwise indicated, all the names, characters, businesses, places, events and incidents in this book are either the product of the author's imagination or used in a fictitious manner. Any resemblance to actual persons, living or dead, or actual events is purely coincidental.

PROLOGUE

It was dark outside—it was even dark in the hotel suite; the lights turned down low, while music played.

She needed to get out of here—she'd only agreed to talk, and this guy was starting to seem a little unhinged—he was really starting to creep her out. But when she headed for the door, he grabbed her. She fought with him—he was so strong!

He just picked her up like she was nothing and threw her on the bed. She opened her mouth to scream, but he put his hand over her mouth so she couldn't.

What was happening?! She had only agreed to come here to tell him that it was over and that he needed to leave her alone!

She realized that he was trying to rape her!

This could *not* be happening to her! She fought with all her strength, scratching and clawing him, but he was too strong. She fought harder and he started slamming her against the bed. Then her head was hitting the headboard, over and over. She fought for consciousness, but she lost the fight.

When she was coming to, not only did her head hurt, but she felt cold and wet. She regained consciousness and saw that she was now naked, and he was putting her into the full bathtub.

She was disoriented—what was happening?

Then she realized—he was trying to kill her. She started fighting again, clawing and scratching, but he was so much bigger and stronger than her—he just looked down at her, almost sorrow on his face, as he held her down under the water with one hand pressing on her chest.

She kept fighting, but little by little she just couldn't. Slowly, she felt it ending. Her last thought was that she hoped that just maybe she would now get to see her parents again.

And then it was just over.

Too Young To Die

CHAPTER

— 1 —

Hey, my name is Blake—Blake Moran—nice to meet you. Yes, I'm aware of the unfortunate initials my name creates—you think that's the first time I've had *that* pointed out to me? That's why I usually include my middle name—Winchester. That look on your face makes me think that maybe you're not convinced that helps—but what can I say, my old man was into guns and old westerns—so how about you cut me some slack? And yes, I know that we can have the whole enchilada by changing just one letter of my last name—"moron"—got it, grew up with it, will be in therapy someday because of it. Real funny. Are we done? Can we move on now?

Enough about that, now about me: I'm currently in my early 30s, in that shadowy valley between that "be all you can be" and that "dang, I feel *old*!" I'm fightin' the years like everybody else—exercising some and eating halfway decent about half the time—so far, so good. I'm about 6 feet, 4 inches tall and just over 200 pounds—depending on the time of year. I have dark hair that pretty much goes in lots of directions at once—so that I get it cut every couple of months, whether I need it or not. Think Italian or Mediterranean—sort of, but not really—and you'll have it. I haven't found *the* girl yet, but not from lack of trying.

Also, I live in Phoenix, Arizona, where the summers can kill you, but the rest of the year is to *die* for!

Everybody has to have a way to turn a buck, so I'm a private investigator. Sounds cool, doesn't it? Yeah, just call me "Sherlock." I guess it's pretty cool, but not *way* cool—at least not all the time. Without getting too technical, I find stuff that tends to be hidden—often stuff that people would prefer stay hidden. You'd be surprised how often you spend a whole lot of boring hours watching for something to happen when nothing is happening. It's only when you realize that you're stuck on a stakeout—and you can't get away, even for a bathroom break—that you curse the foolishness of sucking down that 64-ounce soda from the corner mini-mart. Your 16-ounce bladder refuses to let you forget!

And the paperwork! Sifting for clues through people's bills and letters and trash. Did I say trash? Of course I wouldn't do that! The Internet has helped a lot with the whole investigation side of things, but pretty often you still have to get down and dirty to connect the dots.

Much of the time, the work just isn't very glamorous: background checks for research and development firms, pre-employment investigations, skip traces for small businesses who have been stiffed payment, divorce snooping, "catch 'em in the act," looking for hidden assets to avoid "sharing" with their spouse, searching through marriage licenses or death records looking for genealogical connections, probated wills, property transfers and tax or financial liens on assets down at the county offices. Blah, blah, blah. It's not all laughs and giggles.

But I have to say that this whole P.I. thing suits me—it's about facts, it's about getting to the truth, even when "the bad guy" doesn't want you to figure it out. I like using my head. I'm not necessarily the sharpest knife in the drawer, but I do have a certain "edge" in the old cerebral area. And hey, if I can use that edge to create a little so called "justice" in this world, then why not?

Things had been a little slow lately—the P.I. business tends to be like that. Maybe that's where that "feast or famine" cliché came from. I'd finished up a couple of cases about two weeks earlier, one kind of small, but one was fairly major—I turned some significant coinage on that one. Oh, where would we be without attempted insurance fraud? I did have one ongoing case, the Maxwell Case, but that's pretty much it right now.

So, I was doin' OK, but I had that familiar anxiety of wondering if another case would come stumbling my way or if I'd have to eventually pawn my baseball card collection to feed my fish.

Now, for the record, I don't really have a baseball card collection *or* a fish, but I thought it made the point well, so please just bear with me—I have to make things up—my life just isn't all that interesting.

Since things were so slow, I was sitting in my office working on some of that dreaded paperwork. When I use the word "office," I have to admit that one must use a loose definition of the term. You see, the work I do isn't terribly office oriented, so I don't worry too much about how impressive my digs are to a client. Either that or I'm just cheap to the core and this space is practically a giveaway—it's your choice.

My "office" is actually just two rooms of prime real estate in the industrial section of downtown Phoenix—down the back alley, attached to a cattle feed production factory—my landlord. The factory processes food for lots of varieties of our four-legged friends, not just cattle, and I gotta tell you, you do *not* want to know what goes into those little pellets! Just the aroma that constantly permeates every square inch of my high-powered work area is enough to bring tears to the eyes *and* drop my rent by another couple a hundred a month. So, "silver lining" I guess. Oh yeah, score another one for Blake Winchester Moran; wheeler—dealer—entrepreneur!

Here's the cheap tour: the front room serves as a quasi-reception area—I am just currently missing a receptionist. I'd been through a variety of assistants over the years from the local temp agencies. It almost seemed as though the "offices of Blake Moran" weren't prestigious enough to keep good help—at least not cheap/good help—go figure.

I have to admit that the decorating scheme of the place, along with the aroma, (which might require hazard pay), didn't help. I'd lived in a variety of places growing up, but outside of a damp basement in the mid-west, this was the only place I'd seen that brown, grooved, four by eight feet paneling really *work*! The floor was actually that glue down linoleum that insisted on curling up at various seams throughout the reception area. Then there's the dropped ceiling with a number of tiles with water stains on them, the "print 'em by the thousand" pictures on the walls, the four metal and blue plastic chairs and the metal desk with a decent computer sitting on it guarding the "executive office"—mine. What's not to like?

My office was large enough to contain my "thinking couch," a great place for deep thoughts, and on slow days, even deeper naps. It also had a wall of bookcases with all the appropriate tomes for my profession—although I had yet to come across "Private Investigation for Dummies." Finish it up with a desk, a decent desk chair and two chairs for any clients who would be brave enough to visit my office. You know, when I have to describe it like this, it even makes *me* wonder how I've survived!

OK, on to the case: I'd like to tell you I knew from the beginning how this case was gonna work out—I wish I could tell you that—but I can't. You'd know I was lying, cuz no one could have seen all that was coming. It seemed odd that so much got so weird so quickly, but hey, that's how life goes—sometimes.

But I gotta tell you, that "sometimes" was just getting a little too frequent in my opinion.

But I'm getting ahead of myself. Let me take you back to how it all started—maybe if you get in on the ground floor, the view won't be quite as wacky when we're looking down from the top—at least I hope not.

Any-who, this case all started on a Thursday. Now in general, I typically like Thursdays—they're connected to Friday, so not all that far from the weekend—what's not to like? But this Thursday was different, and not different in a good way. For one thing, it was a Thursday in the Arizona summer where 100 degrees was *way* back in the rear-view mirror!

But as they say, "remember, it's a *dry* heat!"

Uh-huh.

My window air conditioner was blowing like a weekend warrior who just realized that the advertised "run for fun" was mostly *uphill*—but it was still getting the job done. As I transferred data from my iPhone to my computer to complete the final reports and bills from my last jobs, I had the new alternative music station that had sprung up in the valley playing in the background. I didn't like all the music they played, but it at least drowned out the various processing sounds that seeped through the walls. I wish I could say the same thing about the smells.

CHAPTER

— 2 —

So, I'm working away and the phone starts ringing. I don't immediately pick it up because I know Doris will get it. Right before the fourth ring—which will engage the answering machine—I remember Doris isn't with "the firm" anymore—she went all "upwardly mobile" on me and started working a drive-thru window at a fast-food joint.

So, I snatched up the phone, beating the machine. (Score one for "quick draw Moran." Please also note the play off my middle name.) I repeat the obligatory, "Blake Moran Investigations—we find stuff" greeting. OK, so it wasn't like I had an epiphany to come up with that one, but it pretty much told the story. However, by the pause on the other end of the line, I could tell the caller wasn't overwhelmed with confidence by my opening line. Note to self: rethink opening tag line.

I tried again, "Hello?" After another pause, I finally got a "Hello." I don't know how much you pay attention to voices, but this was a pretty cool voice. It sounded like I imagined the voice of God would sound like—at least the voice they would use when they cast God's voice in some movie like *The Ten Commandments*. It was low and vibrant and I'm guessing wishing it *hadn't* called me right about now.

The man went on, "Is this the Blake Moran who investigated the death of Christie Jarvis a few years ago?"

Now that one brought back memories. I'd had a case that I'd done up in Las Vegas a few years back that got lots of press coverage. An attractive news anchor woman had been murdered, but it had been doctored up to pin it on her boyfriend. It had been done well; the dude almost ended up having to take the rap. I was able to uncover a major news story that Ms. Jarvis had been getting ready to pitch to her producer. It was about a big construction company that built casinos, that was also deeply involved in graft and money laundering. Those guys played for keeps because that story cost her, her life. She had been so bent on getting the "exclusive" that she told no one and that secrecy had almost put her boyfriend on death row. I couldn't save Christie, but the truth saved that man—chalk one up for the good guys.

That little bit of nostalgia must have caused me to pause cuz Mr. voice like God said, "Hello?" I snapped out of it and said, "Yeah, I'm here and yep, that's me." When he responded with a "Really?" using that whole incredulous tone thing, I knew I really needed to come up with a different handle for answering the phone.

"Yes, really," I said, trying to convey as much self-confidence with a hint of offense as I could. That seemed to shake him out of it.

"Well, my name is Greg Walker. I'm calling from New York City. I'm an attorney here, and I want to hire you."

Well now I *knew* it wasn't God's voice—I was pretty sure God's name was not Greg. He certainly wouldn't be an attorney, and if He did exist, he wouldn't be hiring *me*!

"The Big Apple huh? That's a long way from Phoenix. Can I ask why me and how you found out about me?"

"I did a search on the Internet for 'private investigators southwest' and the top stories were all about the work you did in Vegas on the Christie Jarvis Case. It made it sound like you were very good at what you do."

I ignored the implied question in that statement—after all, our relationship *did* start out with that "we find stuff" opening.

"OK, I get how you found out about me, but why do you need a Phoenix based investigator in New York?"

"I don't. I need an investigator in Tucson, which looks pretty close to Phoenix."

"Yep, it's just about ninety miles southeast of here." Slipping into my P.I. mode, I grabbed my iPhone and asked, "Is this for a client of yours or for a case you're working on?"

"Neither. It's personal."

The pause that followed was fairly pronounced and I realized that Mr. Walker was fighting for composure.

"I have a sister who lives in Tucson—well actually, I *had* a sister who lived in Tucson for three years. Her name was Kate Walker. Back in January, she was found dead at a local resort. It was clearly engineered to look like an accidental drowning in the bathtub of one of the resort's luxury suites. Kate had some alcohol in her system—but not much, so the idea of being so drunk that she would drown wouldn't work. Apparently, my sister put up quite a fight—she had some bruises on her body from being hit and from being held under the water," he paused again for another composure fight, "and she had somebody's skin under her fingernails."

"I take it that since you say, 'somebody's skin,' they couldn't make a match?"

"I'm sure I don't have to tell you Mr. Moran that DNA is only helpful if you have the perpetrator's DNA to compare it to—they never had that."

"So, what are the Tucson police doing on this case—I know some guys down there and they're pretty good at what they do."

"You're probably right, they're probably very good at what they do, but they're not immune to budget limitations and overworked departments. They've pursued this case for over six months now and while they've made some progress, I'm afraid that this case is starting to find itself on the back burner."

"The inevitable cold case pile, huh?"

"That's what I'm afraid of. Mr. Moran, I loved my sister. Kate had her issues, but who doesn't? Sometimes those issues were with me, but we were siblings—it happens. She didn't deserve to die like this, and I can't just stand by and let somebody kill my little sister and get away with it—that's why I'm calling you."

"Mr. Walker, I'm sorry for your loss and I can pursue this for you if you want, but I've got to tell you, I'm not cheap."

"I wouldn't expect you to be. I do very well here in New York as a corporate attorney, so I can afford to care enough about my sister's death to do something about it. I'm not worried about the money, but I am worried about the time. I'm guessing that the longer this goes unsolved, the colder the trail becomes, so no offense, but are you good?"

Have you ever wondered why people always say, "no offense" right before they offend you?

Me too.

Hearing that awkward silence, he went on, "All I mean is that the article I read was very impressive about how you handled the Jarvis investigation—that wasn't just a fluke was it?"

He might have wanted to insert that "no offense" comment again right before that "fluke" comment—don't you think?

I finally found my voice, "Mr. Walker, if you're asking me if I've ever been able to find my way out of a paper bag all by myself before or after the Jarvis Case, then 'yes,' I do have other cases and specific abilities that indicate I'm 'good.'"

"I've offended you."

"Yep, but that's OK—it's happened before, it'll happen again. And I can hardly blame you—you don't know me except through a couple of articles that you read online and an extremely witty greeting you heard when you called. So, I can hardly blame you—but I'll be honest, I'm petty—so I *do* blame you."

"OK. So, I guess you're not interested."

I started laughing. "Mr. Walker, if I didn't work for anyone who offended me, I'd have to start selling Tupperware to pay the bills—it comes with the territory. I'm not afraid to tell someone when my ever so fragile feelings have been injured, but I'm also not afraid to then take their money and find the answer to their problem—like my greeting said, 'we find stuff.' That's not just an exceptionally clever saying; it's what I love to do. So, we're OK Mr. Walker, I'm just keepin' it real."

"So, you'll do it? Great! What do you need from me to get started?"

"First, I'll give you the information you need to wire me the deposit to get me started—we'll need to start with a $5,000 retainer. I'll keep you up to date with an itemized bill and let you know when that 5K starts to run thin."

"All right."

"Second, I need all the facts you can give me from your perspective, so that I can begin to formulate an idea where to start with this investigation. So, if you've got the time right now, start talking—tell me about Kate."

CHAPTER

— 3 —

Apparently, Greg had time because he didn't miss a beat before telling his family's story.

"OK. Our family lived in the mid-west when we were growing up. There were three kids; I was the oldest son, then my brother Johnnie was three years younger than me and Kate was the youngest and the only daughter—seven years after Johnnie—and was therefore a little spoiled."

"Hold it. Are you telling me you have a brother named Johnny—Johnny Walker?"

"Yes, I am and no, it's not spelled the same as the scotch—it's 'ie' on the end. And since we're keepin' it real, I wouldn't think a guy with your initials would want to do the whole name joke thing."

Smart mouth. Note to self: use middle name more.

"Anyway, our growing up years were all right—fairly normal—at least for me and Johnnie, a nice little family. However, once we left for college, things kind of came unhinged and mom and dad ended up getting a divorce. None of us knew anything was even going on, but there you go. Kate was thirteen when this happened, and it affected her pretty deeply. Her nice little world just fell apart. Dad wasn't there anymore, and nothing made sense. She kind of lost it over the next few years. Kate was a very pretty girl and very popular and when this happened, she started partying and sleeping around and pretty much messed up her life. It was painful to watch, but she wouldn't listen to anyone."

Mr. Walker took a deep breath. "She ended up pulling it back together toward the end of High School. She had always been intelligent and was very ambitious, so she started to focus on a future for herself and she succeeded. After getting a business degree in college, she went into hotel management and started to work her way up through the ranks. She was with some of the smaller chains initially and then moved into the larger hotels—staying primarily in the mid-west. She then took the next big leap into working in the resort industry, working her way up through the ranks again in various resort venues across the nation—she even spent a little time at a Caribbean resort, but she said she missed the states, so she transferred back."

"That's the path she took to end up in Tucson. She was the Director of Marketing at The Palms Resort—a hotel resort that catered to high dollar clientele, including regularly entertaining celebrity clients."

"Kate was thirty-five years old when she died. While I don't know much about her social life, I do know that she dated casually off and on over the years—never seemed to be anything all that serious—and she had never married or had children. I don't mean to play psychologist here, but I always guessed that after what happened to our parents' marriage, she just couldn't bring herself to roll the dice and take the chance herself. So, she was just all about the job and she was good at it. She made good money, lived comfortably and seemed happy enough, although there seemed to be an emptiness in her when she talked about her life."

"How often did you talk to her?" I asked.

"About every other month or so. You know how it is, everyone is busy, but we did try to stay in touch."

"When's the last time you talked to her?"

"About six weeks before her death."

"How did she seem?"

"About the same as usual." There was a distinct pause on the phone. "Well, wait a minute, I take that back. Now that I think about it, she did seem different. I remember really enjoying talking to her because she seemed so up—you know, more optimistic. And not just about her job, but about life in general. She talked about really liking life in Tucson—I remember that now—she was different."

"Hmm. How long had she lived in Tucson?"

"Almost three years."

"Had she ever talked about how she loved living there before?"

He paused and thought.

"She had mentioned the pros and cons of the city—the usual 'hot in the summer, beautiful the rest of the year' stuff and a few other things—but no, she hadn't ever seemed like that before. Maybe she was just having an up day."

"Maybe." And maybe not—I made a note in my iPhone.

"So, she was found drowned in a bathtub in a luxury suite at The Palms Resort with clear evidence of a struggle."

"Wait. All of that is true except the location. She wasn't found at *her* resort—she was found in the tub of a luxury suite at a resort clear across the city."

"She was what?"

"Yeah, I guess I didn't make myself clear on that. Part of the mystery was that she was found at the Casa Hacienda Resort and Spa clear across town. This is another high dollar resort catering to rich clientele—they have quite a few down there in Tucson. The Casa Hacienda Resort has a working relationship with a wellness clinic too, so sometimes when a celebrity or a rich person would blow a gasket, so to speak, they'd go to this resort to get things worked out."

He was right of course, and it wasn't just in Tucson. Phoenix had a bunch of these places too. When the temperature started dropping toward cold everywhere else, the wealthy just couldn't resist a trip to a sunny, 70-degree winter retreat. Who can blame 'em—why do you think so many of us live here?

"Was there an explanation as to why she would be at a competitor's resort? Was there a professional relationship between the two? Was she on a fact-finding mission to see what the competition offered?"

"Well, there was no connection between the two resorts corporately and those places are extremely competitive for business. Her boss, the General Manager of The Palms Resort, couldn't seem to come up with any reason why she should have been there."

"What's his name?"

"Samuel Joyner."

"OK." I wrote that down. "Listen, I'm sure we're gonna be talking a lot more, but I think I have enough of the basics at this point. I need to do some leg work myself so that I don't end up looking at everything through your eyes."

"What do you mean?"

"Well, I'm new to this investigation and don't know much of anything—which has its disadvantages *and* its advantages—one advantage being I have fresh eyes to look at the facts. If I initially see too much of the story through any one person's eyes, their assumptions—right or wrong—will get worked into my psyche, whether I know it or not. I'll end up shaping reality to fit what I've been told instead of actually seeing reality—and that whole "fresh eyes" benefit goes right out the window. So let me chase this some and come back to you when I have questions or need your help in some way—OK?"

"Hey, you're the expert."

I blushed, but then I blush easily.

"Why thank you," I said demurely.

"One last thing—can I get ahold of your parents to get their take on some of this?"

"I wish you could," said Greg sadly, "our parents died in a car accident seven years ago—yet another blow to the Walker family. Though divorced, they were traveling to an event together when it happened."

"Oh, I'm sorry."

"Thanks."

We exchanged contact information and hung up. I sat back and took a deep breath—immediately regretting that move—apparently, they were experimenting with some new pellets next door—I just about lost my lunch.

Time to think a little: the statutory definition of homicide is the "unlawful killing of one human being by another." Sometimes the phrase "with malice" is included to differentiate from issues like war and executions for crimes. "Malice" doesn't necessarily convey hatred or even ill will, but rather a conscious desire to inflict serious injury or cause death. Did you know that close to forty percent of all murders in America go unsolved?

Well, that's a bummer!

As a side note, Honduras often has the highest homicide rate in the world at 85 per 100,000 per year, followed by Jamaica, South Africa, Brazil and Tanzania. This may be why you so seldom hear someone yell, "Hey, let's vacation this year in HONDURAS!" For the record, in case you just really wanted to know, Japan typically has the lowest rate, with only one homicide per 100,000 per year.

I got up from my desk and started to pace—still thinking. When I tired of that, I laid down on my "thinking couch" and added more thoughts. I stared up at a water spot on one of the ceiling tiles and thought. When I realized I had drifted into looking for little animal shapes in the water spot, I knew it was time to quit thinking and start "detecting." Great investigative minds are like that—they miss nothing.

It was time—Kate Walker was waiting for justice.

CHAPTER

—4—

I don't know if you've ever seen a picture of what they call "Crooked House" on the Internet, but it's a classic example of what *not* to do when it comes to an investigation. The problem with the house was not what was built above ground—it was falling over because the foundation below ground wasn't done right.

When building a case, you have to start with a foundation—defined, strong and true—but just a big picture view of what happened. You can then add solid facts to this little by little, to hopefully end up with a solid building—or case, in this case. Since this crime took place in Tucson, I printed off some facts about the city to read up on while I drive there. Yeah, I said, "while I drive." I know it's a bad habit, but I get a lot of reading done when I drive. Got it—I shouldn't do that—I am appropriately reprimanded. Well, *you* shouldn't bite your nails—so there—I guess we all have something.

After getting some pages to read—not too many, there can be such a thing as too much foundation—I closed up shop and headed home to pack. Before I left, I changed my machine message and directed them to my cell phone—I wasn't too sure how long I'd be gone or be on this case. I'd hate to miss any other good ones.

"Home" was a pretty nice, three-bedroom, two-bath condominium with something you don't see too often in Arizona—a basement. While basements are commonplace is much of the United States, the soil in Arizona is so hard in most places that you pretty much have to call in the demolition experts to get that hole called a basement. Read this as expensive! The first time I saw someone using a pickaxe and then a jack hammer to dig a hole for a tree—I knew we weren't in Kansas anymore. (Please click your heels together to complete this obscure reference to *The Wizard of Oz.*)

Any-who, my condo is in Chandler, a cool suburb on the southeast part of Phoenix. It has three levels: you walk into a living room with a den off to the right and the kitchen and bath toward the back. Upstairs there are three bedrooms—and a bath. I obviously only need one bedroom, but this condo had three and I *really* wanted the basement.

In case you were wondering how this works, they put the basement in a hole in the ground *under* the condo—go figure.

Basements are cool—literally, being down in the ground and all—but I mean way cool to have. You don't have to worry about what your basement looks like—it's where everything falls. It's the best for storing stuff and I thoroughly enjoy mine. I'm a simple man.

So, I went in, tossed my keys on the kitchen counter, and bounded up the stairs to my room. My room was done in what I like to think of as Early American Bachelor. Outfitted with bedroom stuff from Wal-Mart, Target, and IKEA, it had all the spice of an egg with no salt, but that was OK—it was home.

I grabbed all the clothes I'd need out of the closet and the dresser, added my unmentionables, (odd that I just mentioned them), and I then pulled out all the bathroom stuff I'd need and put it on the counter. I ran down to my cool basement, picked out a suitcase and a bathroom bag, and went back up and packed it all in. I carried it all out, locked up my place, tossed it all into my truck and was ready to head to Tucson.

My truck. Now I'm not real big on stuff, but I do dig my truck. It's a late model Toyota Tacoma, double cab, 4X4 with extra-large wheels, chrome rims and jacked way up. It's a beautiful black with leather interior and a killer sound system. It is a thing of beauty—and it was time to drive!

I jumped on I-10 East and headed for Tucson. If you've never seen this area, allow me to give you a pictorial description—*desert.* Lots of cactus, lots of scrub brush and lots of sand. The ninety miles to Tucson is pretty unremarkable—except for a little action at about the halfway point at Casa Grande. It's pretty much desert and mini-mart gas convenience stores.

And you know what that means—it was time to read! This mean machine of mine would pretty much drive itself, so after I got out of the burbs, I set the cruise, grabbed my stack of papers, and started laying the foundation for my case—with at least one cautious eye on the road—most of the time.

Most of what I know about Tucson revolved around the long sports rivalry between Arizona State University in Phoenix and the University of Arizona in Tucson. By and large, they had us in basketball—Coach Lute Olsen and his team had won the National title back in 1997 and did fairly well after that up till he resigned in 2008. When Coach Sean Miller got there, he started rebuilding the program to be great again. In the past, we've been ahead in football, but U of A's program started to get better—and then it wasn't again. I'm sure there's more to that whole sports rivalry story, but that's what I pay attention to.

It turned out that greater Tucson was kind of an interesting place. Its population is about one-fifth the size of the greator Phoenix area, but that means that there's still well over one million people in Pima County. What's kind of weird about this is that for all that apparent size, Tucson is called the Old Pueblo or the Old Town because it still has kind of a small town feel for a city this large. Apparently, this has been by design in the past—it says here that the city has had lots of N.I.M.B.Y.s in their government. That stands for "Not In My Back Yard," meaning that they like their town the way it is and don't want it to become just another big city, (read this as Phoenix), so their laws and restrictions tended to reflect this. This doesn't mean that the signs driving into Tucson read, "Welcome to Tucson—now GO HOME!"—just that the city hadn't perhaps been as welcoming to outside interests as other cities had been. I guess they liked their backyard just the way it is.

THUMP, THUMP, THUMP, THUMP. Oops—guess I was drifting a bit into the other lane—no car crash—so no harm, no foul! Gotta love those Botts' dots!

Don't know Botts dots? That means it's trivia time! Those bumps in the road between the lanes that just saved my life were invented in the 1950s by a guy named Elbert Botts who worked for the California Department of Transportation as the chief of the highway pavement division. A little-known fact: Mr. Botts passed away before he got to see his invention implemented on a large scale. The reason? It took them a bunch of extra time because they couldn't figure out the right *glue* to use. Crazy, huh?!

And you thought I was just another pretty face.

Back to Tucson history: going way back, the whole place kind of got started with the San Xavier Mission being established back in 1699. Fast forward to 1775 and the official birthday of the City of Tucson when Hugo O'Conor established the Tucson Presido. Here's a weird fact—Tucson became a part of Mexico in 1821 after fighting for independence, but then after a thing called the Gadsden Purchase in 1854, it fell under the jurisdiction of the United States. They came *that* close to *really* liking mariachi music with a penchant for accordions!

Have to take a break from my reading—gotta pay attention while I get through all the stuff around Casa Grande. Somehow, I'm just not sure that our friendly local police officer would find my study habits humorous.

OK, got passed the exit to Interstate 8 to San Diego—man, I sure wouldn't mind spending a little time "investigating" there! Maybe next time . . .

All right, paper shuffle time. So, Arizona officially becomes a U.S. territory in 1863 and then becomes the 48th state in the Union in 1912.

By 1950, Tucson's population was up to 120,000—one decade later in 1960, it had nearly doubled to 220,000 people. Since Pima County was over one million people, less than fifty years later, the N.I.M.B.Y.s clearly weren't keeping *everybody* out!

ZZZZZZZZZZZZZZZZZZ. I know you're thinking I was catchin' some Zs as I drive, but nope—it's those grooves on the side of the road that sound so cool on your tires, reminding you you're about to die in a vehicular fiery death! Hate for that to be the last sound I ever hear, so pull it back on the road Blakester!

You know, as I'm getting into the Tucson area, one thing I can see that's different than Phoenix is the lack of grass. It looks like most people have "rock lawns" here—that's wild! Gotta be a reason—gotta be here someplace.

Here it is. Tucson has a bit of a water problem. Phoenix has lakes like Pleasant, Canyon, Apache, Saguaro and Roosevelt and has been accused of having more boats per capita than any other U.S. city. How weird is that? That many boats—in the middle of the desert! Go figure.

Anyway, what Tucson calls rivers don't actually have any water—which in my mind kind of *ruins* the whole concept of "river!" What they call rivers, like the Rillito River, is dry most of the year except during monsoon season when it runs like crazy—and then it goes dry again. They have to bring some of their water in from other places through things like CAP, which gets water from the Colorado River. That may explain why the city fathers are a little concerned about growth—they don't want to go thirsty!

Hmmm. Good stuff. Not sure if it'll help me with Kate Walker's investigation, but I have more of a feel of the place where her murder went down. I'm on the outskirts of Tucson now, so it's time to find a place to land and set up my "base of operation" or what you lay people—not in the high end, rarified air of the "Private Investigator," might call—a hotel room.

CHAPTER
— 5 —

Now just because Greg Walker was paying the bill, did *not* mean I had to get all extravagant—but it did mean that I wasn't about to stay in some dive called the "Dew Drop Inn" or anything like that. So, I ended up finding a nice place not far off I-10 that offered what I would call a "Sweet Suite" for a higher, but not a nosebleed price. Translate that into a price that Greg wouldn't freak out about when he got my itemized bill. The view alone of the Catalina Mountains was spectacular—and you might have guessed by now that I'm not the kind of guy who uses the word "spectacular" lightly—or even *at all* for that matter—but there it is.

My base of operation is called, "The Hermosillo." Is that name cool, *or what*?! You gotta love the Southwest culture. I'd pay extra just for the *name*—well, actually I guess I'd have *Greg Walker* pay extra just for the name. So, I got settled, put all my clothes and stuff away, set up my "work area" on the table and was ready to investigate. I have to tell you though, having a TV in each room was a little overwhelming—which one to watch, oh *which one to watch*?! You might be thinking, "I thought you were ready to investigate?" Oh, you simple, naïve, lay person. I needed to get a feel for the community by watching some local news—*or* having two TVs to choose from in two different way cool rooms was just too much temptation for me to bear—*your call.*

So, after about an hour of "investigation," it was time to start the process. I called down to the Tucson Police Department to see if I could track down a contact I had in the department—a homicide detective named Trent Burgess. He and I had ended up working together on a job a couple of years back. Now please understand what I mean by that—by and large, cops don't really "work together" with P.I.s—they don't even *like* us that much. Many of them tend to view us along the same level as "rent-a-cops" or perhaps "Mall Security." We're the guys who couldn't make it on the "real force" and sometimes they're right. But if you do your job well, are actually helpful to solving a case, and aren't trying to show them up or make them look stupid, you can earn some pretty significant grudging respect. That's what happened with me and Trent.

Much to my surprise (not), they put me on hold to jam to a little elevator "*Muzak*," not to *ever* be confused with actual music.

I gotta tell you that I've always thought that Trent's first name was a pretty cool name—but I have to warn you that the name doesn't really reflect the man. Don't get me wrong—Trent's a pretty good guy—he's just not really a "Trent." It's kind of like when your sister sets you up on a blind date with a girl she knows named Tiffany. Just from her name, you get a bit of a mental image of what she looks like—and then you meet her and . . . well, let's just say your mental image ended up being a little "mental." (Not that this has ever happened to me.) That's Trent for you. I hadn't seen him in a couple of years, so I won't assume anything, but I'm guessing the dude might surprise you a little.

Believe it or not, I was able to have that whole little musing with you and I'm *still* on hold—oh the joy of technology! The receptionist finally came back on and told me that Trent wasn't responding to her little "summons" and asked if I wanted his voice mail. I asked if I could just have his cell number and she notified me that they were unable to give out that information. I explained that I knew Trent—I even mentioned that I was from Phoenix to see if me being from the "big city" would make her eyes sparkle a little—nope, same answer. She even dared to wonder aloud that if I "knew" Trent, why didn't I *already* have his number? (Crickets from me.) Do I have a way with women or what?

I caved and said I'd talk to his voice mail. I kept it simple, "Trent, this is Blake Moran and I'm in town on a job—call me."

To be fair to me, it had been a long time since I'd talked to Trent, so I didn't have his cell number anymore, but hey, I'm an investigator—I am not without resources. I called a mutual friend in California and got his number—and you wonder why I make the big bucks!

I rather smugly dialed Trent's cell number, just wishing that receptionist could see me now . . . I had time to wonder if her name was Tiffany . . .

"Yeah," Trent answered. This dude had always had a way with words.

"Hey Trent, its Blake Moran."

Pregnant pause. You know how it is—someone calls you and you're sure you should recognize the name and the attached face *and* there is some vague recollection deep down in the gray matter. However, your personal brain computer is still searching through all your gray matter documents for the thread that will unravel the information you seek—thus the aforementioned, "pregnant pause."

Now a polite person would give the guy a break by supplying a little more information that would help jog the memory—jolt those old synapses toward success—I however just waited.

"Blake Moran," Trent repeated, about as slowly as was humanly possible, while his search engine frantically looked through his database.

I finally gave in—I do have a heart after all—plus I was getting bored. "Two years ago, Tracy Alderman embezzlement. He never got to spend the money—we found most of his booty, but not all of it." As you can see, I'm a student of the old *Dragnet*, "the facts ma'am, just the facts."

That did it—the computer found the file. "Oh, Blake! How ya doin'?"

"Good, how about you?"

"Can't complain—we'll I could, but what's the point?" Trent

chuckled at his own wit. Some might say that in a battle of wits, Trent was unarmed—not that *I* would say that, just that "*some*" might.

Anyway, Trent's a little goofy, but I gotta tell you, he's a pretty darn good investigator. So, I obliged him with a chuckle before I went on.

"Yeah. Listen, I'm in town on a job. Happened around the first of the year—the Kate Walker murder over at the Casa Hacienda Resort and Spa. The perp was never caught."

"Yeah, I know that one—it wasn't my case, but I know it."

"Listen, could we get together, and you could fill me in a little—maybe give me an introduction to the lead detective?"

Pause. "I don't know Blake—who you working for?"

"Greg Walker."

"Oh, the Vic's brother."

I always thought it was interesting how often cops referred to those involved in a crime with these terms. It wasn't like he didn't know the "Vic's" name—I just *told* him it was Kate Walker, and he knew about the case—yet it wasn't "Kate's brother," it was the "*Vic's*." But I do get it—I think it helps them to keep a professional distance from the crime and its victims. To be fair to them, if I had to be exposed to that much carnage, violence, and death on an ongoing basis, I'd work on the distance too—I don't know how else you'd cope.

My situation was different though. I didn't have to always deal with violence and death, so when I did, I wanted to *know* the victim, I wanted to *feel* what they lost and what the world lost. I didn't want to help the Vic, I wanted to avenge "Kate." With me, I *need* it to be personal—it helps me to be passionate. I want to look into the eyes of the evil that ended their life, spit in their face and say, "Not on my watch"—and then see them pay. You may think I'm going all "Dirty Harry" on you, but it's the major perk of the job for me—it's fulfilling.

Speaking of filling, I filled Trent in. "Yeah, Kate's big brother from New York called me and wanted me to look into this. Don't take it wrong Trent—he spoke highly of the T.P.D. and the work they had done.

He simply understood that after this many months, budget constraints would hamper T.P.D.'s ability to continue to chase this one full bore. He's a stand-up guy who just wants to find the slime ball who killed his little sister—and he's got the bucks to afford me."

Then I waited—kind of holding my breath. This was the moment in any investigation when you found out whether you would be working with or against the police department—it was their call. Either way was doable, but working *with* them made your job a lot easier and provided a much higher probability of success.

Still waiting. Big breath and heavy sigh on the other end of the phone. Finally, "I'm not promising anything Blake, but let me ask around a little and see what I can learn and then we'll talk."

PHEW!

"That would be great Trent—thanks. When can we meet?"

"I've got a little time left today and I'm heading in. Let me talk to the detective in charge and see what I can learn and then we'll talk."

"How about I buy you some dinner tomorrow night—would that be enough time?"

"Sure—but it depends where you're buying!" Again, the chuckle. Trent did love his food!

"I know just the place—I saw it on the way in—one of my favorite places. I'll meet you at the Texas Roadhouse up off Cortaro and I-10 at six—an amazing steak on me. After that, we can come back to my digs and see what you know and what you don't. How's that sound?"

"You got yourself a date."

"Well Trent, let's not call it that—I just threw up in my mouth a little—I'll see you tomorrow night at six." I hung up to him laughing—leave 'em laughing, always leave 'em laughing.

CHAPTER
— 6 —

Since I was eating some major cuisine the next night, I ran over to get some fast food for dinner. I saw the Subway sandwich shop and thought about some of their sandwiches on the healthy side of their menu—and then I got in the drive through line at McDonalds. Hey, at least I "thought" about healthy stuff for a minute—that should count for something!

I took my super-sized dinner (I probably didn't need to admit that, did I?) and went back to my castle to eat it. I wanted to get out some paper and just start writing down what I knew so far. It's kind of a surreal experience, but sometimes being able to "connect the dots" in an investigation starts by just staring at all the jumble of facts in front of you on a piece of paper and literally connecting the dots.

And what did I have to lose? I had time, and for all those channels on both those TVs in either "way cool" room—there was nothing on—I already checked.

So, I got my "dinner" set up on the table and started inhaling it. You could almost hear my arteries closing down, but it tasted *so* good! After dinner, I still had about half of my diet Coke left for the caffeine I would need to think through my facts. Yes, I said "diet Coke." You made me feel guilty, so I ordered a diet Coke to offset what I ate—and I don't like diet Coke.

Don't look at me like that! It's something—it's not much, but it's something.

I flipped over the little paper mat they use on the trays at the burger joint to write on. Yes—I ran in and snatched one, maybe two or seven from the joint. Don't shake your head at me—your judgemental-ness, (Is that a word? I don't think it is), is *really* starting to get on my nerves—come on, I have a murder to solve here!

I started writing down everything I knew, and I quickly discovered something. I found out right away that I knew *very little*! I told you this method works!

I knew that after living almost three years in Tucson, Arizona, a successful woman named Kate Walker had been murdered at the age of thirty-five at a fancy Tucson resort. She had worked for a different fancy resort in town from the one where she had been found. Cause of death—drowning. She had what sounded like a nice upbringing until the age of thirteen when her parents divorced. She clearly took it very hard and rebelled until her later High School years when she finally got it together. She had two brothers, Greg and Johnnie, and Greg believed she had never pursued family life because of what happened with their parents. One thing that Greg had realized was that there seemed to be a subtle change in Kate when he had spoken to her six weeks before her death—one that he described as very optimistic and "up."

I sat back and stared at what I had. I knew it wasn't much, but it was a start. That different resort with no affiliation to where she worked bugged me—that meant something—I just didn't know what yet. That subtle change in Kate was weighing on me too. I knew that it could be nothing; we all have extra good days when we just feel good. However, her brother Greg had subconsciously picked up on it. He knew Kate and it stuck in his mind as something significant, even though he didn't realize it at the time. That mattered—at least it might. It's been said that "The devil is in the details" and I have to tell you that has *often* been true in my investigations. I'm searching for a "devil"—someone who does not want to be found. If I find the little scumbag, who is hiding from the truth like a cockroach from the light, I'll probably find him because I paid attention to the details.

I finally threw in the towel and called it a night. I flossed and brushed what was left from dinner out of my mouth and went to bed. I didn't go to sleep for a while though—I just lay in my bedroom at The Hermosillo listening to the air conditioner cycle off and on while I stared up at the ceiling and thought. Kate's murderer was out there—I knew that. My advantage was that he didn't know that I was looking for him—that now I was out there too. Before I gave in and turned over to go to sleep, I said to the ceiling, "Hey dirt bag—ready or not, here I come."

I have this superhero thing that I tend to do in my head, and that made me feel tough. That's our little secret.

CHAPTER
— 7 —

I woke up Friday morning a little confused. I'm often a little confused, but this was that unique confusion you get when you wake up in a strange place and briefly can't remember where you are, what day it is, or why you're there. I'm also confused by the fact that no one will let you count potato chips as a vegetable in your diet—I mean, it *is* a "chip" from a "potato"—but that's somewhat unrelated to that whole waking up in a strange place thing.

It all came back to me pretty quickly—Kate Walker and Tucson. I glanced around the room to get my bearings—reminded myself that I was totally digging staying at The Hermosillo—and then I was up and at 'em! I did the whole morning bathroom routine, got my teeth shining nice and white and then threw on some shorts and a shirt to run down to the lobby. This place had that whole "continental breakfast" thing going on and I needed a little caffeine and empty calories to shift my body and brain from neutral into drive.

With my tray suitably weighted down with a couple of coffees and some of those flat pastries with the filling residing in the middle, (could this count as a fruit perhaps?), I headed back to my rented castle to prepare for the day.

I set up my breakfast on the table and flipped the TV on to the local news to catch the local weather. I could have caught the "local on the eights" on the Weather Channel, but it seemed like the locals got it a little more accurately *and* the local news would give me a little more flavor of the community. "Blake Moran, P.I.—always on the job, even during my continental breakfast." I briefly wondered if I should use that handle to replace my "we find stuff" opening, but decided it wasn't that much of an upgrade.

Now if you've never been to Arizona, you might not appreciate the job of the weather guy or gal—I mean the "Meteorologist." Across our illustrious "fruited plains," there are many options to the weather, but here in Arizona, it rarely varies from *hot* and *dry*. The only real question is *how* hot and *how* dry? So, the main requirement of an Arizona Meteorologist tends to be creativity—the ability to say "hot and dry" in so many ways that you can fill your allotted time without the audience realizing the truth—that you're just stalling to fill time. And I have to say that they are good—really good. And when rain does decide to show up—like during the monsoon season—the meteorological excitement is almost too much to bear.

Today however, was the hot and dry variety—as was to be expected—and the high was going to hover around a balmy 103 degrees—a fairly typical summer day in Arizona. And it only took the meteorologist about seven minutes to tell me *exactly that.*

As far as getting some of the "flavor of the community," it didn't seem all that different from Phoenix except that it wasn't quite as slick, which was to be expected since Tucson was significantly smaller than Phoenix. It really was a larger city that had kept its smaller town feel.

The food was now gone, and the coffee was giving me that early morning caffeine buzz—I was wired and ready to rock and roll. I had a plan, and it was time to work that plan.

Here's the deal—I had the whole day until I met Trent for dinner, so I decided to use the day to investigate "incognito." Now for the uninitiated, to investigate incognito means—and I quote from the dictionary, "having one's identity concealed, as under an assumed name, especially to avoid notice or formal attentions."

Now you can just read it this way—I was about to get my "sneaky" on!

Here was my plan: I wanted to spend a little time at each of the resorts that I would be including in my investigation—both The Palms Resort where Kate worked, and the Casa Hacienda Resort and Spa where she was killed. However, I wanted to have a "look see" *before* I declared myself officially—there's something to be said for seeing things as they *are* before people start arranging things to look the way they *want.*

So, since by Arizona standards it was going to be just a tad warm today, I put on my "dress shorts" and a bright, floral print button down shirt, a floppy hat, my shades, and my Birkenstocks. I was going "incognito" as a *tourist*—and I was very convincing—if I do say so myself. My goal was to hide in plain sight and "observe." Am I a crack investigator or what?!

I decided to start where Kate had worked—The Palms Resort. I went out and climbed up into my mean machine after first removing the expected bird poop from my black paint. What's up with birds? Do they get together and say, "Whoa, look at that paint job—watch what I can do?" Is it a way to impress the girl birds? Is it personal? Did I offend them somehow? Such deep questions. It's *way* too early to figure out these important questions of the universe.

Having thus undefiled my "triple B" truck, (big—bad—beautiful), I cranked up the air conditioning and some tunes and started across town to "incognito" my first resort of the day.

CHAPTER
— 8 —

The Palms Resort was nestled right into the base of those way cool mountains I told you I could see out my window at the Hermosillo. They're called the Catalina Mountains. While Tucson has the Rincon Mountains and the Tucson Mountains all around it, I would have to say that my favorite had already become the Catalinas.

So, I headed east across town on the surface streets. This was kind of wild for me, being so used to going everywhere on interstates in Phoenix. Tucson is pretty much behind on that score—besides I-10 running around the city and I-19 running down to Mexico—off I-10, they didn't have much of an interstate system—and it was kind of a pain. It just took too long to get around town—but hey, I didn't pay taxes here, so I guess I don't get to have an opinion. (But just between you and me, even though I'm sure I'm hiding it really well, I *do* have an opinion anyway—don't tell.)

Pulling up to The Palms Resort was a treat—these were some nice digs! Since I didn't want some scrub driving my fine machine, I avoided the valet parking and parked her myself—way out and by herself. Climbing down from my perch as I looked around, I had to admit that this place rocked! Just the landscaping tab would have put most places under! It certainly lived up to its name—there were palm trees everywhere! Big palms, little palms, fat palms, skinny palms, tall palms, short palms, (are you getting the picture?), allow me to sum up—*lots* of palm trees. It looked great. There were also falls and fountains all over the place and the sweeping driveway that ran under the tall column portico was wide enough to accommodate a six-lane highway. People were coming and going through the broad entrance, and I was glad to see that I was indeed "incognito"—tourists everywhere, dressed "snappy," just like me—so I went into my tourist mode.

I've found an interesting chink in human nature and observation—when someone moves with confidence and acts like they belong, and knows what they're doing—people tend to subconsciously view them that way and let them be. It's fascinating where you can end up and what you can do when people believe that you're supposed to be there doing that.

So, meet Mr. Confident Tourist from Anywhere, USA—that would be me. I smiled and nodded and moved into the lobby with a sense of purpose and confidence—having absolutely *no* idea where I was headed or what I was going to do. Is being a P.I. fun or what?!

Just inside the door I passed a grand piano and some pretty amazing artwork—not amazing because I liked it, but amazing because I *didn't* like it. I have the kind of artistic taste that the value of a piece of artwork is directly proportional to how much I *hate* it—the more I hate it, the more it tends to be worth. As a matter of fact, this reality is so certain that if I ever get out of the P.I. game, I may just become an art appraiser and just over value all the ugly stuff—the art world will think I'm a *genius*!

Being the observant sleuth that I am, I noticed some sofas and chairs down lower in a recessed area where people were talking. I found a seat there and began to casually look around—I was casing the joint.

The sheer size of this room was impressive—it must have been close to fifty feet from the floor to the ceiling. The floor was marble—with the shine it gave off, I could have seen enough to pick a chive out of my teeth—that may have been too personal. More of those formal columns where scattered all over the lobby and the waterfalls and fountains seemed to have followed me in from outside and just the sound made for a soothing place to sit and talk. The resort desk stretched across much of the lobby and could clearly accommodate hordes of people during "rush hours."

Down lower was a fancy bar setting with multitudes of flat screen TVs and lots of expensive wood finishes everywhere. Even further down to the next level was the first of a number of resort restaurants—the kind I wouldn't be eating in—even Mr. Greg Walker, attorney at law, might balk at me eating at those prices. Everywhere was chrome and glass and cloth and *rich*.

Throughout this lobby, where you could toss a football and not worry about hitting a wall, was a view that was breathtaking. Huge glass walls. Below you could see the many pools and Jacuzzis, along with beautiful landscaping and water works—and straight ahead and straight up, the awe-inspiring cliffs of the Catalina Mountains. This was a "Wow!"

I took a moment to take all this in and to appreciate that someone or a group of someones really knew what they were doing to create this place. Sometimes you just have stop and admire a job that's exceptionally well done.

I had just learned some things about Kate. Kate had been a part of one of the premiere resorts in the nation—if not the world—and she had been one of the top people. This meant that this lady had been very sharp, capable, and sought after in her profession and I admired her for that already—even if I didn't know her and even if it was unfortunately a posthumous admiration.

That admiration ticked me off—I was mad that someone had taken Kate Walker, who had worked hard to be this special—and they had just wasted her life and all her effort by killing her. I didn't pretend to understand life and have all the questions answered, but I knew this was wrong and I took it personally—and I felt that it was now my job to right the wrong.

CHAPTER
— 9 —

After sitting for a while in the middle of decadent opulence and reveling in some good honest seething at the crumb bum who killed Kate, I got up and got back to my job.

I wandered across the lobby and walked up this huge, carpeted stairway till I got to the third floor. Now this was a sight. There was a huge open area up here that looked down on the way cool lobby below. The ceiling for this room was still close to thirty feet—part of those thirty feet we started with down below—and the inlaid workmanship and gold fleck work was something to see. The glassed-in walls of the room displayed the sheer cliff of the Catalina Mountains in the back and what must be an amazing nighttime view of the city lights of Tucson—all of which added to the feeling of the size of the room. The staff was setting up for some big "shindig" with large round tables and ornate chairs and a band or orchestra on an elevated stage positioned so the city lights would twinkle behind them as they played. Best I could tell, I was going to miss a *very* cool party.

I headed to the end of the room into a hall where the rooms of the resort began—I just wanted to get a feel for Kate's world. I walked down hallway after hallway until I came to a maid who was just finishing making up a room—time to get my "confidence" on.

I smiled and said "hi" to her as I walked into the room as though it was my room—she smiled right back at me and hurried to finish the last of her cleaning. By the time I had stared out at "my" breathtaking view for just over a minute, she was politely excusing herself to move on to the next room. The door clicked and the room was mine.

Now this is where it can get a little dicey—you see, no amount of confidence will convince the *actual* owners of this room that I belong here if they return and find me—so the clock was ticking. I was clearly standing in one of the resort's luxury suites. The ceilings here were a mere sixteen feet, with floor to ceiling windows in the enormous "lounging room." You could seat eight to ten people at the dining table and probably pay a few of my larger expenses for a year with the price of the chandelier that was hanging over the table.

Off either side of this room were bedroom suites with lush bathrooms—they even had those bidets. I never really got those—let's just say I had a bad experience with one when I couldn't get it to flush and leave it at that! There were separate showers and whirlpool tubs, double sinks, and separate rooms for the toilet/bidet action—all done in recent American *wow*! It was very cool and very out of anything close to my price range.

This whole place was extremely impressive, but it was time to make like a tree and "leave." (Insert laughter here as a nod to my exceptional wit please.) My adrenalin level was pretty high, cuz if I got caught in here, even my fast talking probably wouldn't save me. Exit, stage right.

After making a successful recon of the hall—meaning I stuck my head out the door and looked both ways—I made my way through the resort to the mega-pool area. Now you might think this an odd escape route, but I wanted to get a feel for the whole resort *or* I just wanted to check out all the fine ladies sunning themselves around the pool. Scholars may debate the merits of each position for millennia to come. You can just decide which one you think it was, and you don't even have to tell me—am I a good guy, or what?

So, I put on my Mr. Confident Tourist and slowly strolled throughout the mega-pool areas—where the "scenery" was as impressive as the aforementioned Catalina mountains. (Ah, the beauty of nature.) I then went back through the lobby and back out to my fine ride. I will admit to you that it was a *very* nice walk. Oh, and just for the record, there were a lot of palm trees around the pool areas too—you just gotta admire their consistency.

CHAPTER
— 10 —

I have to tell you, there's a particular feeling that goes along with building a foundation for a case—and it's kind of cool. Here I was in Tucson—a place I'd only been a couple of times, driving over to the Casa Hacienda Resort and Spa—a place I'd never heard of before this case. Here I was, investigating the murder of a young woman who I'd never met—and I felt like I was already getting to know Kate Walker. I had just walked in her world and soaked up some of her history, and it helped me to know her. It might just be a couple of puzzle pieces in one of those 1,000-piece puzzle jobs, (those are *so* tough), but I could feel it—I was already starting to strain a little to try and see a picture starting to develop.

I also had another feeling—my "continental breakfast" had worn off. So, I stopped at a sub shop where I could get a nice healthful lunch and for a quick bathroom break. Now the fact that I got pastrami on rye and a bag of potato chips is irrelevant. First, it came with coleslaw, which is kind of a vegetable—right? It's true that I didn't actually *eat* the coleslaw, but it did *come* with coleslaw. Also, note that I said this sub shop was a place where I "could" get a nice healthful lunch—look for yourself—that's what I said. I didn't say I *did* get a nice healthful lunch, so stop with that condemning look already!

So, adequately reinforced with food from a place where one "could" get a nice healthful lunch, I drove on over to the Casa Hacienda Resort.

My odometer told me that the two resorts were almost twenty miles apart from each other, but with that lack of freeway help here in the "Old

Pueblo," my GPS told me it would probably take about thirty to forty minutes on the surface streets with normal traffic. Who designed this place?! Anyway, just a little factoid for Mr. P.I. to add to his "stuff" list.

When I got there, the Casa Hacienda Resort and Spa had a different feel than The Palms Resort from the start. The Casa Hacienda was situated in the Tucson Mountain range and had what I'd call a "lower profile" approach all the way around to match the lower elevation of its mountains. Don't get me wrong—it wasn't necessarily a lesser quality; it was just a *different* quality.

For instance, instead of the big opulence of The Palms Resort, the Casa Hacienda Resort was all about the western, cowboy, rustic theme with the resort almost molded into the mountains. I was a little concerned that my "incognito" outfit might make me stick *out* instead of fit *in*, at least if the patrons of the Casa Hacienda Resort were as cowboy themed as the resort. I took my floppy hat off just in case, and longed for a decent cowboy hat—especially because I really didn't want to walk around with "hat head."

After I parked away from the entrance and started to walk in, it turned out that the people heading in and out of the Casa Hacienda were a little more "urban cowboy" than "the wild, wild west," and many of them were just regular tourists, so I was ok—I looked somewhat like the rest of the crowd.

As I was walking in, I saw to my left that this place had stables—lots of them—and beautiful horses for the guests to ride. Maybe I was just up wind, but I couldn't smell the stables—now *that* would be impressive if this much money could even stop *horse manure* from smelling!

To my right was a big restaurant—a cowboy themed place, clearly known for grilling large slabs of beef over mesquite wood—and I have to tell you that it smelled "heavenly." I know I just ate, but that "good meat cooking outside smell" was already calling to me—I was having that "Pavlov's dog" thing going on. Greg Walker may just need to buy me dinner here one night!

That thought reminded me that I was meeting Trent at 6:00 tonight for a good steak, so I'd better get moving.

Like I said, the whole resort had a low profile—it was all built in a Santa Fe, adobe style—but whoever put it all together really knew how to create an impression. While everything at the Casa Hacienda seemed more laid back than at The Palms, the attention to detail and the professionalism were the same.

The lobby stretched on and on with various height ceilings throughout and lots of big wood beams and rustic thrown in everywhere. The furniture just *looked* comfortable, and the noise level was a steady buzz as the guests hung around and talked or read. The view out the back windows was the Tucson Mountains with Saguaro cacti and desert vegetation that looked like a painting. (Yep, the word cacti *is* plural for two or more cactus. How about that? Did you know that the word coccyges is plural for your tailbone or "coccyx?" Weird—but it's a totally unrelated, and not all that interesting fact—I guess it's a good thing we each only have one!)

The Casa Hacienda had all the pools and water works too, but some were designed with exercise in mind, like a lap pool, a current resistance pool and some shallows for water exercise. They clearly had a different clientele in mind when they designed this place—the "active vacationer" instead of the passive one.

I walked through the lobby and started looking for a maid's cart, but I came on a carpet cleaning service getting ready to clean a large suite first. Being the quick-witted investigator that I am I saw my opportunity and said, "The manager asked me to take a quick look through this suite before you started."

Now I have to tell you that there are times when you just have to go with your instincts—and this was *not* one of them. You see, it didn't occur to me in that flash of insight that the following would be true: 1) me saying this would imply that "my manager" was concerned that he and his workers might *not* be highly trustworthy—read "you're a bunch of kleptomaniacs"—not exactly the best way to win friends and influence people! 2) The fact that he immediately glanced at my attire made it clear that he had some *serious* questions trying to reconcile the idea that a guy dressed like me was on the job at the Casa Hacienda Resort and Spa. 3) There was always the chance that he would utter the words, "Who's your manager?" *and* that he might know the management at this resort if he did work for them contractually.

Bottom line: *wow*, that was a screw up!

My only chance was to plunge on and try to cover it *before* he asked that unfortunate question or summoned resort security.

I put up my hands in surrender. "Hey, that came out all wrong. We had a guest who last stayed in this suite call us. She asked us to look and see if we could spot a bracelet that she thinks she may have lost. She said it didn't have much monetary value, but it had sentimental value to her since her mother gave it to her, and has since passed away. So, I get this call to come take a quick look to see if we can help her out. I was helping host a resort party, but I figured I could shoot up here real quick and take a look. I promise—five minutes tops and it's all yours."

I don't know where that stuff comes from, but I think I covered everything. (Checklist: hey, you're honest and I know it, I'm also dressed funny, but don't ask questions.) Sometimes I think I'm a savant in shoveling the "hooey." OK, maybe her mom passing away was a bit much, but I was hoping a little tugging on the heart strings might distract him from being offended or asking questions.

Big breath and wait to see if he bought it.

He looked at me a little longer than I hoped, but then I realized that just maybe he thought I was giving him a little too much information. Finally, he said, "All right, but hurry it up—I don't want to be paying these guys to just stand around and do nothing."

"You got it," I said, trying not to let the relief show on my clearly "pure as the wind driven snow" face.

I ducked into the suite, very conscious of my time limitations. The room was beautiful, but in that rustic way the rest of the resort was. The furniture was big and welcoming, the wet bar was impressive and well stocked. The bedroom had a bed with about the biggest wood bed frame I'd ever seen. Over in the corner of the huge room was an in-floor, sunken Jacuzzi with a lounging couch next to it and plants surrounding it. An elaborate bathroom was off the bedroom with a large tub, a separate dual shower enclosure, dual sinks, and a separate room for the toilet. The Casa Hacienda Resort and Spa didn't apparently care for the whole bidet experience, which was oddly comforting to me—the Old West should not have a bidet—just saying.

All in all, this was a great resort with a great feel and great rooms—but not a great place to die. What place is? I didn't know how close I was to where Kate had taken her last breath, but I did know that this place was part of the answer to the question of Kate Walker.

As I stood staring at the bathtub, I heard some sounds of people starting to move around in the other room. My time was up—time to make a run for it. I walked out of the bedroom shaking my head and shrugging to the carpet guy to indicate I'd been unsuccessful in my search. He didn't seem too interested—which I was happy to see—so I just said, "Thanks" and got out of Dodge.

Please note the appropriate use of the cliché, given the resort theme.

A sizzling slab of beef and Detective Trent Burgess awaited the Blake-mystery.

CHAPTER 11

By the time I'd booked back to The Hermosillo and grabbed a quick shower and a change of clothes, I was "fashionably late" for my dinner "date" with Trent. I wasn't worried he'd leave—this was free food we were talking about.

Seeing as it was night and we were eating at what would officially be called a restaurant by anybody, I got pretty slicked up. I wore my best black jeans, my shark skin cowboy boots, a white button-down shirt, and a light sports jacket—dark gray—to complete my ensemble. With a spray of Polo cologne—green, not black—I was ready to go. If I just had a toothpick to hold in a lazy way between my teeth to compliment the self-assured look on my face, I would've been the whole package. Maybe they'll have some at the restaurant.

Since it was time for me to start getting into my P.I. mode a little more fully, there was ONE more item I was wearing—my gun. I typically wore it either in a hip holster or a shoulder holster. With the sports jacket, tonight was a shoulder holster night which meant I had my gun and two extra clips. Don't worry; I have my CCW—Carry Concealed Weapon Permit. What do I look like, a lawbreaker?! (Hopefully, I look a *little* like a lawbreaker—I think it's a good look on me.)

Now I don't know how much you care about guns, but in my line of work, I need to care. Plus, I just think they are cool. I have a number of guns, but when it comes to packin', I tend to lean toward my Glock 40 caliber. I also have a Smith and Wesson 9mm that I can carry, but for sheer stopping power I just think the Glock is better. My 9mm is great for target practice since the rounds are so much cheaper and the recoil is a little lighter, but when I'm getting serious, I carry what a lot of police departments do—my Glock. Maybe it's just psychological, but that little extra makes me feel more confident. I also use Hydra-Shok® expanding rounds so that if I need to stop someone, I don't have to ask nicely. I'm not going all *lethal weapon* on you—and I'm not *compensating* for anything, so cut that out! It's just that when things suddenly get serious, I can't afford to be polite.

Since a Glock 40 is semiautomatic—with one round jacketed and a fourteen-round magazine, I could be ready with fifteen shots—but that's the cop way—I just settle for fourteen rounds and figure I'll cock it the first time—it just feels safer to me. But I gotta tell you that if I ever end up needing more than fourteen rounds, I'm really going to hate myself! Just in case, I usually keep an extra magazine or two with me when I think I might need to be ready for something to go down. So, with the comfort of "Molly" under my arm, I was off to steak and Trent. (Oh, in case I neglected to mention it—I named my gun "Molly.")

Thankfully, the Texas Roadhouse was right around the corner, so I pulled up and walked in. The Texas Roadhouse is exactly what its name implies—lots of wood siding, wood tables, wood benches and some seriously *great* steaks! Lots of cowboy motif going on too, and a metal bucket full of peanuts in the shell on every table. Not too sure what the point of that is—lots of the shells end up on the floor—but it creates a nice laid-back atmosphere. The menu features things like a "Cactus Blossom"—a deep fried onion—and Chicken Critters and Rattlesnake Bites along with a cartoon armadillo in a cowboy hat. They had lots of different steaks to decide between too, but as far as my favorite menu name, it had to be "Roadkill"—I don't eat it, but I have to give them "kudos" for the clever name.

So, I make my entrance with all my tough guy machismo, but the only person I think I impressed was the hostess—and I'm not actually certain about that. I'm still going to go with that to make myself feel better. When I'd finished my entrance, I looked around and realized that apparently Trent was *more* fashionably late than me. I hate that—a perfectly good entrance wasted! All that work for nothing!

I decided to go ahead and get a table—this place would fill up pretty quick *and* I wanted to get started on that bread they bring you—I was hungry. That pastrami on rye and bag of chips was long gone. Trent could catch up when he got here.

The hostess seated me where I could see the steaks on the grill—and that sure worked cuz it just made me hungrier. I quickly checked my phone to make sure I didn't have any messages—especially any cancellations from Trent. Nope. When the cute waitress, (bonus!), went by my table and dropped off the bread and butter, I was *ready*! I ordered a beer—and being the classy guy that I am and wanting to make a good impression on Trent—I even asked for a glass.

As I ate the "Hot, Freshly Baked Bread" slathered in their signature "cinnamon butter"—*so good*—I sat back and tried to piece together what I'd seen today. Both resorts that currently played a role in Kate's life and subsequent death were beautiful, well appointed, well maintained, and designed for a wealthy clientele. Kate had worked at one and, at least one time, apparently stayed at the other. If nothing else, she sure had good taste in accommodations.

In the middle of this deep reflection, I saw a movement that caught my attention. I looked toward the front entrance area and there was Detective Trent Burgess. As he was talking with the hostess, undoubtedly asking if I was already there, (I *am* a Private Investigator after all, I miss nothing), I got his attention and waved him over.

Now you may recall that earlier I pointed out that while Trent was a pretty cool name, the name does not necessarily reflect the man. As I said, while he's a pretty good detective, let's just say he's probably *not* on the short list for the next "Hang up the Hunks" calendar.

Trent was pretty well as I remembered him: a little over forty by now, he still liked those suits he could get off the rack at the mall—they never fit great—but you could mix and match your chest and waist measurement and they wore forever! His tie was blue silk, but it was pulled down and moving over toward the side a little with the top button of his shirt undone. He had a stain on the tie about two-thirds of the way down—I'm assuming remnants of his lunch. He accented all this with what looked like police standard issue black shoes. Trent had always been about thirty to forty pounds above "ideal"—carrying most of it around his middle—and he had some male pattern baldness that was compensated by a perpetual five o'clock shadow.

Having said all that, the total package kind of worked. He had the charm of a guy who just didn't give a rip about fashion, or self-image, or about what anybody thought, and the resulting confident persona he exuded kind of filled in the gaps. Trent was all right.

He made his way over to the table. I stood and we shook and smiled and started to catch up. The waitress interrupted us long enough to take our steak orders—Trent taking time to appreciate the aforementioned "cuteness" of the waitress. We got one of those fried onion things, a first beer for Trent, sans the glass—apparently Trent was *not* trying to come off classy with me—and a second beer for me. Then we continued to catch up.

Trent had gone the way of so many of our fine men and women in blue—his stressful and demanding occupation didn't fit well with marital bliss. The divorce rate for police officers is shockingly higher than the general public. His ex-wife's name was Marilyn and they had two cute kids—Trent "the second" and Jessie, who they just called Jess. They weren't really *kids* anymore—Trent II was now a few years into his teens and was getting ready to start driving, and Jess was just getting ready to move from Tween to Teen—scary times for a dad!

By the time we'd finished the Baby Cactus Blossom—perfect for two people to share—and our salads, I'd heard all about the kids, complete with pictures from the wallet. Trent was clearly a great dad and a "Triple P"—pretty proud papa.

During the steaks—I had the "Fort Worth Ribeye"—I heard about Marilyn. It was kind of sad. They'd been divorced for three years, but Trent was still clearly smitten with her. He was resigned to what seemed to be a fact that they couldn't make it work, but the feelings were still there. Trent said that Marilyn had started dating in the last year and while it was a passing comment, I could tell it really bothered him.

I thought it was wild that he would tell me all this personal stuff, but I'd seen this before. It seemed that since we were in similar occupations and I was someone he didn't have to see day after day, Trent felt he could talk freely about his personal life—and it seemed therapeutic for him. I don't try and play amateur psychologist—I'm self-aware enough to know that I have enough trouble just trying to figure out my own life—so I offer no answers, but I can listen. And that seems enough for Trent.

So, while Trent is all stretched out on the proverbial "shrink's couch," the food was *glorious.* I switched over to water after two beers and noticed Trent stopped after one—must be *trying* to watch those extra pounds. We finished the meal reliving the various facts surrounding the Tracy Alderman embezzlement, and subsequent murder—the case we'd worked on together earlier. All and all, it was a great meal and a pretty OK time.

I grabbed the check when the waitress dropped it off, (did I mention she was cute?), paid for it with my credit card and gave her one of my signature winks—I'm quite the Casanova. I told Trent to follow me over to my digs at The Hermosillo so that we could talk about Kate Walker.

CHAPTER

— 12 —

When we got over to my room, Trent started looking around—you know how those detectives are—and he decided he liked the place. After he made a pit stop in the bathroom, we made room on the table so that we could talk about Kate.

Trent took out a manila envelope and laid it on the table and then did the unthinkable—he pulled out a small, hand-sized flip spiral notebook and opened it up.

"Please tell me you don't *really* use that Trent," I said.

"What?" he asked.

"Dude—that is classic old timer—like *Dragnet* stuff—how *old* are you?! If you say, 'Just the facts, ma'am, just the facts,' I am *so* outta here!"

(Now this is *not* the time for you to remember that when I was trying to remind Trent who I was with that first phone call, *I myself* actually used this same *Dragnet* line. That would seem to imply some level of hypocrisy on my part. However, if you remember, I said that line *in my head*, not out loud, so that was *our little secret.*)

Ergo, not hypocritical.

Now back to our regularly scheduled broadcast . . .

"Are you through?" Trent asked.

I cocked my head and assumed a thoughtful expression on my face. After a moment I nodded and replied, "Yep, I guess I'm pretty much done."

"Thank you."

"All right, here's the facts," he ignored my groan, "A single Caucasian female of thirty-five years of age was found dead on Saturday,

January 4 at the Casa Hacienda Resort and Spa. She was found in one of the luxury suites, room 322, by one of the maids—a Maria Ortez. Mrs. Ortez found her at approximately 1:15 in the afternoon because the 'Do Not Disturb' sign was on the door. Since checkout was at noon and the suite wasn't booked by the same occupant for another night, the maid finally assumed that the sign had been left on in error, and used her pass card to go in to the room. After calling out and not getting a response, Maria began to clean up. It was only when she walked into the bathroom area that she saw the Vic in the tub floating face up. She made no attempt to resuscitate the victim—she ran screaming from the suite and one of her fellow maids actually called 911 and notified the Casa Hacienda management."

He flipped the page.

"Trent, isn't all this information in the official report?" I asked.

"Yeah."

"Then why are you reading it out of your little notebook?"

"I thought you said you were through."

I scanned my mind for a loophole—nope.

"Sorry," I replied.

"May I continue?"

"Please do."

Deep breath by Trent—a little melodramatic if you ask me.

"Emergency personnel arrived at 1:42 and it was quickly determined that the Vic was dead. T.P.D. officers arrived and immediately called Homicide. When the detectives arrived, they observed the following: it did not seem like there had been a struggle throughout the suite. They did observe a bottle of wine that was open—it was about half empty—or I suppose about half full—depending on your philosophic bent."

(Did Trent just try to make a funny? I think he did.)

"They could only find one wine glass. However, when the staff was questioned, they stated that each luxury suite was always stocked with two wine glasses, not one—one had apparently disappeared."

"When they eyeballed the bath area, they noted that every bath towel and hand towel—four and two respectively—along with the bathmat, were soaked and piled together. Both the floor and baseboard were tile and were completely dry by this time, but there was a wooden handle hairbrush that was on the floor. The wood was still dark with water it had soaked up somehow. It appeared that there had been lots of water on the floor that had been soaked up with the towels."

"Not a shocking discovery, tubs can overflow."

"The weird thing is that the tub was still almost full to the top—it clearly had been filled again after the flood—or just shut off and left full. Now it could have been that the Vic had accidently overflowed the tub, cleaned it up with the towels, and then filled it up again to take a long bath, but something just didn't fit for them. If this were the case, and the Vic cleaned up all the water—using all the available towels to do so—why would she then just fill it up again and climb in knowing that she had no towels left to dry off with when she was done?"

Trent looked up. "Now given the wine bottle in the living room suite, it seemed possible that alcohol was involved. However, the detectives felt that if the Vic was aware enough to clean up that much water with that many towels, then she would have also been aware enough to realize that she was *now without any* towels and would have a problem when her bath was over. It wasn't conclusive, but it was an observation."

Back to his notebook: "The Vic was observed to be face up, naked, with no visible scars, tattoos or piercings—except for her ears. She had longer, below the shoulder, dark hair, and dark eyes. She had some visible bruising—around her wrists, in the middle of her chest and on the back of her heels. They left the rest of the evaluation to the Medical Examiner."

"Another thing that seemed odd as they looked around is how clean everything seemed. The Vic had obviously been in this suite for at least some time. However, while the bed was unmade, the rest of the suite looked untouched—a little like a human being had not been there."

"The Vic had long dark hair, but there was no hair on the floor, on the counter or in the sink. There was no toothpaste or water spots in the sink—the toilet looked unused. Basically, the detectives felt that the place looked wiped down. They called the coroner and released the body to him."

Another page flip: "The autopsy took place on January 7 and was done by Dr. Leo Alvarado—Detective Rios was in attendance. By this time, it had been discovered that the Vic's name was Kate Walker, age thirty-five, born in Madison, Wisconsin, who had been living in Tucson for about three years. She had lived up in a place called Rancho Vistoso, a nice, planned community in Oro Valley, a suburb of Tucson. She had worked as the Director of Marketing at The Palms—a high-end resort at the base of the Catalina Mountains—a job for which she was paid very well."

"The autopsy itself revealed a few more issues. The Vic was determined to have been in excellent condition before death—clearly took very good care of herself or was just genetically one of the lucky ones. She was 5 feet 7 inches tall and would have weighed about 120 pounds in life. Examination of the pubic and vaginal area revealed that she had recently been involved in intercourse—however, there was no semen remaining, so he either didn't finish, pulled out, or wore a condom. There was also some internal bruising, so it was either rough consensual sex, or Kate was raped. There were also pubic hairs found in the tub that were not the Vic's. The hairs could have been left over from a previous guest taking a shower or bath, but in a resort of the quality of the Casa Hacienda, that lack of cleanliness was highly unlikely."

"The cause of death was ruled drowning given the water found in the lungs—not a great surprise. The M.E. set the time of death from midnight to 2:00 a.m. based on the extent of rigor mortis, taking into account the fact that the Vic had been mostly submerged after death. There was alcohol in the Vic's system—but with only a reading of .03 percent—less than fifty percent of the legal limit—so she hadn't had much to drink.

It wasn't the Vic who had consumed very much of that half of a bottle of wine that was gone."

"The M.E. noted that the Vic had sustained a blunt trauma blow to the back of the head that was concealed visually by her hair. Now this could have been explained by the Vic slipping in the tub and hitting her head, then drowning, although that would have made more sense with more significant alcohol intake than her bloodwork indicated. However, there was more evidence that indicated that this was not the case."

Trent went on: "The bruises on the wrists and chest indicated extreme pressure being applied to the Vic before death. Now this could have taken place before the Vic got into the tub, but given the nature of the bruising, not too much before that time."

"The bruises on the back of the heels had the same appearance, which seemed to imply that they all took place at the same time. It certainly was not difficult to construct a scenario where this woman had been struck, then struggled with someone, then been held down forcibly under the water while kicking her free legs, striking them repeatedly on the tub edge."

Trent looked up as I began to ask a question. "Yes, we did check the tub edge for any indication of damage, but it was a marble tub, so too hard to reveal anything."

"It could not be determined if the Vic had been involved in consensual sex or subjected to rape, although the bruising could be partially the result of rape. Since the room is at the end of the hall and is secluded, along with the low occupancy of adjacent rooms that night, we couldn't rule out rape based on noise the Vic would have made. And with that blow to the head, there's a chance she could have been raped while out cold."

"The final clue was the presence of skin under the Vic's nails. She had those salon acrylic nails—French manicure if you care to know—and she used them. Somebody got scratched up pretty good before she died—she clearly put up a good fight."

Trent closed his spiral notebook and looked at me. "So, here's where the detective's investigation led them: this appears to be an amateur attempt to cover up a murder. They are guessing that the murderer was a male. They are not assuming that just because she had intercourse, since it was possible that the man who had intercourse with her was not the one who killed her. However, as you know, statistics would certainly point toward a male. In addition to this, two things—the blunt trauma blow and being able to hold such a strong, in shape woman under the water for an extended amount of time, while she fought for her life—would both require quite a bit of strength."

"So, starting with an acknowledged assumption that it was a man, they added the missing wine glass, the tidied-up room, the soaked towels and the wiped down surfaces—this all screamed of a cover up. What the murderer didn't realize was that when he wiped down all the hard surfaces, he didn't just wipe off his prints—the Vic's prints were wiped away too. So, here's this woman who had clearly been in this suite for some hours and yet she didn't leave any prints?! Come on! The *absence* of her prints was one of the biggest indicators of foul play."

"Trent—tell me you didn't just use the term 'foul play,'" I said, "You just *have* to stop watching those late night 'who done it' reruns."

Trent just gave me his best "Clint squint" and moved on.

"We got no help from who paid for the room, since it was paid for in cash and no one remembers who it was. We did take note of the fact that the room was not reserved in advance, but rather rented on Friday afternoon, January 3. It did seem that this may have been a last minute, more spontaneous idea, rather than a planned out get together—for whatever that's worth."

"Since that time, we've done all the usual investigation—interviewed her family, friends, neighbors and co-workers. I'll tell you that the Vic was very well liked and thought of, but was a bit of a loner—nice to people, but not one to get real close to others. She seemed to pretty much live her job and was apparently very good at it. She worked out at a local fitness club, ran some, read some books, traveled periodically and only socialized some."

And that was the summation . . .

CHAPTER
— 13 —

Trent closed his spiral notebook and looked up at me.

"Just being straight with you Blake, I gotta tell you that the fact that she only socialized 'some' was a shocker to every guy on the force—or any male who has ever walked on the face of this planet, I would imagine."

I realized that Trent was looking right at me, clearly expecting a response from me.

"What? Am I missing something? I don't know what you mean."

"Oh, come *on* Blake—you're a single guy! Even if I was still happily married to Marilyn, I would have just about fell over! You just don't see something like *that* very often in the course of your whole life! Don't play that 'am I missing something' routine with me!"

You know, I don't use the word "befuddled" very often in life, but I was clearly supposed to know something here that I didn't know—and I was befuddled!

"Trent, what *on earth* are you talking about?!"

"Come on Blake—that Vic may have been the most exquisitely beautiful woman I have *ever* seen in my life!"

Now I was just getting annoyed.

"OK, first of all Trent—the 'Vic's' name is *Kate*! If she was so beautiful, then how about we just use her name! Secondly, I just got this case yesterday morning over the phone, so I have *no idea* what Kate looked like. Her brother just told me that she was—and I quote, *without* looking at a spiral notebook, I might 'note'—'a very pretty girl' when she was younger! So, you can *stop* giving me 'incredulous'—I really don't know what you're talking about."

Trent looked at me for a moment to see if I was being straight with him and then he reached for a manila envelope. He took out a number of items—three 8 by 10 glossy head shots, two professional advertising brochures for The Palms and a few amateur pictures that someone had taken casually. He then almost reverently spread all of these out in front of me.

I have to admit that I was not quite ready for what I saw. Now I love women—their hair, their shape, the way they move, the expressions on their face, the way they smell—you get the point, I *love* women. In my opinion, God, or nature or whatever, did a really good job when women showed up! I look at women *every* chance I get. Like most men, it's one of my favorite hobbies—if I could figure out a way to turn it into a paying career—I would. So, I guess you could consider me a connoisseur of looking at women, like most men on the planet. But I admit it—I was shocked—and Trent was clearly enjoying his unspoken "I told ya so!"

I'm not sure I can explain this clearly, but I can start here—Kate Walker had been *beautiful*—but that doesn't do it. Kate Walker had been *stunning*! Nope, not enough. Kate Walker had the kind of raw, sensual beauty that you just don't see in one package—not even in Hollywood. Kate had been so amazing that The Palms had wisely used her as the primary model in their brochures. She was throughout the pamphlet on The Palms—in the rooms, the restaurants, the nightclub, on the tennis court and at the pool. She had the perfect skin tone to offset her jet-black hair. Her face was perfectly proportioned with the cutest nose, perfect straight, white teeth, and full, pouty lips. Her legs were shapely and tone. Her figure was the one that a plastic surgeon would dream about—when plastic surgeons dream. Yet, she seemed completely unaware of the camera—a total natural beauty.

What was wild was that it wasn't just the posed pictures—we all know the power of "air-brushing" and how it can make people look pretty doggone perfect. But the amateur, casual snapshots were the same—if anything Kate was even *more* beautiful—this woman may have been the most unbelievable beauty that I had *ever* seen!

While Trent was sitting there getting a kick out of my shock, he probably thought I was falling in love with Kate Walker—apparently a good number of the detectives did—but I really wasn't. Kate Walker wasn't someone I could even think about in that way just because she was so perfect. She was *way* too much out of my league—out of pretty much *anybody's* league for that matter. She was like a Rembrandt—you could be amazed at it and admire it from a distance—but no one should ever have it as their own—it is a gift for all the world to enjoy.

Bit much? OK. Let's just leave it that Kate Walker had been one of the most amazingly beautiful women who had ever walked on the face of the earth. That just about sums it up.

I looked up at Trent's smug face. "All right—you win. She was shockingly attractive."

Trent smiled and nodded to acknowledge the obvious.

"Like I was saying," Trent continued, "the fact that 'Kate' only socialized 'some' was a shocker to all of us."

I acknowledged the use of her name with a wave of my hand as I shook my head and muttered, "That's an understatement."

"We looked into that and found that while she dated a little here and there, there really wasn't much of that. What a waste," he said, shaking his head.

"Would you calm down Trent?"

He just smiled.

I said, "OK, I assume that you've had to move this investigation to the second tier by now since it's been over six months."

He frowned, then sighed.

"Yeah, you know how it is—crime never sleeps and never stops—and manpower demands we chase the cases that are giving us something to work with. It ticks the whole department off that some amateur perp is somewhere out there walking free, but it happens sometimes when the trail goes this cold."

"So, what do you think my chances are of being seen by the detectives on the case as an *asset* instead of a *pain in the butt*?"

Trent smiled. "Well, as you know, we're not allowed to admit that we'd like the help now that we've been made to move on, but I think the detectives on this case will be secretly glad somebody's still on it."

"Do you think I'll get at least some cooperation?" I asked.

"I already called and talked it over with Detective Richards—he was the lead on this case. After I vouched for you, he told me that they could offer you some basic assistance—but he emphasized basic—mainly informational. He told me that back in January he was lead on a number of cases—you know how a New Year makes the crazies come out—so most of the work on the Walker case was done by Detective Who. Richards said you should just talk with that detective."

"Very cool. Tell me where to call and I'm all over it."

"I figured you'd feel that way, so I called Detective Who and set up a meeting for tomorrow morning at 9:00. Does that work for you?"

"Trent, I could kiss you—but then that 'date' comment you made earlier will start to creep me out again."

There was Trent's chuckle again.

"All right. Be down at our Westside substation at Miracle Mile and North Flowing Wells tomorrow morning at 9:00—I'll meet you there to introduce you. Detective Who is getting in an early workout, and then will meet with you in one of our conference rooms."

"Thanks Trent—I owe you one," I said.

"I'll tell you what," Trent said, his face turning all serious and tense all the sudden, "you figure out who killed this Vic—I mean Kate—and we'll call it even."

"Deal."

CHAPTER
— 14 —

After Trent left, I turned on the TV in the living room and mindlessly flipped channels for a while. I needed to think about something else for a while. I was kind of emotionally spent after going over all the particulars of Kate's murder, and even more connected to the case now that I had Kate's perfect form and face as the icon of this investigation in my three-pound, gray matter computer.

I ended up watching a late-night talk show for a while—it was mildly funny—I liked the "Top Ten" segment, but the actor they interviewed about the latest action movie was a *really* boring interview. It always amazed me that some actors could be so good at repeating lines that someone else had written—and make millions doing it—and then be such a dolt when it came to making up their own words on the fly.

They went to commercial. The first ad caught my attention. The guy had dark, spiky hair, (Serious hair products!) saying that he was, "sorry it had come to this," of course making me wonder "come to what?" He then says, "I didn't want to have to do this." He then looked right into the camera as it went to close up and said, "I dare you to try Desert Christian Church. I double dare ya! I double DOG dare ya!" The camera panned out as the music stopped and you heard a sound like an old record scratch. Back to the guy who paused, shook his head and then said regretfully, "I'm sorry I had to do that." The ad cut to some music with Mr. Spiky Hair doing a little dance in the background while the words on the screen and the voice over said, "Desert Christian Church—we double dog dare ya!"

I found myself laughing—that was funny. Talk about a different ad for a church! That was pretty good. Now I don't know why anyone would *ever* want to actually *go* to a church, but I gotta give that church high marks for effort and creativity.

When the commercial break ended, the talk show host started announcing his next shtick and I decided I was over it, so I shut it off.

The darkness was all around as the light faded, so I walked over and flipped on the light above the table. There lay Kate's pictures. I stood there and stared at them all—one by one. I was still shocked by her appearance—it was still hard to believe that someone that pretty had even existed.

I'm going to admit something to you, but you have to promise not to tell anyone else. Promise? OK.

I know the unofficial rules say that we're not supposed to care about how people look, but we're human beings and the reality is that we do—at least some—we all tend to respond to people in part, based on their appearance. I don't know if that's a changeable characteristic of human beings or not. However, I do know this—seeing Kate and how perfect she had been, was going to help me do my job even better.

Here's why: do you remember when I saw where Kate worked and how cool of a place The Palms was? It showed how capable and exceptional Kate had been in her work. Her hard work had paid off and she was at the top of her game. And it ticked me off that some scum bucket had come along and taken that all away from her. Even without knowing all the "whys" and "how comes," I knew that taking this away from her was wrong. I can't tell you where that belief was coming from—I just knew.

Well, when I saw how perfect physically Kate was, I had a similar reaction. Now I know that apart from staying in shape, being fashionable and doing her hair and makeup in a great way, Kate wasn't responsible for her good looks. Apparently, she won the genetic lottery or something. But for whatever reason, Kate Walker had been extremely special physically—one of those rare angels on earth—and that had been taken from her. She may not have earned what she had—she may have not even deserved it, but she had it, and it was taken from her—and that ticked me off! How dare whoever it was think that they could just kill this angel with impunity.

Nope, just *not* OK.

And while I'm admitting things, I might as well tell you something else—I think I might have a clue. Now you might think I'm a male chauvinist pig, but you'll have to get in line—news flash—you're *not* the first. You see, my clue is based on something that I think is generally true about women statistically—most women want to get married someday and most want to have children. Now I get it—I know that many 21st Century women put the whole family thing on hold for a while as they chase their career—and some never do the whole family thing, but they are still in the minority. Whether it's the "biological clock" ticking or whatever, it tends to start "chiming" for most women at some point.

Now, I think Trent and his detective friends were right to be "shocked" that a woman as breathtakingly beautiful as Kate only socialized "some"—but maybe it was more than just a surprise—maybe it was a clue.

The fact that Kate dated periodically indicated that she apparently liked men and was drawn to them—and there was *no* question whether men would have been drawn to her! I'm surprised she didn't have to employ full time *bodyguards*!

But for whatever reason, Kate wasn't finding "it." She had been at the top of her game vocationally for some time—she had arrived—she had been thirty-five years old, and the clock was ticking—so what was the problem? This woman could have virtually *any* man in the world—and she'd traveled a lot of it. It wasn't just her beauty either; they had found that she was well liked and respected too. She clearly indicated interest by dating some, but it was still a no go. Why? What was she looking for that she wasn't finding?

So, I know you're on the edge of your seat right now, awaiting my amazing revelation about what all this means. Sorry. I didn't say I had any *answers*—I just think that there is something there that might be a clue. When the pieces of the puzzle don't fit together very well, sometimes looking a little closer and keeping the puzzle pieces close at hand is a key to success when it all starts to come together.

And sometimes it just ends up being a large pile of puzzle pieces that *make no sense*. Let's hope that doesn't happen!

Either way, I'm beat! I'm off to my bathroom bedtime ritual and then I gotta catch some Zs—I've got a big meeting tomorrow with Detective Who.

(Now you know I could really have some fun with *that* name—but I'm guessing I'd better not if I want any help.)

CHAPTER
— 15 —

My second morning waking up in my new digs was a little more familiar than the first. Weird how your psyche adjusts to that, huh? I had a little grogginess going on—*no*, it had nothing to do with the beer! My mouth felt as old as a pair of sneakers after an hour-long basketball game, and probably smelled about as good—I'm pretty sure you can blame that one on that "Baby Cactus Blossom!" So, I was anxious to get to my bathroom routine and do a little "damage control."

I had to hurry a little—my internal clock failed to wake me up at 7:00 a.m. I know I should have done that whole wakeup call thing, but I have to tell you that those *freak* me out! That whole, from a dead sleep to a ringing phone in the ear, is just a *crazy* way to wake up! I could have set my cell phone to wake me up, but I usually can set my internal clock—it was just off by about an hour this morning. Maybe it was set for 8:00 a.m. because it was Saturday.

I told you, it wasn't the beers! You gotta let that go!

I got my shower and shave and put my best jeans on with my favorite cowboy boots—I was in a phase right now of gettin' my *western* on—oh yeah! I added a pullover short sleeved shirt and a hip holster for Molly and I was ready. I did a quick stop for a little continental breakfast on the way out and jumped into my mean machine—I'd have to eat on the way. Curse that internal clock!

I hit I-10 East and headed for Miracle Mile—it was under ten miles, so I had to eat quickly. When I made the exit, I overshot Flowing Wells—I didn't realize that it was right off the freeway. As I looked for a place to commit a "U-E," I perused "Miracle Mile." I was pretty much just seeing a metal savage yard, a strip club, one-hour "no-tell" motels, and a bowling alley. You have to give high marks to whoever named this stretch of road—I'm guessing they were a "glass half *full*" sort of person!

I found my turn and headed back to the Westside sub-station. Now *that* place was impressive! It was clearly pretty new, and I'd guess that just having this many cops coming and going on this street would probably help clean up Miracle Mile eventually! The place was huge and really nice. It looked like a warehouse with an impressive facelift, which I found out later is exactly what it was. Apparently, this whole corner had at one time been a K-Mart that went belly up. A number of businesses had tried to make something work, but it looked like the police department had finally found the answer to all that space—crime unfortunately tends to be an industry that continues to grow and expand. Right next to it was a brand new 60,000 square foot crime lab—nice digs!

The external facade of the sub-station was done in colored metal and stucco with high roof lines that lent an impressive feeling to the entrance area—and it did a great job hiding that this used to be an old K-Mart. It was all strictly upscale business feel, and I found myself signaling my inner approval to the designers who had created the look of this substation. I'm sure their collective hearts would be all a twitter to know that Blake Moran, Private Investigator, approved of what they had done.

After all, I DO "find stuff."

I walked into the lobby area and admired again. It was all done in cool floor tile with impressive artwork on the wall and granite counter tops—very cool. I went over to the officer behind the bullet proof glass and told him I had an appointment with Detective Burgess—he said he'd call him. I was a couple of minutes early, so I sat down to wait and just enjoy the lobby.

I heard the door to my right buzz open about three minutes later and there was Trent. He clearly was off duty—the suit was replaced by some jeans and a sweatshirt with a University of Arizona logo splashed across the front. We shook hands and he led me back to the door and got us buzzed in.

Trent had already done the paperwork to have me there, but he had to sign it, then have me sign it. He then glanced down at Molly and did that eye roll back up to my face where you leave your head down and just barely look up under your lids—it's that classic "you gotta be kiddin' me" routine.

"What?" I responded.

I know, I know—what can I say, I've always been really good at that 'spur of the moment' response. It's like poetry—it's a gift.

"Don't 'what' me," Trent said, "What are you packin' for?"

I could tell the officer behind the desk was enjoying this moment.

"This isn't my only stop today Trent—packin' a piece is part of my job." I thought that was a pretty good response.

"Yeah right—more like part of your machismo tough-guy 'look.'"

Curses—he was on to me. Mr. Desk Officer didn't even *try* to hide his grin.

"You realize I will now have *more* paperwork to sign to keep your gun here while we're inside?"

I didn't want to seem ungrateful, but this was a bit much.

"Dude, you and I both know it's just another form to hand over with the gun, so don't get your shorts in a bunch."

Trent stared at me for a moment and then chuckled as he shook his head. "Give me the form," he said to the desk officer.

"Her name is 'Molly' if you need that for the form," I said to the officer.

"You *named* your gun?" Trent asked, once again giving me "incredulous."

"Yeah, doesn't everybody?"

Trent just stared at me, then turned to sign the other form and then slid it over for me to sign. Yeah, that was a *lot more paperwork* Trent! I didn't say that out loud, but I thought it!

The officer buzzed us back through the next door into the world of the Tucson Police Department. It was all very cool, police officers all over the place, coming and going—and the digs were sweet! We went past the assembly rooms, the workout area, the gym, and shower rooms down a hallway to the conference rooms. A couple of them were occupied, but it looked like Trent had the third one on the left reserved for us.

We went in and sat down at the large table. Trent pointed over to the side table if I wanted coffee, which I did. He told me that he'd go check on Detective Who and was gone.

I got a "cuppa Joe" with seven packets of sugar and four of those little cups of creamer—God forbid I should actually *taste* the coffee—and I was set.

I sat back down and waited.

Just a couple of minutes later, Trent came walking back with three other people, two men and one really fine-looking woman. They walked in and I stood up—my momma always taught me to be polite.

Trent said, "Blake Moran, this is the lead detective of the Walker investigation that I spoke to you about."

Now I am an investigator—I pick up little clues and file them away for future use, so I didn't hesitate—I turned to the Asian male in the group, shook his hand and said, "Detective, it's nice to meet you."

You know those awkward moments when everyone in the room knows something you don't, but you have no idea what it is—this was *almost* like that. It was clear that *two* of us had no idea what was going on—me and the woman officer—Trent and the other two guys were already starting to laugh.

Trent then says, "No Blake," as he gestures to the woman officer, "*this* is the lead detective."

All right, I admit that I had stereotyped a little here. When I heard

"Detective Who," I did assume a mental picture of an oriental male detective—my bad.

Now I don't know about you, but I try hard not to end up as the butt of a joke—I'm an investigator, so I try to stay on my toes and see if something is coming my way—but I walked right into this one. I said exactly what Trent had planned and was hoping I'd say.

Trying to recover some semblance of professionalism and dig myself out of this hole, I turned, extended my hand, and addressed the female detective with a smile, saying, *"Detective Who."*

CHAPTER

— 16 —

When I said, "Detective Who," I knew something had just happened. The men burst out laughing, practically doubling over from laughing so hard. At the same time, the woman's very attractive face immediately began that pink crawl from the neck toward the face indicating that I had just stepped in it. I wasn't sure what "it" was, but I knew I had stepped in "it."

Her face was registering something close to dislike as she stared at me. Probably the only thing that saved me was the look of total *ignorance* and *confusion* on my face—one thing I can tell you—I do ignorance *really* well.

As I looked back and forth between the howling men and the clearly angry woman, Detective Who composed herself, straightened her back, held out her hand to me and said, "Hello, my name is Detective Rios."

Now the look on my face showed I could do *confusion* really well too, cuz I was totally confused.

Ms. Rios continued, "Mr. Moran, I apologize for my immature colleagues—I can see that you aren't in on their juvenile joke."

It was a little hard to hear her over the gasping for breath of her "colleagues."

"My name is Cindy Rios. Unfortunately, when I joined the force, one of my superiors noted that my middle name is Lou—Cindy Lou. Being from Georgia, this was a common name."

She spoke in a matter-of-fact manner, as though this wasn't the first time she'd had to explain this little story.

"That superior very quickly made the jump to the famous Dr. Seuss character from the TV special, '*How the Grinch Stole Christmas*'—'Cindy Lou Who.' From that time, my infantile colleagues have periodically engaged in what you have just witnessed."

I turned to Trent who was still laughing.

"So, you set me up last night for this?"

"Yep," he confirmed as he gasped for air.

"And these guys are?" I inquired.

"Just fellow detectives who wanted to see it. And I was counting on the fact that my bringing in an Asian guy would really seal the deal."

Now I knew that Detective Rios was pretty ticked off at them, and not at me yet, and that she had had to put up with this joke for a long time.

However, I've always believed that a good scam deserves kudos—it's one of the laws of the jungle.

So, I had to say it: "Well done, Trent my man—well done."

Trent accepted the accolades with a nod of his head while Detective Rios rolled her eyes and I'm pretty sure placed me into the ignoramus column with her "colleagues."

Oh well, you win some, you lose some.

Trent was ready to move on. "Anyway, Blake Moran, Detective Rios—Detective Rios, Blake Moran. I've already filled Blake in on what I could, so I'm going to finish up some paperwork—I'll be in my office if you need me."

He and his "colleagues" made a noisy exit—laughing and backslapping each other—still enjoying the moment of a good joke, well played.

I don't think Detective Rios was enjoying it quite as much.

CHAPTER
— 17 —

After the door closed, I looked over at her and "Cindy Lou" was regarding me with quite an accusatory look.

"Come on—I didn't do it and it *was* funny," I tried.

Detective Rios just stared at me for a moment. "I would think someone with the name Blake Moran would be more sensitive to name jokes."

Whoa—that was fast—she was good.

"How many name jokes are you coming up with right now—one or two?" I queried.

"Two."

Dang it—I gotta start pushing that middle name!

"All right—I'm sorry."

Kind of playing both sides of the street here, aren't I?

"Forget it."

Detective Rios went over to get some coffee which gave me a chance to check her out—forgive me, *or not*—I'm male, it's what I do.

Cindy Lou Rios—not Who—was medium height—about 5 feet 5 inches—and in great shape. She looked like she was a mixture of Hispanic and Caucasian, heavy on the salsa. Her hair was dark and currently pulled back into a ponytail, a thick, full ponytail. Her eyes were surprising, being ice blue instead of brown, and they kind of jumped out at you from the dark complexion of her face. Even though she was wearing some designer sweats after her workout, you could see that her body was tight and shapely when she moved over to get her coffee.

That was about all the time I could risk "investigating" Detective Rios—I was already kind of on her "bad list" for extending kudos to Trent for the joke. All I needed was for her to turn around and catch me staring at her body, and I'd probably find me and Molly sitting on the curb faster than you could say, "The Cat in the Hat."

Get it? I crack myself up sometimes—I don't think I'll share that little joke with Cindy Lou.

"Listen Mr. Moran," Cindy began.

"You can call me Blake."

That got a glance. She continued, "Anyway Mr. Moran."

OooooooKay.

"I typically don't involve Private Investigators in one of my investigations."

Is it just me, or did Detective Rios just refer to "Private Investigators" with the same attitude that one typically reserves for finding that one has just stepped in a bit of doggie doo?

"However," she continued, "in spite of Detective Burgess' sense of humor and gender, he *is* a good detective, and he has vouched for your abilities."

Did she say in spite of his gender? Please tell me I don't have a man hater on my hands.

I decided to go on the offensive, so when she turned around with her coffee, I hit her with my 100-watt smile—guaranteed to win over any member of the opposite sex.

It didn't even seem to start a thaw on the frost.

I cranked it up to 200 watts—not usually advisable within closed quarters like this—I didn't want anyone to get hurt.

She was still giving me Frosty the Snowman—and us here in the desert!

I realized that another tact was called for.

"Listen Cindy—can I call you Cindy?"

"Detective Rios will do."

Uh-huh.

"OK, listen Detective Rios, this is how I see it: I'm not your enemy, I'm on your side. Given the fact that I'm sure that Tucson has its share of crime, I'm guessing that a crime like Kate Walker's murder that is now over six months old has had to been put on the back burner. Your superiors would have made you do this by now—budget constraints alone would demand it."

I could tell I'd scored a point there.

"Since I imagine that you are a good detective, I'm guessing that having this woman's murder unsolved really bothers you. The problem is that, as much as it bothers you, you don't really have much of an option—you can't devote hardly any more time to it."

I'm not all that good at Jeopardy, but I'm pretty good at guessing this kind of stuff.

"So here I show up, just as cute as a button," (that comment threw her a little, so I moved on), "and guess what? I've got time. Kate had a brother named Greg, who is short on closure and long on cash, who wants me to help find his sister's killer."

"Now as I see it, that makes me your ally—I have the time and resources that you don't have, to help you solve a murder that you don't want to go unsolved."

"All I'm asking from you in return is a little cooperation."

I paused and waited. She just stared at me—thinking. Many times, the key to moments like this is having the patience to just wait it out until something breaks. I've never been good at that patience thing—so I suddenly blurted out:

"But wait, there's more! If you act now, we'll throw in the Ronco, two in one coffee maker and garden fertilizer for only $19.95, that's right, only $19.95—but you must act NOW!"

I don't know where I come up with this stuff, but believe it or not, Cindy Lou Rios actually *smiled*—and it was a nice smile—and then she laughed outright. Chalk one up for my lack of patience—and my Ronco shtick!

After staring at me for a moment, Cindy Lou said, "All right Mr. Moran, I'll drop the attitude. You're right—not being able to solve this murder drives me nuts, but I unfortunately can't spend hardly any time on it anymore. If you're as capable as Detective Burgess believes, it would be in the best interest of the case to spend whatever time I can spare, helping you to investigate."

"Thanks," I replied.

We spent the next three hours going over all the facts, implications and assumptions presently being made about Kate Walker's murder. T.P.D. had clearly done their job well. I made copious notes on page after page as I caught up on six months of investigation.

(Please note my use of the word "*copious*" above—absolutely *no* reason for me to use that word except that I'm trying to *impress* you. Thank you for your kind attention to this fact. In case you missed the opportunity offered you earlier—feel free to now be impressed.)

It was a nice way to spend a Saturday morning—two professionals putting their heads together to fight for justice and the American way! I'm sure that you know that the fact that Detective Rios was a total babe and smelled awesome had *nothing* to do with how nice the day was—it would have been just the same experience if *Trent* had been the lead detective.

Mm-hmm.

CHAPTER — 18 —

After leaving the substation, I started looking for some place to eat—I was starving. I also wanted to sit and think for a while—I'd just been handed a large amount of information and I needed to digest it all—along with some greasy pizza, if I could find some.

I ended up on a major surface street called Oracle and I stumbled on the Tucson Mall—and if it's in America, a mall pretty much has to have a Food Court. I parked my black beauty around back by Dillard's where I saw a parking garage—here in the desert you can read that as *shade*! A coveted commodity here.

So, I parked way out in the lot away from other door dingers—commonly called automobiles—and hoofed it into the mall with my notes. And it must have been my day, cuz right there to the left of Dillard's was an outside entrance to the "Food Court." Score!

They had a pizza by the slice place—maybe not as greasy as I would have liked, but what's a boy to do? At least my notes wouldn't get all stained.

I settled myself by the large windows overlooking the parking lot—it was quite scenic—and dug into my pepperoni pizza and sucked down about half of my soda. I then tried some of the cinnamon pizza dough bread sticks dipped in frosting—can't imagine they did anything for my health quotient, but what ya gonna do?

Having started to digest my food, I sat back and stared out at the parking lot while trying to start to digest what I'd learned so far in my investigation.

One thing that it seemed everyone could agree on is that this *was* murder—that whole accidental drowning con that the Unsub tried to play didn't fly with anyone.

For the record, the term "Unsub" is a term used to designate an *unknown* or *unidentified subject*—and I feel pretty cool when I use it. We knew we had us an Unsub since this case was definitely a murder. It was my job to find that scumbag—my even cooler term for the Unsub.

Having said all that, I had other stuff in my life besides my investigation into Kate Walker's death—and I hated that. I don't know about you, but I do best when I can focus on one thing at a time—I'm not a great multi-tasker. Even when I eat, I eat one type of food and then move on to another—I don't like to mix 'em. And don't even try to talk to me when the TV is on—although that's not particular to me—that's the bane of the left-brain male species of the human race.

Ask *any* woman who has tried to talk to a man while he's watching TV!

Any-who, I finally checked my phone, (which I had been ignoring for two days, sending it directly to voice mail—a bad habit, I know), and I was both delighted and a little disturbed that I only had five messages. Less calls to be returned, but feeling a little unloved by the human race.

One call was from Greg Walker this morning, wondering if I had anything yet on Kate's investigation. That's pretty eager if you ask me after only two days *but* you sure wouldn't catch ol' Blake Moran blaming the poor guy. I'd call him to update him either later today or tomorrow.

The only other call that required my attention was from Hailey Maxwell, a woman from Ohio who had hired me to run down her bum of an ex-husband. He had flown the coop to Arizona to avoid having his assets divided and then having to pay alimony and child support. This dude gets caught with his pants down, and subsequently gets served papers by his wife for his "Benedict Arnold" impersonation. He then decides to make some plans and abandon his wife and three kids financially, even though he's wealthy through his Internet business.

Enter Blake Moran—the righter of wrongs and the defender of all that is good and just—who says, "Yeah, I don't think so—punk."

I admit it again, I like to think of myself as a superhero sometimes—another little secret just between you and me. I'm still trying to work out what my costume should look like.

The real shot in the arm on this one for me was the double hit on this bum—if I caught him, not only would he be shipped back to Ohio, but the court papers stipulated that *he* had to pay my fee, (insert big grin), which I assure you will be large and bloated—just for him. Oh, how I love sweet justice.

Like I said, I'd rather focus on one thing at a time, but the problem with that is that jobs don't come at you like that—you don't always get one *as soon* as you finish the last one. So even though I've never been able to figure out how to juggle, I have to run simultaneous jobs and Hailey was calling!

That settled it—I needed to run home to Phoenix. I knew I wouldn't be able to be very productive on Kate's case over the weekend—everybody I needed to talk to would probably be off for the weekend or out having fun. Also, I had some things I needed to do at home.

I could also run down some checks I had going on Newton Maxwell—I kid you not—Newton. Who names a kid "Newton?!" I had some contacts at some city utilities and some in real estate and rentals, along with some pictures of "Newton" and a list of a couple of friends of his in the Phoenix area—the perp was practically mine!

So, I slurped down the last of my soda and then snagged myself a refill for the road. I got into my "foxy auto" and shot across town on River Road, (sans the river of course, since we're in Tucson), hit I-10 and then stopped off at Cortaro to settle things at The Hermosillo.

I asked for the manager and explained that I'd be back and forth to Phoenix some and get him to set up a special for me since I'd be around so much. I hope Greg appreciated my attention to frugality on his behalf, although I doubt it since the rate *still* wasn't cheap!

I arranged to get my room back for next Tuesday night and then hit the road to home. I called Hailey Maxwell and filled her in on what I'd found so far on Newton, which wasn't that much, but then I told her my plans for this weekend. I assured her I was on it and would call her soon with what I had found. She was sweet about it even though I knew she was stressed about whether her ex-husband might get away with his Houdini act and leave her and the kids to fend for themselves. It made me dislike "Newton" even more.

CHAPTER
— 19 —

The man sat in the dark office looking out at the mountains and desert landscape—but he wasn't seeing it.

He was just thinking—and seething.

He'd always had trouble with his temper—he had a dark, ugly side that very few people ever knew existed. He didn't care—as long as he could hide it from people, what difference did it make that he could lose it so easily and do some really bad things—even lethal things?

He'd gotten away with plenty in his life—things no one knew about—but the call he'd just gotten on his cell phone sent his anger meter into the red.

Someone was looking into Kate Walker's murder.

It was just idle conversation from a "friend" who was connected to the police department. He told him about a joke that was played down at the west substation on a Private Investigator from Phoenix. It would have been funny until he made the offhand comment about *what* this guy was investigating. It was all he could do to keep it together and not break something! It had been over six months and they had quit investigating—now this guy shows up!

He'd been able to regain just enough control to casually ask a few questions about this guy and then get off the phone. A quick search on the Internet told him that this Blake Moran wasn't just some hack—the reporting on the Las Vegas case regarding Christie Jarvis showed that this guy was the real deal.

He stood up and grabbed the lamp by the base and with a roar smashed it against the wall across the room. He was breathing hard and desperately wanted to hurt someone. How *dare* this man reopen this case and potentially jeopardize everything!

As he got himself under control, he began to think of ways that he could deal with this new threat. He would study and plan—he was very good at that. Mr. Moran must never be allowed to get even close to him or the truth. Too much was at stake. He knew instinctively that he would do whatever was necessary to stop this man—even if he had to kill him.

Actually, truth be told, that is exactly what he hoped he would get to do.

CHAPTER
— 20 —

I hung up with Hailey and was about to call Greg back to fill him in when it occurred to me that I still hadn't talked to Johnnie, Kate's other brother. Greg had given me his number, so this was a perfect time to follow up on that.

According to Greg, Johnnie lived in Chicago, Illinois and was a jazz musician—apparently a struggling musician like so many, since Greg said that he also worked construction on the side. I guess Johnnie as the middle child didn't pursue the corporate world like this brother and sister.

I wasn't sure I'd catch him in, but I figured I could give it a try and at least leave a message to get the ball rolling. I was kind of surprised when Johnnie picked up on the third ring.

"Hello."

"Hi. Mr. Walker, my name is Blake Moran. I'm a private investigator in Arizona and your brother Greg hired me to look into your sister's murder."

"Oh yeah, Greg called me and told me you'd probably call. And you can call me Johnnie—but no cracks about scotch—it's spelled different."

Bummer, he'd obviously already heard all the good jokes—on the positive side, maybe my name issues were safe as well.

I replied, "I wasn't sure I'd catch you this time of day on a Saturday, but I thought I'd try—I'm surprised I didn't get a machine."

"Whenever I'm home, I always answer the phone. I don't know if Greg told you, but I'm a jazz saxophone player when I can get the work.

I play in clubs all over the city and sometimes do some road trips too. People call for me to do gigs, often at the last second, so I can't afford to let it go to the machine. If they need someone right away, they don't leave messages, they just move on."

"I do have a gig tonight, however," he continued, "so I don't have too long to talk."

"That's all right, I just have a couple of questions," I replied.

"Shoot."

"Can you tell me a little about Kate?"

"Aw, Katie was super—I loved her a bunch. She was born when I was seven and was the best. Just having a baby around can do that, but Katie was something special. Have you seen a picture of her yet?"

"Yeah," I replied, "I just saw a picture of her last night."

"Then I don't have to tell you how amazingly beautiful Katie turned out to be—she was beautiful like that as a baby and a little kid too. She was my little buddy—she'd follow me around like a little puppy—called me 'John-john.'"

There was a long pause at the other end of the phone. I just waited while Johnnie fought for a little lost composure. I used this time wisely by spending it hating whoever killed this little girl even more—I think good time management is important.

Johnnie finally got some control back.

"Sorry about that."

"Don't blame you in the least, take all the time you need."

He took a deep breath and continued, "Katie was just the light of our life and a focus of a lot of fun and happiness in our family."

I was observing something about Johnnie that I thought was pretty cool. Johnnie didn't seem like his smooth, sophisticated and moneyed brother Greg or like his gorgeous and successful sister Kate. Johnnie was a little more common, the middle child working construction and playing his music whenever and wherever he could. And he called Kate—"Katie"—I liked that. She had obviously been just as captivating as a child as she had been as a woman. She was a focal point of much in the family after she came along and yet Johnnie clearly hadn't been jealous of this little cherub invading his world—he had celebrated it and her—and he still did. I don't know if I would have been quite as gracious if it had been me and I liked Johnnie for it. I found myself hoping he got to play a lot of his music.

"I'm sure Greg told you about the change in Katie when my parent divorced."

"Yeah," I said, "sounds like she took it really hard."

"She was the only one of us still at home. I was twenty and had moved out for a failed attempt at community college, and Greg was off at Harvard Law School. The divorce was a surprise and was hard on all of us, but poor Katie took the brunt of it—her whole world just came crashing down."

"It was hard to watch her mess up her life the way she did after that—it was like she was trying to kill herself—or at least bury herself away from the pain. I tried to step in and talk to her a number of times, and hug her even more, but ol' 'John-john' just couldn't pay the freight anymore, I guess. Greg tried some too, but we just couldn't get through."

Another long pause.

"As you can imagine, we were thrilled when Katie came out of all of that and got herself together. It had been a bad, bad road, but much of the good that Katie used to be seemed to come back. It was like that had been her way of dealing with her grief and then she just decided it was time to stop it."

"After that, Katie became the success story we always thought she'd be. I can't say she got that inner glow back that she'd had before the divorce, but she was doing life well. That was another thing that made her murder even harder for me."

"What," I asked, "that she had been doing life so well?"

"Well yeah, that, but that's not what I meant. I talked to Katie about every other week—you know, just about what we were doing and such.

She was always trying to send me money to help me out, but I wouldn't let her. She'd made her way and done well for herself, and I was proud of her and wanted her to just enjoy what she had—I get by."

"But what made the murder even harder for me was that the old Katie had come back in those last few months—a Katie I hadn't seen since she was thirteen."

I sat up a little straighter and drove off the road a little.

"What do you mean Johnnie?"

"That light, that inner glow that she always had seemed back. She was happier and funnier and just seemed more lighthearted than I had known her to be for decades."

"Did you point this out to her or ask her about it," I asked.

"You bet I did, a couple different times—and she would just laugh, almost giggle and just say, 'I'm very happy Johnnie, that's all.'"

"Johnnie, I need you to think hard about this for me—this might be important. How long before her murder did this inner glow show up? You said, 'those last few months'—can you try and pin down when you first noticed this change?"

Silence. More silence. I just waited and tried to stay out of the way—my cell plan had unlimited minutes, so I wasn't worried.

Finally, a heavy sigh and then he said, "I'm gonna say a little over two months before her death. Maybe two and a half at the most. The reason that I remember was because it was such a change, kind of a transformation back to Katie again—it made me very happy for her."

I did some quick calculations.

"All right, starting at January fourth and working our way back, that would take us to . . ." wait for it, "sometime pretty close to Halloween."

"Wait, that's right!" Johnnie said suddenly.

"What?"

"I talked to Katie just a couple of days after Halloween cuz I wanted to tell her about the crazy gig I'd done at a big Halloween party—that was when she seemed like the old Katie! We laughed and joked and talked for over an hour—it was great! That was it, so it was just over two months I guess."

"That may be a great help Johnnie, a really great help," I said.

"How come?" he asked.

"Well, when I talked to Greg, he commented that the last time he had talked to Kate was about six weeks before her death. At first, he said she seemed the same as usual, but then he corrected himself and said that now that he thought about it, she was different—more upbeat and optimistic. He seemed to say that she was just happier in general. The fact that he noticed that stuck with me. Now clearly you were closer to Kate than Greg—perhaps because you were closer in age and lived in the home longer with her—but being closer, you've just given me a closer look into something that I think might matter. I'm not sure how yet, but I think it be a clue."

"Well, if it helps, I'm all about that Blake—I want to do anything I can to help. I don't have the money that Greg does, but if there is anything else I can do, just let me know."

"Thanks Johnnie, I'll remember that. I'm coming into a notoriously bad cell phone area up ahead, so I'd better get off this phone, but if I come up with anything or have any more questions, I'll give you a call."

"Sounds great—I gotta get ready for my gig anyway. Talk to you later—and Blake . . ."

"Yeah?"

"Find the scumbag who killed my sister."

I even liked Johnnie's choice of words.

"I'll do my best Johnnie—I promise—I'll do my very best for you and Greg—but especially for 'Katie.'"

CHAPTER
— 21 —

I got back to my castle in Chandler late afternoon on Saturday. The remainder of the trip back to Phoenix had given me time to add what Johnnie had told me to the rest of the things I'd learned so far in my investigation. Something was starting to stir inside of me—I felt like I was starting to get a grip on a thread on a piece of cloth—if I could keep tugging on that, I think something might start to unravel.

Speaking of which, (cloth, thread, thus clothes), I needed to be a little domestic. I had some clothes to wash and a little cleaning to do on my abode. That's right—it was heading toward Saturday night and I, the tall, somewhat good looking, (or at least presentable), young thirty-something man of high, (or at least passable), intelligence was cleaning his house and doing his laundry. Oh the "life on the edge" existence of a single, male Private Investigator living in a major metropolitan city! It boggles the mind!

So, I put on my apron . . . oh *come on*—I was totally kidding about that! Did you believe me—maybe for a minute? Seriously?! Don't get crazy on me here!

Anyway, I did my cleaning, washed my clothes, went through my mail, all while watching highlights on ESPN. I'll admit it to you if you promise not to tell anyone else—it was a nice night. I'm in no way a "confirmed bachelor"—I am certainly looking for "Miss Right"—but I admit it—even without "Miss Right," it *was* a nice night.

Sunday morning, I slept in and woke up nice and slow. I finally crawled out of bed at about 9:00 a.m., gave my pearly whites a good workout with my brush, and then did the unthinkable—threw on my gym trunks and running shoes, stretched out and took off out my door for a run. I do this a couple of times a week if it occurs to me—but doing so on a lazy Sunday morning is unheard of! Sure, I'm ashamed of myself for doing this, but I don't know what to say—it sounded like a good idea—even if it was a Sunday.

It was already pretty hot as I started to run through my neighborhood—this is greater Phoenix after all—so by the time I'd gone about half a mile, I was starting to sweat and huff and puff. I ran through the local park complete with a fake pond and a fountain shooting up in the middle of it and then on to the High School. I did a couple of laps around the football field while I watched some "weekend warriors" playing a football game on the field. It could just be me, but I felt a kind of brotherhood with these fellow warriors as we fought together against that ancient foe—becoming out of shape old fogies. I resisted the urge to call out, "Fight on brother warriors, fight on!" People always look at you kind of weird when you do stuff like that—all I'll say is, trust me on this one.

I headed back toward my place, sprinting as much as I could the last quarter mile into the strip mall close to my condo. It just so happened that there was a donut shop in that strip mall, and it just so happened that I had cash with me to purchase said donut should the interest arise at the end of said run. Now I don't want you to get the idea that I *planned* this all along and that the run was actually both an excuse and a justification for eating a Boston Crème, a chocolate covered Long John and a jelly filled. Seriously, where *do* you come up with this stuff?! Don't look at me like that—I took them home and had *skim milk* with them! Who feels foolish *now*?!

In addition to my "breakfast," I picked up a Sunday paper. I know, in the age of the Internet, *who* gets a paper?! But there is something about a Sunday paper. The thing is *huge* and *so* fun! I pulled all the ads out of the middle and settled down at my dining table to enjoy breakfast and peruse the paper. (Notice that I didn't just "read" the paper—no, I "perused" it—I am one seriously intellectual snob!)

After about an hour of "perusing," I figured I'd better get at it. I cleaned up my mess and jumped in the shower—half an hour later, I was ready for my day.

Now I know that a guy being able to get ready for his day in a half hour or less is patently annoying to those of the fairer sex—sorry about that. Look at it this way: we can get ready really fast, but there is *no* amount of time we could take that could make us look anywhere *close* to as good as you ladies look. It's a tradeoff. And if I may speak for my male counterparts the world over, (and I may since this is my story), for all the preening, cleaning, plucking, designing, coiffing, waxing, adorning, and applying—we males are *eternally grateful.*

CHAPTER

— 22 —

It was time to put a little work in on Mr. Newton Maxwell—in my mind thought of as "Mr. Take the Money and Run." Dirty dog. It was now after 1:00 on a Sunday afternoon—a great time for a little "siesta," as we say down here in the Southwest—but there was work to do!

Being Sunday afternoon, many of the offices that I needed for my search would be closed, but not Barry Parker—my old friend was a bit of a workaholic. Barry was an older brother of a kid I ran track with in High School—Aaron Parker. One time when I stopped by Aaron's house, Barry was there and we met. Even with the ten years difference in our ages, we kind of clicked. When Aaron said, "This is my brother Barry," I said, "Barry? Barry Parker?" Barry nodded yes and I said, "Kind of like berry picker?" (Admittedly, *not* my best stuff.) For some reason, Barry thought that was really funny, and turned right around and gave me grief about my name.

We've been friends ever since.

Barry is in real estate—he's actually quite successful in real estate. That's probably attributable to a few things: the fact that he's a good talker, that whole "workaholic" thing, and the fact that it's typically tough to fail in real estate in Phoenix. This is especially true when it's winter everywhere else and people would just about sacrifice their first-born to get out of their deep freeze and into the "Valley of the Sun."

So, I put in a call to Barry's office. The phone rang about three times and then a female voice came on the line and said, "Parker Realty."

I froze. I purposely called Barry on a Sunday afternoon because I figured *he* would be the only one in the office and would answer the phone. His agents would be showing houses, and his administrative staff *should* have been off.

Apparently not—the great sleuth Moran had been outfoxed.

You see, I knew the voice on the other end of the line—I'd actually dated the voice on the other end of the line—and all the rest that was attached to it. Her name was Stephanie Flores. I met her through Barry. After one divorce, Barry is now a happily married man with two children and seems to have it as his mission to get me hitched too. His wife Serena, whom I adore, is a co-conspirator on this mission as well. Because of this plan of theirs, I have often heard the phrase, "We have this girl we want you to meet." This mission has yielded a success rate anywhere between "nice" and "train wreck." But don't worry, neither Barry or Serena is deterred by failure—oh no—they soldier on regardless of the cost—*to me*! But I'm OK with it, I kind of like it that they love me.

Stephanie Flores was one of those girls and she was closer to the "nice" side of the scale. But after about three dates, I wasn't feeling the magic that would ever justify me uttering those ominous words, "For better or for worse, to death do us part." You see, I'm a bit of a romantic—I don't want to "settle" in the area of romance—and if there is to be a future Mrs. Moran, I don't want her to settle either. I don't want to "mutter" those ominous words—I want to gladly "utter" them. So, I avoid "mutter" and aspire to "utter."

Well, let's just say that Steph didn't see things quite like I did—she thought we had a future and thought I should give it more time to see. Ms. Flores had some great Latino flavor about her—dark hair, dark eyes—she was a good-looking woman. However, she also had a bit of a temper, and I was on her—how shall I say this nicely—naughty list. Let's just say she wasn't pleased about this Private Investigator's decision to discontinue his investigation into "us."

So, you could say that I'd been "outfoxed" by the "fox" on the other end of the line—I couldn't *believe* she was there! It flashed through my mind just to hang up, but then I realized they probably had caller ID. (I recognize that I may be ruining that whole "superhero" image for you right now, but I don't know what to tell you—I really didn't want to do this with her.)

So, I just took a deep breath, put on my big boy pants, and decided I might as well face the music. Then, I tore off my big boy pants and tried to make my voice sound as different as I could when I said, "Yes, is Barry Parker there please?" (I don't know what to tell you—I panicked.)

Ms. Flores responded, "Yes. May I tell him whose calling?"

CURSES! I did *not* see that one coming!

I thought fast—after all, I'm a Private Investigator—it's what I do. I did a quick search of my gray matter and came up with the fact that Barry was a member at the Biltmore Country Club.

"Yes. This is Curtis Sanders over at the Biltmore—he asked me to confirm his reservation for he and Serena tonight in our restaurant."

Pause.

"Really?"

"Yes."

"Well, 'Mr. Sanders,'" replied Ms. Flores, with force, "it says here that you're calling from the residence of a Mr. Blake Moran to confirm this reservation for your country club. Since you're there, would you be so kind as to turn and ask Mr. Moran, on my behalf, if he would please *take a long walk off a short pier*?!"

Pause. Wow—that was a good one. I hate it that she thought faster than I did. Finally, I said, "Certainly ma'am, I'd be happy to." Don't come out of character—don't *ever* come out of character!

"Excellent! I'll put you through now."

That was just not at all how I saw that going down.

CHAPTER 23

Barry got on the phone. "Hi Blake."

Curses again—didn't fool her!

"Do you want to explain to me why Stephanie just told me that Blake Moran was on the line pretending to be Curtis Sanders from the Biltmore because he's too much of a coward to face her after blowing her off?"

I thought about it.

"Nope, I'd have to say that she summed it up quite nicely—that's pretty much it."

"Blake, you do realize that there is no Curtis Sanders over at the Biltmore and that Serena and I don't have any reservations for dinner there tonight? I would have pointed this out to Stephanie, and she would have come back and questioned you even if she hadn't seen your number."

"Oh, sure Barry, everybody's a critic when they're sitting in the cheap seats. What can I say? I panicked. I figured she'd be off, and you'd answer the phone on Sunday afternoon—I was unprepared!"

Barry started laughing. "Just as smooth as ever, aren't' you Blake? We gotta find you a bride Blake, just to protect you from yourself!"

I hesitated to remind him that the aforementioned awkward situation I'd just been through, was somewhat a result of him and his lovely wife *already* trying to find me a bride.

"That reminds me," continued Barry, "Serena and I are having a party out at the house and there's this girl we want you to meet."

"Oh, I'm busy that night."

"Blake, I didn't tell you what night the party was."

Man, I am *really* off my game today!

I tried again.

"Oh. Well look Barry, I really am in the middle of this murder investigation down in Tucson, so I'm going to be gone quite a bit for a while."

"OK—no problem. I'll let Serena know and we'll just arrange the party for when you'll be in town."

Pause. I'm thinking . . . I got nothin'.

"All right."

"Great! Serena and I will look forward to that. I think you'll really like this girl."

I cut in before Barry had me married with 1.7 children and mowing my grass in the "burbs."

"Listen Barry, I wanted to see if you could help me out with another case I'm working on."

"Sure, what do you need?"

"I've got a runner," I continued, "a deadbeat dad who doesn't want to pony up the cash for his family back in Ohio, even though apparently he's got a lot of it through his Internet business. He's used to nice stuff, so my guess is that he changed his name so that he could keep up his lifestyle without being found."

"Sounds about right to me," replied Barry, "what do you need me to do?"

Barry was kind of "into" this detective stuff—he always liked it when I called, and he got to hunt the bad guy.

"Could you call some of your real estate colleagues and see if they've had any moneyed clients in the last six months who have gotten their wealth through an Internet business? Also, it's probable that the initials of this guy's new name will be N. M. or M. N.—perps tend to keep the same initials in some combination."

"Really?" Barry asked. "What was his real name?"

"Newton Maxwell."

"Seriously? The dude's name is 'Newton'?"

"I don't name 'em Barry, I just report the facts."

Chuckle.

"All right—when do you need this?"

"Yesterday. I got a wife and three kids in Ohio who need a little justice from a philandering crumb bum who needs to face the music and pay for his sins. Any chance you could call around now?"

"Sure, I know just the people to call—I should be able to call you back in a couple of hours if I have anything."

"Thanks Barry—I owe you—again."

"No problem. I'll get right on it—and don't forget about that girl—she's a good one. I'll let Serena know to get with you about the party."

"OK." Doesn't this man forget anything?!

"Oh, and 'Curtis'—I'm gonna cancel those reservations for the club tonight—Serena and I are just going to stay in tonight."

Funny man. I hung up with him still laughing.

CHAPTER
— 24 —

While I waited on Barry, I got busy on the Internet looking up the friends of Mr. Maxwell in the Phoenix and surrounding area from the list that Hailey gave me. Given the wealth of the friends he had here, I was able to just "Google" their names with "Phoenix" and I found information about them fairly quickly. Using that information, I was then able to cross reference it with the areas where they lived and narrow down the search area. I found three of the friend's addresses, phone numbers and where they worked just through that search.

Not to my surprise, the other two were seeking the anonymity of being unlisted, but I knew how to get to them too—it would just take another step, but that would have to wait for tomorrow when the utility offices would be open. You might be nice and rich and try to be invisible, but everyone needs water, electricity, trash service and other utilities and we all pay taxes. If you have the right contacts in the right places—and I do, (said Blake Moran, P.I., modestly), it's only a matter of time.

I then sent Barry an email with an attachment. I wrote, "Barry, attached is a picture of 'Newton Maxwell.' If you find any of your associates thinking they might have worked with our perp, please forward this picture to them. Also let them know that if Newton—or whatever he's calling himself now—really went for it, he may have had some cosmetic work done. He may have changed his nose or lips and most probably changed the color and style of his hair. Tell them to focus on the eyes and the structure of the face—basically, does the face look 'familiar'? One way to do this is to have them stare at the picture and then half close their eyes to blur the particulars—the structure can become more clear through this. Let me know if and when you have something. Thanks."

A lot of investigating was hard work and research with a nice dollop of luck on top. Barry's research was key to this investigation *if* Newton had changed his name, which I think he had. I'd already done credit card searches for any hint that he had used his existing credit cards or any new cards that he'd hidden from his wife or gotten after the divorce. I hadn't found any.

Newton was following after, what I guessed was his namesake, Sir Isaac Newton—he was being smart. But we would soon see if Mr. Maxwell had what Sir Isaac Newton referred to as "gravitas," a word that he used that came to be known as "gravity" in our English language. (The Latin word, "gravitas" means "weight.") When it came to being pursued, would Newton Maxwell have the "gravitas" to get away with it? We would see—oh yes—we would see. (Insert evil genius laugh here.)

In the middle of my evil genius laugh, I realized that my donuts had worn off and I was really hungry. I had a little time to kill while I waited on Barry, so it was time to grab something to eat. I flipped ESPN on and then did a quick survey of my kitchen and decided I had enough stuff to put to test my culinary abilities.

I admit that I don't know much about cooking, but there are a few things I can do—one of which was a mean grilled ham and cheese. While I heated up my electric griddle, I buttered four pieces of wheat bread on one side and set two of them to browning on the griddle. I then got out the ham. I'll admit that it was a mite bit slimy, but it smelled OK, so I decided I'd take the chance—I was really hungry. I slathered the bread with mayonnaise—a key to the taste—and then the slimy ham went on both slices of bread. I then piled grated cheddar and Monterey Jack cheese on, topped it with mild pepper rings and put the "lid" on with the other two pieces of bread. I then put the other two, already buttered pieces, on the top, and flipped each of them over to brown the top piece of bread and melt the cheese—oh yeah!

While I waited for the sandwiches, I got out some potato chips, (which as you know I think should be counted as a vegetable), and popped open a Mountain Dew (Which has "corn syrup"—a vegetable, *and* orange juice—a fruit.) Clearly a well-rounded meal.

I sat down and focused on the sports channel while I fed my face—happy as a pig in slop. (Perhaps I should have come up with a better simile.)

I was almost done when Barry called with a smile on his face that I could practically *hear* through the phone.

"Blake my man, I'm like the Sam Spade of Real Estate and I bring you good news."

"I'm all ears Mr. Spade, tell me what you know."

"I called my sources . . ."

(Sources? His colleagues were now "sources?" My friend Barry had been watching too many Crime Scene Investigation shows . . .)

". . . and I gave them all the information that you gave me and three of them thought they might have worked with a guy like you were looking for. They weren't sure they should "out" this guy—since they had worked for him. However, I told them generally what Newton had done to his family, and then convinced them to look at the picture you sent me. Two out of the three identified the guy and it was just like you said—he changed his name but kept his initials. He also changed his face a little—apparently a nose job. His new name is 'Nelson Montgomery' and I got them to give me his new address and his phone number."

I was a little dumbstruck.

"They gave you all that?"

"Well," Barry replied, "one of my friends was a little more incensed than the other—it's a woman realtor who had this happen to her—and she wants this guy nailed. After I had the information from her, I was able to just confirm it with the other guy."

Maybe Barry Parker *was* Sam Spade.

"Wow Barry, I don't know what to say. I was just hoping for some possible leads to follow up on, but this is amazing! I'm going to have to give you *my* fee."

Barry was clearly enjoying the praise—and I was totally blowing about giving him my fee—he didn't need it, and I did.

"All in a day's work my friend, all in a day's work! Seriously though, with everything you gave me, it wasn't that hard—a heavy hitter like that who can throw around that kind of cash, kind of sticks in your mind. All his money is going to end up being bad luck for him."

"You got that right. Well thanks a ton Barry—with just a few phone calls, you just gave me what I need to fix Hailey and the kid's problem back in Ohio. I hope that feels good to you."

"It does," said Barry.

"Good," I replied, "cuz I'm not really going to give you my fee."

Once again, I left him laughing.

CHAPTER

— 25 —

After I put down the phone, I steepled my fingers and in my most convincing cartoon voice, actually said out loud, "Mr. Maxwell, I have you now!" It's kind of that superhero thing that you promised *not* to say anything about. However, now that I think about it, I could've done an even better line: "Mr. Maxwell, your coffee break is *over*!" Get it? "Maxwell"—coffee break—from paying money to his family? Dang it! I hate it when I think of a better line later, even if I was just sitting by myself in my house! Oh well, life goes on.

I called Hailey Maxwell and filled her in on what I had on Newton. I told her that her ex-husband had changed his name to "Nelson Montgomery" and altered his face a little through a nose job. I could tell that it was sobering to her that this man who she had once loved and with whom she had children, was now willing to go to such lengths just to avoid caring about his family. I felt bad for her. When you see the ugly underbelly of humanity like this, it can be pretty unsettling.

I explained to her that I would now call the Phoenix Police Department who would in turn call her precinct in Ohio to get the arrest warrant in front of them. They would then verify my information and then make the arrest. I explained that "Nelson," aka Newton would then "lawyer up" to fight extradition back to Ohio. Since he has so much money, it will take a little longer, but it won't work. He *will* be returned to Ohio to face charges. His assets will also be frozen so that he can't pull anything. However, he may have already tried to hide some of his assets just in case, but they will probably be found. I also pointed out that since Newton has proven he is a flight risk, you should be able to fight for and get a "bail denied" decision. That will give him the privilege of enjoying the deluxe accommodations at one of your fine jail facilities in Ohio. I told her that in my opinion, this would be good for Mr. Montgomery/Maxwell—he'll see why he doesn't ever want to try and pull a stunt like this again.

Finally, I told Hailey that I would be sending her my bill and that she shouldn't freak out when she sees how high it is. That got her attention.

"Why do you say the bill will be so high?"

"One of the things I do in situations like this is if the victim is paying the bill, I lower my rates, but if the perpetrator has to pay out of his resources, I double my rates. I figure he caused all this mess, he ought to pay the premium price through the nose."

Hailey thought about it. "I see your point, Mr. Moran—I won't freak out."

"Great. Just put the invoice into the settlement and the court will take care of the payment out of his remaining assets."

"Mr. Moran, thank you. I can't tell you what a relief this is for me." She began to cry. "I'm sorry, it's just been hard enough feeling so betrayed by Newton because of the adultery, but then to watch him endanger our family in such an uncaring way, it's just demoralizing."

I thought about that for a moment while she cried.

"Mrs. Maxwell, I'm guessing you are a strong, capable woman—you certainly did not take this abandonment lying down. I would suggest that you work at not letting this bad man have any more control over your life or over how you feel about yourself. He has the problem—not you, and not your children—don't let it infect you and your life."

Silence. Oh great, I thought, I just had to go into my "Blake Moran, life philosopher/psychologist" mode.

Finally, Hailey spoke up.

"You know Mr. Moran, I think you're right—this man has done enough damage to me, my self-esteem, and my family—enough is enough. I think maybe it's time for me to get on with my life and leave 'Nelson' in the dust."

"Good for you Hailey—good for you."

I like her style—and maybe I should think about that psychologist thing . . . naaah.

CHAPTER
— 26 —

Sunday night was nice. I didn't think I'd have the night off—I even thought I'd be working on the Maxwell case through Monday. Barry really came through for me there, so I'm guessing I'll have to go to his and Serena's faux party so they can try and fix me up with the latest "Miss Right" in their opinion. Oh well, I could always go as my alter ego, "Curtis Sanders" from "the club." Hmmm. I'm guessin' that ship has already sailed.

I had two calls that I needed to make. I first called my contact at the Phoenix Police Department and gave him all the pertinent information on Newton Maxwell, aka Nelson Montgomery. The officer said they'd get in touch with the Ohio precinct and work out the preliminary extradition issues, and then serve the warrant. "Newton's" high life was about to take a serious downturn and I didn't give a "fig" about that. (Think about it . . . get it? I really crack myself up sometimes.)

I then returned Greg Walker's call from yesterday. I checked the time difference in my head for New York before I put the call through—after all, I'm a classy guy. Given the later hour in New York, I tried his home first—I'm a P.I.—I know how to figure out stuff like this. A woman answered the phone and indicated that she was Mrs. Walker. I identified myself and she seemed to know about me, and let me know she'd get Greg right away.

Greg and I did the usual human ritual of "How are you?" and I even added a nice personal touch by asking him about his wife and if he had any family. I'm a regular graduate of Dale Carnegie's *How to Win*

Friends and Influence People, aren't I? It turned out that Greg had three kids—a son who was fifteen, a daughter who was twelve and a baby girl who was only two. I expressed surprise at the ten years between the last two, thinking that maybe Mrs. Walker was actually Mrs. Walker the second. You see that starting a second family thing pretty often in blended families. Greg just laughed and said that their little girl was their "love child," a nice way to say "oops"—I'm sure a wonderful oops—but still one of those, "didn't see that coming!"

I then shifted gears and told him what I'd done so far, and what I knew, and what my next steps would be on Kate's case—heading back to Tucson tomorrow. I explained to him that while everything so far was preliminary, that's how most cases started out. I would just keep scratching the surface till something started to bleed. I'm not sure, but I think ol' Greg thought my analogy was kind of gross. He may have a point. I told him I'd call him again when I had more and that he could reach me anytime he needed to as well.

Having taken care of that call, I decided to watch a made for TV movie that was on while I had some microwave popcorn and a brew. It was fun, but I have to admit that I had this nagging feeling that I should probably grow up and start thinking about the future a little bit more. So, I started to think about it, and then got over it, and decided I'd think about it tomorrow—or maybe the next day.

Finishing up Newton's investigation so quickly meant that I could get back down to Tucson a day early and see if I could get some traction on Kate's investigation. I called The Hermosillo to see if I could get my room back a day early, which I did, and then I started getting my plan in place to ferret out the perp.

CHAPTER

— 27 —

After a good night sleep, I cleaned up the place one more time, so it would be nice when I came back—then I loaded up and headed out. I knew what my plan of attack was going to be now, and I was anxious to start tugging on that thread a little harder.

(I decided I agreed with Greg's take on the "scratch it till it bleeds" approach—gross. So, I'll be "thread tuggin'" from here on out.)

I stopped by my office before I headed out of town to look through the mail. Having been gone from my high-powered executive suites for a while, I just about passed out when I stepped out of my truck. Whatever internal organs the cattle feed factory was grinding up today, to turn into pellets for our four-legged friends to munch on, just about put me down for the count! I had to hang on to my side view mirror mount for a moment, bending over and breathing into the sleeve at the crook of my elbow. I finally took in whatever air I could find and bolted for my office door. Once inside, the air quality went up by about twenty percent—not much, but I'll take it.

Having been gone from the, let's just say "nuances," of my office space for a while made me wonder if just maybe I should start thinking about some different office space. Along with the overwhelming odor, there was the impressive wood paneling, the water-stained ceiling tiles, and the glued down linoleum that was pealing up in various places—what's not to love?! I could tell that staying at The Hermosillo was starting to make me a little snooty.

Don't worry, I'll always be the good old, Blake Moran that you've come to love and cherish.

Too much—too soon?

OK.

Any-who, in the middle of my disdain, I looked down on that linoleum floor through my watering eyes, where the mail had been pushed through the mail slot, and right on top was my office rent bill. I knew very well how much that bill was—and it wasn't much—and suddenly as I looked around my "power suite," I decided my offices had "character." It's amazing how cheapness can change your whole perspective.

I spent about an hour in the office doing the bills and getting the checks that had come in ready for deposit—basically some general tidying up. As I started closing up to leave, I noticed that my eyes weren't even watering much anymore and that if I worked real hard, I could imagine that I smelled a hint of something like a food smell in the stench. It was all good.

As I traveled toward Tucson, I started reviewing what I knew about Kate's murder so far, and where I was headed now in the investigation.

I probably need to fill you in on something here: you have to understand that when it comes to reasons for committing crime, I've always believed that the criminal world suffers from an acute case of PMS—no, not what you're thinking—that would just be weird. I'm talking about three things: power, money and sex—the "why" behind most crimes can be tracked back one of these reasons. There might be some other reasons that could be added, but I don't think so, *and* I don't want there to be. You see, that's a pretty cool acronym I came up with there—I don't want another letter to mess it up!

Another thing you probably need to know; statistically, most people who are killed are done in by close relatives, friends or acquaintances, *not* by strangers. This fact means two things: 1) that I always start looking there first and so do the police, and, 2) you might want to think about that little statistic as you look around at your "loved ones." (I'm just messing with you on that one . . . but seriously; do keep an eye on them.)

Anyway, because of these realities, this is what I always start looking for—how the "Big 3" might relate, and who was close to the victim. These are the threads I start tugging at to see what unravels—and that's what I was headed to do now.

CHAPTER
— 28 —

While I drove, I put in a call to The Palms, asking for Samuel Joyner, the General Manager of the resort, who had been Kate's immediate boss. As you can imagine, the dude was a pretty hard guy to get to, given his executive position, running this posh resort. However, never let it be said that Blake Moran, P.I. is timid—I can be a tenacious little jerk sometimes.

After fighting my way through the front desk and then two secretaries who were sure they could "handle whatever I believed I needed to speak to Mr. Joyner about," I was put through to his "Executive Secretary" in the Executive Suites.

Now I know I'm probably supposed to be intimidated by all this wealth, power, and opulence, but I'm just not. Hey, I have "Executive Suites" too! OK, given I could still smell a hint of my "Executive Suites" on my clothes, it was not a great argument. But hey, we're all just people, so lighten up already!

The phone clicked and I heard, "This is Mrs. Coleman, Mr. Joyner's Executive Secretary. I'm told you wish to talk with Mr. Joyner—how may I help you?"

Oh dang. This lady's cold tone sounded like the real deal—I think my fingers on the phone took a little frostbite when she spoke. I pictured a lieutenant colonel in a dress with a riding crop—scary lady. I'm guessing she knew her job, she had the clout, and she knew how to use it.

Bummer.

I found my voice and said, "I need to speak with Mr. Joyner please."

"I see," she replied, "As you can imagine Mr. Moran, Mr. Joyner is an extremely busy man running such a beautiful and exclusive resort. Part of my job is to make sure his job isn't made more difficult with unnecessary interruptions. May I inquire as to the nature of your business with Mr. Joyner?"

"Sure," I replied.

Pause. I just waited. I know I shouldn't be like this, but when people say things like, "May I inquire as to the nature of your business" in such a snooty way, it brings out, shall I say, my petulant side. (Really childish—really, really immature.)

"Well?" she responded.

"Well, what?" I asked ever so innocently.

"What is the nature of your business with Mr. Joyner?"

"Oh good—I didn't think you were *ever* going to 'inquire.'"

I was having a real chuckle on my end of the phone, but I'm pretty sure Mrs. Coleman was not enjoying my wit as much as me—I think she was giving me "harrumph." I figured I'd better get on with it before "Mrs. C" harrumphed me right into a dial tone.

"My name is Blake Moran and I'm a private investigator from Phoenix."

I paused—nothing. So, I plunged on.

"I've been hired by Greg Walker to continue the investigation into the murder of his sister, Kate Walker, who worked at your resort before her death."

Pause.

"I see," said Mrs. Coleman.

Is it just me, or did "Mrs. C" say those two words a lot? However, for some reason, when she said it this time, it felt like Mrs. Coleman thawed out a little. I pushed on.

"To pursue further investigation effectively, I am going to need to begin to talk to those people who were closest to her, and those who work at The Palms are the obvious candidates. I could try and track all these people down in their personal life, but the most efficient approach would be for me to try and talk with them at The Palms. I was hoping for permission from Mr. Joyner to do this."

"I see." Silence.

I didn't know what the deal was, but I figured I'd made enough of my case to either get put through or not, so I waited for the ice queen to issue her decision.

Finally she said, "Mr. Moran, I was quite fond of Kate."

You could have knocked me over with a feather when she said this. Her next statement was in a lowered voice.

"For Mr. Joyner to end up being agreeable to this request of yours, you will need to be able to assure him that your activities will not be overly time consuming for the employees, and will not adversely affect his operating of this resort. Mr. Joyner is a fair man, and an excellent businessman, but he will need some convincing that your efforts will not get in the way of what we do here."

I was shocked. Mrs. Coleman had gone from locking and securing the gates, to giving me insider advice on how to succeed, apparently simply with the utterance of the words, "Kate Walker."

I found my voice.

"Thank you, Mrs. Coleman, I believe that I can give Mr. Joyner those assurances, and should he allow me to proceed, I will seek to honor those promises." I could talk kind of flowery when I needed to, and this seemed like a good time to do so.

"Mrs. Coleman," I continued, "whether I'm able to do these interviews at The Palms or not, would I be able to talk with you soon about Kate?"

"Yes Mr. Moran, I would be glad to help in any way I can."

"Thank you."

"Please hold Mr. Moran," she continued, "and I'll put you through to Mr. Joyner."

Cool.

CHAPTER
— 29 —

There was an extended pause while I set on hold and listened to *Muzak*—that elevator music everybody pipes in. I was right in the middle of a fully orchestrated version of "Havin' My Baby" when a voice came on the line.

"This is Samuel Joyner. Judith tells me this is regarding something to do with the investigation of the death of Kate Walker?"

OK. Right to business. Guess we're not going to engage in that ancient form of humanness where we meet and greet each other.

Also, I figured out pretty quickly that "Judith" was Mrs. Coleman's first name.

What can I say? I'm an excellent private investigator.

"Yes, Mr. Joyner. My name is Blake Moran and I'm a private investigator from Phoenix. I've been hired by Greg Walker to continue the investigation into the murder of his sister, Kate Walker."

"Listen, Mr. Moroon, is it?"

"No, Moran, Blake Moran."

"Well, Mr. Moran, the police were all over The Palms for some time with their investigation. Why do you have to repeat their efforts?"

"I wouldn't be repeating them sir, I'm hoping to continue them."

"Aren't they still investigating?"

"Well, Mr. Joyner, the answer to that is 'yes' and 'no.' Being in business, I'm sure you have to deal with allocation of resources on a regular basis—so does the police department. Because of this, after a case has lingered for some time and leads have seemed to dry up, the case has to be moved into a cold case category while the department focuses on cases that are generating leads. There is little 'active' investigation at this point, but if a lead presents itself, that cold case can come back onto the front burner as an active case. Being that it's been over six months now since Kate's murder, her case has been moved to the cold case category. I was hired by Kate's brother Greg to try and shake loose some leads, so that we can hopefully make sure that a murderer doesn't get away with killing a wonderful woman."

Silence.

Then, the gruff voice returned. "Mr. Moran, I'm sympathetic to the family, but I have a large and extensive business to run here. I can't afford for that to be interfered with. I've got to tell you that the police investigation was quite unsettling to our operation, and I can't allow that to happen again."

Score one for Mrs. "C's" intuition.

"In addition to that, we currently have a major client base in our facility right now—a repeat customer—holding a large conference that is bringing potential clients from all across the country to be at our establishment. I can't have that conference disturbed in any way."

"Yes sir, I understand that. Typically, a police investigation is by nature fairly intrusive, but that would not have to be the case with me sir. I'm just one man, who would need just a few minutes of time from some of your employees. I've already met with the detectives responsible for the investigation, and I have all their notes. After that initial talk, there would be only the potential of a few follow up questions. I would be as non-intrusive as possible Mr. Joyner."

Silence.

"When would you want to do this Mr. Moran?"

"I'm driving into Tucson right now sir. If I could start later this afternoon, that would be great."

Another pause, then a heavy sigh.

"All right Mr. Moran, I'll allow it. Kate was a wonderful woman, exceptionally capable at her job—it never set well with me that her murderer wasn't caught."

Mr. Joyner—you old softy.

"However, if you start to make a nuisance of yourself, or impede my staff's ability to do their job, I'll have to toss you out of here."

So much for Mr. Softy. I'm not sure, but from the sound of his voice, I think he may have been able to toss me out if he needed to.

"Yes sir, I understand. Thank you, sir."

I found myself listening to a dial tone. Mr. Congeniality he ain't.

CHAPTER
— 30 —

I stopped by The Hermosillo and dropped my stuff off in my room. I unpacked enough to get Molly out and strapped on with my shoulder holster. I was anxious to get over to The Palms and get started, but a boy has to eat. I found a chain restaurant close that had a sports bar in the middle, and I bellied up to the bar and ordered lunch.

While I was sippin' on a Coke—a *real* Coke this time—and digging through a plate of nachos, (What? They had tomatoes on them—those are vegetables!), I was planning my "storming the gates" strategy.

I probably need to tell you a little something about this job: I'm about to go out of my way to tell everyone that I meet what I'm doing here in Tucson—making it clear that I'm here to track down Kate Walker's killer—and I'll be handing out my business card like I'm a ticket vendor at a local sports arena.

But there's a reason—there's always a reason.

When there's a perp out there who apparently got away with a crime, it's improbable that he's going to squeal on himself. He might get comfortable, and end up making a mistake by doing or saying something he shouldn't, but even then, if no one is really looking anymore because the case is so cold, chances are even that will get missed. So, part of the job of the Private Investigator is to spread around the word that he is on the case *and* give at least the impression that he is making progress. The reason for this? To make oneself *bait.* That's right—part of my job is to become a 200-pound piece of cheese and hope that the perp will react so I can spring the trap.

Now as you can imagine, this approach is not without its dangers—getting *killed* being pretty high up on the list! There is a person out there who has already killed a gorgeous young woman for some reason—the idea that they would kill a mutt like me if I became a threat to them, isn't even *close* to far-fetched. And killing again is easier than killing the first time—if Kate was their first time.

So, let's just say that it is an occupational hazard of being an effective Private Investigator that people begin to *want* to and then *try* to—hurt or kill you. The weird thing is that it's your *job* to try and instigate this response. (What am I going to say? My grades in high school weren't good enough for med or law school.)

My "storming the gates" strategy basically consisted of trying to get a "successful" killer to try to kill again—this time me! Maybe my mom was right—maybe I should have found a nice trade to throw myself into.

Nah—I love the *action*!

I ended up pushing back from my nachos—all of a sudden they were landing pretty heavy in the old breadbasket—probably all those tomatoes causing the trouble. Either that or the idea of becoming bait for a murderer had ruined my appetite . . . yeah, I'm guessing it was that one.

Hmmm. I *think* I love the action.

CHAPTER

— 31 —

I headed across town on the surface streets, and as I was driving, my eye caught something familiar—Mr. Spiky Hair church dude's picture on a bus bench—actually three different benches along my route. Each started with the phrase "The Church for the . . ." and then different big words: "Unchurched, Unconvinced and Unchallenged." I gotta admit, that got me thinking—I wonder what they meant by that? I gotta say, I don't know if "Desert Christian Church" was any good as a church—whatever the heck that even means—but they did have some intriguing ads.

So, I pulled into The Palms and once again parked my own mean machine. I head into the lobby, this time not having to be Mr. Incognito. This time, I was greeted by large groups of well-dressed people everywhere. The signage informed me that some major conference of large-scale new car dealerships was actively going on—and they clearly were sparing no expense. There were two different light musical groups playing at different venues, and the food and drink was flowing like there was no tomorrow. All the signage showed the smiling face of a good looking, fifty-plus man, welcoming them to his conference. Based on the signs, he owned multiple new car dealerships across the southwest and about six surrounding states. I briefly wondered what it would be like to be worth that much money—but I digress.

I went up to the elaborate marble check-in desk and asked where the executive offices were located. Apparently, that was too big of a question, because they asked my name and made a call first. After being given "grace from on high" I guess, they then pointed me to a special elevator and gave me a key card to operate it. Cool. It took me right to the top floor and opened right into an elaborate reception area. The receptionist directed "Mr. Moran" down the hall and to the right. The next secretary—or administrative assistant, (I'm never sure on that one), directed me through a couple of fancy doors and suddenly I walked into a "wow" office, that I was pretty certain Mrs. Judith Coleman, Mr. Joyner's Executive Secretary, occupied.

Mrs. Coleman was about what I expected: thin and quite tidy, somewhere north of sixty years old—her gray hair not trying to disguise that fact. She had eyes that didn't miss anything, and intelligence and enough steel in her spine that made me not want to mess with this lady. I wasn't even tempted to *try* and be clever—and I'm *always* tempted to try and be clever!

"Mrs. Coleman, I'm Blake Moran—we spoke on the phone."

I gotta tell you that I almost got a case of the giggles right there. Whenever I hear myself trying to act or behave like a grown-up—it always cracks me up. However, I won the battle with my face and kept it straight.

"Hello Mr. Moran, it's a pleasure to meet you. Mr. Joyner authorized one of our conference rooms for you to meet with our staff. I have it set up for you, so you may begin right away. I assume you have a list of people with whom you would like to talk? If you would provide that list for me, I can begin to organize the interviews."

"OK," said Mr. All Business Now, (now that I had suppressed the giggles), "I narrowed the list down from the initial report to just five people with whom I would like to talk—you and Mr. Joyner being two of the five. Perhaps I could talk with Mr. Joyner now if he is available and then that would give you a few moments to organize the next interviews in an orderly way. Would that be OK?"

I could tell that she was quite taken with my efficient use of time management principles—but hey, what can I say? I'm a professional.

“That would seem to be an efficient approach,” she replied, perhaps even visibly impressed—but perhaps not. “Why don’t you give me the list and then let me check with Mr. Joyner and see if he’s available at the moment.”

I handed over my list and got my game face on—it was “go time.” I’m not really sure what any of that means, but I liked saying it—almost as much as you liked hearing me say it.

CHAPTER
— 32 —

I only had to wait for about ten minutes for Mr. Joyner to get off an overseas phone call. I was then promptly ushered into his well-appointed office and placed carefully in one of the chairs in front of the aircraft carrier that apparently doubled as his desk. I'm not kidding you—this thing was enormous! For the life of me, I could not imagine why *anyone* would *ever* need a desk this size, unless they planned on seating the Mormon Tabernacle Choir for a lovely meet and greet dinner. OK, that's a bit of an overstatement—which is *so* unlike me—but you get the point. Desk—really big.

Now in my head, I was right in the middle of a really funny shtick about this battleship of a desk—it was just about to escape the cage of my teeth—when I looked right at Mr. Joyner—and stopped cold. Call it my insightful, investigative side that misses nothing—but "shtick" was *not* gonna sail with this man.

Mr. Joyner came around the desk to meet me, (he had to stop at a mini-mart on the way for some sustenance just to make the trip—oh, sorry about that—I fell in the shtick), and the guy was about 5 foot nothing. You can read that as extremely short for a man. But what he lacked in height, he made up in intimidation. I don't know what to tell you; he was mostly balding on top—no comb over for this guy—had the fringe thing going, well-groomed and a suit that probably cost about what my truck did—read that as *nice*! I don't know if it was how he carried himself or what, but I'm guessing Mr. Samuel Joyner was *never* called "Sammy"—ever—even as a little guy—I mean a little-er guy—you know, a kid. I already felt guilty like I'd already done something wrong just for meeting with him.

Let's just say, "Awkward."

So, I was going with the "sans shtick" approach and keeping a close eye on my P's and Q's—whatever *that* means.

We got the compulsory handshake out of the way, (did I just see him wipe his hand off on a handkerchief?!), and I waited the ten minutes for him to walk back around his desk, (oops, shtick again), and he settled in and gave me "the nod." I just nodded back and tried to force a smile through my fear, when suddenly I realize that the great one had just given me permission to speak—even directed me to speak. I was *on*!

I kid you not—I drew a *blank*! This dude had me freaked out and everything was starting to go kind of white. You might begin to question my "I'm a professional" statement earlier, but please don't—I'm being vulnerable here—I'm fragile right now.

Just kidding, you can question it—I was!

Suddenly I found my voice—it was just a little too much of it. "I appreciate you meeting with me Mr. Joyner," I shouted. He jumped, and I think I did a little too. Nice start Moran—don't *earn* a letter change in your name!

I took a deep breath and lied, "Sorry, I have Tourette's." At the look of concern—and maybe a little fear—on his face, I realized that probably wasn't the best approach. "No, not really—I was just joking." I wish you could have seen the confusion on his face at the idea of someone "making ha-ha" with him. I realized that I'd better just move on.

I cleared my throat: "I've found that often a technique that works effectively is to have someone briefly tell me about the victim—in this case Kate—and to work backward from there. Could you do that for me?"

Mr. Joyner considered the "technique" for a moment, then nodded his head as he raised one eyebrow—as though that might be a good approach. I gotta tell you that I liked the combination and made "a mental note to self"—work on the nod/raised eyebrow combo.

Mr. Joyner steepled his fingers in front of his face, took a deep breath and began, "Ms. Walker was an exceptional employee; talented, creative, personable and professional. She took her job seriously and had an ability to accomplish difficult assignments in surprising ways. As Director of Marketing, she had to deal with a variety of personalities, not all of them pleasant, and she had a knack for making it all work. She 'marketed' this establishment well, which might not seem all that difficult, looking from the outside in—it *is* an exceptional property. However, there are exceptional properties all across the world—it is a very competitive business—and Ms. Walker was very good at winning the competition."

"So, she was playing in the big leagues and still knocking it out of the park," I offered.

The confusion on his face indicated that Mr. Joyner wasn't a big sports analogy fan—I'd clearly lost him.

After a pause, he continued, "However, it always seemed that Ms. Walker struggled with *living life*—as opposed to just going through a process to get through life."

Now, I have to admit two things here: First of all, the idea that Mr. Joyner gave any credence to actually *living* life shocked me—I would have guessed that this dude was *all* about the process, *not* the living. I would have thought that a concern of "living" life would be "mundane, banal, prosaic" to our Mr. Joyner. (You have to add the snotty tone when you hear me say this, to get where I'm drifting here.) I just had trouble picturing ol' Sammy here kickin' back with a brew for a little "Miller Time."

Secondly, this was a remarkably personal and perhaps insightful evaluation by a man who I would not have guessed paid attention to the personal side of those around him. That Mr. Joyner—he was just a plethora of surprises!

"Mr. Joyner, you had commented earlier about Kate's qualities—one of which you said was 'personable.' How do you square that with what you just said?"

"Oh, Ms. Walker was quite personable—on the job. She was the consummate professional who knew how to work with people and make them feel cared for and important. But when it came to simply living her own life, Ms. Walker seemed a little lost. Granted, I didn't see Ms. Walker often in that setting, but when I happened to, that quite amazing woman seemed a little more like an insecure little girl. It was odd. I assume you seen pictures of Ms. Walker?"

"Yes."

"Then you are well aware that someone with both her level of beauty and abilities would be a bit of a conundrum should they ever seem 'lost.' That seemed to be the case with Ms. Walker—she 'had it all' and yet one wondered if she even realized that reality in her own life. It seemed a shame."

Mr. Joyner was almost "pensive." I think that all 5 foot nothing of this man had actually felt *sorry* for Kate! And I kind of liked him for it. He'd looked passed the drop-dead beauty and saw a young woman who seemed a little "lost"—and it disturbed him. I almost wanted to reach across that desk—as if I could reach that far—and grab his little bald head and put a smoochie right on it. However, I had visions of security being called—so I restrained myself.

"That's pretty much the extent of what I saw in Ms. Walker—a delightful and capable worker who never seemed to quite figure out life."

I suddenly realized that with that sentence of summation of Kate Walker, Mr. Joyner was ending our moment together.

"Were there any facts or observations leading up to the time of the murder that might have any bearing on my investigation?"

"I assume you read the record of my comments to the police?" replied Mr. Joyner.

"Yes sir, I did."

"I know of nothing that I could add to that record."

And with that, I was dismissed. I thanked him for his time and for allowing me to conduct these interviews—I'm a classy guy after all—and I was outta there!

CHAPTER
— 33 —

When I scooted out of that office, Mrs. Coleman was at her desk, working away. I wouldn't have ever thought that talking with Mrs. C would be a relief, but after Mr. J, I looked forward to it.

Mrs. Coleman took out her notebook and informed me that she had set up interviews with each of the individuals I had requested, allowing twenty minutes per interview. She then pointed out that I was a bit ahead of schedule—a point that she seemed to approve of—and stated that we should proceed down to the conference room for our interview.

Well, "chop chop" Mr. Private Investigator!

She led me down the ever so softly carpeted, super wide hallway to the last door on the left. The conference room was huge—making it seem even more so by the two walls of glass and the twenty-foot ceilings. One view was the sheer rock of the Catalina Mountains and the other looked over the city of Tucson. This place was amazing!

Mrs. Coleman and I sat down at the end of the huge table, and I commented on what an amazing property The Palms was. Mrs. Coleman looked around like someone who worked here every day and forgot how extraordinary it really was—and then agreed with my assessment.

"Mrs. Coleman," I began, "you commented to me on the phone that you were quite fond of Kate. I was hoping that perhaps your connection to her might provide me with some insight that would help me to take the next step in my investigation."

"Well Mr. Moran, I don't know what knowledge I would have that would help, but if I can help, I certainly want to. Kate Walker was a treasure."

"Could you tell me about her please?"

"Certainly. Kate was one of those rare people who possessed grace, beauty, and talent, while not behaving as though she did. She was a thoughtful, and at times ingenious professional, but at her core she was a genuinely nice person—to everyone. It was almost like she was unaware of the uniqueness she possessed as a person and simply was Kate with everyone she interacted with—from world traveler, to celebrity, to colleagues, to maintenance staff. Kate Walker was easy to like, even love, which made her murder even more callous and wrong. Having said all that, I'm not sure what more I would know that would help your investigation."

"Mr. Joyner had some interesting comments," I interjected, "that I was wondering if I could get your take on?"

"Certainly."

"He described Kate as an amazing professional, but surprised me when he said that he believed Ms. Walker struggled with living life—as opposed to just going through a process to get through life. He also said that when it came to her personal life that he *had* observed, Kate could quickly come off as an insecure little girl instead of the amazing woman that she was. Given her qualities, he found that odd and sad."

"Mr. Joyner said that." The question was implied.

"Yes ma'am."

Mrs. Coleman sat back and pondered.

"As surprised as I am to say it, I would have to say that Mr. Joyner may be right."

I think she saw in my eyes that I thought she was dissin' Mr. Joyner—which I admit surprised me. She quickly corrected me.

"I don't mean that as a slight to Mr. Joyner—he's a capable professional. I simply meant that it surprised me that he caught that element of Kate when it eluded me. But he is right—truly living life was not Kate's way—the process of getting through was."

However, she then did that little squinty eyebrow that gives you the wrinkle right above the nose. She then looked at me.

"Yes?" I inquired.

"What?"

"You furrowed your brow."

"I what?" she replied.

"You furrowed your brow—and I was wondering if you could tell me why?"

"Well, I was just thinking—Mr. Joyner's insight into Kate was accurate, but not entirely—at least not toward the end."

"What do you mean?"

"One of the reasons that Kate's death was especially hard on me—even though I hadn't realized it till just now—was the fact that something was happening in Kate's life during the last couple of months—something good."

I felt a little shiver run down my spine, "What was happening?"

"I'm sorry, but I don't know. All I know is that what Mr. Joyner described—which I now realize was accurate—was going away. Kate seemed happier, more self-possessed, and seemed to have developed a focus to her life—her personal life. I wondered if perhaps she had met someone special, but I never got that indication. She just seemed different—like she was finally figuring things out and it was changing her—it seemed for the good."

"And you have no idea what could have been happening?"

"I'm sorry, no. I wish I'd asked, but as I said, it didn't actually register till you pointed out what Mr. Joyner said. I wish I had more to offer—but that's all I know."

"Well thank you Mrs. Coleman—I'll take what I can get—you never know which piece of the puzzle will fall into place and show the picture—I'll just add that to the pile of pieces."

CHAPTER
— 34 —

While I waited in the conference room for the next person to interview, I stared out at the beautiful view and became quite "pensive." Mrs. Coleman gave me more than she knew. Both of Kate's brothers had commented on the difference in Kate over the last couple months of her life—now Mrs. Coleman came to that same reality on her own as well.

Something was afoot! (I don't know why gumshoes are supposed to say that—probably that whole Sherlock Homes thing—but it's in the contract—we have to say it.) I needed to find out what changed for Kate during that time—it may have been nothing, but since people noticed it, it may end up being a key.

I heard the door open that shook me from my reverie, (that's a funny word, don't you think?), and I turned to my next interviewee. I knew from my notes that this guy's name was Todd Brooks. I chose him because of some of his comments in the police interview, and a few comments by others, caused me to go, "Hmmm."

Todd was the Director of Guest Services—it was his job to make sure that their clients enjoyed their experience at The Palms. The jacket I'd read said that he was thirty-two years old. Now it wasn't my day for guys, but Todd was a good-looking dude—topped out at about 6 feet 4 inches, and probably weighed in at about 225 pounds—and it clearly wasn't weight from too many nachos, (Wait, I just remembered I had nachos for lunch), I mean too many pizzas. Todd was obviously no stranger to the gym. He wore nice duds, had good hair, and carried himself like a guy who *already knew* everything I just told you *and* would agree *and* add a few more positive observations that he thought I'd missed.

I already both hated him and wanted to *be* him. (That may seem petty and juvenile—I get that a lot.)

We did the introduction thing and I explained why I wanted to talk with him.

"I wanted to ask you about something that some of your colleagues mentioned in passing when they were interviewed by the police."

"All right," he said, shifting in his seat.

"It was pointed out that you had shown an interest in Ms. Walker toward the end of last year, and that you had pursued her romantically."

Todd stared at me—I gathered he was not amused.

"Is that a question?"

"I can see why you'd wonder, since it didn't end with a question mark, but yeah, that was a question." (My, aren't we snippy!)

"OK," he said with a sigh, "I did have an interest in Kate, and I did try to get a date with her."

"The individuals said you tried to get her to go out with you numerous times, and that she continued to tell you no, and that this took place over the course of months."

Todd stared again.

"Once again—still not hearing a question. What's your point?"

"I'm not so much trying to make a point as trying to understand the things going on around Ms. Walker up to the time of her murder."

"Did Ms. Walker give you a reason for not accepting the offer of a date from you?"

"I just assumed she must be gay," he replied.

I felt my stomach clench and I suddenly felt the weight of Molly on the shoulder holster. Now I didn't like this guy for a *whole* other reason!

"In the two years that you've worked at The Palms, you've never known Ms. Walker to date anyone?" I asked.

Todd fidgeted a little.

"I'm sorry—didn't you understand the question? There *was* a question mark that time."

"Fine—yes, she dated some."

"And were these people men or women that she dated?" I asked.

"They were men."

"So, I can only assume that since you knew this, and yet still said what you did, that this comment must spring from some deeply held belief on your part that any woman who would have the power to say 'no' to you must clearly be 'gay'—even if all the evidence points in the exact opposite direction.

Todd's face was red at this point, and he moved forward in what I think he imagined was a threatening way. I just gave him my best "Clint Squint" and let my jacket fall open enough for him to get a good look at Molly. He slowly set back in his chair.

"Todd, you seem like kind of an angry guy—maybe even the kind of guy who would get pretty ticked off at some beautiful woman who continued to refuse his advances."

Todd just glared at me—to be fair, I hadn't put a question mark at the end of that one either.

"Check the record dipstick—I had two people who verified where I was that night."

"I saw that. The first one is a woman who is very interested in you romantically, upon whom you periodically shower your favors, and the other was a bartender at a sports bar restaurant that you frequent regularly—who, by the way, turns out to be a friend of yours."

"What's your point?"

"Not great alibis Mr. Brooks. The police ran out of time to keep looking, but I have time—so I'm going to *look*—a little closer . . . at you."

Todd leaned forward and used all 225 pounds to make his point: "Listen Mr. P.I.—I didn't do anything. Fine, she wouldn't go out with me—big deal. But you try and pin this on me, and you and I are going to find ourselves with a problem. And from where I'm sitting, I'm thinking you will be the one with the biggest problem."

This last statement was punctuated with a slight flexing—nice touch.

"Why Mr. Brooks, I believe you just threatened me—a threat that emanated from anger when things did not go like you wanted. That scenario seems strangely similar to an idea I'm tossing around about what might have happened to Ms. Walker. Could we be seeing a pattern of behavior surfacing here? I wonder."

Again, the glare. Then, "I'm not messing around here—you leave me alone or you and I are gonna dance."

"Oh sorry—you clearly get confused about this a lot—I'm not 'gay' either, so you'll have to fine some other dude to 'dance' with."

I kinda thought me and ol' Todd were about to have a moment right there in that beautiful conference room. I was ready—I have some skills that ol' Todd would be very unhappy to discover. Finally, Todd worked through his Anger Management 101 list and stood up, gave me one last hate-filled stare and then stomped out.

"Well, that went well," I said to myself.

CHAPTER 35

I let Mrs. Coleman know that she could send for my next appointment. While I waited, I looked over the police report.

Her name was Bailey Sanchez. She had worked for Kate as her assistant. She ended up getting Kate's job as Director of Marketing after Kate was murdered. Since the three major reasons for crimes were power, sex and money—remember that whole PMS thing—and she had two out of the three—I thought a closer look at Kate's successor made some sense.

Ms. Sanchez made her entrance—and it was a pretty good entrance. Bailey was probably 5 feet 9 inches tall, without her spikes on, and she had legs that went all the way to the floor—if you know what I mean. She was dark—dark hair, dark skin—being that she was Hispanic, great figure—she was one fine-looking lady. I was starting to wonder where they were finding all these knockouts.

About the only negative I could see—or in this case detect with my nose—was that Bailey was a smoker. She clearly tried to hide it with nice perfume, and probably some type of mouth freshener, but it was still there—faint, but there. Still, all and all, dang!

But Bailey wasn't just attractive—she "played" the part. The way she stared into my eyes when she shook my hand, the way she sat down and arranged herself—the whole thing felt like a performance. Don't get me wrong, it was a nice performance, but it was still a performance—and that came off kind of hollow. She clearly knew that she had "*it*," but she was working a little too hard trying to "sell" *it*—you know?

We did the introduction thing and then I said, "I appreciate you meeting with me Ms. Sanchez."

"Oh, I'm more than happy to meet with you Mr. Moran."

What was with the Marilyn Monroe, "breathy" voice, and the eyelashes? I looked around to make sure we weren't sitting in a bar all of the sudden. Don't get me wrong—I can get flattered as quickly as any guy, but this was just weird. I'm a moderately attractive male, but with a guy like Todd Brooks walking around, I wasn't going to make Bailey swoon. Clearly this was a way of life for Bailey—she was trying to use her flirty sexuality as a form of currency to trade with. Now typically I'd be OK with this, but in this setting, given what we were trying to figure out, it just seemed grossly inappropriate and a little suspect.

"Ms. Sanchez, could you please tell me a little about Ms. Walker?"

"Please, call me Bailey."

"I'm going to keep it Ms. Sanchez, just to keep it professional. Tell me about Kate please."

Now, I know that I refused to use her first name, and yet immediately switched to "Kate" from Ms. Walker, but it was on purpose—crafty devil that I am.

Pout. Wait. Even "poutier" lips. Wait. Finally, she gave that up and started talking.

"Kate was all right, I guess. I think she thought a lot of herself, was pretty self-absorbed and just wanted to get to the top—not to speak ill of the dead of course."

Which of course, she just did.

Now this was interesting. This was the first truly negative evaluation I'd had regarding Kate. I couldn't help but feel that Bailey had just described herself, not Kate.

"So, I take it you weren't too fond of Kate?"

"She was just someone at work. I don't know why people made such a fuss over her—she wasn't *that* pretty! It was always, 'Did you hear what

Kate did,' 'Did you hear about her new promotion,' 'Did you see Kate today' and I just got sick of all her self-promotion."

Whoa—the claws sure came out! ME-OW!

"So, are you saying that Kate was arrogant, and always trying to make herself the center of attention, and took all the credit for any success? It's odd, I haven't got that from anyone else."

As I said this, I opened a notebook and sat posed to write down what she said. This is a little trick I use when I think someone is blowing about something that they would *never* want to have to back up, or have other people know they said. People think harder about what they say if they think what they say may be read back to them or others at some point. Think of it as the classic, "You don't mind if I record this, do you?"

Bailey looked at my pen for a moment, and then quickly secured her feet in the proverbial peddles for the predictable "back peddling" to begin.

"Well, I wouldn't say that," (although she had), "it's just that our personalities didn't connect very well."

"And why was that?"

"It just seemed like Kate got all the breaks, and everyone was always making over her like she was some goddess or something. Oh, and speaking of 'goddess,' when I saw she was looking into religion, I knew I just couldn't connect with her."

"What are you talking about? Was she looking into some kind of New Age religious stuff—is that what you mean by 'goddess'?"

"I don't actually know what it was—I just saw her reading some pamphlet, and I turned it over and looked at it when she left it on her desk. The title said something about how to 'get right with God'—whatever that means—so I knew it was some religious thing. Sounds like just the kind of stupid thing that Kate would get involved with!"

That last part of said with some serious venom. Bailey looked up like she'd just noticed I was still in the room, and tried to qualify her hatred with, "Oh, I'm not religious."

Yeah—*got that*—not exactly a shocker.

I finished the interview, excused Ms. Sanchez and watched her sashay out of the conference room. And I'll give her credit—the woman *could* sashay!

Sorry, I didn't *like* Bailey—she was annoying—but I *am* a guy. You could read that as, I wasn't unhappy that she was leaving, but I liked watching her *go*.

We men—we're such *complex* creatures.

I sat thinking for a moment. Bailey Sanchez had benefited greatly by Kate's death—at least professionally—which provided motive. In addition to this, it was obvious that Bailey was *extremely* jealous of Kate's beauty, success, and likeability—in spite of her own physical qualities. In short, she kind of hated Kate for being so "*Kate*." She also had no alibi for the night Kate was killed—but since the police thought the murderer was male, she wasn't pursued.

Hmmm.

And besides all that, what is this "*looking into religion*" stuff? That was the first I'd heard from anyone about this. Even the fact that Bailey had to "turn it over and look at it"—the little sneak—showed Kate was keeping whatever she was doing on the "down low."

So much to think through—but I was on to my next suspect—I mean person.

CHAPTER

— 36 —

My last interview actually *was* on the list because he stood out as a possible suspect based on what the police report said. His name was Lester Jenkins and honestly the only reason he had initially gotten a second look was because when TPD ran people at the resort, ol' Lester had a sheet—a rap sheet that is.

Lester was a fifty-two-year-old male who had worked at The Palms for about five years—as a cook. He wasn't a chef, but he worked doing basic cooking in one of the resort restaurants and worked some of the special event banquets to make some extra coin.

He had come to TPD's attention for two reasons: he had a "sheet" that included various charges of domestic violence against women, attempted rape, and other crimes, for which he had spent time incarcerated—and he had paid unwarranted interest toward Kate Walker according to other members of the staff.

When Lester walked in and sat down, I gotta tell you I was pretty creeped out. Lester still had his apron on, stained with food—which I think was intended to tell me that he didn't sweat me. Lester looked every year of his fifty-two years and then some; this was a guy who had lived a hard life. He had that thin, sinewy build, that was typically surprisingly strong and agile. His hair was combed back in that old "duck tail" swoopy style, and it was impossibly black—had to have had some help straight out of a box, to be that color. His face was deeply lined with wrinkles. Lester reeked of smoke, and I could see the outline of the pack of cigs in his t-shirt pocket.

Top all that off with a sneer of contempt, that at least bordered on hatred for—I'm guessing here—the entire human race, and you've pretty much got the big picture!

I was guessing this was gonna be fun.

"Hello Mr. Jenkins, I appreciate you meeting with me."

"Wasn't aware that I had a choice."

I ignored that.

"I wanted to talk to you about Kate Walker."

Silence.

"I understand you had some interest in Ms. Walker."

An ugly gleam came into his eyes as a leering smile spread across his face. "Oh yeah, I had 'some interest' in her."

This jerk was baiting me—and it was working.

"Did you ever see her? That was one fine piece walking around this place."

Steady.

"Members of the kitchen staff stated that you seemed to have an infatuation with Ms. Walker—that you often tried to take detours to look at her, and that you often said lewd, sexually explicit things about her to them. I also see here that you were even reprimanded officially by the resort for this on one occasion."

He just stared at me with the vacant stare. Finally, he said, "Do you hear me denying it? I wanted some of that and I said so—that's no crime."

"But given your history, saying so makes you suspect—that's why we're sitting here now."

"And you think that somehow I care? I don't. Listen, that lady was so fine that I took every chance I could to get a look at her. And if I could have found a way, I might have just taken what I wanted—how do you like *that*?! But I couldn't find a way, so I didn't do the crime. You think I'm afraid of some P.I.? If you want to pin this on me, then *prove* it. Until you can do that, don't think I'm gonna go all weak in the knees, cuz some 'rent a cop,' whose taking off time from his mall gig, called me in and tried to 'scare' me."

I just sat staring at the little pervert. He just admitted to me that he was obsessed with Kate and would have raped her if he could have found a way. I guess my not being a "real cop" had loosened his lips a little. Then he sat there and smiled that ugly little leering smile, and dared me to try and prove that he actually did just that—and then murdered her too.

I realized that I was sweating, and my breathing had become rapid. I could feel the adrenaline rushing through my system and I became very aware of the weight of Molly strapped under my arm. I realized that I wanted to kill someone—not metaphorically—but for real. And not just *generally* kill "someone"—I wanted to *specifically* kill Mr. Lester Jenkins—*now*.

I needed to end this "interview." Things were spiraling out of control—"things" specifically being *me*.

I took a deep breath and leaned forward: "All right you little *perv*, here's how this'll go down: you're officially *on my list*. Your alibi is weak, and just the fact that you would talk about this nice woman, who was murdered like this, makes me want to bust you up, whether you did the crime or not. So, I'll be around, checking on you from every angle I can think of, and just hoping you do or have done something stupid—please feel free to do so. I hope you enjoy your upcoming anal exam—cuz I know I will—now *get out of my face*!"

There was a satisfactory moment when a quick shadow of concern passed behind his shifty eyes and then it was gone—but it was enough.

Lester stood up and sauntered out of the conference room, taking a moment right before he left to abuse me with a two-handed, single finger salute. I think he was just trying to regain that moment of lost "I'm bad" attitude, and then he was gone.

I had to sit there for a moment—not even noticing the amazing view—while I tried to get myself under control. Lester Jenkins was a bad man—I could only hope that I could be at least a part of the sack of bricks that would hopefully fall on him soon.

CHAPTER
— 37 —

I thanked Mrs. Coleman for her help and assured her that it had indeed helped in the investigation. I mentioned that one person had commented on Kate "looking into religion," and asked if she knew anything about that. She assured me that if Kate had been doing that, she was unaware. She asked me to let her know if there was any good news and I told her that I would.

I used my fancy key card to activate the executive elevator and then dropped it back off at the front desk on my way out. After I walked out the opulent front entrance, I heard someone saying, "Excuse me sir." I turned to see an older man in a maintenance staff uniform hurrying toward me. I stopped and when he got closer, I saw that his name plate said, "Jesus."

Now I don't pretend to know very much about all that Bible stuff, but I would have guessed that Jesus would've been *taller*—oh, and *more Jewish* instead of Hispanic.

This investigation was kind of *blowing my mind*. Think about it: I had gotten to hear the *"voice of God"*—found in a New York attorney named Greg, and now I was meeting *"Jesus"*—courtesy of a janitor, working at a fancy, Tucson resort.

Quite the spiritual journey for me!

(Now lest you think I'm a total moron—yes, I know that this is actually pronounced "Hay-SOOS" and is a common Hispanic name. I *do* live in Phoenix—give me a break!)

Remember, it's "Moran," *NOT* "moron!"

So, I stopped and waited.

Jesus caught his breath.

That is a funny sentence. I try not to chuckle out loud. I succeed, which for me is personal growth!

"I was told that you are here to investigate Ms. Kate's murder."

Ah, the workplace grapevine.

"Yes, I am."

"I just loved Ms. Kate—she was like an angel from heaven—such a beautiful person, and not just in face and form. She always had a good word for everyone, and she was so nice. She knew many of the maintenance staff here and even asked about our families. I was hopeful that she might even find a family of her own, but I guess that didn't work out."

I was getting ready to thank Jesus for his interest, and assure him that I would do all that I could to find Kate's killer when what he said registered with me.

"What do you mean Jesus, when you say, 'I guess that didn't work out'?"

"Oh, I just meant that man who she was seeing," he said.

"What man?"

"Uh, I don't really know. I just saw them from a distance three or four times, down in some of our secluded garden areas talking and hugging."

OK, hold the phone.

"Jesus, this is the first I've heard of this. I need you to describe this man to me—everything you can think of."

"I'm sorry sir, but there's nothing for me to describe. It was always at a distance while I was working on a maintenance project—otherwise I would have never seen them. Since it was always in these gardens, it seemed that they were seeking privacy."

"What time of day was it?"

Jesus thought.

"I think it varied—there was no specific time."

"OK. Can you remember what the timespan was? A few weeks, a few months?"

Again, he thought.

"I remember the first time I noticed them, I was working up on one of the HVAC units, but it was related to the heat instead of the air conditioning. Around here, the earliest that could be would have been late October or early November. The rest of the times were after that."

"Were they all closely placed or spread out?"

"They were somewhat spread out—like I said, I would just happen to be in the right location to see them."

"Do you remember the last time you saw them?"

Pause.

"Yes, I do. It was over the holidays between Christmas and New Year's, because I was called in to work on another unit that had gone down—and that's a very busy time for us."

"Could you tell what they seemed like—happy, sad, agitated?"

Thinking.

"It was typically just a look and then a hope that maybe Ms. Kate had found someone, but I do remember that it usually seemed like serious talking. But that last time had been some time since I had seen them together, and I think they were fighting."

My heart sped up.

"Why do you say that?"

"It was just an impression, but I remember feeling a little sad when I caught sight of them because they seemed to be fighting—and it was the holidays."

I first of all asked Jesus his full name—if he said "Jesus Christ," I was going to absolutely lose it! He didn't—it was Martinez.

Then I said, "Listen Jesus, here is my card with all my numbers. What you've told me may be nothing—but it might be something—so thank you for telling me. If you think of anything else—even if it seems insignificant to you—please call me. Everything I've discovered about Kate tells me that she was a wonderful woman, and I want to nail the piece of dirt who killed her."

Jesus beamed.

"I will try and remember more sir—I also would love to help you nail this 'piece of dirt.'"

CHAPTER

— 38 —

He sat in the sedan and watched Blake Moran leave The Palms. His hands clenched and unclenched as he stared—he was in a stage of "black rage" at the problems that this moron was potentially creating for him.

He saw Blake get into a black, lifted Toyota Tacoma—he made a note of the plate number—never know when that might come in handy.

Having him here where Kate had worked was not good. Having him do interviews with some of the people who had known and worked with Kate was dangerous—it was too close.

Too much of a chance that he might stumble onto something.

Too much of a chance that he might stumble onto *him*.

He fought down the rage and decided that it was time to start doing something about Mr. Blake Moran.

CHAPTER

— 39 —

OK, now *that* was a revelation.

Back in "Black Beauty," I tried to assimilate what I'd just been told. This was new information to everyone—I don't think Jesus knew to tell the police what he'd seen—or the potential significance of it.

Unless Jesus had somehow gotten it wrong, Kate had a beau—or at least was entertaining the idea. That one fact could alter the whole scenario of Kate's death. Given the reality of Kate clearly being drowned by someone, the violence of that act would tend to lead investigators to another belief; Kate had probably been raped. The autopsy revealed that sexual intercourse had taken place recently. However, the introduction of a possible romantic relationship into the mix might mean there was consensual sex, and then, for some reason, things turned ugly. This second scenario fit typical patterns better because most murders result from someone the victim knows.

This was *big*!

And then there was that other thing: what "religious stuff" was Kate looking into? I had heard *nothing* about this—from either of her brothers, or from anybody else. Was this some idle curiosity or did this have something to do with the case?

I started my truck and headed back across town. As I drove, I put a call in to Kate's brother, Greg, in New York. Since it was his private line, he answered after three rings.

"Yeah?"

"Hi Greg, its Blake down in Tucson."

"Oh hi," he said.

"You got a minute?" I asked.

"About that—I'm just getting ready to run to a deposition, but I can talk for a moment."

"This won't take long. I've been doing some interviews with the staff at The Palms, and I've come up with some interesting information. However, there were two things that I wanted to run by you. First, did you have any reason to believe that Kate was involved in a romantic relationship during those last few months of her life?"

"If she was, she never mentioned it to me," Greg said, "but her silence wouldn't surprise me. Kate was never all that interested in men because of what happened with my parents getting a divorce. So I would have to believe that it would have to become pretty serious before she would bring it up to me—or Johnnie for that matter. She knew that we both really wanted her to find someone to love—that we would like it if she had someone to take care of her—no matter how chauvinistic that sounds. She probably wouldn't mention it to us unless she actually started seeing someone seriously. Why? Was she involved with someone?"

"To tell you the truth, I'm not sure—but there is some indication that she may have been," I told him.

I went on. "OK, how about this one: did you have any indication that Kate was looking into any kind of religion?"

Silence.

"Religion?"

"Yeah."

"What kind?"

"I have no idea—yet," I replied. "I get the idea that she was keeping it to herself, but there seems to be some evidence that she was at least looking into some kind of religion."

"Huh," said Greg. You know, for a big-time New York attorney, this guy could really be articulate.

Big sigh.

"Well, no, she never gave me any indication of this, and we never really had any of that stuff growing up—frankly I'm surprised to hear this."

"Why is that?"

"Well, um—are you religious Blake?"

"Nope—well, except when I'm watching the NFL."

He chuckled. "I just didn't want to offend you."

A lawyer *and* a politician—dang!

"OK."

"All I wanted to say was that Kate was one of the smartest, the most capable and beautiful women I've ever known. The idea that she would consider something like religion would shock me—she was just too together for stuff like that."

"Hmmm." (I could be articulate too.)

"Well listen," I said, "it might be that there is another explanation for her looking at this stuff, or even the idea that she might have been in a relationship—I'll pursue them further and let you know."

"OK."

"Well, I'll let you go save the corporate world from those evil higher capital gain tax rates—or whatever it is you guys do. I'll keep you informed."

Greg was chuckling as he hung up.

So, no indication to the brothers on either issue.

I had an idea, so I called Trent. It sounded like he was in the squad room when he answered.

"Hey!"

"Hey yourself," I responded.

Alright, enough with the witty banter.

"Are you back in town?" Trent asked.

"Yeah, I'm back on it and I wanted to see if I could catch a favor from you."

"Uh oh."

"Nope, this one is probably easy."

"What is it?"

"Could I look at Kate's effects? You probably still have all her personal effects stored somewhere, since this is 'technically' an ongoing investigation—right?"

"Yeah, I think we still have it stored away—at least the basic stuff," he said.

"I have a lead or two that could be helped with a little look see—whacha say?"

Pause.

"You being straight with me—you're not doing anything hinky here?"

"All above board Trent—I am the opposite of 'anything hinky' here—whatever that means."

Pause.

"All right—hang on." I heard keys typing. "OK, here it is—her stuff is right by the station here—yeah, you can take a look."

"Excellent. Listen, I'm heading over to the Casa Hacienda Resort to try and check out the room where Kate was killed. It's the slow season, so I'm hoping it won't be booked. I'm coming from The Palms, so I'll be driving right by—any chance I could get a look in about twenty minutes?"

"Sure Blake, I've got nothin' to do—let me just drop everything I'm supposed to be working on, and just rush to do whatever you want," said Trent.

"Excellent!" I said. "That's just what I was hoping you would do!"

"I was giving you "*incredulous*," you moron! Do you even *get* the concept of sarcasm?! You're supposed to realize that I'm *incredibly* busy and that *you're asking too much*!"

"Oh. I've never been good at that subtle, secret message, hidden between the lines stuff."

"Subtle?! Hidden?! You'd have to be blind and deaf to not get . . . oh never mind. Fine, get your butt here, but I'll have to go in with you—chain of evidence and all that—but you know that."

"Yeah, I know. Thanks Trent, I owe you one."

I could hear him sputtering, "You owe me one—you owe me *ONE*?!" as I disconnected the call.

CHAPTER
— 40 —

I was glad that Trent had twenty minutes to calm down—he seemed OK by the time I got to the fancy police digs at I-10 and Miracle Mile. He came strolling out of the back area to the waiting area where I was, well, *waiting*—and I was encouraged that his gun was still in his holster.

We're all good.

He told me to follow him around back, so we headed out the door and around the side of the building, back to a large, warehouse structure. We went in through a regular door, and immediately found ourselves in front of a built-in counter with an officer sitting behind it. It wasn't terribly bright in there, given that it was primarily lit by the ambient light that came through skylights that were scattered across the ceiling—the aforementioned ceiling being about twenty feet in the air. The place was huge.

"Hey Danny," Trent said.

"Hey Trent."

"This is Blake Moran, a P.I. from Phoenix whose doing some extra work on one of our cold cases."

I kid you not; ol' Danny boy looked at me like you'd look down at something you stepped in, that you really wished you hadn't. I didn't know if it was my name, or that I was a P.I. or that I was from Phoenix, (I was guessin' it was the P.I.), but I could hardly contain myself. I wanted to point out to "Danny" that at least I didn't sit around behind some desk "guarding" a warehouse full of "stuff" and call it police work!

While I was getting myself all worked up, Trent saw it too and assured Danny, "He's one of the good ones."

That seemed to be enough for Danny and suddenly, apparently, I was accepted. I just wanted to skip and leap and dance for joy—on his *face*! Wow, that seemed unnecessarily violent—maybe I *do* have anger issues . . . naw!

"So whatcha need?" Danny asked.

"We need to look at the personal effects of Kate Walker—a Vic from back in January," Trent informed him.

A quick search on the computer and Danny had the section, row, and bin number for us. He had us both sign in and off we went into the belly of the building, leaving ol' Danny boy to "guard and protect" his counter.

Whatever.

It took us a couple of wrong turns and about ten minutes to locate the appropriate coordinates, (Lewis and Clark we are *not*), but we finally found it.

We had to use one of those super tall rolling stairways—which I thought was way cool—but apparently Trent is not a fan of heights. He started up to get the boxes, at which point, I pushed the stairs and rolled him forward. It was at this moment that Trent uttered some quite colorful expletives that were 1) clearly aimed right at my laughing face and 2) shan't be recorded here lest smaller eyes behold them.

I was just going for a little "Ha-ha," but Trent decided that maybe I should be the one on the rolling stairway. That was fine with me—remember, I was of the "way cool" camp when I saw the stairs.

So, up I climbed up to the proper number—provided for us by the always vigilant protector of the "stuff," Danny boy, (should I get over that? Nah, that would be way too mature for me), and I retrieved the boxes of Kate Walker's effects.

Once I had them all down, we carried them over to the end of the aisle where there were tables set up at specific points, for the purpose of searching through effects. We spread the boxes out and started opening them up and looking at their contents.

This moment is usually pretty depressing. We all know our own mortality—i.e., we're all gonna die someday. However, we're all pretty good at either ignoring it, or we quickly pack up and move to a whole new state—the "*state of denial.*" Moments like this are a rude reminder that everybody eventually gets reduced to their "effects."

Wow—I should write greeting cards for *Hallmark*!

We had just gotten all the boxes opened when Trent asked me, "We lookin' for anything particular or are we just pawin' through her stuff on a fishing expedition?"

I was trying to play my hand pretty close to the vest—but I never was that great of a poker player.

"I'm looking for two possibilities: is there any evidence of a *romantic* interest or any indication of a *religious* interest?"

Trent looked at me for a moment in a thoughtful sort of way, then did the slow nod and raised one eyebrow at the same time. I couldn't believe it! He did the *same move* Mr. Joyner had done in his office—the combo that I'd made a note to work on later—and Trent had already *mastered* it!

I was going to have to move that practice up the ol' priority list—apparently it was catching on—and it really did work!

We went back to the search and things were quiet for the next half hour. Most of the items were what you would expect—just personal items that anyone has. However, Kate had some great taste in things, and apparently enough money to buy them too. Some of the search just felt kind of dirty when I came to her personal stuff.

While Trent went through her itemized list of larger items and pictures of the same, I got to her music and book collection. Clearly most of her music was on her phone that was never recovered, (read *suspicious*), but she still had quite a few CDs from "the old days" when that's how we listened to music. I noticed that she had had a pretty broad range of music tastes—some of which I really liked—and some highbrow stuff that I would choose going to the dentist for a *root canal* before listening to that!

That thought got me drifting off, trying to remember when the last time was that I'd been to the dentist to get the ol' choppers checked. Suddenly, I realized that I had been working through some things that weren't music CDs—they were DVDs. So, the image of the dentist drilling on my teeth faded away as I drew my attention back to the matter at hand.

As I looked, there were *scores* of DVDs, apparently all from the same source. I picked one up and looked at it—it said, "How to Have Real Self-Esteem Part I." I was thinking some self-help, guru stuff, but then I looked at the picture on the DVD and got a *shock*. It was spiky, dark-haired dude from those TV commercials and bus benches. I looked on the DVD and saw that it said, "Desert Christian Church."

OK, this just felt weird.

I looked at some of the other DVDs. I saw that this wasn't just some self-help drivel—there were a variety of titles: "Why God Wants to Help Us Fix What We've Already Broken," "How to Stand Strong in a World that's Trippin'," "Why the Exchange Rate for Sin is Way too High," "How to Beat the Giant in Your Life," "How to Deal with Depression" and "How to Avoid Spiritual Cardiac Arrest." There must have been thirty or forty DVDs from this church.

Then there were some seminars that had both DVDs and books—some of those titles were: "Facts Behind the Faith," "Why Bad Things Happen to Good People," and "Creation Versus Evolution."

Huh.

Clearly Kate *had* been looking into a little religion—Miss Bailey Sanchez had been right—and this was more than "a little." The idea that it happened to be this church that I kept seeing advertising around town was wild. However, the more I thought about it, it didn't seem quite as surprising. I'd only been in town a little while and already I'd seen a couple of TV commercials and some bus benches. I suppose if someone wanted to look into something like this, Desert Christian Church seemed to have a corner on the "church advertising market" here in Tucson—if there was such a thing.

Still, it was an interesting coincidence, and I'm not real fond of "coincidences."

Trent hadn't found anything else of note—actually *not even like a note* from a guy—that would indicate any romantic involvement. Looks like we were striking out on that one.

I showed Trent all the DVDs and books from Desert Christian Church and asked him what he knew about this place.

Trent was surprised they hadn't noticed this. "Not a lot," he admitted. "I mean, everybody in town knows *of* Desert Christian and can recognize the Pastor from the advertising, but beyond that, I don't really know much. I have some friends on the force who go to church there."

"Do they ever say anything about it?" I asked.

"Well, they're pretty careful about it in the work environment, but a couple of my friends on the force have invited me to give it a try—I'm just not interested."

"Are these *friends* not exactly the sharpest knife in the drawer or something."

Trent laughed.

"Actually, these guys—oh, and one woman—are some of the best people I know. And they're great cops. I'd have to say that if the people I know who go to this church are any representation of what this church does—it's impressive."

Hmmm. (Insert long pause while the old Blake-myster brain processes all this . . .) Not at all what I expected to hear about a church.

"Listen Blake, I gotta get going—I know it's hard for you Private Investigators to understand, but we *real cops* have a thing we call '*work*' that we have to do. If you want, I can explain it to you some time—and I promise I'll use small words so that you can understand it."

"Real funny Trent." But his eyes were laughing when he said it.

We packed everything back up and I took it back up the way cool stairs and put it away. I was tempted to make Trent do it for that crack about work, but 1) he was about *half right* about that whole "work" thing and 2) ya just never know when you'll need to cross that bridge and I'll need to call Trent again—so I best not burn said "bridge" now.

We walked back to the front, where I got to lovingly say goodbye to my buddy "Danny boy," then back around to the front of the building where Trent bid me farewell. I remembered to thank him again for the help, but I was fairly deep in thought about Kate and what she had been up to before she was murdered. I had a new clue—I didn't know what it meant—but I knew who might.

CHAPTER

— 41 —

Back in my big, bad, black machine, I got back on I-10 and headed toward Casa Hacienda Resort and Spa for my appointment—which of course I hadn't made.

Ah, the joy of surprise!

While I tooled East on I-10, headed for I-19, I took out my phone and the DVD that I'd palmed from Kate's stuff.

(All right, you can get that look off of your face—I needed some information, there were *plenty* of DVDs there to get whatever facts they needed, so I just "five-fingered" *one*. What do you mean that's not "right?" Is it "right" that Kate was killed?! I'm the good guy here—I'm the one trying to "right" a wrong! So just keep your highfalutin morality to yourself—I have a *job* to do!)

You have to admit, I do "*righteous indignation*," along with *moral relativism* with a tall pile of *self-justification*—really, *really* well! Oh yeah, it's a gift!

Any-who—I got the phone number off the DVD and called "Desert Christian Church."

If I thought I was going to just talk to Mr. Spiky Hair when he personally answered the phone . . . not so much. I had to first get the answering service to let me talk to the office administrator—no small feat—so I didn't just have to leave a message. Then she clearly planned on "vetting" me and handling my questions—but I wanted to talk to "the guy." I kept telling her that I just wanted to talk to the guy on the commercials, and yet she just kept asking how she could "help" me.

"Ma'am, I just want to talk to him—why can't I?"

"Well sir, if you could tell me why you're calling, I would be able to help you more effectively," she said.

"But I don't *want* you to help me," I responded, "I just need to talk to the guy on the commercials."

I was kinda being a pain here—I knew that—that "special kind of pain," a pain in the butt.

"I'm sorry sir, but as I'm sure you can realize, with our multiple locations and thousands of people who attend Desert Christian Church—as well as the whole greater Tucson area feeling a familiarity with Pastor Brian from all our advertising, we have to help him filter things a bit for him to do his job well."

"Oh." I hated to admit it, but that seemed reasonable. Curses!

"OK. Listen, I really think that I'm one who should get through to talk to him. I'm a Private Investigator from Phoenix, who is here investigating a murder that took place back in January. I just came on some evidence that indicated that the woman who was murdered had some connection to your church—at least she had a lot of your DVDs, seminars, and books. My hope is that Pastor Brian might be able to provide some help."

Wait for it . . . wait for it . . . would I get passed the keeper of the gate or not?

"Could I have the woman's name please?" she asked.

"Kate Walker."

Another pause. "Hmmm. That name doesn't ring a bell with me, but as I said, thousands of people attend Desert Christian each weekend and with the multiple locations, I might not know her. Could you hold for moment?"

"Sure."

It was more like three or four moments, but when she came back on the line, the keeper of the gate said that Pastor Brian would meet with me if I could be there at 10:00 a.m. tomorrow morning.

I took a moment myself to pretend that I was looking through my schedule to see if I had that slot available—just to maintain a little self-respect—and then told her that it looked like I could squeeze that time into my busy day. I'm not sure she bought it, but I was sure selling it!

She confirmed Tuesday morning at 10:00 a.m. at their "West Campus," whatever that meant, and then politely said goodbye.

I mentally made a note to do some research on "Desert Christian Church" online before my appointment—just so I had a clue what I was walking into. My "religious training" was somewhat lacking—OK, it was basically non-existent. But I wasn't trying to join up—believe me—I just needed some answers from Mr. Spiky Hair church dude—and I wasn't sure he was gonna like my questions.

CHAPTER

— 42 —

Twenty minutes later, I pulled into the parking lot of Casa Hacienda Resort and Spa. I once again avoided the valet parking and did my own dirty work. Walking into the resort, I still couldn't get over how they were able to mask the smell of all those horses in the stables—things like that intrigue me. Especially since it had some *real-world application* in *my life*! I would love to figure out how to mask the aromas that emanated from the cattle feed place by my office in Phoenix. Oh well, an investigation for another day.

This time, instead of avoiding everybody official and sneaking into a room, I needed some help. So, I walked right up to the fancy granite registration counter and asked if I could speak to the manager. When politely asked the reason, I simply said, "I'm investigating the murder that took place here in January." I made sure that I said it loud enough to be heard, but *not* loud enough to spook off the clientele—*yet.* On the one hand, I didn't want these people to get mad at me—as I said, I needed their help. However, I did want them to know that I also possessed information that I was guessing they would prefer was *not* spread around the resort to the paying guests.

Something about murder is just so messy and passé, after all. Paying clientele at expensive resorts just tend to be put off by such things.

Apparently, my approach had the desired effect on the "guest service representative" named Heather—according to her name tag. (Didn't they used to be hotel clerks?) Her eyes bugged out just a little—she quickly looked left and then right to see who might have heard me—and then with a forced smile she asked me to wait for just a moment.

Excellent.

She was only gone a couple of minutes and out she emerged from the bowels of the resort with a woman I could only assume was the manager.

Oh yeah, I'm good—I am an investigator after all!

She introduced herself as Jane Alexander and I returned the favor and gave her my card. She looked to be a little north of forty years old, somewhat overweight, but with clothes that were so well made it hid the weight quite effectively. She also had medium dark, medium length hair that was just a little bigger—and let's say "*bouffant*"—than was currently in fashion. (As you can imagine, I am quite the savant in determining what is "in fashion.")

I have to admit; I couldn't help but stare at her "high hair" a little longer than was probably safe. It intrigued me—how *did* she get it to stay up like that?

She asked me to step into her office—probably to avoid me telling her, and the entire lobby, why I was there.

Her office was right down a plush carpeted hallway, just a few doors on the left. Her large window looked out at the entrance of the resort—I could see Black Beauty parked down in their lot.

"Now Mr.," she looked down at my card, "Moran. My assistant tells me you are here to investigate the murder from earlier this year. I see from your card that you are a Private Investigator . . . ," she paused and looked closer at my card. All of the sudden I realized that what gave her pause was that she was looking at my motto—"*Blake Moran Investigations—we find stuff*"—on my card.

I really may need to consider thinking up a new catch phrase—I don't seem to be catching much with this one.

She looked up at me with a quizzical look, then shook it off and continued. "Anyway, as a Private Investigator, what is your interest in this case?"

Translation: "What jurisdiction do you have here gumshoe, and why should I bother to help you?"

"I've been hired by the deceased woman's brother to continue the investigation, since the police department has naturally had to move this case to the 'cold case' pile. He really wants to discover who killed his sister and bring them to justice. That's my 'interest.'"

Ms. Alexander held my gaze for a moment—I just looked back at her and let her figure it out.

"What is it that you are wanting from us Mr. Moran? Obviously, we have a large enterprise to run here, so our involvement would need to be limited. We already cooperated extensively with the police in their investigation."

"Yes ma'am, I understand that. All that I was hoping to do was to look at the actual room where Miss Walker was killed, and see if I could speak to the resort staff member who discovered Kate's body. I think most of the rest of the information I can get from the police report."

"Oh, and if you could also tell me *how* you are able to hide the smell of the horses down at the stables, that would be awesome too."

Her incredulous stare caused me to realize that I'd overstepped.

"Or . . . *maybe just the first stuff* I said."

She was clearly hesitant, but my silent staring, leading to quite an uncomfortable silence, finally broke the dam.

"I suppose we could arrange for you to visit the room and speak to someone, but I have to emphasize that beyond that, we will not be able to assist you any further."

"Thank you, Ms. Alexander. I'll try and complete my investigation as quickly as I can and get out of your hair."

She jerked her eyes back up to glare at me, and it was only then that I remembered her out of fashion "bouffant" hair. Honest—it may have been a subconscious reference, but that comment was totally innocent. I'm not sure that she thought so though.

I turned my most appealing 100-watt smile on Ms. Alexander—I was selling it, but I'm not sure she was buying it. She just looked at me with that accusatory look, then subconsciously patted her bouffant and said, "Yes, well see to it that you *do* complete your investigation quickly sir!"

As she turned and marched out of her office, my smile faded as I realized the "sir" clearly meant that my "sell" hadn't landed. She left me out in the waiting room for about twenty minutes to contemplate where and how I had started losing my touch with the fairer sex when it came to shoveling the hooey.

Maybe I should spend some time working harder on my smile . . .

CHAPTER
— 43 —

I waited for a few minutes in Ms. Alexander's office, but then it just started to feel weird, so I went back out into the hallway and retraced my steps back out to the lobby.

I stood where I figured "Heather" could keep a wary eye on me, while I made sure they didn't forget about me. See how helpful I was being—looking for the win/win?

It was actually about twenty minutes before anything happened—I'm guessing about fifteen minutes longer than necessary just to punish me for that comment about Ms. Alexander's hair. I still say it's unfair to blame me for that—but whatcha gonna do?

The woman who came out to help me seemed very nervous. She was Hispanic, a little heavyset, was probably somewhere between forty-five and fifty-five years old. She was wearing the same maid's outfit that I'd already seen around the Casa Hacienda. Add all this together with the nervousness and the fact that her name tag said, "Maria," I was surmising that I was meeting Maria Ortez—the maid who found Kate.

I know—astounding deductive reasoning. What can I say? It's just what I do . . .

"Ms. Ortez?" I ventured.

"Mrs. Ortez," she responded. She spoke so quietly that I could barely hear her.

"Thank you for helping me."

She nodded slightly and began to walk away. I barely heard her say, "It's this way."

I followed her down a hallway and around a corner into a service area. There were other service personnel who grew quiet as Maria led me by them to some service elevators.

She led the way onto the elevator and pushed the button for the third floor.

Big shocker here—we rode the elevator in silence.

When the doors opened on the third floor, Maria stepped out and turned toward the left, down the hallway. She then turned right down a final hallway that housed the luxury suites at Casa Hacienda.

She stopped at the end of the hallway at suite 322, took a deep breath and swiped her pass card. At the click, she opened the door and led me into what had been Kate Walker's crime scene.

After stepping into the luxury suite, the door clicked shut behind us and all was quiet. It was quite a place—huge, comfortable looking furniture like I'd seen on my stealthy "peek" into a room before—but these rooms were even more luxurious and impressive.

The rooms appeared to be at least twice the size of the room I'd seen, and the view was spectacular. I was confident that the view at night with the mountains and the clear night sky would be even more stunning. The large, secluded balcony would be quite a place to sit and stare.

I walked through the room, almost forgetting that Maria was standing close to the door, nervously looking down at the floor.

I walked through the suite, trying to reconstruct what might have happened here, based on what I knew from the police reports and from my own investigation.

I stepped through the living area into the bedroom. It had the same large windows and amazing view—and a bed that seem to just go on and on. In the room, there was a sunken Jacuzzi hot tub, similar to the one I had seen before, except that it was about twice as big as the other one—like everything in this suite.

After looking around and trying to "see" the room through the eyes of the crime, I walked through the bedroom into the final scene of the crime—the bathroom.

Like the rest of the suite, it was huge and beautiful, tiled floors and part way up the walls, with listels throughout. Mirrors were everywhere and I was surprised to see that this suite *did* have a bidet. Apparently, that was *not* too uppity for the Casa Hacienda—if you were at the top of the food chain and could afford their best.

My eyes finally settled on the huge bathtub—the place where Kate had lost her life. I stood there trying to imagine the scene, while putting it together with the crime scene photos that I'd studied.

I'd stood there for some time staring when I heard barely audible whispering behind me. I jumped and spun around, only to find Maria standing there, seeming to be repeating something over and over.

I have to tell you that I'm not really very proud of my reaction to this: first, my ninja hearing must have been on the blitz because a fifty-ish woman just walked right up behind me and I had not a clue. Secondly, my ninja reflexes didn't send me launching into my surprise aggressor, but rather had me cowering like a little girl at a spider convention. Thirdly, my heart rate was racing so fast I had to stop and take a couple of breaths to calm myself down.

Not exactly "Manly Man of the Year" stuff . . .

So, what say you and I just keep this between us? I'm not sure that Maria even noticed since she was so engrossed in whatever she was doing.

This is the kind of stuff that can really hurt a guy's "rep."

I promise I'll try and do better next time.

So, our little secret? Pinky swear? Oh, probably not too manly again . . .

Anyway, after I caught my breath, on closer inspection I realized that Maria was praying. She was whispering it over and over, and I realized that it was one of those Catholic prayers—I had no idea which one.

"Maria, are you OK?"

She looked up at me and I saw real fear in her eyes.

"Maria, are you OK?" I asked again.

She nodded slowly.

"Maria, you don't need to be afraid—I just wanted to ask you some questions."

"But you are *Federales*?" she whispered.

Now I admit that my Spanish isn't all that good—being able to order a taco and chimichanga is pretty close to my limit—but I do know that *Federales* are the police in Mexico, and I'm not that. Perhaps she was in the country illegally and that was where her fear was coming from, but all I cared about was any help she could provide regarding Kate.

"No Maria," I assured her, "I'm not *Federales*—I'm just an investigator."

At the confused look on her face, I tried to think how to explain it to her. Then I had it.

I pointed to the bathtub and said, "You know the women you found in this bathtub?"

She nodded her head.

"Her name was Kate Walker. She was a very nice person. Kate has a brother named Greg and he hired me to try and find out who murdered his sister. I'm not with the police—the *Federales*—I'm with Kate's brother.

Maria looked surprised, but it seemed that she understood what I was saying to her. She immediately relaxed—I guess she really didn't like "*Federales*."

Wanting to seize on her better disposition and knowing from the crime report that she had had virtually nothing to say to the police, I asked her, "Maria, was there anything that you can add to what you already told the *Federales*?"

She looked nervous again when I asked her that.

I tried another tack.

"Maria, do you have sisters?"

She nodded yes.

"What about children?"

"Si, three niños." She said this with some pride.

"Well Maria, Kate Walker was somebody's sister and somebody's daughter—and they loved her like you love your sisters and your children. If you know anything, I could really use some help in catching Kate's killer."

She stared at me for a long moment, apparently letting what I said sink in.

"No *Federales*?" she asked.

"No *Federales*—this is just between me and you Maria."

She stared again, looked over at the oversized tub, and then back at me.

She then quietly whispered, "I saw him."

CHAPTER

— 44 —

The shock that ran through my body felt almost electric.

"You saw *who* Maria?"

"The man who visited the woman," she replied.

I was trying to keep my emotions in check to keep Maria calm, but I was struggling.

"You saw a man who visited Kate?"

"Si," she replied.

"When?"

"The day before I found her in the bath. I ended up having to stay late to finish some rooms and right before I left for home—around 7:00—I had to drop some extra towels off to a room on the third floor. After I handed over the towels, I heard someone knock on a door down the hall. I glanced that way and that's when I saw him."

I couldn't believe what I was hearing! Maria very possibly saw the murderer!

"Maria, what did this man look like?"

She took a deep breath.

"I didn't get a very good look at him," she said, "I didn't know it was important at the time. The door was opened after he knocked, and he went inside. Also, his back was to me, so I didn't get a look at his face."

My exhilaration deflated a little—so much for the sketch artist that I was hoping Trent had on speed dial.

"So, what did you see?" I asked.

With a shrug, she said, “Not really anything I can describe, just the back of a man.”

Witnesses often know more than even they know that they know if led the right way, so I tried another tack.

“How tall was he?”

“I don’t know,” she responded.

“Hmmm—can you follow me out into the hallway for a minute?”

We walked out of room 322 into the hallway.

“Now to which room were you were delivering towels?” I asked.

She pointed about fifty feet down the hall. “Down there at room three-one-one.”

“OK, go ahead and walk down there and stand in front of that door where you were standing.”

She walked to room 311 and stood there, clearly a little confused as to why.

“Now Maria, I would like you to close your eyes and try and ‘see’ what happened again, but only in your mind. I’m going to knock on this door, just like the man did, and I want you to try and ‘see’ in your mind as you are turning and looking.”

“But why Mr. Moran—I don’t remember.”

“Let’s just do this anyway.”

She shrugged her shoulders and closed her eyes and faced room 311. I gave it about three seconds and then rapped on the door loudly and very fast—in a way that no one would knock unless they were also yelling, “This is the police, open up!”

Maria opened her eyes and turned and said, “No, that’s not the way he knocked.”

I suppressed a smile and asked, “How did he knock, show me.”

She reached up to the door of 311 and somewhat softly knocked three times right in a row. Thankfully no one was occupying room 311 at the moment.

"OK, I'll do it like that this time—go ahead and close your eyes again and try and picture the scene."

I gave her a few seconds again and then knocked three times just like she did.

She kept her eyes closed as she tried to replay the recording in her head.

I gave her a minute and then asked, "Now Maria, how tall was he?"

She turned and looked at me and said, "I told you, I don't know."

I turned my back to Maria, just as the man had, and squatted down about a foot.

"Was he this tall?"

"Oh no, he was taller than that."

OK, we were getting somewhere.

"OK Maria, this time I want you to look at the door of room 311 and when I knock, turn just like you did and compare his size with mine."

Maria was starting to get how this worked, so she turned and waited.

I waited a few beats with my back to her, then I knocked and waited.

Suddenly Maria said, "He was tall like you, but he was bigger in the shoulders."

Excellent.

"That's great Maria, we just learned something. I'm 6 feet 4 inches, so this man was taller than most, but also with a bigger build. Did he seem overweight to you too or just bigger in the shoulders?"

"Close your eyes and see if you can tell."

She shut her eyes and I could see her searching. She seemed to be struggling.

"Maria," I called, "try and look around his center area and his legs—did he have a waist or was he square or round."

She closed her eyes again and saw it.

"He wasn't fat—his shoulders were big, but his bottom was not."

All of the sudden Maria heard what she had just said and turned a little red.

"That's great Maria—you're doing great. Now what was he wearing?"

Maria looked confused. "Clothes?"

"Yes, but what kind—shorts and a shirt, jeans, a scuba suit, a dress . . ."

Maria actually laughed.

"No, none of that sounds right." She closed her eyes again and furrowed her brow she was trying so hard to see.

"A suit," she said all the sudden.

Her eyes popped open, and she had a look of surprise on her face.

"Excellent. Did the suit look cheap or expensive—well used or well kept?"

"I don't know," she replied.

"Here's how to know. When you glanced over at him, do you believe that he looked good, that the suit fit well, that it seemed well cut, that it complimented his body—or not?"

She closed her eyes.

"It did look good—very good—I think it was probably a very nice suit."

"OK, great. Now, what about his hair?"

"I'm sorry Mr. Moran, I don't remember."

"OK—was his hair long, over his collar or maybe all frizzy?"

She laughed, "No, it was shorter."

"Try and see in your head—was his hair over his collar at all or was it shorter?"

She thought for a moment.

"It was shorter."

"So would you say kind of professional, like a businessman might wear?"

"Yes, I would."

"OK—was it a bright blonde or red?" I asked.

"No, it was dark."

The look of surprise on her face when she heard herself immediately say that, was priceless. I just let that statement hang there because I could tell that she wasn't completely satisfied with the statement.

"Wait," she said as she stared off into space, "not completely dark. It had gray around here," she signed around the temples," "and some around the back."

I just looked at her down the hall for a moment.

"You're doing great Maria. Just one more question: as you see this tall, not fat, well dressed, dark haired with some gray man—is he standing tall, with good posture, or is he slouching some with poor posture?"

With each statement with my back to her, I mimicked what I was describing.

I looked around and saw she was staring at me as she thought.

"Standing tall," she replied.

I turned and walked the fifty feet to Maria and surprised her by giving her a big hug.

"You did really well Maria—really, *really* well."

CHAPTER

— 45 —

I finished up with Maria and we went back downstairs where I walked by the front counter and saw Ms. Alexander. I thanked her for her help, without staring at her bouffant hair, and then I headed for the exit.

I got back to Black Beauty and fired her up and tore out of the Casa Hacienda resort. While waiting at a stoplight, I dialed Trent and put the phone on speaker.

"Hey Blake, what's up?" Trent said.

"What, no chit-chat, no 'how's your day been'?"

"You do know I have a real job, right?" Trent asked.

I ignored his apparent attack on private investigators—after a while I've gotten used to how police tend to view what I do—I don't like it, but I've gotten used to it.

I have to admit that I kind of like it that Trent decided to try and give me a psychological "wedgie" right then. It made what I had to tell him that much better.

"Oh, you're right, I'm sorry," I said, "I shouldn't be bothering you while you're doing your 'real job,' just to give you a description of Kate Walker's murderer. Just give me a call when you have some time."

And I *hung up*!

You know all that talk before about getting used to how police view what I do—I was just blowing; pretending that I handled it with maturity and class. Yeah, right! I can be as petty and juvenile as anyone, thank you very much!

You might be surprised to hear that not ten seconds later, *my phone rang*! And who should it say was calling but my buddy, Trent Burgess! Go figure.

"Hey Trent—what's up?!"

"Real funny."

"Yeah, I thought so," I replied.

"So?" Trent asked.

"What?" I replied.

"Really?" Trent asked.

"Yeah—I'm that petty and I've come to terms with it. You wanna know, you gotta ask."

Heavy sigh.

"OK, Blake, what was that you said about having a description of Kate Walker's murderer?"

"It might have landed better if you had added 'O great investigator' Blake . . ."

Silence.

"Too much?" I asked.

Silence.

"That's all I'm getting?"

Silence. I looked at the phone, starting to wonder if we'd been cut off.

Finally, "Blake, if you don't cut the bull and just tell me what you know, I'm gonna hit you with an obstruction of justice charge and provide you with free room and board courtesy of the Tucson Police Department."

"Whoa, did somebody steal one of your donuts this morning?!"

Cops just *love* that stereotype!

But I told you, I'm petty and just a little immature—maybe a lot at times. But enough was enough—jail time simply wasn't on my schedule—although I think Trent was just huffing and puffing.

So, still laughing, I started the story with Trent.

"It turns out that our murderer is most probably tall, not fat, well dressed, dark haired with some gray and has good posture. So that means that he is probably fit, most probably has money and has some age on him."

Silence.

I gotta say, Trent was *really* good at the silent treatment.

Finally, Trent said, "And you know this how?"

"Sorry my man, no can do," I said, "my unnamed source has a real phobia about cops."

That landed like a burrito in a stomach with an ulcer.

"I don't care what her 'phobia' is—you're not a journalist with some 'unnamed source' to protect, and this is a murder investigation!" Trent not so quietly informed me.

"I know, I know," I responded, "but let me try and handle her. If she has to talk with someone more official eventually, I'll get her there. Maybe I could have her talk to someone calm and controlled like you are—I'm sure *that* won't scare her!"

Silence. But this time I waited him out.

"Fine. But she has to be available if we have to have her."

"Absolutely—if you *have* to have her."

CHAPTER
— 46 —

As I drove back to The Hermosillo, I evaluated the day and decided it had been a pretty big success. I'd learned a lot of things that I hadn't known—and for that matter—even a few that the police hadn't known. I was getting closer, and I felt jazzed by that.

I also was hungry. Before I headed to my "home base," I needed some sustenance. Given the way I'd been eating, I figured I'd better try and eat a little "cleaner"—as they say. (Honestly, what normal human being talks like that?!) Anyway, I'd seen a "Chili's" close to my hotel, so I figured I'd go there and clean up my act a little.

When I pulled into the parking lot, it was only about half full, so that was a good sign—I mean because I probably wouldn't have to wait long to get fed. I still went ahead and parked Black Beauty out all by herself toward the end of the lot—couldn't take a chance some family in a minivan would park next to me and ding *"her excellency."*

When I walked in, I was able to get seated right away—which was good, cuz I was hungry! I began to peruse the menu—it had *lots* of choices. I focused on *"healthy"*—they even had some indications of the *more* healthy choices. I read all of those and resolutely planned my healthy choice. I felt pretty good about it too.

When the waitress showed up to take my order, I looked right at her, glanced back at the menu, and heard myself say, "I'll take the *'Chicken Crispers.'*"

Now, let's just say that was *not* my plan! *"Chicken Crispers"* are my *favorite* at Chili's—they are *awesome*! However, they are *not* exactly in the "healthy choice" aisle, if you know what I mean. They are these amazing chicken pieces, (so hey, that's better than red meat, right?), that they cover in this delicious batter and then *deep fry* it to a golden brown. They then add a pile of French fries—so a vegetable—*and* a piece of corn on the cob—another vegetable! Now you can't knock the corn on the cob—and yes, I *do* eat it. Mainly cuz you can't imagine how good it is covered in butter and salt and pepper. (I'm guessing I'm hurting my argument with the slathering of butter.)

OK, how about I just had *water* instead of a soda?! That's right, whose healthy *now*?!

Can I get any credit for *meaning* to eat healthful food? What ever happened to "It's the thought that counts"? Wow, you are such a food Nazi!

As I ate my "not fast food" meal, (OK, I'm reaching here), I thought over my day. I'd really had one of those rare days in my profession since I'd driven back from Phoenix this morning—a day where I'd learned *a lot*! Now, as I dipped my *"Chicken Crispers"* in ranch dressing, (yeah, I'd pretty much given up at this point, but *oh, so good*), it was time to do my best "P.I. Ponder."

All the interviews at The Palms had been helpful, but when taken all together, they really started to construct an interesting picture. Todd Brooks' clear romantic interest in Kate and his tense body language sure made one want to take a closer look at him. He fit some of the description from Maria, but maybe was not old enough. Bailey Sanchez, (my that was a good-looking woman), oops, got distracted—she clearly did *not* like Kate, obviously from jealousy. (Did I mention she was one fine looking woman?)

Then there was Lester. Lester the pervert. Just thinking about that jerk was making all that fried food turn a little in my stomach. Yeah, that dude needed to go down—just not sure if it was for what I was investigating.

Then there was the bombshell from Jesus—that's Jesus of the non-Messiah variety—that there *had* been a man in Kate's life romantically. However, given that Kate's brother Greg didn't know about it, I wasn't sure how serious this "relationship" could have been.

And what about this whole "religion" twist?! Clearly there was something connecting Kate to this church called "Desert Christian Church". Given how much stuff she had from there, it would be hard to think of this as just a superficial interest.

And finally, there was Maria—an eyewitness to some man—maybe the romantic interest, maybe not—who interacted with Kate right before her death. Her description, unearthed from her subconscious, was a *major* leap forward in the case.

Yep, it was a *very* productive day! I wiped my hands with my napkin—kind of tough to get that much grease off of them—and then stared at something—the dessert menu. Oh, leave me alone, I didn't have any—I just looked and then resisted. I don't care what you think, I'm counting that as a "win"!

When I got back to the hotel, I actually washed my hands with soap a couple of times—that really was a lot of grease! Then I stripped down to my boxers and settled down with my laptop to start some research. I had "*Sports Center*" on in the background for noise, but I was pretty focused on my research on "Desert Christian Church." With my appointment happening the next day with Pastor Spiky Hair, I wanted to have some background before I started the interview.

CHAPTER

— 47 —

The guy moved carefully at the edge of the dark parking lot—just a shadow. It was the middle of the night—actually more like the very early morning hours, when nobody was awake or moving around.

The owner of the lifted black Toyota 4X4 had done him a favor by parking out at the edge of the parking lot. Idiot. Was he trying to get it stolen? It *was* under a powerful light, but at this hour, who was going to be looking? He looked into the cab and saw the make of the security system and knew what he would have to do to disable it once he got the door opened. It would make some noise, but he could probably stop the noise in about three seconds—and then he would wait to see if anybody would notice it in the middle of the night.

It was a very good system that would make the truck undrivable until the actual key was put in the ignition—but that was OK—he wasn't here to steal the truck. Although, if he could have, he would have—this was one nice ride! The system would also be turned off when the owner went to the car, but there wasn't anything he could do about that.

After sitting in the dark for a while to make sure nobody had seen him looking into the truck, he quickly moved toward the truck and went to work. It took less than a minute to get the door opened and the alarm went crazy. He quickly went to work under the dash and was able to shut the alarm down in about five seconds.

He then quickly got out of the truck and moved back into the darkness, close enough to see the whole parking lot, and yet still far enough that he could dissolve into the shadows if someone came running.

He waited a full fifteen minutes to make sure that no one was going to respond. He then returned to the truck with the package and stowed it, hidden away so that the owner wouldn't find it. He then stuck the magnetized GPS locater toward the back of the truck, attached to an inside panel.

He then shut everything up, re-locked the door, and quietly returned to the darkness—all in all, it only took about five minutes total—not bad. He stood for a moment in the darkness to make sure there would be no response and to stare at the truck a little more. It was really a shame he couldn't figure a way to steal it—he could make some *serious* money off of this one.

CHAPTER — 48 —

Tuesday morning, I woke up in one of those "where am I?" zones—totally confused about my whereabouts. I slowly began to remember the hotel and Tucson, but I had really slept *hard.* Guess I needed it.

After a little time in the bathroom, I looked around for some eats. After my healthful meal at Chili's, I decided to have a couple pieces of fruit—that's right—you heard me, so *there*!

I'd been up pretty late researching the church, so I was going to have to keep things moving to get to their "West Campus" on time—wherever that was. It occurred to me that I didn't even know how far away the church was, so I'd better start there. When the Google Maps on my phone said it was about ten minutes away, I chilled; I had more time than I thought.

I grabbed a shower and relaxed in it a little and then got dressed in my "going to church" attire: jeans, shirt, jacket and tie—this *is* the Southwest after all. I didn't even pack Molly—I wasn't expecting a shootout with the Pastor.

I headed out to my triple B, 4X4—she looked awesome and shiny, baking there in the early morning Arizona sun. Walking up to her, I hit the clicker to turn off the security system and nothing happened. Weird. I tried again—still nothing.

I tried the door handle—locked. Hmmm.

Now I realize that it is humanly possible that I would forget to set the alarm on my little beauty—but not *really* possible—especially when I am parking in a different city *and* in a public parking place all night!

In addition to that, I *know* that I would never actually physically lock the door with my key—or if I had to, I would certainly remember doing it, cuz it would be that random.

So, the fact that the system was *off* while the door was *locked* meant somebody had messed with me—and I started feeling some heat that had nothing to do with the balmy 90 degree "good morning" heat of SW Arizona.

I looked all around the truck first to see if anything was damaged—nope—good there. Then I carefully unlocked the door with my key and looked around the cab. Everything was still there—especially all my expensive upgrades and stereo system. Hmmm.

I looked around and nothing seemed out of place, vandalized, or gone. Weird again. Don't get me wrong—I was happy about this, but it didn't make a lot of sense.

I supposed that someone could break into Black Beauty and have the alarm go off and freak and run—but what would make them actually *lock* the door again? In addition to that, after going off for a while, the alarm would stop and would reset. It hadn't.

No doubt about it—something was hinky. I didn't know what had happened, but since everything seemed in place—and I didn't have time to keep standing here and thinking about it, I had an appointment to get to, plus, I was *dying* in this heat.

So off I went, confused and just a little thankful that nothing serious had happened to my girl.

CHAPTER

— 49 —

The trip to Desert Christian Church didn't even take the full ten minutes. I drove in with two minutes to spare, so it gave me a little time to look around.

The campus was pretty cool—it looked a little more like a walking mall than it did a church. There was a fair amount of grass—a commodity not found often in the Tucson area—and some interesting water features around the campus. The landscaping was beautiful—they had some great Palm trees too. There was an area labeled "Food Court" with tables and chairs and an outside stage. Kid's play equipment systems, volleyball courts, a play fountain, a man-made pond, what looked like a huge in ground hot tub, a rock wall—and if I wasn't mistaken—a long zip line. OK, *that* was extra cool—certainly not like any church I had ever been to—not that I'd been to many.

There were a number of different buildings, the largest clearly being the "sanctuary"—or seems like from the signs here—they call it the auditorium. Classrooms were scattered around the campus and up in front, I found the offices. It was about time, so I went on in.

I was kind of surprised when I stepped into the office space because it *wasn't* all that impressive. It was nice enough, but the offices were small and unassuming. The lady behind the desk said "hi" and asked if she could help me. I was guessing that she was the "keeper of the gate" that I had to work so hard to get past yesterday.

I told her my name and that I was here to see the Pastor, and she said, "Oh yes, we talked yesterday."

Nailed it!

"Have a seat," she said, "and I'll let him know you're here."

I did and she did.

I didn't have to wait long, but while I did wait, I was reminded how much I didn't like churches. For some reason, I always felt like I was in the principal's office, about to get in trouble. I don't know if that's cuz I had *spent a lot of time in* the principal's office or because religious people are always telling everybody else how to live.

I decided to blame my discomfort on *them* instead of on me.

When the Pastor came out, it was indeed Mr. Spiky Hair. Dark hair, about 6 feet tall—but somehow, just not what I thought a Pastor would be like. He said "hi" and introduced himself, as did I—handing him my card—and then he led me back to his office.

After we got settled, Pastor Brian leaned back with a smile and said, "How can I help you Mr. Moran? I see from your card that you 'find stuff'—what can I help you 'find'?"

Oh, funny guy! I was *really* going to have to change my tag line!

"Well Pastor, you can call me Blake—I hear Mr. Moran and I start looking around for my father."

He laughed and said, "OK, and you can just call me Brian."

"Really?" I was a little surprised.

"Yep, just one guy having a conversation with another guy. My office manager said that this had something to do with a murder and that whoever was murdered came to Desert Christian. May I ask why a Private Investigator and not a police officer is investigating this?"

"How did you know I was a P.I.?"

"Well, you *told* my office manager that you were when you called for the appointment yesterday—she told me. Also, it *says* so right here on this card you just handed me."

"Oh." I probably should have figured that one out. I may have just hurt my credibility *as* a P.I. that I missed all that.

"And for the record, I like your slogan—it gets right to the point."

I wasn't sure if he was kidding me or not. Now I was conflicted about whether I had to rethink, "we find stuff."

"Well, I was hoping that you knew the young lady or had had some interactions with her that could be helpful. Her name was Kate Walker."

I watched closely for some sign of recognition, but there didn't seem to be any "tell."

"No, I'm sorry, but that name isn't familiar to me. That doesn't mean that she didn't go here. We have a lot of people who go to Desert Christian—and then there are other satellite locations as well. Could you describe her?"

"I can do better than that," I said, "here are a number of different pictures of Kate."

Once again, I watched closely.

"Wow, she was really beautiful, wasn't she?"

"Yes, she was," although I wasn't sure that pastors were allowed to notice that.

After looking at the different pictures, he said, "I'm sorry, I don't recognize her—she doesn't look familiar. It's so horrible that she was murdered."

Again—I saw no "tells."

Bummer.

"Well, here's the deal—I talked to a person who worked with Kate who described her as investigating 'religion' before she was killed—although it seemed to be a little on the 'down low.' So then when I looked through her effects, I found probably thirty or forty DVDs of what looked like—what are they called—sermons? And then there were other DVDs with books that looked like seminars. All of them were from Desert Christian Church. Now as far as most people around her, they didn't know that she was looking into any of this. For the life of me, I cannot figure out *why* a woman like this would be looking into religion."

Pastor Brian just stared at me with a half-smile on his face and this quizzical look. I've learned over the years that one of the best interview methods is to wait out the other person—so I just looked back and waited.

And waited . . .

Dang, this dude was good . . .

"*What?*" I finally asked.

CHAPTER

— 50 —

Detective Cindy Lou Rios was sitting at her desk at the Miracle Mile Substation, working on one of her current cases. The place was loud—which was normal—but inside her little cubical, you could at least hear yourself think.

Cindy was currently running down a model, make and year, from an eye-witness of a hit and run. She had a partial plate and color—which narrowed it to 100s of cars instead of 1000s—hurray!

As she was beginning to feel the obligatory headache come on from her search, Agnes stepped into her cubical. Cindy smelled her before she saw her.

Agnes was an interesting woman, a chronic chain smoker. Because of her smoking, she tried to cover that with prodigious amounts of "ode to make your eyes water" perfume. The combination of ash tray and "ode" was truly an experience for the ages.

Agnes probably carried a good seventy-five pounds more than was good for her, she wore shocking amounts of, let's call it "loud" makeup, and she had her hair dyed, well, let's call it "magenta." Agnes' whole persona kind of screamed *"hello!"*

And now she was in Cindy's cubicle.

As one might guess from her persona, Agnes could be a bit abrasive. Now to be fair, Agnes ran the Crime Stopper program—a call in number where people could call in and anonymously report information that they believe dealt with a crime. So even though it was to be anonymous, it was part of her job to try and pry out of these people who *want* to help and yet *want* to be anonymous—who they are.

Not any easy job—certainly not one Cindy would want.

But given that Cindy was starting to feel that headache come on, she was actually happy to see Agnes. You had to admit that she was an interesting character.

"Hi Agnes."

"Rios." (Agnes could really make you feel all warm and fuzzy inside.)

"What can I do for you?"

Agnes threw a printed piece of paper on my desk.

"Had something come in on the hotline—guessing its gonna land on your desk."

"Why is that?"

"Got a call about some guy trying to sell some drugs out of his truck around the Foothills Mall. They gave me a lot of information—description of the truck and the guy and even the tag number. Couldn't get 'em to tell me who they were, but none of 'em wants to do that. It was a vanity plate, so I ran it.

"OK."

"It was a Toyota Tacoma 4X4 with the plate, TOY4BOY."

"Sounds like a very mature person," Cyndy said ironically.

"Ya think?"

Agnes wasn't good at irony.

"Anyway, I ran the plate, and it came back from Phoenix. The owner is a guy named Blake Moran—a Private Investigator."

The world kind of froze for a split second.

"Now I'm not trying to be nosy, but I couldn't help but remember that tall drink of water that walked in here last week with Detective Burgess—wasn't his name Blake Moran?"

Cindy looked back at Agnes.

"How could you possibly know that Agnes?"

Agnes colored a little.

"Well, when I saw him walk in, I happened to be over at intake and happened to notice his name on the paperwork."

Now *that* was an awful lot of "happening!" Cindy pondered that Agnes was *always chasing* men.

"Anyway, I was guessing you'd end up with this, since he was helping out on one of your cases. I sure hope he's not dirty—cuz he's *way* too fine to be doin' time."

Cindy just stared at Agnes, wondering if she was into rap.

Agnes finally got uncomfortable.

"So, there you go. If you find out that this isn't true, could you let me know? Maybe put a good word in for me?"

Cindy stared more in quiet disbelief.

"OK," said Agnes and off she went in a cloud of bad perfume and even more smoke.

All I could do was look down at the paperwork that had just become potentially toxic to my case, at least if ol' Blake Moran—that "tall drink of water"—was dirty.

CHAPTER
— 51 —

Pastor Brian continued, "So I'm curious Blake; when you say you're surprised that a 'woman like this' would be looking into what you call 'religion,' do you mean that Kate was a horrible, godless, hateful, hideous excuse for a human being?"

"O gosh, no—quite the opposite. Kate was clearly such an awesome person, that no one can figure out a reason why anyone would kill her."

"OK, good—but that still has me wondering what you mean by 'a woman like this,' and wondering why she would be looking into what you call 'religion'?"

"You know," I said forgetting myself a little, "a woman this beautiful, this cool, this fine, this successful—that stuff."

Pastor Brian got an amused look on his face and said, "So you think that Kate had too much going for her physically for her to consider God?"

"Well, yeah."

Why did I all the sudden feel like I *was* in the principal's office again?

He paused for a moment, then said, "Listen Blake—I have to believe that for you to effectively do your job as a private investigator, you'll have to have an objective view of the elements that surround your case. Is that accurate?"

"Well, yeah." I was starting to feel a little inarticulate here.

Pastor Brian continued, "If I could make a suggestion; if Kate was considering God through the resources that Desert Christian offers, it will probably be important for you to avoid any inaccurate presuppositions that you have, if you hope to discover what she was going through."

"What inaccurate presuppositions?" I asked defensively. This guy was really starting to tick me off.

"Well, it would start with your own personal view of what you refer to as 'religion.' You clearly have a less than positive view of this—a view that would seem to *not* be shared by Kate when she was alive, and honestly is not rooted in the real world. If you use your starting point that is negative about what you call 'religion' when apparently, Kate was not of the same mindset, you'll logically arrive at inaccurate conclusions based on an incorrect starting point."

"Who said I was negative about religion? I don't have an opinion one way or the other."

Pastor Brian actually laughed.

"Blake, you just informed me that in your worldview, only unattractive, unsuccessful and uncool people would be interested in what you termed 'religion.'"

This guy was really starting to tick me off.

"I did *not* say that."

"Oh, but you did—according to you, that was the whole basis for the 'WHY'—the confusion on your part as to why Kate was looking into this. Blake, please understand—you haven't offended me—I actually get why you might feel that way."

"Honestly, too often, the only thing that the world sees is weird, supposedly 'religious' people, doing odd, illogical things, and acting in strange ways. Since that is all they are exposed to, they discount the reality of 'normal' people or even what you would think of as 'exceptional' people considering God—people apparently like Kate. I get it."

"Having said that, let me ask you a question—are there embarrassing, or bad, or even corrupt, private investigators?"

"Sure there are, and they really tick me off!" I said defensively. "I work hard to do my job right because I think being a P.I. can have honor and those guys make the real deal—like me—look bad."

I think that would classify as a "*tirade*," but I'm sorry—that subject really gets me worked up.

Pastor Brian just looked back at me saying nothing, but having his eyebrows raised.

"What?"

"Did you hear what you just said? You said it with passion, because you care about what you do, and how those who either don't care or who do it wrong, reflect badly on you."

"Yep, I do."

"And there ya go."

"And there I go—what?"

"Blake, there are embarrassing or bad or even corrupt people in *every* field there is—no one is exempt—and that includes in what you call 'religion.' I am *just* as passionate about God, Jesus, and the Bible, being judged negatively based on *some* people's behavior as you are about your profession—probably more so because I'm dealing with eternal issues."

"Here's why I point all this out Blake—you are a detective—an investigator—and if you're trying to right a wrong and bring some justice for Kate and her family—I want you to succeed. That is going to *demand* that you have clarity in your view of what happened—and that includes a more accurate view of people who consider God. People as awesome as Kate."

"For instance, look at that picture on my wall."

I looked at where he was pointing and saw a beautiful woman in what was clearly a newspaper article. OK, now *that* is a weird picture in a Pastor's office.

"OK," I said cautiously.

"I think you'd agree that she is beautiful. She was a local news anchor here in Tucson for some years and even got to do some national work for a short time."

"OK."

"That's my wife, Kristi, and she is really committed to God, Jesus, and the Bible—and she loves this church. Oh, and by the way, happily *she loves me too*." He smiled.

"Really?" I said as I stared at the beautiful woman in the picture.

"See what I mean Blake? Even in your response, you were incredulous—still surprised that exceptional people would pursue God. But I don't want to mislead you, so let me say it clearly: *it doesn't matter* how beautiful OR unattractive, *how* cool OR uncool, *how* successful OR unsuccessful a person is—they are just *people*—and when people take the time to really *think* and *investigate* with an open mind—not 'religion,' but the real God—you'd probably be surprised where they end up."

"The quicker you understand that, the more you'll be able to understand Kate and what she undoubtedly was going through and therefore pursuing."

Hmmm. I couldn't argue his point—often investigations get messed up because people see what they either *want* to see or what they *think* they saw based on a skewed view from the beginning.

Could he be right? Was it possible that I could be missing important clues or information because I was starting with a bias against this whole religion thing—a bias clearly Kate didn't have? I could have sworn I honestly had *no* opinion on all that religion stuff, but maybe I did—well actually *obviously* I did. Pastor Spiky Hair had just shown it to me.

I was *really* starting to *not* like this guy!

CHAPTER

— 52 —

Detective Rios pushed everything else aside, grabbed the poisonous paper Agnes had thrown on her desk, and went in search for one Detective Trent Burgess.

When she found him over in the snack room, she was not in a good mood.

"Hey Cindy," he said cheerfully.

"Detective Burgess."

That caused him to do a double take.

"Yes."

"Just exactly how well do you know our little, 'I want to help you solve a murder' P.I. from Phoenix?"

"Blake? I don't know—I worked an embezzlement case with him a couple of years ago—why?"

"Agnes came to visit me."

"OK."

"Had some info come in on the hotline—anonymous of course."

"Yeah."

"Do you have any reason to suspect Mr. Moran of any drug use or possible distribution?"

"What?!" Trent said, clearly incredulous. "I don't know the guy well, but that seems pretty far out there."

"Well, whoever the informant was, they had all the facts on him when they called—right down to his tag number and description."

"Hmmm." Trent was good at understatement.

"Trent, you know I gotta follow up on this. If this guy is dirty, he'll do *immeasurable damage* to my case—he may have *already* done it."

Trent was clearly feeling fairly uncomfortable—given that *he* was the one who brought Blake in *and* was the one who vouched for him.

"Listen," Trent said, "let's do this together. This was my bad if Blake is dirty, and I'd like to help you clean up my mess if that's the case. We can find him and confront him together."

"Alright, but Trent, if this guy is dirty, *no favors*—he goes down—just like anybody else."

"Listen Rios, if Moran *is* dirty, I *want* him to go down—*hard*—this was *my* support he's been cashing checks on—you'll have no beef with me if we have to bust him."

"OK, just so we're on the same page."

"Oh, we are" said Trent as he started calling Blake's cell number.

CHAPTER

— 53 —

My cell phone went off—the old Dragnet theme—so I knew it was a cop, but I felt stupid having that happen right in the middle of my interview. I quickly dismissed it.

"Sorry about that."

"No problem," said Pastor Brian.

"OK," I said, "then forget all the beauty and success—just in general, why would Kate be looking into religion. Oh, and why do you keep saying 'what you call religion'?"

"Now you're asking some great questions."

I *do* enjoy a little unsolicited praise!

"Let me start with the second question first: when you use the term 'religion,' it is being applied across the board—anything that points to any kind of spiritual behavior. So, this could be anything from Christianity to Islam to Hinduism to Baha'i to Mormonism to Catholicism, even to Satanism and more. The problem with that is that is *doesn't make sense*."

"Every one of those so called 'faith' groups says *very* different things about the major areas of life—in short, they all *disagree* with each other adamantly on virtually everything important. That's *why* people think religion is so *foolish*—they are trying to combine world views that are *completely contradictory* to each other—it's *never* going to make sense. So, the idea that they are lumped together is just bad thinking."

"Well on what basis would you ever pick just *one*?" asked the great theologian, Blake Moran.

"Great question—very logical."

Told you so.

"In my first year of Bible college, it occurred to me that I needed to struggle with that very question. I had been raised in a Christian home—my dad was a Pastor—but I knew that I couldn't just accept all this on the basis of my upbringing."

"It occurred to me that if God was real—and if we really are made in the image of God—there would be some level of *logic* to the answer to this question. It made sense logically that only *two* possibilities existed: one, either *all* religions are lies or *false*—which explains why they all contradict each other—which would logically lead to the only conclusion—*there is no God.* The second possibility as that *only one* religion was *true.* And if one was true, then God would have to *show* us that it was true. Based on that, I set out to look at all the major religions in the world. Based on extensive research, I discovered that *only* the religion that is called *Christianity*—the religion of God, Jesus, and the Bible—could *prove* itself to be true."

"Whoa—what? *Prove*? That's quite a claim! Isn't the whole basis of religion what people call 'faith'?"

Much to my surprise, Pastor Brian smiled and said, "I'm so glad you said that—it shows you have a presupposition that most of the world has—that the word 'faith' actually means *blind* faith—meaning devoid of facts or proof. That may be how many people *use* that term, but that was *never* God's use of the term."

"In the Bible, specifically in Hebrews 11:1, God defines what true faith is—He says, '*Faith is the assurance of things hoped for, the conviction of things not seen.*' Around Desert Christian, we say it this way: 'faith is being *sure* of what you can prove, so that you can be *confident* of what you can't prove.'"

Now it was my turn to be incredulous.

"Wait—you're telling me you can *prove* God."

"Yep. God, Jesus, and the Bible."

"That's *crazy*."

"And yet I can—it's the reason that I can be a Christian, let alone a Pastor. Now I'm not expecting you to accept that I can do this on '*blind faith*,'" he smiled here, "I'm just trying to give you an answer to your good question. For the record, we have a seminar called, 'Facts Behind the Faith' where I do exactly what I'm claiming I can do with a workbook included to provide the documentation."

"Wait," I said, "I remember seeing that seminar in Kate's effects."

"Oh good, I'm glad to hear Kate was looking at that. It's the foundation for real faith."

"Anyway, to get back to your question—the reason I keep referring to 'what you call religion' is because until you *limit* your understanding to the only 'religion' that can *prove* itself to be true—that of God, Jesus, and the Bible—the whole picture you get will be *muddied* and *confusing*—cuz you're mixing the provable *true* with the provable *false*.

"It's like trying to mix *grape* jelly with *petroleum* jelly—you shouldn't be surprised that when you take a bite, it is *disgusting*."

"Since Kate was looking at the provable truth found in Christianity, you will be helped in your investigation by keeping the water free of mud by just focusing on that. Try not to let your own beliefs or presuppositions get in the way. That will help you to understand what was going on with her."

My head was swimming—this was some crazy stuff I'd never heard about before. I have to admit that I liked that he even used "grape jelly," my favorite, to illustrate his point.

I needed a minute, so I went to one of my best moves: "Could I take a moment to use the restroom?"

What can I say? I'm quick on my feet.

CHAPTER

— 54 —

"*You* have *got* to be *kidding me*!"

He said this as he threw the lamp in the office across the room with such force that it broke into multiple pieces when it hit the wall. It wasn't the first time.

The rage was overwhelming him, and he was starting to hyperventilate.

The door to his office was thrown open and his administrative assistance rushed in.

"Sir, are you OK?!"

"GET OUT of my office!" he roared.

She ran out like she was terrified—because she was.

He could *not* believe what he was seeing—according to the tracker he placed on that stupid P.I.'s truck, he was currently sitting at the West campus of Desert Christian Church. How could he have *possibly* put Kate and that church together? That church had messed everything up for him and he hated them. What kind of danger did they pose to him now?

This P.I. may be better than he thought initially. If his little ploy of planting the drugs in his truck didn't detour him, he might have to start thinking about a way to do something a little more *permanent* regarding Mr. Blake Moran, P.I.

CHAPTER
— 55 —

Time out completed, business done and hands washed, I returned to Pastor Brian's office.

"Now where were we?" I asked.

"I answered your second question, so now let me circle back to your first question of why Kate might be looking into 'religion.' While I didn't know Kate, there are clear reasons that a person—any person—would consider God. The primary one is often that they start to *think* about life instead of just passing through it."

"What do you mean by that?" I asked.

"Well, by and large, most people spend at least part of their life putting one foot in front of the other—just getting life done. This often consists of growing up, getting through school, finding a job, or getting even more education, and maybe getting married—for others, it is just surviving life."

"However, a time comes for most people when they have a chance to sit back and take stock of what they call their 'life.' They sit back and *think* for a minute. Whether they are successful at this point or a failure, the question for both tends to be 'What's the *point* of all this?' and it's a fair question."

"If they've been *successful*, they look around and realize that for all of their efforts, they're still not as happy or fulfilled as they hoped they'd be. And then when they consider that they're doing all this, even if they *are* pretty happy, and then they're just going to *die* and it's *all over*—so now they're *really not* happy. Again, the fair question is 'What's the *point*'?"

"On the other side, if they've *failed* in life, they look around and believe that in life, you work and try and fail—and then you *die*. Once again, 'What's the *point*'?"

"You see, as soon as people buy into the idea that this world and this life is all there is, there quickly becomes a sneaking realization that there is *no point* to this life. Let's face it, if we're just *accidents* that happened in some primordial soup, millions of years ago, then *of course* there's *no point* to life."

"Wait a minute—are you taking on evolution now?" I asked.

Pastor Brian smiled.

"To really have that discussion, you'd have to define your terms. If by evolution you mean MICRO-evolution or the principle of '*adaptation,*' then no—God most certainly designed adaptation qualities into the DNA of creation—we see it all around us."

"If, however you are referring to Darwinian MACRO-evolution or even Neo-Darwinism—which based on your question, I believe you were—then *absolutely* I'm taking it on."

"I know we don't have time to go into it now Blake, but we have a seminar called, 'Creation Versus Evolution' that is four hours of science, *not faith*. Once again, I'm not asking anyone to just believe the Bible and what it says, I show God revealing Himself through science."

"And for the record, this seminar *destroys* the theories of MACRO-evolution and Neo-Darwinism—*scientifically*—it really is something to see!"

Pastor Brian was really getting worked up about this! I think he realized it.

"Sorry about all the enthusiasm—I really love the fact that no matter where you look, God can be seen."

"Now that you mention it," I said, "Kate had that seminar too."

"That's great, it sounds like she was looking into what we call '*The Big 3*' around here."

"The Big 3—what's the third one?" I asked.

"Our third seminar is called 'Why Bad Things Happen to Good People.' You see, we have to clearly answer the question most people have—'If God is so good and a God of love, then how to you explain all the *bad stuff* that happens in the world?'"

"It's a great question, and one that keeps a lot of people from God because they've *never* gotten a *clear* answer. Most of those asking the question are thinking of a bad thing in *their* life, and they need to know 'Where was God?' We give them that *very clear* answer in this seminar."

"Really?" OK, color me *intrigued.*

"Yep. Anyway, back to our discussion, it's this realization that life seems to have *no point* that often causes people to begin to *think* and want to know if there actually *is* some reason for life—ergo, a consideration of God. Given how successful and beautiful Kate was, she very possibly was looking around thinking, 'is this *all* there is'? That would explain her looking for God at Desert Christian. Our step-by-step approach to help those 'thinking people' could have been just what she needed to search and decide for herself about God."

"I have to believe that understanding why she was investigating God—understanding her frame of mind at the time—*might* just help you to piece together some of the clues you'll need to find her murderer Blake."

I just sat there, staring at him. My head was so full of stuff it felt like it might start dripping out of my ears.

After a beat, "Blake, are you OK?"

That snapped me out of it.

"Yeah, I was just thinking."

"Great, I hope you do."

Was it just me, or did Pastor Brian just challenge *me* to do some of that "*thinking*" he was talking about?

Hmmm.

CHAPTER

— 56 —

Pastor Brian had to run to another meeting, so I made my exit. I sat in my truck for a moment and tried to think a little about what I'd heard. It kind of blew my mind. I'd just been told that God could be proven, Macro-evolution could be scientifically DIS-proven and that the classic question, "If God is a God of love, then how do you explain all the evil in the world?" *could* be answered.

My head was reeling.

The thing that surprised me was that this guy didn't just *say* these things—he offered lengthy seminars that he said *did* these things. The tough part of that is that I could simply watch them and blow him out of the water—*unless* he really *could*!

The other thing that confused me is that this guy was *not* weird—quite the opposite. He sure could converse on seemingly anything. I was having a hard time seeing a guy like that making some outrageous claims if he *couldn't* back them up. And he kind of handled himself like a private investigator—looking for the facts and proof and letting them lead wherever they did—I couldn't help but like *that* approach!

Well, Pastor Brian was getting his wish—I *was* sitting here "thinking" about it.

I started Black Beauty and headed for The Hermosillo. I remembered that I got a call from some cop, so I looked at my phone to see who it was. Turned out it was Trent. I had hands free calling through my sound system, so I called Trent back.

"Detective Burgess."

"Hey Trent, its Blake. I saw you called. I was in a meeting, and I couldn't pick up. What's up?"

Silence.

"Trent, you there?"

"Yeah Blake. We had a development and Detective Rios and I were wondering if we could talk to you about it."

"What development?"

More silence.

"Um, one that we'd rather sit down and talk about rather than do it over the phone."

My turn to issue silence.

"OK. I'm heading back to my hotel right now—do you want me to meet you somewhere?"

"Hang on." Sounded like Trent was talking to someone.

"We'll just meet you at The Hermosillo—say in thirty minutes?"

"Wow—you're coming to me—this must be quite a development!"

Silence. Dang, lighten up Trent!

"OK, I'll see you there soon."

I had just enough time to grab something to eat. I wish I'd had a little more time to get something nutritious, but you work with what you have!

I went through the Jack in the Box drive thru and got three of their monster tacos—it's like they fry the whole taco—and some fries. Gotta love Arizona where you can get such an awesome combo!

I showed up at my hotel—full, but greasy—so I parked and ran inside to wash up a little. One might think I was hiding my poor eating habits, but one could also applaud my commitment to cleanliness. Yeah, let's go with that one.

I'd just finished cleaning up—even hit myself with a little more Gucci "Guilty," just to smell nice when I heard the knock on the door.

(No, this was *not* because Detective Rios was coming over and that is *not* why I cleaned up the room either!)

I went to the door, prepared my best handsome and debonair look, and opened the door.

"Hi Trent—hi Cindy."

"Mr. Moran," they said in unison.

Uh-oh.

"Detectives," I said in a deep voice, trying to lighten the mood.

Didn't work.

"Come in."

We all went into the living room—Detective Rios sat on the couch, and I sat down on the chair. Trent stood.

"Is everything alright?" I inquired.

"We need to ask you a few questions Mr. Moran," said Trent.

Mr. Moran again—what was going on?

"OK."

"Have you recently been at or around the Foothills Mall," asked Detective Rios.

"I don't think so," I replied, "I don't actually know where the Foothills Mall is."

"It's about ten to fifteen minutes from here on Ina Road and La Cholla," said Trent.

What? Are they tag teaming me?

"I don't know those roads, so I don't think I've been around there. Why?"

"Have you interacted with many people in Tucson since you've been here?" Detective Rios asked.

What's with this acting like I didn't even ask a question?

"Some, but not too many. Why?"

"Where have you been today?" asked Trent.

Hello! I asked a question!

"I met with the Pastor of Desert Christian Church this morning for almost two hours. Why?"

"Where did you meet?" asked Cindy.

I stared at them for a beat. "At the Satanic Temple—we sacrificed a goat and then argued over who would get to eat the heart."

That pulled them up short.

"He won—but I got the liver and a kidney."

More silence and stares.

"Listen," I said, "I don't know what's going on here, but I'm done feeling like I'm being ganged up on here and getting interrogated like some criminal!"

Trent and Cindy looked at each other.

Cindy took the lead.

"Mr. Moran, we have received some information that accuses you of selling drugs at the Foothills Mall."

I waited a beat for the punchline—nothing.

"Seriously? And what exactly is the source of this 'information'?"

"We got an anonymous call on our Crime Stopper line."

Silence.

"OK, well, I didn't do it. How's that for the classic denial?"

Trent jumped in: "They had you and your truck described accurately. If you didn't do it, would you be willing to allow us to search these rooms and your truck?"

Now I was getting mad.

"Yeah, Trent ol' buddy—you two go right ahead and have at it."

And they did. They searched the rooms, and to their relief, and not a bit to my surprise, they found nothing.

They clearly were starting to feel a little sheepish, and I was getting madder as we walked out to my truck. Cindy even had the nerve to comment about what a nice truck it was—but I was ticked, so I didn't care.

I opened up Black Beauty and gestured for them to go ahead.

They did the external search first—under the bed and in the wheel wells—and then they got inside. Less than two minutes later, Trent came up from under my seat with a bag of white powder separated into individual baggies—clearly cocaine.

I couldn't believe what I was seeing!

All of the sudden, Detective Rios came up behind me and twisted my arm behind my back. As I heard the first cuff click shut, she began to say, "You have the right to remain silent. Anything you say can, and will be used against you in a court of law. You have the right to an attorney. If you cannot afford an attorney . . ."

CHAPTER 57

I could not believe what was happening! Little Miss Cindy Lou Who was *mirandizing me*!

Moments like that kind of get frozen in your mind. It's odd what your mind does at these moments.

For instance, did you know:

In 1964, the Supreme Court had ruled in Escobedo v. Illinois that since the police refused Escobedo's request to consult his lawyer during an interrogation, they had violated the Sixth Amendment. Just two years later in 1966, Miranda v. Arizona changed everything when the Supreme Court again sided with the plaintiff, saying his Sixth Amendment rights had been violated. Since that time, the necessity of "Mirandizing" a suspect *before* questioning became the standard in law enforcement. Honestly, it has been a major pain for law enforcement—but to be fair, it was probably needed.

And you just thought I was a pretty face!

Hey, I don't just "*find stuff*"—I "*know stuff*" too!

Back to the real world . . .

As Detective Cindy Lou Who finished her Miranda statement, (OK, so I'm getting petty now—sue me!), the other cuff clicked shut on my other wrist.

All I could think to say was, "You have *got* to be kidding me!"

Trent was still standing there, "holding the bag"—that's kind of funny—but he was glaring daggers at me.

"Come on Trent—I'm being set up—I did *not* do this!"

"Really," said the clearly angry cop, "do you have any *proof* that this is a set up?"

OK, that was a problem. What proof *did* I have?

My silence clearly offered all the proof they needed. They each took an arm and started escorting me toward their cop car.

"Wait!"

"What?" he said.

"I just remembered—this morning when I went out to my truck, the security system was off. I always set my alarm—especially when I'm away from home."

"So, what's your point?"

"Someone must have put those drugs in my truck last night!"

"That's it, Mr. Moran?" Rios asked, "'Someone must have' is your defense? Any proof this happened?"

Silence.

Dragging me back toward their car.

I swiveled my head around.

"Wait!"

"What now?"

"Look over there!"

They both turned and looked.

"And over there!"

They turned back and looked.

Security cameras—numerous cameras—covering the whole parking lot.

"Yeah, so?" said Trent.

"Before you go and drag me down to the station on some bogus charge, just ask to look at the footage from last night and see if someone messed with my truck."

I could tell they were thinking about it, but I didn't have them yet. So, I went for my "Hail Mary."

"Guys, just think about all of the *paperwork* you'll have to do to put me in the system—all for *nothing*—if you then come back later and find someone on that footage!"

That did it—the police officer's "*Achilles' heel*"—paperwork. Detective Burgess and Rios did a quick "confab" and decided to investigate a little *before* subjecting themselves to the dreaded bureaucracy.

As they started to lead me toward The Hermosillo offices, I had to object.

"Guys, seriously? You're going to haul me in handcuffs into the hotel where I'll still be staying *after* you find out how wrong you are?!"

I was hoping that giving them a little "incredulous" would alter their plans—after all, I do have some self-respect—*well I do*!

They seemed a little lost about how to fix this since I was under arrest. I came to their rescue.

"I have a jacket in my truck—at least throw that over my shoulders so I can look like I'm just walking with my hands behind my back. Come on, give me a little dignity!"

They went for that, and we were soon moving toward the office—with me sporting a jacket in the Arizona midday heat well over 100 degrees. I hadn't really thought that through. Oh well, I guess I'd rather look stupid than guilty.

When we got into the lobby, we headed for the front desk, and everyone snapped to attention. Have you ever noticed how uniformed police officers have that effect?

Trent requested to speak to the manager, and he was quick to show up. He was probably mid-forties, and introduced himself as Jordan Smithe—with a hard "i" instead of "smith-e." I wondered if he made that up to sound more sophisticated, but to be fair, I could be being catty, cuz of the way he was looking at Miss Cindy Lou. Look at me being all possessive . . . of that which did *not* belong to me.

He shook the hand of each officer and when he turned to me, I quickly did the head nod and affected an angry tone, launching into my belief that my precious truck had been tampered with the night before.

I think that move prevented the coming awkward moment when Mr. Smithe went to shake my hand and got bupkis from me. Pretty quick thinking for a future ex-con, huh?

Any-who . . . when Jojo heard my concern over my truck being tampered with, (OK, that was catty again), along with the presence of the officers, he offered his regrets and agreed to lead us to their security room. I'm guessing he wanted to get this audible discussion of the vandalism of vehicles at his establishment *out* of his lovely lobby.

CHAPTER — 58 —

After taking us through a maze of hallways, Mr. Smithe introduced us to his security officer who would run the equipment for us and then he left. I was glad—I didn't want Detective Rios to have to endure any more longing looks from him—those were *my* job!

Mr. Smithe said, "This is Waldo—I mean Kenny—he'll help you find what you need." And he was gone.

I couldn't resist, "Waldo?"

Kenny started to turn a little red.

"Oh, that's just what they call me around here. I'm always out patrolling the property—which is huge—so they were always asking, 'Where's Kenny'? Someone joked one time with 'Where's Waldo' and it kind of stuck."

I couldn't help it—I have an inquisitive nature.

"Ever think about wearing a red stripped shirt and hat?"

Kenny turns redder. "No."

"Oh well, research says that wouldn't make you any easier to find anyway."

OK, I'm kind of a smart aleck too—even in handcuffs.

"Moving on, here's the deal," I said, "I got back to the hotel last night probably a little after 10:00—so this would have happened between then and sunrise this morning—say around 6:00 a.m."

"Eight hours is going to take some time to go through," Kenny said, "I have some fast forward capability, but if you go too fast, you can't really look for what you want to see."

I could see my captures getting a little antsy at that statement—I'm guessing they were thinking that maybe the paperwork *would* be faster.

So, I jumped right in.

"How about we try to narrow the search down some? If I was going to try and do this, I would make sure that it was *late enough* that everybody who had been out partying had gotten to the hotel and in their rooms, but *not so late* that the early risers were getting up and about. Ideally, I would think that from about 2:00 a.m. to maybe as late as 5:00 a.m. would be the best time."

I suddenly realized that both detectives were looking at me as someone who was thinking entirely too much like a criminal. I'm not sure I was helping my handcuff situation with talk like that.

"Alright," said Kenny, "Getting it down to that small of a window will really help *if* you all help me. Sir, where was your truck parked?"

I told him where it was and was even able to point to where Black Beauty was sitting right now.

"It was within a space or two of where it is right now."

"Oh, that's your ride?"

"Yep."

"That is *SWEEEET*!" said Waldo, "I noticed it right away."

"Thanks!"

"What did those huge tires and chrome rims set you back?"

Suddenly two detectives were clearing their throats and moving their feet.

"Oh, sorry," said Kenny. He manipulated the equipment to come up with the time stamp of 2:00 a.m.

"Here's how we can do this as quickly as possible," Kenny said. "We have quite a nice security system here and the truck would have been covered by four different cameras from four different perspectives. If each of you will simply take one screen each, I'll put them all into as fast of forward as we can and yet still see movement. We'll continue until one of us—or probably all of us, from different angles—see movement. OK?"

Everyone was up for it and was assigned a screen—and we were *off*!

Whoa, this was weird. Since it was so late, each screen looked almost stationary. So, trying to stare at it was a little tough, cuz it just looked like a picture. Every once in a while, we would all scream, because there was some movement, but it was usually an animal moving across the parking lot.

Right around the 2:50 mark, we had some excitement when a man holding a bag in his hand was walking toward and then around Black Beauty. The excitement abated when we slowed it down to real time and realized that it appeared to be a drunk guy—and we were pretty sure we knew what was in the bag.

My excitement turned to horror as I watched this guy clearly admire the truck and then unzip and *urinate* on the back wheel.

The *rage*—the unmitigated *rage* that I felt! It didn't help that when he looked over at Cindy, she was laughing.

"Detectives," I said, "I'd like to report a crime!"

Both detectives just looked at the guy and shook their heads "no."

Oh, the humanity! Was there no justice in this world?!

Waldo put it back into fast forward and the waiting began again. I was starting to wonder if I was going to have to get comfortable in an orange jumpsuit—and I'm sorry, but orange is just *not* a good color on me.

Then at 3:41 a.m., we all yelled at the same time.

There was someone there, moving back and forth, seeming to be checking at my truck from the shadows. He just waited and looked around for another five minutes and then he approached Black Beauty.

When he got near her, he was in the light, because of course I parked where it was all lit up—safety first!

As he walked toward her, you could see that he was carrying something under a jacket. After he looked at the door of the truck and then into the truck, he took that thing out from under his jacket and place it on the hood.

It was a bag of white baggies!

I couldn't help but look over at my captors with *haughty derision*—a squinty eyed stare that said, "How *dare* you arrest such a pillar of the community!"

Both detectives had the decency to look appropriately embarrassed.

We finished watching as the perp opened Black Beauty and then disarmed her. He then spent all of about a minute in her, and then locked the door and shut it. Then he walked toward the back on the truck and reached under the truck and did something—well *that* certainly got our attention! Last we saw, he disappeared into the shadow again, this time without his package.

I turned to my captors with my hands thoughtfully still behind my back and said, "I think we have some things we need to talk about."

CHAPTER
— 59 —

After thanking Kenny for all his help, we began to make our way back to the lobby. Just as we were almost there, Mr. Jordan Smithe found us. Apparently, Kenny had called him immediately.

"Mr. Moran," he began, "I am so sorry to hear about this unfortunate event taking place on our property. If there is anything we can do to help with this, please let us know. Again sir, we are so sorry for this."

Now the whole time this is going on, I'm just trying to respond in a way that will not require me to try and shake his hand. I'm still the great "cuffed one" and really didn't want anyone here to see that.

But doggone it if ol' Jojo didn't put his left hand on my shoulder and reach his right hand toward me right at the end.

And doggone it if ol' Trent didn't jump right in and save the day!

"Mr. Smithe," he said, "if you could have Waldo—er Kenny—download that camera footage and forward that to my email on my card here, I would appreciate it. We have some people who are savants at getting as much as can be gotten off of video like that—you know what I mean?!"

Wow, back slapping, and all. Nice save detective.

We moved on through the lobby with Mr. Smithe still apologizing to me—to which I offered a nodding acceptance.

Finally, we got back to my room. Believe it or not, we all just stood there in front of my door for a second or two until I said, "Sorry guys, but my hands are a little tied up right now—can ya give me a hand?"

Maybe *they* could forget I was still handcuffed, but I sure didn't!

Finally got those nifty steel bracelets off my wrists—they were nice, but they simply did *not* go with my outfit!

"Thank you," I said, while I was definitely still giving them some indignation.

It had only taken us a few minutes to get out of that office and back to my room. We closed the door and then just looked at each other for a moment.

Trent spoke first, "Well, I guess we can now be sure that Kate was murdered, and he is still around."

Way to state the obvious Trent.

"Unless you're just a jerk Blake, and there is some other reason some perp in Tucson doesn't like you and wants to frame you."

Trent's sense of humor was a little illusive—you couldn't always tell if he was serious or trying to be funny.

Trent grinned, now clearly just trying to take away some of the—shall we say "awkwardness" of just trying to fit me for an orange jumpsuit?

I just stared at him for a beat and then turned and said, "Detective Rios, what are you thinking?"

"Oh, please, it's Cindy."

What just happened? She had just *corrected* me and told me to call her Detective Rios! Oh, that's right, that's when I was a drug dealing perp—and *yes*—I did that on purpose, just to rub it in how *wrongly accused* I had been by them. Again, I'm petty.

I was also wondering if this mistake on their part could play in my favor with Miss Rios—so I was *shallow* too.

"OK, 'Cindy'—what are you thinking?"

"Well obviously you have somehow done something that attracted the killer, and either the killer or someone he hired has decided that you are getting too close and need to be neutralized."

Don't you love it how law enforcement uses sanitized words for what they are really saying? You can basically read what she just said as, "they want to *kill* you," but *"neutralized"* is supposed to soften things a little. Almost makes you feel all warm and gooey, doesn't it?

"Sooooo, any ideas?"

"Well, we should have forensics go over your truck and see if we can get any prints or fibers to try and identify this dude—*if* he's in the system. Oh, we need to check out what he was doing under your truck at the end of the recording—I'm guessing he was placing a tracker. We'll need to remove that."

"Hmmm."

I *thought* that pretty much said it all, but Trent and Cindy didn't seem to get where I was coming from—so I elaborated.

"So, the murderer somehow knows about me and is aware of what I'm trying to do. It would seem that my going over what I've been doing since I got here and who that would involve, just might give us some insight into who *might* have been put on notice by my actions. He may have just given us some clues, simply by letting us know that *he* knows."

"Secondly, what about actually using this against the murderer. *We* know now that *he* knows, but *he* doesn't know that *we* know that *he* knows." (I was getting a little dizzy here.) "We may get some advantage by *leaving* the tracker on Black Beauty and spook him further as he tracks where I'm going."

"You named your truck?" asked Cindy. "You call her 'Black Beauty'?"

"Please Cindy, let's stay on topic," thinking I may have just lost the edge I had with her for the almost wrongful arrest.

"Thirdly, if I need to go somewhere that we don't want him to know about—because it might tip him off to what we know about him—we just take the tracker off for that trip. All of this is assuming that he *really did* place a tracker on my truck."

See what I mean, I said, "Hmmm"—*who wouldn't get all this from that*?

Trent stared at me for a moment. "You realize that by doing what you've said, we'd be using you as 'bait,' which means we'd be putting a huge bull's eye on your back? This guy has killed before—he might well decide another kill isn't that big of a deal."

"I do. I've made myself bait before—it typically is kind of part of the job. I realize there's a risk—but huge potential reward too."

Now I can't be sure about this, but if I'm not mistaken, I think Trent just got a little look of *respect* in his eyes! Oh yeah, break out the Aretha Franklin!

(Give me a minute while I bust a move to R.E.S.P.E.C.T . . . OK, I'm done.)

Now Trent's giving me his best "Clint squint." That was sure short lived!

CHAPTER
— 60 —

Cindy broke into my reverie by asking, "So, where *have* you been since you started this investigation?"

Hmmm. Thinking back.

"It would seem that any place I've been that was innocuous—meaning I did *nothing* relative to the case that would alert anyone—would be off the table. So, all the places I've eaten or gotten gas, wouldn't matter."

One might say that those places could all be the same . . . Get it? What can I say, I'm a funny guy.

Any-who . . .

"Somehow the perp was able to follow me to The Hermosillo, since I've done nothing here that anyone would know about relative to the case. So, that would leave The Palms resort, the Casa Hacienda resort, and your police station. Oh, also your evidence storage. Hey, do you think ol' Danny boy could be the leak?" (I admit it—he got under my skin with his attitude—and I hold a grudge.)

"I'm guessing no," said Trent, "but I guess we'll have to consider that there *could* be a police connection—but let's hope and proceed based on it's being *unknown* by the officer if he or she *is* the leak."

Wow, Trent believed and trusted in the basic goodness of the human race—at least those in the T.P.D. . . . what a schmuck!

Something else occurred to me.

"Oh, we'd also have to include Desert Christian Church—although it could only be the Pastor if that's the leak. I only talked to him about it."

"What were you doing at Desert Christian Church?" Cindy asked.

"During the investigation, I found out that Kate was looking into religion—oh, scratch that—she was specifically looking into Christianity."

See, I was listening to what Pastor Brian said.

"We found no such thing when we investigated."

"Yeah, I know."

OK, that sounded *smug*—it felt smug—was I being smug?

"Oh, I was also able to get a general description at one of the resorts of the guy I think was the murderer."

"What?!"

"Yep."

Cindy just glared at me. "Don't be *smug*."

So, I guess the answer was *yes*—I was being smug.

"I got some information out of one of the witnesses that they chose *not* to share with you."

"Who would that be?" she asked.

"Sorry, I promised to shield them unless we *had* to have them—they have a phobia about all you great defenders in blue."

Cindy tried the "Clint squint" on me—*it didn't work*. She was just *too cute*—it just came off as adorable—like if a koala bear quit munching eucalyptus long enough to try and growl. Like I said, "*adorable*."

So, I said, "Don't worry, if we need them, I can produce them—but I don't think we will."

"Well, you'd better," Cindy said, trying to sound tough—I'm telling you—*absolutely adorable*!

CHAPTER
— 61 —

Trent and Cindy got ready to leave, but actually took the time first to tell me they were sorry about the whole arrest thing. I thought that was a pretty stand-up move for them to say that, and I thanked them. They also told me that they would stop at Black Beauty and see what was under the back of the truck, then they would text me what they found. If it was a tracker, then the plan would be to try and use it against the perp.

By this time, the day was almost gone, and I needed to compose my thoughts . . . which means I was hungry and needed to veg out in front of one of the TVs.

I walked next door to the restaurant that claimed to serve "home style cookin.'" I looked at the menu and decided to have some light fare—chicken fried steak, covered in gravy, with biscuits and honey on the side.

Mmmm!

I headed back to my room, and I can report that the food was as good as it sounded—perhaps not for my heart or my cholesterol numbers, but for my tastebuds—let's just say they were *dancing a jig*!

About halfway through me scarfing down that delectable food, I got a text from Cindy—*it was a tracker*. When she told me the make and model, I knew it was an expensive one—so we were good to go on our plan.

Good to know.

I flipped around from channel to channel—you know how it

is—100 channels and nothing to watch! I did see another commercial from Desert Christian Church—that must be some kind of advertising budget!

There were a bunch of car dealership ads too—and guess what? There was a *sale*! At virtually *every* car lot in Tucson! And it was *only this weekend*!

Who saw *that* coming?

I realized as I was watching, that it was the same guy who I saw on the signage at The Palms—the one who was putting on the conference. Apparently, he also does lots of commercials for various new car lots—and it looked like he in fact *owned* them all. It didn't mention the car dealerships in six other states, but once again, I pondered how much I'd like to have *that* guy's portfolio!

Any-who, after I finished my meal, I practically had to take a shower to get all the "remains" off my body—but it was *so* good! Maybe that should be the basis for knowing how good food really is—do you have to take a shower afterwards, or not?

I sat down and tried to organize my thoughts about where we were in this investigation. Out came those paper mats I "borrowed" from McDonalds, turned them over and started writing.

There's lots of value in the written word—I gotta tell you that if you don't write it down, things tend to get lost in translation. Just think about all the stuff that has to go on just for communication to happen: most people aren't trained to listen, they drift off, pick and choose what they want to hear, forget something said, and often misinterpret what is said. If you take a conversation and try and reconstruct it a day, week or month later, it is shocking what is missed, forgotten, added to, or flat out embellished. (A nice word for "liar, liar, pants on fire.")

And if you add *emotions* to the mix—*forget about it*! It really gets weird. So, taking the time to write it all down tends to clarify that which is unclear—and I needed it all to be clear.

I first wrote down all the things that Pastor Brian had pointed out—

at least the pertinent parts—but I was surprised how much that ended up being. He made some really interesting points—even about being an investigator—maybe I didn't dislike him after all. Well, just not as much as I thought.

Then I wrote down all that we now knew, after my little brush with the "fuzz" and the almost incarceration of yours truly. It all added up to quite a lot.

Now all I had to do was figure out what it all meant—and then what to do about it.

But that was for tomorrow—the Blake-ster was *tired*. Threats of prison and becoming some large man's "girlfriend," can really do that to you!

So, it was time to catch some ZZZZZZZZZZs.

CHAPTER

— 62 —

I must have been fairly tired—I didn't wake up the next morning until my phone started playing the "Jaws" music. I know it's an annoying ringtone, but I paid $2.99 for it, and I'd hate to just delete it.

"Yeah," I answered.

Sometimes my penchant for the pithy wordplay amazes *even me*!

"Hey Blake, this is Pastor Brian."

I looked over at the clock—it was 8:52 in the morning—who calls someone at such an ungodly time?!

"Hey," I said, adding even more to the pile that is my poetic use of the English language.

"Guess what, I 'found stuff'!"

Pregnant pause.

"Get it? Your tagline?"

Yeah, I got it—too *much* spiky hair dude—too *little* caffeine!

When I didn't say anything, Pastor Brian went on.

"Alllll—righty. Anyway, I talked to my wife and told her about our conversation, and she said that she talked to Kate for a little while one Sunday. She thinks she may have some things to add for you. I wanted to see if you wanted to talk with her."

OK, now I was ready to quit pouting like a little girl because he joked about my tagline. I found my voice—it was that scratchy morning voice—but it was my voice.

"Yeah, that would be great—when can I meet with her?"

"She is going to be here at the West Campus around 10:30 doing some work—can you meet her then?"

"Sure—I'll be there."

"Did I wake you up Blake?"

"No—of course not—it's almost nine!"

Is it a bigger sin if you lie to a Pastor? I'll have to ponder that.

CHAPTER

— 63 —

It was actually a bit of a rush to get there by 10:30 since I still had to get a shower, get dressed, and find something to eat before getting over there. I had to settle for the "Continental Breakfast" of those pastries with the jelly in the middle—SO good!

I had planned on a sensible, healthful breakfast, but I just didn't have time this morning.

(I can't imagine it's that big of a deal if I lie to *you*!)

I made it to the campus with a couple minutes to spare and headed for the office. Of course, it was on my mind that the killer would know that I was at Desert Christian Church, and I wondered if that would mean anything to him.

The administrative assistant was there and told me that I could go in to see the Pastor—he was expecting me.

Pastor Brian said "hey" and I said "hey"—but enough of the witty banter.

"My wife is over in the auditorium working on some things—you can just go over and talk with her. I probably already told you, but her name is Kristi. She's expecting you."

"OK—thanks."

I walked across the campus—it was already warm, but this was Tucson—what did I expect? Not as hot as Phoenix, but still *hot*.

I walked into the auditorium and looked around. The temperature was pretty cool in here given the heat outside—and I didn't hear any AC running. The stage was at the other end and there was a lot of nice band equipment—they clearly had a large band—the drums had the double bass kick and lots of cymbals—it was huge. Clearly, there were tons of stage lights, so this looked like quite a light show. All and all, not what I expected "church" to look like.

Sitting at what looked like a café table on the floor by the stage was Pastor Brian's wife, Kristi—I recognized her from the newspaper article on his wall in his office.

She was as fine looking as that picture on his wall. That's all I have to say about the Pastor's wife—and maybe a little more than I *should* say.

I said "hi" to a woman who was working in what they called the "Resource Center" at the entrance and walked up to Kristi.

"Hi, I'm Blake Moran."

"Hi, I'm Kristi. Let me guess—'you find stuff.'"

Wow, Brian even told his wife—everybody's a comedian! I really have to work on that tagline!

"Yeah, that's the rumor."

She smiled. It was nice. She was forgiven.

"I can't tell you how sorry I was to hear about Kate. I only got to talk to her for a short time, but she really was a very sweet woman. She was conflicted when I talked with her, but she asked some great questions and seemed really eager to get some clear answers."

"What exactly was she conflicted about?"

"Typically, I wouldn't be able to tell you, since she told me in confidence. However, given what happened to her—and my wondering if what she told me might have some bearing on the case—it seems like you need to know. That's why I wanted to talk to you."

It felt like the blood in my veins was zinging a little quicker. "Go on."

"I ended up talking to Kate after she had been coming to Desert Christian for just a few weeks. She really seemed to love it and seemed to really want to just take it all in. She asked me some vague questions, so I just told her that even though we had just met, I could really be a lot more helpful if she could ask exactly what she wanted to know. She just looked at me for a moment—I was getting the vibe that opening up to people was a struggle for her—but then it was like she decided to do it, nodded once and started her real questions."

"Her questions had to do with a romantic relationship and how she should handle it. She had been involved for a short time with a man whom she thought was pretty special, and it had recently become a sexual relationship. She had discovered that he was married—he had hidden that from her—and she was devastated and angry. She didn't know how to deal with the betrayal; by this man of both her and his wife—and what she felt was her betrayal of his wife, though she didn't even know about the wife."

"I gave her a brief explanation about God's design of sexuality and that His whole point to confining sex to marriage was to protect her from the 'broken' feeling she was having now. That seemed to surprise and even intrigue her. I told her that God designed sex to be much more than just the physical. However, God had some real answers for her now that she was on this side of this situation. I noted our seminar, 'Why Bad Things Happen to Good People,' and some other teachings we had that could help her. I then took her back to our Resource Center and introduced her to our volunteer who was working that day. I then gave her a big hug and told her if she needed anything else at all, I was always around, so don't hesitate to ask."

She was clearly done.

"Did she ever talk to you again?"

"No, I saw her here and there over the next few months—you certainly couldn't miss Kate—she was so beautiful. We'd say 'hi' and smile—but she never engaged me again."

So, I'd learned some things—but I wished for more.

"However," she continued, "I actually do have a little more to offer. That volunteer in our Resource Center, the one I introduced Kate to, is right back there doing some work. I wanted to schedule this when she would be here, so that you could talk to her—she just may be helpful to you."

I glanced back at the woman in the Resource Center who I had said "hi" to—she looked up at me with sad eyes.

I looked back at Kristi.

"I had to tell her about Kate—she didn't know—just like I didn't know. She's pretty broken up about it."

"OK, thanks."

"I hope you find the man who did this Blake—Brian and I are praying for you while you look."

Nobody had ever said anything like that to me before—I'm not sure *anyone* had ever prayed for me before. It felt weird—but I had to admit that I was glad and appreciated it—I could use all the help I could get.

CHAPTER
— 64 —

Kristi took me over to the Resource Center and introduced me: "Blake Moran, this is Isabella Fuentes."

She nodded to me, and I said hello.

"I'm going to have to get going now. Isabella—are you sure you're OK?"

"Yeah, I'll be OK—it was just such a shock."

"OK, I'll let you two talk then. Let us know if there is anything else we can do Blake,"

"Thanks. What you told me was really helpful."

"Good. See ya."

I turned back to Isabella—her eyes were somewhat red, so I knew she was taking this hard. So, I started easy.

"Can you tell me how you knew Kate Walker?"

She took a deep breath and started,

"I met Kate, apparently the day that Kristi met her. Kris had given her a number of ideas of teachings and seminars that could be helpful for her and sent her here. Kate was so sweet—easy to talk to—and clearly wanting to just soak everything up that she was hearing here. I remember the feeling when I first started coming here—things you'd never known or understood before were becoming so clear—so I could relate."

"She and I got a chance to talk most weeks for somewhere around three months. She was always getting new teachings and usually wanted to talk a little about what she had just learned from what she'd either heard that day, or from the last teaching she had gotten from the Resource Center the week before."

"I was so sad when she just disappeared—I could not imagine what could have stopped her from being here—she was just so excited about all this. Clearly it wasn't the excitement that died—I just cannot believe someone would kill such an exceptional woman. We really do live in a very broken world."

I just stood there—what was I going to say?

She went on. "After about six weeks of us talking each week, Kate commented to me about how, for the first time in her life, life actually made sense, and she understood what it was all about. Once again, I could relate."

I interjected: "That's great that she was finding that. Did she ever say anything that might be a clue to anything I'm investigating regarding her murder?"

Isabella went quiet and was clearly thinking.

"She did make a comment the last time I saw her. She said that she was going to have to deal with an issue from before she started coming to Desert Christian—and she didn't seem very happy about it. She said, 'it just refuses to go away.'"

"I didn't know what she was talking about, but I told her that I would be praying for her while she tried to deal with it."

"And that was the last time I saw Kate," she said sadly.

Thinking back to what Kristi had told me, I asked, "Is it possible that this 'issue' might have been a past romantic relationship?"

"It certainly could have been. When I think back over some of the teachings and seminars we got, coupled with how obviously stunning Kate was, I have to admit that I was guessing that direction."

Hmmm.

"That's pretty much all I have—I wish I knew more, but we try not to pry around here."

"Nope, you did great Isabella. You gave me another piece to the puzzle—thank you."

"You're welcome. I will be praying for you Blake. This evil person needs to face justice—Kate needs justice."

Is it just me, or did Isabella just get *fierce*?!

I nodded at her, said goodbye, and left.

I could *not* agree more!

And now someone else is "praying for me?"

This is just weird.

CHAPTER 65

I thanked Isabella for all her help and told her I would do my best to provide that justice for Kate. I then headed back over to the office to see if I could talk to Pastor Brian.

The administration assistant checked, and he could talk, so in I went.

"Hey Blake—how did it go? Was it any help?"

"Yeah, it really was. Your wife's talk with Kate confirmed that there *was* a romantic relationship—something that I only had a small indication about before. Also, that it progressed to sexual involvement and then she discovered that the man was married—something that he had hid from her. Kate then broke it off."

"Then, Isabella answered a question that I've had since I first started this investigation. I've been trying to figure out what happened in Kate's life somewhere around about three months before she was murdered? Both her brothers, Greg and Johnnie, stated that over the last three months or so of her life, Kate was very different—happy, content—really seeming to be doing life well. They said that for all of her qualities, she just never seemed to be particularly happy. Someone at her job pointed out the same thing, saying she seemed to be finally figuring things out and doing life well."

"So, what was it?" asked the Pastor.

"Well, as far as I can tell, everything seems to line up perfectly with the time she showed up here."

"Really? I'm glad we could help her."

"In addition to that, Isabella told me that the last time she saw Kate here, Kate told her that 'she was going to have to deal with an issue from before she started coming to Desert Christian. She also noted that she 'didn't seem very happy about it.' Kate told Isabella that, 'it just refuses to go away.'"

"Less than a week later, Kate Walker was dead."

Heavy sigh from the Pastor.

"Well, I was glad you were able to get some answers for your case."

"Yeah, me too. Talking about answers, can I ask you something?"

"Sure."

"I'd be lying to you if I said that what I'm finding out about Kate and this church wasn't causing me to rethink what I thought I knew about relig—I mean Christianity."

Pastor Brian smiled at my correction.

"I admit that our conversation made me think—and then seeing the impact it clearly was having on such an extraordinary woman as Kate is making me think even more. I admit that I've always consider religion—any religion—to be dumb, money grubbing, and for losers. I didn't *know* I felt that way, but now that you pointed it out, I have to admit that I did."

Pastor Brian laughed!

"Come on Blake—don't sugarcoat it *for me*—tell me how you *really* feel!"

I laughed.

"Just keepin' it real."

"So, I'm curious about what you said—are you seriously telling me you can *prove* this stuff?"

"I am. We have a whole seminar to do just that."

"But *how*? How can you possibly do that?!"

"Well, the seminar takes three hours, but I can give you a 'cliffs notes' version if you want.

"OK—please."

"I first of all explain how we got the Bible historically, then establish the reliability of the Bible as compared to all other works of antiquity—you can just read that as before the printing press. The Bible is historically *by far*, the most reliable document of antiquity—there really isn't any competition. The reason I do this is to establish that we can trust the Bible historically in what it says. I make it clear that for all the bogus claims of 'mistakes' in the Bible, there has never been even one that can be proven. Someone might choose to *not believe* the Bible, but what is called its 'historicity,' cannot be logically questioned. Archeology plays a role in this as well."

"I then go over a good number of what are called prophecies in the Old Testament about very specific cities. Anywhere from 100s to sometimes 1,000s of *years* before these things happened, they are prophesied in the Old Testament. Yet Blake, they *all* happened, just like God said they would."

"Wait," I said, "couldn't that just be the Bible being written *after* these things happened and then *pretending* to be before it happened?"

"Good question."

"Thanks," I said modestly.

"I address that in the seminar—we have clear proof of when these documents were written through the manuscripts that comprise the Old Testament—they simply could *not* have been written after the fact. It's all in the seminar."

"Oh."

"And while all that can be very impressive, the real 'kicker' comes when you look into the Old Testament prophesies about what is called the 'Messiah'—or Savior. There are over three hundred prophesies about the Messiah—*all* of which are fulfilled by Jesus Christ."

"OK—is that a big deal?"

"Yeah, it really is. What you have to understand about this is that we can *prove* that there is *no way* that could happen—unless it was done by God."

"How is that?"

"I first of all prove that the Old Testament—which contains *all* these prophecies about the Messiah, *had* to be completed *at least* two hundred and fifty years *before* the time of Christ. This is because of a thing called the '*Septuagint,*' the Greek translation of the Hebrew Old Testament, published during the reign of Ptolemy Philadelphus."

"Oh, what's that rascal been up to now?" I said.

Pastor Brian chuckled.

"The important thing is that it proves that all of these over three hundred prophecies actually *were* prophecies—written *long before* they were fulfilled by Jesus. Think about that—over two-hundred and fifty years—*at a minimum*—is more years than the time the United States of America have even existed."

"So, God made all these prophecies that long before they happened, and yet got them exactly right."

"I then am able to use the known laws of probability and the 'Father of Probability" himself—Dr. Emile Borel—to show that it is *statistically impossible* for any one man to fulfill even a handful of those prophecies—*certainly less than fifty*—and yet Jesus fulfilled them *all*—over three hundred."

"Dr. Borel states clearly that the laws of probably demand that this could *never* happen *in any area*, no matter how much time was allowed, or how many chances were given—yet, it all happened with Jesus. This can *only* be explained through God's interaction and direction—what would be called '*supernatural intervention.*' It simply *cannot* logically be explained in any other way."

"These laws of probability are used constantly in our world, even in areas like the mortality tables, and in this case, they *prove* God, Jesus, and the Bible."

"Really?"

"Yeah, they really do. I have to tell you Blake, if I couldn't prove all this, I wouldn't be a Pastor—I wouldn't even be a Christian."

"In the eighteen hundreds, a guy named Soren Kierkegaard came up with a thing called 'religious existentialism.' It says that '*religion' is based on blind faith* that so many religious people follow—even many churches. But that is *not* God's way—ol' 'Soren' can keep that for himself. The Bible says quite the opposite—God has *always* provided proof of Himself."

"And you do all this in that 'Facts Behind the Faith' seminar?"

"Yep."

Hmmm.

"Listen Blake, in the seminar, I challenge each person to sit as the '*Judge*'—just hear me out, and then *decide based on the facts.* I would never do this stuff if I wasn't sure about it, but you can look at the facts for yourself—*or not*—it's your life and your call. But I hope you'll look."

I looked back at Pastor Brian. I think he was honestly just tossing the ball into my court—and to be fair, I *did* ask—so I'd have to think some more about it. I didn't mention to him that I already *had* the seminar from Kate's effects—some things are better kept to yourself.

CHAPTER

— 66 —

I thanked Pastor Brian for all his help and hit the administrative assistant with one of my 100-watt smiles—I figured she'd earned one. I am one gracious dude after all.

I decided that I wanted to head back over to The Palms for three reasons: 1) I had to figure that if my going to Desert Christian Church meant nothing to the killer tracking me, then my going back to The Palms would tweak the murderer something fierce! 2) The major guy I could think of who *might* have had the "resume" to be having a secret relationship with Kate was Todd Brooks—Mr. *"gift-to-the-world-stud-muffin."* Of course, he denied that he'd made any progress with Kate, but he *would* deny that, if he had in fact killed her. There was no question that dude had some *serious* anger management issues!

3) Honestly, I couldn't think of anything else to do.

I realize that last one is kind of weak, but sometimes in investigations, when you've run into lots of dead ends, all you can do is throw some chum into the water and see what bites.

Now that I think about that last statement, I realize that *I'm* the one who will get bit! Oh well, Blake Moran—*living on the edge*!

Could that be a new tagline? No, I'm not sure that would be any better than *"we find stuff"* . . . well, maybe a *little* better, but let's face it—that was a pretty low bar to start with!

When I got to The Palms, I once again avoided the valet parking, (never shall they touch this Beauty), and took the far away parking that was starting to feel like "my space."

Since I knew that it might be iffy as to whether I could get to Todd again, given that Mr. Joyner had made it clear that my investigation needed to be limited and relatively brief, I thought I'd start with something that I had yet to do—walk around and get a feel for the outdoor resources of The Palms.

I can assure you that the fact that this would eventually take me past some of their pools had *nothing* to do with this decision—absolutely *nothing*!

A quote from Shakespeare's Hamlet leaps to mind: *"Me thinks he doth protest too much."*

That's right, I'm sophisticated and well read—I know where stuff comes from!

Well, to be completely honest, I think I read that on a cocktail napkin in a bar once, but I still *read* it!

Any-who, (see—sophisticated), I strolled around the north side of the building and took in the property. This was really a beautiful place—and it seemed to go on forever! It was a little after lunchtime—and with the Tucson heat—I didn't run into anyone enjoying the "sweat" with me.

As I came around a corner of the building, I saw to my right a secluded area that appeared to be a designated smoking area. It was surrounded by foliage, but there was an opening to the grounds in one part of the high bushes. It looked like a pretty nice place if you were really "jonesing" for a smoke.

I started to move on past it when I heard a muffled sound—like a high squeak being stopped. Now *that* was weird! So, I backtracked and went to the opening in the bushes and looked in. I didn't see anything but some nice outdoor chairs and tables—all empty.

Hmmm.

I turned to leave, but then I heard a low sound, almost like a growl—and it didn't sound pleasant. This was just getting weirder. So, I turned back and looked again, wondering if a coyote or a bobcat had perhaps gotten into the smoking area. As I looked to my left, I realized that there was an alcove that was out of my view, so I quietly moved toward it on high alert. I really wasn't anxious to confront a wild animal.

What I saw took a split second to register. There was a wild animal, but it was the *two-legged kind*—not the four.

I was looking at the back of a thin, ropey muscled guy with that impossibly black hair in that stupid "duck tail" style, with one hand clamped over a woman's mouth and the other holding a knife in front of her face! Mr. "*domestic violence and attempted rape*" was living up to his titles—that prick Lester Jenkins was trying to do his thing.

The woman he was pressed up against was Bailey Sanchez and she was clearly terrified! Her skirt was pulled up to her waist, her blouse was torn open—the buttons pulled off the blouse.

It didn't take a keen detective mind to figure this picture out!

Bailey's eyes found me and screamed "help" as well as if her mouth had done it. Lester, being the accomplished criminal that he was, saw the look in her eyes and threw her to the ground and swung around to face me in a fighting stance.

"Lester," I said, quite Zen-like.

"What do you want, you stupid P.I.?! Just walk away!"

"So, here's the deal," I continued, in my Zen-like voice, "you have two choices right now. You can put that knife down, surrender yourself, and we'll call the police and send you away for assault and attempted rape."

"Your second option is that you can keep your knife, come at me, and I will do the very thing that I've wanted to do to you since the day I met you, you slimy excuse for a human being. I will kick your butt for as long as I think I can legally get away with it—and *then* we'll call the police and send you away for assault and attempted rape."

Lester sneered and started to speak.

"Oh," I interrupted, "for the record—*before* you decide—I want to suggest that you take the chance that you can beat the fool out of me and get away with this. Please select '*door number two*'—I *BEG* you!"

"I told you the day I met you that I hoped you would do something stupid so I could destroy you—and now you've gone and done it—*right in front of me*! And who knows, maybe an old, skinny idiot like you *can* take me . . . and we'll never know *unless we 'dance.'*"

Now I realize that this was juvenile, immature—whatever you want to call it—but you have to admit, I *never* said I *was* a grown-up!

Don't you think what I said had some of the magic of Dirty Harry's, *"So, do you feel lucky—PUNK?!"*

I know it could be said that I was just asking for it, but that is *only* because I *was*!

Lester's face was a beauty to behold—it just got screwed up in a rage as he rushed toward me and swiped at me with his knife. He got a little closer to cutting me than I meant for him to. I felt the air go by as I ducked and side-stepped him, hitting him hard with my right fist in the solar plexus.

Watching the air leave his body was fun. I took a quick glance at Bailey to make sure she was OK, and then I hit Lester hard, right in the middle of his face. It was satisfying to feel his nose break, and blood went everywhere.

To his credit, whizzing, bleeding Lester actually came at me again, and I did what no man is supposed to do to another man—I kicked him with everything I had, *right between the legs*—right in the jewels. Given that had been the source of his planned crime, it seemed fitting that I destroy them—and it gave me great joy to do so.

The look on Lester's face—the disbelief, followed by the *unspeakable* pain—of which, of course, is the pain of which I am currently *speaking*—was a joy to behold. As he went down—and actually passed out from the pain—my only sorrow was that it was over.

What a slime bag!

I kicked the knife away from Lester's crumpled form and turned to Bailey. I carefully helped her sit up, sat down next to her, and held her while she sobbed.

"Are you OK?"

She couldn't answer for a minute, so I just let her cry—while keeping one eye on the perp.

He still wasn't moving.

Finally, I told Bailey, "Look, I'm just going to call 911 and get the police and some paramedics here—then I need to call Mr. Joyner—he'll need to be in on this too."

She gave a slight nod—at least I think she did—and I called 911. I was still trying to get through to Mr. Joyner—trying to explain what had happened to Mrs. Coleman, so that she could tell him—when I heard the sirens in the distance.

So, I just sat back and held Bailey until people started showing up—I was guessing that was the best thing I could do at the moment.

CHAPTER
— 67 —

It ended up getting very busy, very quickly, back in that smoking area. You had the Pima County Sheriff officers, paramedics, hotel staff and your usual "Looky-Loos."

After cuffing Lester, they mirandized him and half carried him to put him in the cruiser. I had clearly hurt him bad—and I wasn't a bit sorry. His hateful, arrogant act was now replaced with fear—and that was just awesome. I hoped he ended up being somebody's "girl-friend" in prison—it would serve him right.

After examining Bailey, they decided to take her in to make sure that she was OK—I'm guessing to try and deal with some of the psychological stress she was going to feel. I was glad she was going to the hospital—she needed some kind faces and helpful people around her right about now.

The Sheriff's officers took my statement. I tried to just give them the facts of what I saw and did—I even admitted to kicking him in the "boys"—which certainly elicited some bug-eyed looks from the officers. Initially, I'm not sure the officers knew how to think about such an assault on a "fellow man."

However, then I explained what I was doing in Tucson. I told them about my interview with Lester, including his hideous comments about Kate—a murder victim. At that point, there was more *admiration* for the shot to the *"no-nos"*—which replaced the looks of *"oh, no he DIDN'T!"*

The paramedics did a once over on me too, but I was fine except some bruised knuckles—my badge of honor.

Mr. Joyner stood over with Mrs. Coleman, watching all this happen. When I was released, they asked me to come with them, which I did.

Once we were up in his executive office suite, he had me explain what had happened, all over again. He was a little confused as to why I was back on the premises in the first place—I guess "following up on some leads" wasn't quite landing. But given what I have prevented from happening, Mr. Joyner could not have been more thankful to me.

Mrs. Coleman looked at me like I was Ironman, and I'd just saved the day. (I gotta say that I kind of liked that. As I've told you, I sometimes have these thoughts about being a superhero—again, our secret.)

Mr. Joyner was in the middle of saying, "If there is anything we can do for you Mr. Moran, please just let us know. We could not be more grateful to you for protecting Ms. Sanchez."

Now I'd have to think about *that* offer.

At that moment, there was a knock at the door. Mrs. Coleman got up and answered it—and who should stroll in? The "always on TV," car dealership guy!

It was weird to see him in the flesh.

Mr. Joyner jumped up and came around his desk, saying, "Mr. Whitlock, so good to see you! We have a bit of a situation going on that we are currently dealing with—what brings you by?"

"I happened to stop by The Palms to check out some dates for future conferences and I heard what happened. I wanted to stop in and offer anything I could to help."

"So good of you Nicholas, but I think we have it under control at this point."

Mr. Whitlock was looking at me as clearly the only person in the room that he didn't know—Mr. Joyner noticed.

"Mr. Whitlock this is Blake Moran, a Private Investigator from Phoenix who is following up on the death of Kate Walker from the first of the year. Mr. Moran, this is Nicholas Whitlock one the clients at The Palms, and a member of the Board of Directors."

Oh, *now* I get Mr. Joyner's differential tone—this is one of his *bosses*. I stood up and shook his hand.

"Mr. Moran," started Mr. Whitlock, "from what I've understood, it appears we owe you a huge debt of gratitude for what you did today—thank you."

"Glad to do it sir—actually, after interviewing Mr. Jenkins about Ms. Walker's murder, I have to admit that I thoroughly enjoyed doing it. He is a horrible excuse of a human being."

"Yes, it would seem that 'The Palms' will need to address our employee screening process a little more closely. We aren't in the business of rehabilitation."

I could feel the tension in the room over that statement. Having no desire to get immersed in corporate politics, I just said, "Maybe so."

With that, it seemed that everything had been said, so I made my excuses to leave and left. They thanked me again and said goodbye. It could just be me, but I think Mr. Joyner was in for an awkward meeting.

With everything that had happened since I got there, it seemed like a bad time to try and confront Todd Brooks. It was now getting late, so I decided to pack it in and head back to The Hermosillo.

If I told you that the looks of admiration and waves that I received from the hotel staff on the way out the door felt awesome, do you promise not to tell anyone else?

In that case—it felt awesome!

"Ironman has left the building!"

Too much? Yeah, I guess you're right.

It was still worth a try.

CHAPTER

— 68 —

I called ahead to the Tucson Police Department and found out that Detectives Burgess and Rios, (read Trent and Cindy), were "in station," (why do they talk like that?) and would be there finishing up some paperwork for the day.

I asked the receptionist to relay to them that I needed to stop by and inform them about the ongoing Kate Walker investigation. (Now there *I go* talking like them!)

It only took me about twenty minutes to get across town—and Trent only took about five minutes to come to the front and get me. Believe it or not, he had to complain *again* about the "paperwork" to leave Molly at the front—it was *one* signature on *one* sheet!

"You have *got* to get some new material Trent," I told him.

I just got the "Clint Squint" again, but he finished with the one eyebrow up! Now *that* was cool—I just *have* to learn how to do that!

When we were almost to his desk, he commented, "Hey, did you hear that the Sheriff's Department picked up a call on an attempted rape/assault at The Palms a few hours ago? We heard it come across our dispatch."

We'd just walked up to his desk and "Cindy Lou" was right there—so, what was I supposed to do? I mean, the last time they saw me, they had me in *cuffs* and were giving me my Miranda rights! Now it's the *next day* and I was a "hero." (A superhero, but remember, we agreed not to tell anyone that part.)

So, I took a deep breath and simply said, "That was me."

Trent looked at me for a second. "You were the perp on *another* crime?!"

It took me a moment to comprehend the confusion—I was busy assuming my superhero stance.

"What?! *NO*, I was the guy who *STOPPED* the rape/assault!"

Now I had the ears and eyes of everyone in the cop bullpen.

"What are you talking about?" asked Cindy.

So, I told them—from the start to the finish. I explained that I went to The Palms after Desert Christian Church, in part for the purpose of having the killer be aware I went back to these places. I need to freak him out and force his hand. In the process, at The Palms, the whole thing with Bailey happened and I dealt with Lester. When I recounted the fight with the knife wielding Lester, every *male* within the sound of my voice cringed when I got to the part about the final kick to the "boys."

When I saw that they were struggling with my completely out of bounds final move, I simply informed them of all the horrible stuff Lester had said about Kate during my interview with him. With that information—I went from *zero* to *hero* again.

When I finished, as the officers left, I got a lot of pats on the back and "atta boys"—I'll admit, it was nice.

Now that it was just Trent and Cindy again, I told them that I wanted to update them on some things I'd learned regarding the case.

Cindy said, "Well, by all mean, now that you're a superhero and all."

I know she was joking, but I'd be OK if she thought of me that way.

So, I told them about my conversation with the Pastor's wife, Kristi, and then with Isabella Fuentes. We had now confirmed the existence of a personal relationship. Up to now, that was just based on the speculation of Jesus Martinez—who had gotten the impression that Kate might be in a romantic relationship. However, Jesus' description of the last encounter that he'd seen between them, indicated that the relationship might have gotten confrontational toward the end.

I noted that Kate had told Kristi that it had turned into a sexual relationship, that then turned sour because the man had been hiding from Kate that he was married, and she found out.

I then told them about Isabella's ongoing interaction with Kate for around three months at Desert Christian Church—the three months, I reminded Trent and Cindy—that both Kate's brothers had stated that Kate was so different, happy, and content.

Kate's unhappy comment to Isabella about having to deal with an issue from before coming to Desert Christian Church, that "just refuses to go away," was a bit of a bombshell.

"Well, *that's* interesting," said Trent.

"I thought so too, but something else occurred to me that made me feel even more on point with whomever this guy is. See if this seems odd to you two: here is this romantic relationship—where we might guess that he wanted it to continue, and she was done with it. Now *if* this guy did nothing, doesn't it seem like this guy would have come forward to provide some information that might help to provide justice for someone about whom he had cared?"

Trent and Cindy thought on that.

"I'm not sure," said Cindy, "since we know he was married and clearly wanted to cheat without getting caught. Maybe he would feel he couldn't come forward and risk that?"

Could be.

Trent chimed in, "But he could have at least provided information on an anonymous basis—a tip line, or some other means. I have to say that this guy not saying anything tilts the field a little more *toward* his guilt instead of *away* from it."

That was my take too. I could tell that made some sense to Cindy Lou too. (Just wanted to rhyme there at the end.)

CHAPTER

— 69 —

We talked for a while about what we knew and what we didn't—the scale feeling like we were starting to tilt toward more of what we *did* know.

Trent said he had to "*skedaddle*." That was so like Trent—he would *totally* be the guy who had to "*skedaddle*." He said that we were going to get to spend some time tonight with Trent II and Jess—his son and daughter. He seemed genuinely stoked about it.

Don't look at me like that—yes, I said "*stoked*." That is *nothing* like saying "*skedaddle*"—apples and oranges, people—apples and oranges!

Any-who, Trent was outta there.

I looked at Cindy and asked, "So, do you eat food?"

I know that is a lame start, but I like to get a woman saying, "yes" with the first question.

Cindy squinted her eyes a little and said, "Yeeeesssss?"

(She really did draw it out like that, and there was a question mark at the end too—as though she was concerned that she was perhaps being *drawn into a trap*. How *crazy* is that?!)

"Well, as it turns out, I also eat food—regularly. As a matter of fact, it just so happens that I plan on eating food *tonight*! I was wondering if just maybe you would be willing to join me?"

She just looked at me for a moment.

"Are you asking me out on a date?"

I looked back at her, unable to gauge what she was thinking.

"Yes, I believe I am."

She looked some more. I was really hoping that maybe the whole "this dude was a hero today" thing might put it over the top.

"OK—I'll meet you somewhere."

Now that was both a *win* and a *loss*. Yes, she would go out with me—*WIN*. But she would drive herself just in case I'm a total bust so she could avoid the awkward car drive home—*LOSS*.

I'll take it!

"Great. Since it's your city, any specific place you'd like to go?"

She thought about it. "I like El Molinito on Ina Road at Thornydale—it just so happens that it's close to The Hermosillo and I haven't been there in a long time. They have some really good Mexican food." Looking around at her paperwork, then looking at a clock, she said, "I can meet you there by 7:00—does that work?"

"Works for me—see you then."

I walked out of the station a few inches above the ground—I even forgot to get Molly back. The deputy had to call me back to get her and do the "*paperwork*," meaning, once again, *one* page Trent! Needless to say, Molly was *not* amused at my oversight! I needed to get back to The Hermosillo—time for me to get all dolled up!

CHAPTER

— 70 —

I had a couple of hours to get ready by the time I got back to The Hermosillo—and I'm sorry, but no matter how bad I look, I would *never* need *two hours* to get ready. Sorry ladies, the male species knows all too well that you gals can *easily* burn through two hours getting ready—and we *greatly* appreciate the outcome. Can I say "*magnificent*"? But you ladies have all kinds of tricks that you can do—talk about a lot of "bells and whistles!" It's just not all that complicated for the "dudes"—only so much "help" that is available to us.

We're a little like, "just sign on the line here Ma'am that you are accepting him in *'as is condition.'*"

So, I took some time to arrange my thoughts and write down a few observations from my extremely busy and profitable day. Between my time at Desert Christian Church, The Palms, and the police station, I had made some good progress.

Now to be fair, *most* of that progress was that I felt like a superhero, (our secret), and I got a date with Miss Cindy Lou Rios! But I had also added some to the case, so Greg Walker was getting his money's worth!

I left myself about thirty minutes to get ready. I got a shower but decided to stay with the scruffy face. I was going for the "rugged" look—you know, simply too busy saving damsels in distress to take the time to shave.

(OK, I get it, time to stop reveling in the "hero" thing.)

Since I was in the Old Pueblo, I went with my best jeans. This is odd, because they are ripped—but "*professionally*" ripped—they came that way, and they *really charge* for such professionalism!

A pull over shirt finished the process and then I spritzed myself with Creed Aventus cologne.

Now if I didn't just impress you, it can only be because you are unaware that Creed Aventus cologne is *the most expensive cologne for men*. Seriously, the cheapest you can find it at major retailers is OVER $400 for 3.3 ounces!

Are you impressed now?!

But hey, *I'm worth it*!

Well, actually, *not really*. You see, I'm a *big saver* as opposed to being a *big spender*. So, I found a Creed Aventus "clone" called Armaf Club De Nuit Intense Man—and it smells *"magnificent!"* (There's that word again. You know, that's one word that is just *not* used enough!)

So, bottom line: when I say "Creed," I'm actually wearing the knock-off—but dang it smells good! And at a much better price! The bottle is surprisingly cool looking too—square, black, and chunky.

I jumped into Black Beauty, and I was off for my date. It didn't take long to get to the El Molinito restaurant—although if I'm not mistaken, I think the "El" is "the" in Spanish, so I just said that I got to THE, The Molinito—which even I know sounds stupid. I'll try and avoid that around Cindy.

I was a few minutes early, so I just sat and waited, letting the radio play. The restaurant looked authentically Mexican with its mustard yellow walls and its Saltillo tile roofline. It smelled good too and I realized I was really hungry.

Cindy pulled up right about then in a really nice yellow Camaro. It was the newer body style and I'd always liked the newer ones—they just *look* fast.

I'm not sure how she had done it, but somehow, she had come from the station looking like she had spent the whole two hours getting ready. She was wearing a skirt with a blouse tucked in and knee-high black boots. Her dark hair was down—which I hadn't seen yet—and it was thick and dark and beautiful, and pulled to one side with some kind of hair trickery. (That's how guy see all the magic you ladies pull off—pure trickery!) Her face was glammed up with makeup, done just perfectly—and those crystal blue eyes just jumped out of that beautiful face. WOW, this was one fine looking woman!

(Of course, for the record, I was only interested in her mind and her personality. Uh-huh.)

By this time, I was standing by my truck, just staring at her as she walked toward me. I'm guessing I was looking a little like Cro-Magnon seeing a woman for the first time—not my best moment.

"Hi," she said.

"Hi," I stammered out.

"Are you OK?" she asked.

And in that moment, I was at a loss. I just looked at her and then blurted out, "You look so beautiful!"

I could have *kicked* myself—if I were that flexible. I sounded like I was in Jr. High, hoping the girl would go to the prom with me. What a *horrible* start! But I didn't know how to save it.

She looked at me for a beat and then giggled—I am *not* lying to you—Cindy Lou *giggled*! She then smiled that beatific smile and said, "Why thank you Blake, you look nice too."

Well, what do you know—the Jr. High schtick can actually work! Who knew?!

So, I gave her my arm and we walked toward the restaurant. We'd only gone a few steps when she turned to me said, "I don't know what cologne that is, but you smell *magnificent*!"

I KID YOU NOT—the woman said "*magnificent*." I told you this stuff was good!

I just smiled, said "Thank you," and led this angel into the restaurant.

CHAPTER

— 71 —

We didn't have to wait too long to be seated, and the whole time I had to fight to not just *stare* at Cindy—I'm telling you—she looked *good*! I really could get lost in these blue eyes, surrounded by that thick dark hair. And it wasn't just me—every male eye in the place was appreciating all her effort to look that good!

After we got seated in the main area, we did the small talk thing while they dropped off some chips and salsa—which was very good, by the way. We took a little while to look at the menu and figure out what we wanted, and then we ordered.

We had come to that moment that often can be the beginning of the end—the "talking." I was well aware that since we were currently "collaborating" on an investigation, this "date" could quickly turn into an extension of the case—which was *not* my goal. This needed to be a *non*-work date where we were just two people getting to know each other. I needed to make sure to not take the easy way out and just land where we'd both feel comfortable—Kate Walker.

Can we all just admit that the girls are *much* better at this dating and talking than the guys? Which, for the record is statistically a primary reason why guys drink in bars—so they can "*talk to women*." Alcohol loosens them up—which, as we all know—is *not* always a *good* thing! I don't know what our problem is, but we just don't do the "gab" thing as well as "*the fairer sex*."

I heard a guy talking one time about guys being more "left brain" oriented, while the ladies are more "right brain" oriented—and the "talking" part resides in the right hemisphere brain. I think he called it the "language hub."

For the record, the emotions reside there too, so that whole "get in touch with your emotions" thing can be a real stretch for those of us blessed with that "Y" chromosome.

However, I really wanted to just stare at Cindy—and talking to her gave me the chance to do just that!

So, over the years, I have learned a little trick—if I dare call it that. Having said that, I *am* in my early 30s and still *not* married, So I guess you'd have to say my little "trick" is *not* delivering the goods!

Any-who, my *trick* is that is I ask her questions about her. This comes pretty naturally to me with the whole "investigator" thing—but this isn't the aggressive questioning style—just "*tell me about yourself.*" Doing so shows interest in her—which I'm thinking is flattering—and that tricky thing called conversation tends to spring from answers to my questions. It can become downright interesting—and just maybe wrestle my left brain over to my right brain.

Here's hoping!

Let the conversing begin!

"So, you told me when we met—you may remember the whole 'Cindy Lou Who' schtick—that you were from Georgia—what part?"

Score one for Blake Moran, P.I. who "*finds stuff*!" I could see that Cindy was both surprised and impressed that I remembered that she told me that when we met. What can I say? I concentrate harder when beautiful women are addressing me.

"I was raised just outside Savannah, Georgia."

"Wow, that's right there on the coast—was that pretty awesome?"

"It had its moments—I did get to go to the beach some, but the threat of hurricanes was also a very real issue that we just had to live with from June to November."

"Have you been through a hurricane?"

"We had a few that hit when I lived there—and lots of false alarms—they are pretty scary."

The waiter dropped by to bring us our food. I had the cheese enchiladas, two tacos with beans platter—it looked and smelled great.

Cindy got the Molinito Asada Special—you know the one—the steak comes out sizzling on a hot skillet and all the "fixings" like onions, rice, beans and more are brought out—along with the flour tortillas. It's an impressive entrance—and I *love* the moment that the waiter tells you to be careful, because the plate is *hot*! (Oh, you mean this skillet that is sizzling with steam coming off it—that's *"hot?!"* Thanks for the warning—I probably would have missed that!)

Cindy had also gotten a Margarita—big glass, salt on the rim, lime wedge—just what you'd expect at a Mexican restaurant.

So, we both commented on how good each other's food looked—it's so funny that we all do that—and then we took a few minutes to dig in and *groan* at how good the food was. I told Cindy she'd made a good choice—this was really good!

CHAPTER
— 72 —

After we'd eaten for a few minutes, I asked Cindy, "So, how did you end up in law enforcement and all the way across the country in Tucson?"

A shadow crossed her otherwise beautiful face—I wondered if I had somehow stepped into *"it"*—whatever *"it"* was.

She finally said, "I just really wanted to try and make a difference and stand up for right against wrong."

"That's a great reason," happy that we seemed to have moved past whatever the "shadow" had been, "how did you end up in Tucson?"

She stopped and set down her fork and seemed to gather herself. She took a sip of her Margarita and then looked up at me. I could tell that something was going on, but I honestly had *no* idea what. I was hoping I hadn't inadvertently veered my "left-brain" right into her "right-brain!"

"Blake, I'm not being completely truthful with you about all this, but I can only tell you if you'll promise me that this will stay between us."

"OK—sure."

A deep breath. "When I was seventeen, my life was the fairly traditional life of a teenager—high school, friends, parties, a job, the beach—just normal stuff. My dad was a carpenter, and my mom was a nurse, and we had a fairly regular middle-class life."

"OK."

"I ended up meeting a guy at a party who was a college senior at Savannah State University. He was handsome and seemed 'worldly'—

whatever that means—and he really intrigued me. We dated a few times and he seemed nice."

"However, on the fifth date, he started trying to move toward sex. We were in his car, and he started coming on really strong, and I told him 'No.' He didn't stop. I tried to fight him off of me and get out of the car, but he was bigger and stronger than me. End of story—he raped me."

I just stared at Cindy. All I could say was, "I'm so sorry."

"Thanks. I finally got out of the car, and he just left me there and drove away. I called my parents, and they came and picked me up. They took me to a hospital, and we made a police report."

"Did they nail him?"

"They went through the process, but he lied and said that the sex had been consensual. When we pointed out that I was only seventeen years old, they acted like that was 'close enough' to eighteen, which was confusing to us. It turned out that his parents were wealthy and well connected, so they had some pull with some officials. They chalked it up to a 'he said/she said' stalemate and nothing happened."

"Wow, I really am sorry."

"So, after that, everything was different for me. Feeling that helpless, with nothing I could do but just let it die, caused me to pretty much stop being a 'normal teenager.' I decided that I could at least try to fight for other people who were wronged by both a perpetrator and the system—and try to give them justice—even if I didn't get it myself. It set me on a path of law enforcement."

"As far as Tucson goes, I had trouble being around Savannah after that—it was almost like everything in life had gone from full color to black and white. So, after I finished my schooling for law enforcement, Tucson was offering some nice incentives for new officers. I thought about it and decided 'why not'? Tucson doesn't have hurricanes or tornadoes or earthquakes or floods or volcanoes—it sounded like an interesting choice. And as much as we joke about the "dry heat," having lived in Georgia with all that humidity, there really is something to that. So, I took the job and have been here for seven years. I went from the street beat to being a Detective, and I really like it—I feel like I'm making a difference—at least at times."

Cindy took a deep breath like that story had taken something out of her—which I think it had. I just looked back at her for a moment and thought.

"I have to tell you first of all, that I am amazed and honored that you would actually tell me what you just did. The level of courage that it took for you to say all that to a relative stranger is remarkable."

Her face registered something akin to surprise.

"Secondly, the level of anger that I feel right now toward some random college frat boy is somewhat overwhelming. While I don't want to offend you—I find at this moment that I have this strong feeling of wanting to protect you—I would *love* to get a shot at that rich, pampered jerk, and do to him what I got to do to Lester Jenkins today—including the shot to '*the boys!*'"

Her face remained stoic and staring.

"Lastly, I'm sorry—so sorry. I hope you know that while pieces of crap men like that do exist, we are *not* all like that. Some of us know how *precious* women can be and that they deserve *respect*—and when it progresses—real love. Some of us even want to "take care of" our girls—even though feminists try to tell us that's wrong. I'm sorry, it's just part of our DNA. I don't know what this jerk's problem was, but my parents raised me right."

Now I was worked up!

Cindy just stared at me for a moment. She was either close to tears or the meal had made her eyes water.

She finally just said, "Thank you for all that. That was surprisingly caring and supporting."

I wasn't sure what to make about the "*surprisingly*" part. I was guessing it might harken back to a guy with *"we find stuff"* as his tagline on his business card, not creating much hope that there's much *depth* to work with!

Well, welcome to the deep end of the pool, Cindy Lou!

She smiled the sweetest smile—and it was a little sad too—it kind of broke my heart.

"Listen," I said, as I took a chance and reached across the table and took her hand, "I really appreciate your honesty in telling me the truth—and this stays right here with me. I get it, you don't want to be 'the victim' in your department. But now that we've got that out, would you be OK if we now went back to the 'light side' of this date and just enjoyed being together? I think we both could use that."

Just so you know, she did *not* pull her hand away when I took it, and it was "glorious" to be holding it!

She said, "I would love that—let's lighten things up."

And that is just what we did! We had a wonderful evening, we laughed, held hands, and even shared an order of Sopapillas with honey—and all the delicious mess that came with them. (For the record, if you've never had those, you really should!)

We then walked out into the night—right up to her Camaro—and much to my surprise and joy, she turned to me, looked up at me and clearly invited me to kiss her—which I promptly did—and it was *magnificent*! (Again, with that word!) I held her for a moment and then she said she would see me tomorrow, got in her car, waved, and left.

I just stood there for a while and enjoyed the moment. Cindy was special, and we had made a real connection. What a night! What a date! Blake Moran is calling this a "win." (Did I just talk about myself in the third person? You bet I did!)

Good night—a really good night. Still wondering about that whole "*surprisingly* caring and supporting" comment, but hey, I'll take it!

CHAPTER
— 73 —

He sat in the car in the dark parking lot of the restaurant. That tracking device had continued to work like a charm, and he monitored it regularly.

The private investigator had been at the Police Station after being at Desert Christian Church and The Palms. He'd been there for hours.

This little adventure to this restaurant had been confusing to him—maybe just food—until he'd seen him sitting in there with Detective Rios. His police contact had mentioned some time back that Rios was the lead investigator on Kate's case. She was so cleaned up that he almost didn't recognize her from her headshot on the department's website. She was an extremely attractive woman when she wanted to be—those police uniforms sure weren't doing her any favors.

He thought that maybe this was actually a date, but the P.I. and Rios had clearly been very serious all of a sudden—they must have been discussing the Kate Walker case.

This whole thing just made him *so* angry! The case had basically been done—pushed to the back burner—and he could move forward with his plans—and then this fool had to show up!

And he didn't seem to be easily dissuaded from pursuing it. He had no idea why the P.I. hadn't been arrested for the cocaine—maybe he found it first and tossed or hid it. For whatever reason, he hadn't been stopped. He was like a dog with a bone.

His rage was just simmering—all the time—he needed to get passed this problem and get on with his plans.

But he really couldn't do that with this fool around. He might have to take some drastic action—this guy might just stumble around enough to stumble into something that could ruin him.

He'd keep an eye on him for a few more days, but if he didn't give it up, he was going to have to end up like Kate. He was not sure how, but enough was enough—he needed to have this thing over.

He'd better get out of here before they left. Just sitting in a dark parking lot would be suspicious—and he couldn't afford any mistakes now.

CHAPTER
— 74 —

Wednesday morning dawned bright and clear—not exactly a *shocker* in Tucson, Arizona!

I woke up in a good mood—well duh! After a date like I had with Cindy, the "glow" tends to last for a while.

I needed to think a little about the case—but I also needed to walk a little—I was feeling a little out of it, not getting any exercise in the last few days.

Now since I was in Tucson, the idea of walking outside during the day was flat out crazy! It was probably already in the nineties, and it was only mid-morning. I grabbed my phone and did what any self-respecting Arizonian would do—along with any geriatric person—I looked up "malls" in Tucson! Time to walk *with* the oldies—or rock *to* the oldies—one or the other.

It appeared that there was an outdoor mall pretty close to me called Twin Peaks—but *come on*—outdoor in Tucson?! That was clearly tailored to the "snowbird" time of year—not the summer. It looked like the big mall in town was the Tucson Mall, (they clearly put some serious time and creativity into naming *that* one), and it was only about twenty minutes away.

I got ready and got out of there, heading for a little exercise and deep thinking.

When I got there, I went ahead and parked in the covered area—to keep Black Beauty out of the wicked sun. I went into the mall through the Food Court and had to stifle my urge to eat immediately. I wanted to get some walking in first and then I would eat something healthful—you know me.

I started walking and thinking. The mall was good sized, a two-story structure with lots of good stores. The place was busy—lots of people around as we moved closer to lunch time.

I have to say that lots of my geriatric brethren and sistren (is that a word?) were out in force. I found myself competing with them a little for speed before I realized what I was doing and cut it out.

And some of them were *fast*!

As far as my thinking went, I found I kept thinking about a certain Detective Rios—and *not* regarding the case! Did I mention that it was a great night?

I finally marshaled my thoughts and started pondering over the case. I was trying to take all the pieces and try different combinations to see what fit together.

I'd been walking for a little over an hour when there was a commotion behind me. I stopped and looked to see a bunch of people behind me gathered around somebody—must be some kind of celebrity. I actually laughed out loud when someone moved, and I saw that the "celebrity" was the car dealership guy from all the TV commercials—one of Mr. Joyner's bosses on the board at The Palms—Nicholas . . . something. I will never get over how just having your face on a TV commercial or a billboard makes someone a "celebrity." I kid you not—the dude was *signing* autographs! Guys! He's just a *car salesman*! OK, a *rich* car salesman, but *come on*!

People are a trip!

With that interruption, I realized that I was really hungry—time for that healthful food! So, I headed right over to the Food Court, did my survey of the various offerings—and walked straight over to Cinnabon! Now just *wait* a minute! I hadn't eaten since my meal with Cindy last night and have you *seen* those? Those huge confections with frosting literally dripping down them? Again, it must be said, "magnificent!"

What could be better than that? Don't worry, I'm not even going to *try* and say that there is *any* healthful benefit in these—not even I could rationalize that.

But they are *so* good!

CHAPTER
— 75 —

After finishing my meal—can I call it a "meal"—I was on a sugar high. So, I took the long way around the mall—to burn off all the calories I'd just consumed, (he said hopefully), and headed back out to the parking garage.

Believe it or not, something had occurred to me on my last walk—maybe it was just my blood sugar talking—but I wanted to check something out.

I headed back over to Miracle Mile to the police station. I've been trying to come up with some excuse for going over there, but all I could come up with was wanting to see Cindy again. (I thought about saying "Trent," but I just didn't think you'd buy it.)

When I got to the police station, I went ahead and locked Molly in lockbox in the cab—just thought I'd save *all that paperwork* for our boys in blue.

I knew that I must be becoming a regular around the station when they let me walk back to the bullpen on my own. I tried to look casual, but my eyes were searching for Miss Cindy Lou. I really hoped she wasn't out on a case—this would be a good paperwork moment.

And there she was! Not done up like last night—dark hair in a sensible "bun"—but my heart still did a little skip.

I walked over to her desk and said, "Detective Rios."

She looked up at me and smiled, "Private Investigator Moran."

All the electricity running under those greetings could have powered the station for the day.

"How are you doing?" I asked.

"Good. You?"

Wow, this was some powerful stuff! The reference to Jr. High came back into my mind.

"Good." Pause.

I gave in. "Last night was really great—thank you."

"It was great for me too—and you're welcome."

"So, is there a chance that you might agree to an encore?"

"Why Mr. Moran—are you asking me out again—even though social convention dictates that you wait a minimum of twenty-four hours so that I'm not repulsed by your cloying eagerness?"

Aw-oh. Too much, too soon?

"I guess I am," I said sheepishly.

Cindy laughed. "Well good—I've always thought social convention was stupid!"

Wait, what?

"Is that a 'yes'?"

"Yes Blake, I thought you'd *never* ask." Another smile.

Dang, I really did feel like I was in Jr. High again—and not the bad parts—the really good parts!

While we were still smiling at each other, Trent came walking up. "What's everybody smiling about?"

What? Is Trent personally offended by happy people?

"What are you in such a huff about?" asked Cindy.

"I had to see my ex-wife last night. The time with Trent II and Jess was great, but that woman really gets under my skin!"

Nothing like a lack of marital bliss to really torpedo a moment!

"Why, what happened?" I asked.

"Oh, nothing—she's just 'her'—and it bugs me!"

"Just maybe you're still hung up on her," Cindy said.

"Well, aren't you the Sherlock Holmes today!"

"That wasn't a 'no' Trent," Cindy replied.

"What are you doing here Moran?"

Smooth change of subjects, Detective Burgess!

Pregnant pause while I searched for something other than the truth.

"He came to ask me out for our second date," Cindy offered.

I almost went into a coughing fit. I would have bet money that Cindy did *not* want it known that we dated.

Trent looked at me and did his best "Clint Squint" and then raised one eyebrow. "You took Detective Rios out on a date?"

Why did I feel like I was being interrogated by a suspicious father all of the sudden? Maybe I *was* in Jr. High. I looked over at Cindy for some help, but she was just laughing.

"Yes, I did."

"Why?"

"What does that even *mean* Trent?! Why?! Do you have *eyes*? Have you *looked* at your partner? She is stunning!"

Whoa. Did I just say all that out loud? Was that going to be too much?

I looked over at Cindy—she just looked pleased with herself.

He looked over at Cindy—she just smiled back at him, clearly enjoying his discomfort.

"Are you going to go?"

"I am."

"Well, you be good to her—you got it?!"

Whoa. Trent, the protective papa bear—I liked it—I think Cindy did too.

"Yes sir, I will."

"I gotta get going." Way to exit an uncomfortable situation Mr. Burgess!

"Wait, I have a question regarding the case for the two of you."

"What?"

"If I was to get some DNA, would you be willing to fast-track it through your lab for comparison to the DNA found under Kate's fingernails?"

"What does that mean, 'get some DNA'?" asked Trent.

"Look, we all know that I'm not as constricted by the law as you two would be when it comes to my investigation. That's one of the perks of being a private investigator. So, I'm not talking about DNA that we would use in court—I understand that this would be classified as 'Fruit of the Poisonous Tree.' However, this DNA would enable us to either nail down or exclude someone who might end up on the 'suspect' list."

"You have a suspect *list*?" asked Cindy—not even acknowledging how impressed she undoubtedly was that I knew about the "*Fruit of the Poisonous Tree*" doctrine.

Hmmm.

"Well, I admit that I'm playing fast and loose with the term 'list,' but I have a hunch that might be absolutely nothing, but it will waste a lot of my time and Mr. Greg Walker's money, if I pursue it. If I could just get a test done, I could know either way."

"I can't authorize a DNA test in a case, based on a hunch—and based on DNA collected not using the legal chain of custody. In addition, it would be totally useless in a court of Law. And this stuff is expensive, especially if we expedite it," replied Cindy.

"But what if we don't have to use it in a court of law, *and* you don't authorize it 'in a case,' *and* I pay for it—or Greg Walker pays for it?"

"Hmmm." Trent always knows just what to say.

"I don't know—this is really unorthodox Blake."

"I know Cindy, but that tends to be the way I win. Let's face it—this perp certainly isn't playing by the rules. You two have to play by the rules—I have more 'freedom.' All this would tell us if my hunch is on point or if I need to move on. All I would need from your lab would be the expedited test—specifically, I would need the comparison to the sample."

Cindy looked at Trent.

"Don't look at me—*I'm* not dating him!"

"What? Come on Trent—what was that?" I asked.

"Just a dig. I can be like that sometimes. Look Cindy, you could put it through under a general investigation tag and by paying for it yourself, it takes it off the books. It can be done—if you want to."

Pause. Thought.

"Also," I added, "since it's my test, I would need to be the one who gets it and reads it—then I can act based on it."

"So, now you're going to see it and we don't get to?"

"While I can give you my response to the results of the DNA test, you can't be a part of it in any way. You need to separate yourself from what I'm doing. I can do it—you can't—'plausible deniability.'"

"Are you good at hunches?" Cindy asked.

"It's often the thing that comes through for me."

"OK, get me the DNA, but don't *tell* me anything about it—this is *your* thing."

"Plausible deniability—you got it!"

"Now, as I remember, you were about to ask me out again?"

"Whoa," said Trent, "I am outta here."

Cindy was still laughing as we made plans—I guess Trent wasn't the only one who liked a good prank.

CHAPTER

— 76 —

Back at The Hermosillo, I was still enjoying that whole interaction with Cindy and Trent. I really liked her—she had a lot of spunk—she would *not* be a boring girl to date.

It was really cool too that she was clearly disappointed when I told her that I couldn't take her out tonight—I think the lady is into me too! I explained that my whole DNA plan had to take place tonight, so I would be on the job. But I promised that we would go out as soon as we could, depending on how this all played out.

So, I got ready for my "off the books" outing. I could be all wrong about this hunch, but it was really bugging me, and I just couldn't afford the time to chase it if it was a dead end.

It was all based on what I had come to know about Kate and what I would "surmise" she might do. You can read "guess" when you see that—but I'm a pretty good guesser. So, I think I'd found a shortcut and I was going to try and take it.

That shortcut took me back to The Palms by about 8:00 p.m., dressed in black slacks and shoes and a standard white shirt—my "uniform" for the night.

When I got to The Palms, I parked way off like I always did, but this time I went around back and entered at the service entry. I employed my "if you seem confident, people who see you will assume you are supposed to be there" persona, and walked right in. As I entered, I did a quick survey and saw what I was looking for—the burgundy server/

busboy jackets lined up on a rack to my left. I did a quick look around and calmly walked up, found one my size, and put it on.

And just like that, I was one of the "waitstaff."

My biggest concern now was that I needed to *not* run into anyone I now knew, or who had met me. Honestly, this would've been easier without the Lester Jenkins fiasco—having people applaud you as a hero tended to cause them to recognize you.

But I was going to keep my head down and try and keep a low profile—or this simply was not going to work.

So, literally looking down while I surveilled ahead of myself, I did a quick walk through the hallways where the ballrooms were. There were a number of functions going on, and I was happy to see that I looked just like any of the waitstaff.

Something that I didn't tell Trent and Cindy—so not *you* either—is that when I had been in the executive offices, dealing with the aftermath of saving Bailey Sanchez from Lester the pervert, I notice that they had a white board on the wall that listed the upcoming functions at The Palms. One in particular had caught my attention—and that was the reason I was here, acting like I was making minimum wage cleaning up after people.

I decided to take a walk past the room where the "eye-catching" function was taking place—just to get the lay of the land. There it was, well on its way, and looking like it might be winding up. It started at 7:00 p.m., according to the board, and even with the usual chit-chat these functions usually begin with, I was guessing it would be over around 8:30, maybe 8:45 at the latest. It was now 8:25.

That's why I waited to get here when I did. The longer I had to walk around the property dressed like this, the higher likelihood that someone would notice that I didn't belong. So, I tried to judge the timing to minimize my exposure.

I took a quick moment to locate my mark in the room, while

keeping my head down—yep, there he was, up at the head table, right in the middle, to the right of the tabletop lectern. Now that I knew his location, I could do my thing when the time came, so I moved on.

Since the function was still going, I decided to take another walk through one of the ballroom hallways so that I looked busy and not out of place. I could just keep making a pass of the room I was watching so I would know when the meeting broke up.

As I was making that pass, all of a sudden, someone said, "Hey, can you give us a hand here?"

Uh oh. I tried to just keep moving.

"Hey buddy—a little help!"

Now I had to turn—and really hope I did *not* know this person.

I didn't.

I turned. "Yeah?"

"Can you grab a tray and clear some of this off for us? We are really slammed and need to get this done."

Uh oh.

"Um, I working the executive suite function and need to get back there to bus them."

He looked at his watch. "They probably won't be done for at least fifteen minutes—come on—help us out!"

This was really getting bad—way too much face time and way too much conversation to be "forgettable," which was what I was shooting for.

"OK, let me bus you one tray full to help out—but then I gotta take a look and make sure my function hasn't broken up."

"Fair enough. Are you new?"

Dang it.

"Yeah, this is my first week."

"Well great—thanks for the help."

"Sure."

I quickly walked into the room and saw the waitstaff trays off to the side. People were everywhere, just talking, but this was bad! If anyone recognized me, I was history!

I grabbed a tray and went over to where there were just enough people so that I wouldn't stand out being by myself. I saw what the other busboys were doing, and I filled that tray like there was no tomorrow—while trying to appear cool.

When it was packed, I followed my fellow busboys out the side door—purposely avoided the guy who had recruited me, (let's not have *another* memorable encounter!) and walked right to the deposit station and put down my tray. While the other busboys headed back, I took my chance and exited "stage right" and hightailed it to where I was supposed to be.

I had to look inconspicuous, but I wanted to run! It was now 8:51 p.m., and I might have really blown it!

CHAPTER — 77 —

As I came around the corner, there were some people coming out of the room. My heart sank! I walked by and glanced into the room and saw that the mark was still at the head table, talking to a few people.

YES!

The problem is that I could see at least *four* people in the room that would know me by sight. And after my little "hero" moment today, there might be more who knew me that I wouldn't even know about.

Curses!

I noticed that there was a curtain behind the head table going across the whole room—I was guessing they used that to section off the room for a smaller venue. I headed around the corner before I ran into someone I knew. I also grabbed a tray to be holding—another convincing part of my "disguise."

Down the hallway were some doors—the first two going into the room I was watching. But right after the second door, I was hoping I would find—yet another door.

I figured that if they had that big curtain set up in case they needed two separate rooms, they would have to have access to those rooms—and access is just a fancy word for "door."

I quietly opened the door—just in case there *was* a meeting in there—but nope—the room was empty.

I went to the curtain by the wall and carefully peaked out. The room was still clearing, but the mark was still at the table talking. I looked carefully at where he was sitting so that I knew what I needed to do, then I closed the curtain and went directly behind the mark to listen to what they were saying.

This was a very dangerous moment, because if anyone came in at this moment, I would have *no* excuse for being there!

Thankfully, it sounded like they were finishing up—just joking around and hazing each other a little. I went back over to the wall by the door so that I could be ready when they left.

I watched them all shake hands—two out of the five people I knew—and then my mark really helped me out by reaching down and taking one last drink out of his glass before leaving.

They all were walking toward the doors and talking. I couldn't wait too long, because another busboy might start clearing off the front tables, so I took a chance.

Hoping no one forgot anything—and that none of them would look back—I took my tray and started clearing the dishes. When I had a pretty full tray, I grabbed a clean napkin off the table and carefully wrapped the mark's glass in the napkin and put it in the outside pocket of the jacket.

Then I needed to make like a tree and get out of there! (Wait, I don't think that's how that goes.)

I dropped the tray of dishes off in the kitchen, removed the glass from the pocket and replaced the jacket. I had to take the napkin too—which technically made me a thief—and I walked out the back door like I owned the place.

And at that moment, I felt like I did!

Blake Moran—007—*OUT*!

CHAPTER
— 78 —

Thursday morning in Tucson dawned bright, clear, and hot—*again*! I hadn't slept all that well—I kept reliving the night in my dreams and kept getting caught—over and over. Dreams are a *trip*—all those synapses firing away in that gray matter throughout the night—*freaking* us out!

I was glad when the night was finally over. Apparently, the night had freaked me out a little more than I thought.

But you can't tell me that "Bond—James Bond," aka 007, didn't have a few "night terrors" too—at least that's what I'm telling myself.

So, I tried to wash all that out of my mind by taking a good, long shower—I did feel better after that.

I got ready to "get my day on"—paying a little more attention to my "attire," since I hoped to see Trent today.

OK, just kidding—I hoped to see Cindy today.

I played with the memory of that Cinnabon from "lunch" yesterday, but I decided against it—maybe something a little more healthful.

So, I stopped at McDonalds and got two sausage and egg McMuffins . . . *and* some orange juice!

I did say "a little more" above—I think that fits the bill.

After stopping at an ATM, I headed down I-10 toward Miracle Mile and got to the police station around 9:00 a.m. I made my way in and started my search for Trent and Cindy.

They ended up being in a task force meeting, so I had to wait for about a half an hour for them to finish up. I just sat at Cindy's desk and looked around—I am an investigator after all. I was really tempted to do a little "snooping," but I was pretty sure that could put the whole "kibosh" to our thing if she found me doing that—so I resisted the temptation.

When Trent came lumbering up, with Cindy right behind him, he said, "Well look what the cat dragged in."

What did I tell you? Trent is . . . just Trent.

I smiled appropriately to his attempt and simply nodded and said, "Detective Burgess—Detective Rios, how are you on this fine morning?"

Another "Clint Squint."

"What are *you* so chipper about?" asked Trent.

"I come bearing gifts—well, A gift."

I carefully extracted the drinking glass, wrapped in the napkin from The Palms and set it down on Cindy's desk.

"What's in that?" Trent asked.

I carefully unwrapped the napkin to show a clearly used drinking glass.

"Where did you get that?" asked Cindy.

"Can't say."

"Who used it?"

"Again, can't say."

"Blake!"

"Cindy, there is *no* reason that you and Trent need to know anything about this glass since it is useless as official evidence—remember the "*fruit of the poison tree*?" In addition to that, you both need plausible deniability in this case—you're just allowing a test—that I'm paying for. It will never be used in any case in any official capacity."

"What do you expect to find on it?" she tried again.

"That I can answer. I would ask that it be tested for both DNA and fingerprints. Then have the DNA compared to the results from the material found under Kate Walker's fingernails, and the results given to me—and only me—in a sealed envelope please."

Stoic silence and stares at me and then the glass.

"Why the fingerprint test?" asked Trent.

"That's more for my peace of mind," I said, "conclusive proof'—if I'm right—that I have the right guy."

"Now, I believe the two tests will be around $200," I said, as I counted out the bills, "and the comparison cost somewhere around another $100?"

Again, just stares.

"If it's more, just tell me."

"Are you sure that you want to do this?" asked Cindy.

"I really am. The war will be *shortened* by years and *millions of lives* will be saved!"

Now they just both looked confused.

"Sorry, just trying to be funny. It will save a lot of time to either exclude or point the finger at the mark—my hunch is either right or bogus, and this fast-tracks the answer—one way or the other."

More silence.

"Guys, this is getting a little tedious—I appreciate the 'strong, silent type,' but it's really only working for Trent. If you'll just walk over to the lab and fill out a short form and give them my money—well, Greg Walker's money—we can find out."

Another pause.

"OK," from Trent.

"Great. By the way, how fast can they turn around an expedited test?"

Cindy thought about that one. "Well, since we haven't hit the weekend yet *and* it's not Monday—where the heavier load from the weekend tends to still be slowing them up—I'm guessing that they can have it done in twenty-four hours."

"Great. Can we plan to meet here tomorrow morning—same time—so that I can look at the results and then respond to our next steps based on whatever we find?"

Thinking.

"It's a date," Trent finally said.

"Trent, you just keep trying to get a date with me—seriously dude, from the first time I called you about this case—the answer is still 'no' big guy!"

Trent walked away laughing—again, always keep them laughing.

I carefully wrapped up the drinking glass in the napkin again and Cindy grabbed an evidence envelope and we put the glass into the envelope.

She then grabbed a form off her desk and filled it out—checking expedited. She then checked both DNA and fingerprinting, and then wrote in the request box that it be compared to the DNA from under the "Vic's" fingernails. She had to look up the case number from Kate's case so that she could indicate *which* Vic. She then sealed it and was getting ready to walk it over to the lab.

"Just for the record," I said, "even though I said 'no' to Trent's advances, I *am* open to going on a date with you, if you're willing."

She smiled.

"Is that right?"

"You betcha!"

"When would you suggest this?"

I acted like I was searching my mental schedule—like a man who actually *had* a schedule.

"Turns out that I am available tonight!"

"What? No skulking about tonight, trying to abscond with evidence to break a big case in a rather unorthodox way?"

"First of all—did you really just use the words '*skulking*' and '*abscond*' in the same sentence? And no, nothing tonight, it's all about you."

She smiled at that.

"OK. Let me see how my day goes, but I'll plan on a date with Blake Moran, P.I. tonight—or should I call you 007 now?"

Now *that* was weird—how did she know I'd been thinking that?

"As long as something doesn't get in the way, I'll text you my address this afternoon and you can pick me up at 6:00. And it's your turn to pick a place to go. Does that work?"

Did you catch that I'd just been *ungraded*?! We weren't "meeting" at some place—I got to pick her up!

Be cool dude!

"Yeah, that sounds great—I'll look forward to it."

"Me too. See you then."

Cindy headed for the lab, and I "floated" out to my truck. This investigation had taken a fascinating turn—in my love life—and it might just be about to take a turn toward getting solved. Things were looking good.

CHAPTER
— 79 —

OK, that's *enough*!

He'd been sitting in his car, parked at the far end of the parking lot among other cars, watching through binoculars, being careful that no one was around to see him.

And he was *seething*.

This P.I. would just *not* let it go! His tracker had told him after the fact that the P.I. had been at The Palms last night. He hadn't seen him, but he'd really like to know what *that* was about.

Now, he'd gone back to the police station this morning—carrying something. He been in there just over an hour—and now came out, looking like the whole "*cat that ate the canary*" cliché!

What is he so *happy* about?!

He couldn't think of any area that he'd made any mistakes up to this point—and he'd been able to casually keep tabs on the case through innocent questions to his contacts in the department. The case had gone cold—he'd been told—and now this!

He didn't know a lot about criminal stuff, but he was smart, and he could see that if this guy kept digging, he might just hit something.

He did know about something that might help—his guns. It appeared that he was going to have to stop this P.I. in his tracks—*literally*. He was a crack shot with a rifle—and he had many to choose from. He had a bunch of meetings today and some conference calls—but then he was headed for the shooting range to sharpen up for what would probably be the most important shot of his life . . . ending this investigation, once and for all.

And this guy was *not* doing himself any favors by parking his truck out away from everything else. With that thick stand of trees right by where he parks, it wouldn't even be a long shot.

Enough, Mr. P.I.—it's time for you to be done—permanently.

CHAPTER — 80 —

I headed back to The Hermosillo—I honestly didn't know what else to do until I knew the results of the various tests.

I had some follow-up work to do on some other cases, some calls to make—I even called my answering service and got my messages.

I decided that I needed to call Greg Walker—after all, it was *his* money that I was spending, and it had been almost a week since I had updated him on what was going on.

With the time difference, it would be early afternoon back in New York, so I called his office number. His assistant told me that he was on an oversees conference call—read *big shot*—but that she would give him the message, and have him get back to me at his "earliest convenience."

Well, what if *his* "earliest convenience" would not fit into *my* schedule?! Oh yeah, my only real appointment in my "schedule" for today was to get a nap after that bad night of sleep last night.

But you never know when I might need to be on an "oversees conference call" myself . . . actually, you do—and that would be *never.*

Oh well.

Greg actually got back to me in less than a half an hour—glad to see that he was still anxious about getting his sister's case resolved.

"Hey Blake—you called?"

"Yeah. It has been a few days and a number of things have happened, so I just wanted to catch you up."

"Great—what do you have?"

"Well, if I remember correctly, the last time we talked, I was asking you about whether you knew of Kate showing any interest in any kind of religion—and neither you or Johnnie—knew anything about that. Do you remember?"

"Yeah."

"It turns out that not only was she pursuing that avenue, but it has also clearly shown itself to be the basis of the good change in Kate that you and your brother saw. And you weren't the only ones who took note of it—other people who were around her down here have commented on it as well."

"Really? Religion? That's hard to believe."

"I probably should tell you that it's not the crazy stuff that you might be thinking. I've met with the Pastor now multiple times, and he is logical and actually presents a persuasive and compelling case."

"I thought you told me that you weren't 'religious' Blake," Greg said, the question implied.

"I'm not—at all. But this guy provided a whole different perspective, not on 'religion'—he was very specific about that—but specifically on Christianity."

"What church are we talking about?"

"It's a non-denominational place called Desert Christian Church—the Senior Pastor actually founded it about twenty years ago. It has a really good reputation here in Tucson as being a good place, represented well by the people who go there. I'll admit to you that I was impressed by their approach. If I *were* interested, that would definitely be a church I would look into."

"And that was the reason Kate was so happy for the last three months or so?"

"Everything I'm seeing says 'yes.'"

"OK, I may do a little research online into this place."

"You should," I said.

"I also discovered that she had been in a relationship with a man, but then found out that he had been hiding from her that he was married, and she broke it off. That may well have some bearing on the case."

"Do you know *who* this guy was?"

"Nope—not the 'who,' just that he 'was.' I've had a couple of people who have confirmed this, even though Kate had clearly kept the interaction with the man unknown to those around her."

"Hmmm."

"A big event was that I was 'arrested' by the Tucson Police for about thirty minutes or so."

"What?"

"Yeah. It turns out that by doing what I tend to do—which is trying to be a bur under someone's saddle—the killer got wind of me and what I'm doing. He decided to break into my truck—or maybe he hired someone else to do it—and plant a fair-sized package of cocaine. He then made an anonymous call accusing me of dealing."

"Really?!"

"Yep. And the cops I'm working with actually bought it until I insisted—well, I was in handcuffs and had just been mirandized, so 'insist' may be a stretch—but I begged them to look at the overnight camera feeds from the parking lot. It was a distance, but we definitely saw the perp around my truck, so the officers got to do 'sheepish' and apologize."

"But you couldn't see who it was?"

"No, but the really helpful part is that we saw him go around to the back of the truck and do something under it. When we went to look, he had placed an expensive tracker on my truck."

"Wow—good thing you saw that so you could get rid of it," said Greg.

"Actually, I—along with the officers—decided to leave it on and use it to try and draw the murderer out. We're kind of forcing him to show his hand, since he doesn't know that *we* know that he is tracking me."

"But doesn't that potentially make you 'bait'?"

"Yeah, it does."

"I don't know Blake—baiting a guy who has already murdered doesn't seem real smart."

"Well remember, I told you I was *'good'*—I didn't say I was *'smart.'*"

Greg laughed.

"Greg, this is what I do. By the time I get to a case, if I don't do some unorthodox things, the perp can just sit back and hope that I don't find any leftover 'threads' and start pulling on them. This way, it can cause him to panic and make some mistakes—which I think he might be doing."

"Well, I really appreciate you putting yourself on the line like that for Kate but please be careful."

"I will. Speaking of being careful—or not—I also saved a woman who worked at Kate's resort from getting raped."

"You what?!"

"Yeah. I was doing some investigating and got to beat the fool out of a total pervert that I'd already interviewed regarding Kate. If you had heard the offensive things this loser had to say about your sister, you would beat him right there!"

"Hmmm. Did you beat him good?"

"Yeah—*Real* good."

"Then you are now *my* hero Blake—thank you."

"Aw shucks."

"Did you just say, 'aw shucks'?"

"Yeah. I'm good with pithy comebacks like that."

"Oh, and you'll probably appreciate that after I gave him a good beating, I finished him off with a hard kick—right to the 'boys.'"

"Whoa!"

"Trust me, he had that coming and more."

"Oh, I do—I just wish I could have done it on Kate's behalf! So, what happened to this guy?"

"Well, he's a multiple offender, so right about now he is sitting in jail, just waiting to find out which prison he'll be going to. He'll be some big guy's girlfriend in prison if there is any justice in the world."

"I'll second that."

"The really big news is that I might be getting close to figuring out who Kate's killer was."

"What? Who?"

"I can't say just yet, because I really may be wrong, but I did some undercover sleuthing last night—the kind of stuff that official police are not allowed to do—and I was able to abscond with some DNA from the guy I'm wondering about."

"Blake, did you just use the words 'sleuthing' and 'abscond' in the same sentence?" asked Greg.

"Yeah." (That's weird, Cindy must be wearing off on me.)

"OK. But what good is this DNA going to do you?"

"Do you remember the skin that Kate clearly scraped off of the perp?

"Oh yeah."

"It's a totally random way to do it, but if I can match that DNA, I'll know who the killer was."

"And then you can get him?"

"Well, not exactly. Because of the way that I went about getting the DNA, as I'm guessing you already know, it would be considered '*fruit of a poisonous tree*'—so 'inadmissible.'"

"Oh, that's right. So, what was the point?"

"I really don't want to waste time—or your money for that matter—chasing down ideas if they are going to end up going nowhere. By either confirming or eliminating this guy, I can either set him up and go after him, or start chasing other leads—it's just a faster lane to get there."

"Hmmm. Well, don't worry about the money—I'm happy to send you more if you're making progress. Do you need more yet?"

"Nope. I'm still cutting into the first $5,000. I'll let you know if that changes. And I'll let you know if I find out that I've marked the right guy—everything will get ramped up at that point if I'm right."

"OK, Blake—sounds great. Thank you again for taking this case—I guess you really do *'find stuff.'*"

We said goodbye as I pondered that he had used my catch line effectively. I really was back and forth on whether to make a change or not.

I wasn't sure what to do next—so I finally settled on that nap—it was a good choice.

CHAPTER

— 81 —

The Sweet Miss Cindy Lou Who texted me mid-afternoon, which pleased me to no end. I now had her address and another date with her starting at 6:00 p.m.

"I have you now, my sweet!" I said in my best evil villain voice. Don't worry, no one was around to hear me.

I'm also going to have to ask that you *not* tell her that I referred to her as Cindy Lou Who—I was just feeling whimsical at getting another chance to be with her. She might not see it quite that playfully—so let's keep this just between us.

Cindy's address took me around the base of the Catalina Mountains—which were beautiful and along a really scenic road called Skyline. The view of the city was epic—unless of course you were driving and needed to keep your eyes on the road—which I was, and I did—for the most part.

Her apartment complex was really nice, and I arrived very close to the appointed time of 6:00 p.m.

When Cindy answered the door—dang! She wore a pair of jeans that we could all thank God for! The blousy top was colorful. The long earrings were riveting—the makeup was perfect. She added spikes to the look and *MAMA-MIA*! And I'm *not* even Italian!

I have to admit—I could get used to this!

I told her how beautiful she looked, and she even blushed slightly.

She showed me around her apartment—it was decorated nicely and had that great view of the city off the balcony.

I told her that I was thinking large, white concrete horse for dinner—she had the same confused look on her face that you do now—so I got the message that this was a weak start. So, I just said, "*PF Chang's*," and she then gave me a nod and a polite smile. Not too smooth Blakester, but at least she said that sounded good.

It only took us about fifteen minutes to drive to River Road—and odd name because it ran beside what *would* have been a big river, but it was empty. In Tucson, they have all these *dry rivers*, (oxymoron anyone?), that are actually called a "*wash*" that both run, and even flood, during their monsoon season. In Phoenix, we have rivers and lakes—real ones—but that's just us!

We got to the restaurant and only had to wait about twenty minutes—so we did the whole "small talk," "how was your day," chit-chat—and then we were seated.

It was a nice, semi-dark ambiance that just made Cindy a "delight" to behold! I really could just stare at her for a lot of the night, but I didn't want to creep her out, so I made conversation *while* I stared at her. What can I say—cue the music—*"He's a smooth operator . . . smooth operator . . ."*

She asked me a little about my life in Phoenix—which is kind of funny because, except for my work, "my life in Phoenix" is a *little light* on "life." A few friends, going for a run or hitting the gym—it wasn't adding up to a lot.

I was running out of "me" stuff and I kind of panicked and said, "I'm thinking about visiting the church that Kate got involved with just to get a feel for what she experienced."

I'm not sure where that came from, cuz it honestly had *not* crossed my mind. Oh, what panic can do!

"Really?"

Already committed—what was I to do?

"Yeah, thinking about it. They have four services—two on Saturday and two on Sunday—so at least it's convenient."

"That's Desert Christian Church, right?" she asked.

"Yeah."

"Are you religious?" she asked.

"Nope. Not in the least. You?"

"No, I've never really thought about it much. I have to say though, I know some of the people on the force who go there and love it. They're good people."

"I hear that from people—it seems to have a good rep."

"Well, what the heck—you want some company?" she asked.

"What?"

"I've been a little curious about that place from what I've seen—if you're going to go do a little 'fact finding'—what do you think about taking me with you?"

This had gone a really different direction than I had planned, but why not?

"I would love for you to go with me—I'd love your perspective on it too. Do you want to go Saturday or Sunday?"

"What time are the services on Saturday?"

I fished out the card in my wallet and said, "3:30 p.m. and 5:00 p.m."

"I like to sleep in on Sunday, so how about the 5:00 service and then I'll take *you* out for dinner?"

"That sounds great—let's do it."

Our food showed up right then and we started the process of gorging ourselves on really good food. We shared some Spring Rolls, and I had the Lettuce Wraps, and she had the Crispy Honey Chicken. We shared and I think her chicken was the better choice—but it was *all* good!

And somehow, I'd gotten another date with Cindy—but a date to *church*? That was a curveball that I had *not* seen coming! Oh well, I had to agree with her—I was a little curious too.

CHAPTER — 82 —

The rest of the date had gone well—some really fun conversation—lots of laughing. I got another kiss at her door at the end of the date—this girl is just *yummy*!

We probably should keep that adjective between us as well—"*yummy*" doesn't exactly scream "strong, manly man."

I slept a lot better than the night before—no more freaky dreams about fighting bad guys—apparently a date with Cindy can erase bad guys from my subconscious.

On Friday morning, I was "up and at 'em" before 8:00 and had time to go down to the lobby and get "a cup of Joe". Well, actually, about three cups of joe, and a couple *huge* muffins—blueberry—if I'm to be descriptive—and I shall.

I watched some news in my room while I ate, and then got dressed and headed for the Miracle Mile Police Station. At 9:30, I was there and anxious to get some answers.

When I got inside, Trent and Cindy were waiting for me at their desks—I think they were as anxious as I was to find out the results of the two tests.

As a side note—can I just say that those police uniforms simply do *not* do Cindy any justice? This woman is *fine*! I've seen her dolled up twice now—and one time in just workout stuff—and this girl has got it *going on*! But you'd never know it in these uniforms! Who designs these? Are they doing it on purpose? And could this mean that *TRENT* has a great figure too?!

Just messin' with you on that one. Insert smiley face here.

About that whole "doing it on purpose" thing; I guess it could make some sense that they might be doing it on purpose. If they wanted to make sure that all the officers—women included—simply look *boxy* (instead of "*foxy*"), and bulky, so that they all get treated more equally by the bad guys.

Maybe even by the other officers too. Might be some common sense working itself out right there.

Hmmm. I'll have to ponder that later.

There was a large envelope laying on Cindy's desk—I was guessing it was the results. I was happy to see that it was in fact sealed, and was currently unopened.

Cindy picked up the envelope and Trent said, "Let's go into one of the conference rooms in case we need to talk more privately."

Conference room "A" was taken, so they pointed me to "C"—I'm guessing to get us further away from everything.

We all got settled at one end of the long table and Cindy slid the envelope over to me and waited.

"Allow me to first of all say, 'good morning' to each of you," I started, just being me.

I'm not sure, but I think Trent *growled* at me.

I looked closely at him, but couldn't tell.

"I hope you had a great time last night, Miss Rios," I said in my best Don Juan impersonation.

"I did," Detective Rios responded, "and it will be the *last* time you ever have with me if you don't open that stupid envelope and tell us what's in it!"

What a "loving" reply.

I smiled as though she hadn't spoken and threatened my life, "I had a great time too—thanks for asking."

She and Trent both started to rise out of their chairs.

"OK, OK, I just thought I'd start with a little friendly banter—calm down."

"You two went out on another date?" Trent couldn't help himself.

"Yeah, we went to PF Chang's—good food—and we . . ."

"*BLAKE!*"

We both cut our eyes to Cindy. I'm pretty sure she was done with the "friendly banter" portion of our meeting.

"OK—here we go."

I opened the envelope. I was just as curious and excited as they were, but I just can't resist a good "tweak" when the tension and expectation is that high—it's how I deal with stress.

I took out the report. It included both the DNA panel and the fingerprint results. I took a moment to read the results of the DNA exemplar that I had provided, and then the comparison with our DNA sample found under Kate's fingernails. I then went on to the fingerprint analysis to make sure I had the right glass—and sure enough—it was!

I have to believe that Trent and Cindy were *freaking out*—trying to read my face—but I really wasn't being a jerk about this—I just needed to be *sure* I was seeing everything clearly before talking with them about it.

Now armed with the answers, I put the pages back into the envelope, resealed it and put it on the table in front of me.

"OK, first of all, I believe *I now know who killed Kate Walker*."

CHAPTER
— 83 —

Bug-eyed from *both* Trent and Cindy.

"Show us the results!" Trent bellowed.

"No can do, my man."

"WHAT?!" Trent started to rise out of his chair.

"Whoa, big fella! This 'evidence' is still '*Fruit of a Poison Tree,*' and you two *cannot* be looking at it. If you ever find yourself sitting in court, you need to be able to say that you had *nothing* to do with this," I said, pointing at the envelope.

"Then tell us what is in it," said Cindy.

"That I *can* do. I want to walk you through the process I went through, so that if you have to add it to your investigation, you'll have the progression clear."

"It turns out that my 'hunch' was right. As far as the DNA comparison, my mark *is* where the DNA that was under Kate's fingernails came from. In addition to that, the fingerprints on the glass match the guy I suspected—so that way we don't have to wonder if we got a wrong glass. It turns out that the mark's fingerprints are in the system because he has purchased a large number of firearms."

Whoa, a guy with guns in Tucson, Arizona—that pretty much narrowed it down to—like *everyone*!

"We might want to remember that this guy has lots of guns as we progress," I said, as much to myself as to them.

"In Arizona, we have to make that assumption with *everyone* we go after!" Trent replied.

"OK." I opened up my phone and looked at the notes I'd made regarding this case and began.

"Please know that I am not pretending that I'm some kind of 'profiler,' but there were a couple of things that made sense to me. First, we're all aware that most homicides are committed by someone close to the victim—friends, family, acquaintances—not strangers—so I focused on those around Kate, cuz that's where the percentages made sense."

"Second, Kate was clearly a beautiful, accomplished woman, who could have dated *anyone* that she wanted. I believe that a woman like that would be quite intimidating to most men—at least men her own age. In addition to that, the divorce of her parents scarred her and even took her off course in life for a number of years. Add to that the loss of both parents in a car accident seven years ago. Any psychologist would tell you that this can lead to some 'daddy issues'—it doesn't have to, but it can. I also thought it was fair to think that Kate might be more attracted to an *older*, probably highly accomplished man—given her own attributes."

Yes, I used the word '*attributes*'—I get like this when I start narrowing in on the 'prey.'

"Third, we found out from people at Desert Christian Church that this guy was married and had hidden that from Kate. That clearly excluded all the unmarried men around her—which meant that Todd Brooks and Lester Jenkins—coworkers at The Palms—probably didn't make sense, even though they had some markers that pointed to them."

"Fourth, the fact that fairly early on, the perp clearly became aware of me and my efforts. He then stupidly tried to torpedo me by getting me arrested," I looked back and forth at Trent and Cindy shaking my head—they had the good sense to look sheepishly down at the table, "told me that this guy was connected. This would have been either to the police department, The Palms, the church—or a combination of all the above. Those are the only places he could have found out about me."

"Fifth, the perp's ability to get into my truck so effectively—clearly knowing how my alarm worked, and that it would reset itself—demanded some knowledge of cars and alarms. Also, the correct placement of the tracker indicated that as well."

"Sixth, the tracker itself was an expensive one, which again indicated the perp might have significant 'means,' i.e. lots of money."

"Seventh, by leaving the tracker in place without the perp knowing that we knew about, gave me the chance to watch and see if anyone started randomly showing up. I'm sure that, like all law enforcement, you simply don't *like* 'coincidences,' or even really *believe* in them. Me either. So, while keeping my eyes open for this, suddenly two times that I know of, the perp just '*happened*' to be where I was, even though I'd never been around him or met him *before* the placement of the tracker."

"Where did he show up?" asked Trent.

"Right after the whole fiasco with my protecting Bailey Sanchez from being raped by Lester Jenkins, randomly this guy shows up to check on what is going on. But he had an excuse—he's on the Board of Directors at The Palms."

They both stiffened when they heard that. I wasn't surprised—anyone on the Board of Directors at The Palms meant *serious* power, money, and influence. Read that as "*tread carefully grasshopper!*"

"All that did though was make my antennae ping a little—it could have been innocent, and he did have an excuse to be there since he's one of the big bosses running things."

That's kind of funny that I said it made my "antennae ping" after just making a reference to "grasshopper"—I just wanted to make sure you didn't miss that.

That however does raise a serious question: "Is it 'clever' if you have to go this far to point it out?"

Hmmm.

"The clincher was when I went to the Tucson Mall—a completely random place where I'd never been—just to walk around and think about the case. However, my secondary reason was that just maybe the perp would be stupid enough to show up there too since he was probably following me with the tracker. As you both know, typically bad guys are kind of stupid in what they do—even if they are usually pretty smart in their real life."

They both nodded.

"So, I'd been at the mall for a few hours when I heard a commotion behind me and I turned to see the same man from The Palms, being surrounded by a few—I guess you'd call them 'fans'—who knew him from his TV commercials. He was clearly taken aback that this happened, and he made the mistake of glancing over at me and then looking away quickly, hoping I hadn't noticed—which I clearly had. By doing this, he just about *told* me that he was tailing me—he might as well have sent me a *'candygram'* announcing it—and he'd been caught by his own 'celebrity.' I just kept on moving, so that he would have no idea that I now suspected him of Kate's murder."

Trent and Cindy both looked concerned again to hear that the perp was also well-known and apparently liked at a distance, by people in the community. Couldn't say I blamed them.

"So, here is this fiftyish, great looking, very fit man, who is married, wealthy, popular, well-known, undoubtedly powerful, and well connected—who was connected to The Palms both by being on the Board of Directors and by holding some of his largest functions there."

"And for some reason, he seems to be following me."

I looked at Trent and Cindy—they just looked back.

"Wanna guess who it is?"

They just stared. They might have even looked a little "green around the gills."

"No?"

Silence.

"OK—the murderer of Kate Walker is none other than—*drum roll please*—Mr. Nicolas Whitlock, your friendly, multi-state, car dealership mogul!"

CHAPTER
— 84 —

I didn't really expect applause—*OK, maybe I did a little*—but I didn't expect the pale, stoic faces that I saw in front of me. It had the distinct feeling as though I had just dropped a large pile of bull excrement, right in the middle of their pristine police department.

When Trent found his voice, he asked, "Are you sure about this?"

Confused, I said, "Trent, I'm not lying about the DNA evidence—it's Mr. Whitlock's DNA under Kate's fingernails—I don't know how else to explain that other than she was fighting him while he was drowning her."

Trent looked over at Cindy with raised eyebrows.

Cindy found her voice, "You have to understand some things here Blake. Mr. Whitlock has been heavily connected to our department and has been *very* supportive financially—he's considered a 'friend' of TPD—specifically all the way up to the Chief of Police."

I looked back at Cindy for a moment.

"OK—first of all, perhaps you should all 'vet' your friends a little better. Secondly, that adds even more to this scenario—if he's 'connected' around here—because that even better explains how he became aware of me so quickly after I got here. Any of the officers could have inadvertently made him aware of my efforts."

Trent waded in, "This guy knows and influences everybody who is anybody Blake. He owns multiple car dealerships in every major city in probably eight to ten states, from Texas up to Washington, and more."

"OK. So, he is rich and powerful—got it."

"He's also planning on running for governor of the state of Arizona in the next election—he's planning on announcing in just a few months. People believe this is just a step he's taking to move to U.S. Senator, with the hope of trying for President eventually. That's President of the *United States*—in case you missed the reference."

"And you just pointed us to him as the *murderer* of Kate Walker," Cindy added.

"Yeah, I did. Conclusively."

Silence.

"Look guys—I get it—Whitlock is *'the man'* when it comes to money, power, and influence, but he's still a stinking *murderer*! I don't care who he is, what he's got, or where he thinks he's going—he doesn't get to kill Kate—he just *DOESN'T*!"

Trent and Cindy just stared at my outburst.

"Blake, we know that, and we agree—we're with you," offered Trent. "What you have to consider is *our* position. You get to come in here and—let's call it '*bend the rules*'—and find this out—and then when it's all said and done, you get to go back to Phoenix. We have to *live* and *work* here."

"OK Trent—I agree—but what does that *mean*?"

Cindy jumped in, "All we're saying is that this kind of mess that you've just dropped here is a *career* and *life destroying* move, *if* we get it wrong in *any* way. That means that we have to make *sure* that we handle this very carefully and that we have Mr. Whitlock '*dead to rights*' when we go after him. This will have to happen, so that none of the '*suits*' or the '*brass*' can respond in any way, but with condemnation and eventual *conviction*."

"Yeah," added Trent, "since the only 'proof' we have of this is 'proof' that we *can't ever use*—even though it convicts Mr. Whitlock. We *can't* pursue this without some ironclad evidence—the *real* stuff this time—usable in a court of Law. Law enforcement is funny when it comes to stuff like that."

"Well guys, I didn't say we were *done* and should go arrest him. But now that we know the perp, we now can focus on how to draw him out and make him make another mistake."

"How?" they both said in unison.

"I haven't figured that out yet—but we will."

All I got was the "Clint Squint" from Trent.

But I was sure—we *would* figure it out.

CHAPTER

— 85 —

While Trent and Cindy sat in the conference room and tried to get their minds around one of the most prominent citizens in their city—in their state and even in the country—being the murderer of Kate Walker, I headed for the "little boy's room" and did what little boys do in said room. When I came back, they seemed like they had regained their composure.

"Alright, first of all, 'Private Investigator, Blake Moran,' Detective Rios and I want you to know that you did a magnificent job on this case, and we are deeply appreciative for all you've done."

Could've knocked me over with a feather! He even used *"magnificent"*!

"Um, thanks guys—I'm glad I could help."

"We really mean it Blake," said Cindy, "Trent and I realized that while we were busy being traumatized by your news, we lost sight of both Kate Walker and all your work—and the potential danger—that it took to bring us to this point. Without that, I'm afraid that Kate's murderer—Mr. Whitlock—would have gotten away with it. So, sincerely, thank you."

Whoa. This was nice, but it was starting to be one of those 'awkward moments'—I didn't even know where to look. So, I just went for the simple, "You're very welcome—I'm glad I could help."

"And just think Blake," bellowed Trent, "you just fulfilled your tagline: *'you found stuff.'*"

OK, that's it—if even Trent can find a way to mock it—that motto has got to go!

"Good one, Trent."

"So," continued Cindy, "since we actually have *no* evidence that we can use—and yet *know* that Mr. Whitlock killed her—what's the plan here to get some actual evidence?"

"Well," I responded, "we're ahead in that we know the perp, but there is no way to get a warrant, because our 'knowing' won't count with a judge. Also, we don't even know what we'd be looking for, so a judge would just see it as a 'fishing expedition.'"

"And they hate that!" said Trent.

"So, basically if Mr. Whitlock does nothing," added Cindy, "he could still end up getting away with this."

"Yep. But that assumes that he is smart," I said. "Now obviously a guy this high up on the 'food chain' is smart—but we all know that doesn't necessarily apply to being a criminal. I am hoping that he's a really stupid criminal for such a smart man."

Trent chimed in, "I get what you're saying, but I'd have to say that *so far*, he has seemed like a *very* smart criminal. He got past us, and you only got to him by going around the law to catch him."

Here we were really cookin', and Trent had to go and throw his wet blanket on the fire!

"OK, so far he's done well, *but* the whole deal with planting drugs in my truck and putting the tracker on *was* dumb because *that's* the way we got to him."

Nice save—the Blakester strikes again!

"So, if the key is to *not* let him 'do nothing,' I figure we're gonna have to *'poke the bear,'*" I offered.

"How do you propose we do that?" asked Cindy.

"Not we—*me*."

"You do what?" asked Trent.

"Here's what I'm thinking: I go and try to surprise Mr. Whitlock at his office late this afternoon—maybe catch him a little tired after working all day. I can do that because he showed up at The Palms and interjected himself into the picture. He put himself in the game, and there's logic that I would talk to him. I'll use the fact that he was introduced to me as being on the Board of Directors, and since he's one of the bosses, I wanted to talk to all of them about Kate."

"What if he asked around and finds out that you're not talking to other directors?" asked Cindy.

"I actually hope that he does. If he finds out that I'm only talking to him, it could spook him into doing something stupid quicker."

"I'll ask him specific questions about Kate—see if he admits to knowing her or denies it. I'll then ask him about the Casa Hacienda Resort and Spa where she was killed—stuff like that. Basically, I'll try and come across as just questioning harmlessly, but ask enough to rattle his cage and get him to act."

"You do remember *why* his fingerprints were on file? All those firearms?" reminded Trent.

Wow Trent, you are really being a *"Debbie Downer!"*

"Yeah—it's not a perfect plan. I just don't know how we progress in this case without forcing his hand."

Deep breath from Cindy.

"I agree with Blake on this—I don't see another way. I also agree with Trent—you need to be very careful because forcing his hand could cost you everything—and I find that I kind of like having you around."

Trent just rolled his eyes.

CHAPTER

— 86 —

We talked for another hour, throwing out ideas of what to say and what not to say. By the time I left, we had a game plan and I told them I'd let them know what happened.

Trent gave me the big bear back slap—about knocked me over—and Cindy walked me out and gave me a kiss before I left.

That was awesome, but I have to say that it *felt* a little too much like they were potentially saying "*good-bye*"—just in case.

Well, that sucked!

However, as I drove back to The Hermosillo, I couldn't help but dwell on Cindy's comment—*in front* of Trent—"I find that I kind of like having you around."

OK, I admit that I was grinning like a fifth grader with a crush when I thought about that—but it was just me—well, you know now, but I know you're not going to tell.

You aren't, are you?

It was early afternoon by the time I got over to the Northwest side, so I stopped at a roadside food truck to get some grub. It's an odd thing in the Southwest part of America, but there are "portable restaurants" along the road. We have an odd name for them: "Roach Coach."

Mmmm—yummy!

However, while it can be a little hit or miss, some of the best grub can be had from these restaurants on wheels. I got some cheese quesadillas, some beans and homemade, (read Roach Coach made), chips, along with two tacos. The smell was making my mouth water, and once I was in my room—*fiesta*!

When I was done—I cleaned up and then began a search for Nicholas Whitlock's car dealerships in Tucson—it turned out he had three.

That in itself might prove to be problematic—which property held his offices? In spite of the fact that he had car dealerships scattered across the West side of the country, it did seem that Tucson was his base of operation.

I put Whitlock car dealership's executive offices into the search engine and whatcha know? It spits out Whitlock Chevrolet on Auto Mall Drive. The Internet can sure tell you a lot! I looked up the address and it was right down by the Tucson Mall—I guess that explains the "mall" part of "Auto Mall Drive".

Don't be amazed, I'm an investigator—deductive reasoning is simply what I do.

That was only about twenty minutes away, so I had some time—and honestly—nothing to do.

So, I took a nap. It was becoming my "go-to" move.

CHAPTER
— 87 —

That was a totally unnecessary nap—but it was nice!

After I shook it off a little, I started figuring out how to approach this—and then it occurred to me: *the tracker*!

I'd completely forgotten that a *huge* way I could freak out ol' Nicky was to just *park* at his place! That's genius! (Can I say that about my *own* idea? Oh well—I hope so, cuz I just did.)

I got everything I needed together, (paying attention to Molly being loaded and ready, just in case—after all, we already knew the man had lots of guns!), and jumped into Black Beauty to head over to Whitlock Chevrolet.

I was there by about 4:30. I pulled into the parking lot and stopped long enough to look around the property. Very cool place—I'll give the murderer that! But I was looking for something specifically—the executive offices.

And there they were.

You couldn't miss them—the word "*ostentatious*" comes to mind. You could just imagine the deep pile carpet, the solid wood furnishing, the piped in "*muzak*"—before you even went in. Lots of chrome and glass and I was just sure the great view would be reserved for "The Man."

So, I parked in direct view of what I was guessing was the office of the President and CEO of the Whitlock Corporation.

And then I went shopping.

Actually, all I was doing was killing time—giving Mr. Whitlock the chance to check the tracker—only to find that I was parked in *his* parking lot, right below *his* window.

Talk about *"pokin' the bear!"*

I practically got attacked by salesmen, wanting to sell me something. Told them I was just looking for now. I did get some good comments on Black Beauty, so that was fun.

I walked by the new Camaros—made me think of Cindy.

Then I saw the new Corvettes. I have to admit that while I love *"America's Sports Car,"* I was *not* a fan of the new mid-engine design that started in 2020. Don't get me wrong, it was a pretty car, but it felt like a "poor man's Ferrari," because that's what it looked like. I'd probably be called a "traditionalist," but if it's "*America's Sports Car,*" don't make it look like a *European sports car.*

I know why they did it—a mid-engine car performs better on a track than a front engine Corvette—better weight distribution—and Corvette has always been big about winning on the track—lots of success. But for most of us, that's not the issue.

Having said that, I may well be in the minority, cuz the first few years of the C-8, they sold out.

I guess I'm "old-school" on this one.

It *was* a pretty car though.

Remembering why I was there; I went to the other side of the Corvette so that I could casually glance up at the executive offices—faking like I was looking into the car. When I did that, I could just make out that Mr. Nicholas Whitlock, President and CEO of the Whitlock Corporation, was standing at his window, *looking right at me.*

Maybe this dude was *not* as smart as we thought!

He must have been monitoring that tracker pretty closely—I'd only been on his property for about twenty minutes!

Since I knew he was watching, I called the salesman over and asked him one thing about the Corvette—which style it was—1LT, 2LT or

3LT Stingray—I was just doing this so Mr. Whitlock would see. I then thanked him and said that I was needing to speak with Mr. Whitlock. Naturally he balked—I'm guessing nobody just "talked" to "The Man."

I told him that I met Mr. Whitlock at The Palms, where he is on the Board of Directors, and he said that if I needed anything, I should just let him know.

Now *before* you flip back to my first encounter with Mr. Whitlock at The Palms—I'll save you some time:

That was *A LIE*! He never said that.

But it worked—chalk one up for the morally compromised! The salesman pointed right up to that window, right at Mr. Whitlock—who *never saw* it coming and was totally *caught*! Even at a distance, he was like a deer in the headlights! I could not have choreographed it better if I had tried—which I guess is what I *did*!

I already had him back on his heels before I threw the first punch! So, I waved at Mr. Whitlock—who just looked back in shocked disbelief. I thanked the salesman, (for the cameo role he had played without knowing it), and headed to see "*The Man*."

CHAPTER

— 88 —

By the time I got up to the top floor of the executive offices, I was guessing that Mr. Whitlock would have had time to compose himself—he was a very successful businessman after all—he would know how to handle a meeting.

I gave his executive assistant my name and she immediately asked me if I had an appointment.

"No," I said, "but I met Mr. Whitlock at The Palms, where he is on the Board of Directors, after I had just saved a woman in his employ from being raped. He thanked me profusely and told me that if I needed anything, I should let him know. I do, so that's why I'm here."

I've got to say that I think I told that lie the second time, with a little more "*panache*" than the first time I told it to the salesman. Apparently, practice *does* make perfect.

She asked me to be seated and got on the phone and relayed this to Mr. Whitlock. She listened and said, "Yes sir" and hung up the phone.

"Mr. Whitlock is in the middle of something at the moment, but if you'd care to wait, he said that he could speak with you momentarily."

Sure, he's busy, I thought, watching the tracker he put on my truck and then staring in disbelief out his window at me on his car lot! Maybe he's busy plotting his next murder? Maybe hoping it can be me?! What a douche!

I thought all that, but I said, "I'd be happy to wait—I'm sure he's a very busy man. I just appreciate his willingness to see me unannounced."

So, I sit down and ol' Nicky tries to pull a power move—makes me wait for him—cooling my heals in his waiting room—for thirty-five minutes. It was almost 5:30 by the time he called his executive assistant and had her show me into his office.

This was OK with me, since I knew he was in there freaking out—and it was just building—I was as cool as a penguin on his very own ice shelf.

When I got into Mr. Whitlock's office, it was pretty much as I expected. Huge. Great view out of the floor to ceiling windows that made up two walls of the office. Behind his desk was the "Power Wall"—the wall of pictures of him all over the country, shaking hands with "celebrities" and "power brokers." He had pictures with several governors of various states, some on the "Red Carpet" with a number of Hollywood stars, some with U.S. Senators, and even one yucking it up with former President Obama.

The other wall was filled with awards and newspaper articles about Mr. Whitlock, plaques about his philanthropic endeavors, and various accolades about this "great man."

After looking around the room, I think I may have just thrown up in my mouth—just a little.

I shook it off and accepted Mr. Whitlock's hand and thanked him for carving out some time for me "in his busy schedule." Hey, I can kiss up with the best of them.

That seemed to settle him a little that I showed some deference to him—which was exactly my goal.

He walked over to the seating area next to the windows and we settled on the leather couches.

I started, "After we met at The Palms, it occurred to me that since you are on the Board of Directors, you may have your fingers on the pulse of the place and could help me with something."

"I'm not sure if I can, but I can try. What is this regarding?"

"You may or may not recall that Mr. Joyner mentioned to you that

I am here investigating the death of a former employee at The Palms, Miss Kate Walker."

"Yes, I recall."

"I was wondering if perhaps you ever had occasion to meet or to know Miss Walker?"

There was a fleeting panic that flashed behind his eyes as he forced a smile and said, "Well, Mr. Moran, as you can imagine, The Palms has many employees. Being on the Board has more to do with overall direction of the enterprise, rather than in on going, day to day, interaction."

"I'm actually on the Board of Directors of a number of business enterprises, not just The Palms."

My, my, my—aren't *you* so important?

I choked back my gag reflex and came at him again.

"I was guessing that might be the case, but I noticed on the board, when I was in the executive offices, how often your 'enterprise' here, had been having events or functions at The Palms. I thought that might have brought you into contact with Miss Walker—she really was quite memorable and beautiful—so beautiful that she was used extensively on The Palms advertising and brochures."

His jaw clenched, "Well, I was certainly made aware of the death of one of our employees when it happened. However, as you can imagine, I have people for all of the set up and interaction with staff for all events—I simply don't have time for that myself."

That "I have people" comment was *so* condescending—I just wanted to throttle this jerk!

"So, you *hadn't* met Kate and *didn't* know her?"

"That's correct."

"Then how do you explain your DNA being found under Kate's *FINGERNAILS*?!" I shouted!

Did I get you? I'm laughing, cuz *I think I got you.* Of course, I didn't *say* that! I was just messing with you! Remember, I have proof that can't be used *as proof*! But wouldn't that have been *fun* to say that?!

OK, back to our story . . .

"OK. Are you familiar with Desert Christian Church?"

The abrupt change in topics clearly unsettled him—which was the point.

"Um, I've seen their commercials on TV and heard them on the radio—why?"

"Apparently, Kate ended up going there over the last months of her life and was really benefiting from it—since you are so embedded in the community, I thought you might know something about it."

I changed direction again, "Are you familiar with the Casa Hacienda Resort and Spa where Kate was murdered?"

That shook him—which was again my intention.

"No, I've never been to the Casa Hacienda Resort and don't know anything about it."

"Also, did you say *murdered*? I'm sorry—I wasn't aware that this was considered a murder investigation. My contacts at the TPD indicated that they had moved this to a cold case because they couldn't prove it to be a murder."

Easy, Mr. Killer—you're playing your hand too openly. You have been spinning the tale that you're too busy and powerful to really know too much about this "happening," yet you just *told me* that you're *keeping tabs* on the on-going investigation of a crime that you claim you know little about. *Rookie move!* I'm guessing this will occur to you later and you will freak out—which gives me great joy.

"It is true that they didn't have the manpower to continue to pursue Kate's murder as an active case—that's why one of her brothers hired me to continue the process."

"But you said, 'murder,' what is your basis for calling it that?"

Careful big guy, your respiration is getting a little thready and your neck and lower face are starting to flush—I'm betting you have anger issues galore—you'd better reign it in!

Time to drop the hammer—or shall I say, *"Hammer-time!"* Cue the music!

"Well, a number of things stand out: the scene was clearly wiped down to start with—no prints whatsoever. Had the killer known what a dead giveaway that was, he would have just wiped the surfaces that he had touched—not all of them—cuz people who are in a hotel room naturally leave fingerprints."

The flush moved higher.

"There was also the absence of one wine glass."

"Wine glass?"

"Yeah, housekeeping always keeps two in each of the top end suites, but one had been taken, indicating *two* people had been there—not just one—and the other person didn't want anyone to know that they'd been there."

"Then there was the bruising on the back of Kate's head. This could have happened just from her slipping and falling, expect for the fact that there was bruising on her upper chest and the back of her heals. She clearly was held down and fought against her attacker."

Full face flush.

"Then, of course, there were Kate's fingernails."

"Her fingernails?"

"Yeah. Kate had those nail salon acrylic jobs that are so pretty, but they are dangerous as well. Kate must have been quite a fighter—she scratched her attacker up something *fierce*! She ended up having quite a bit of *his* skin under *her* nails."

I looked deeper into his eyes.

"So we actually *have* the killer's DNA."

This guy might just start hyperventilating!

"Oh, and then there's the *witness*."

"The what?!"

"The witness. That's a new clue that I discovered. One of the staff actually *saw* the man who entered the suite where Kate was killed. She only got a view from the back and from a distance, but I was able to help her to give me a fairly clear description of the parts she *did* see."

OK, I may have a real *dilemma* here; if this jerk actually *strokes out*, do I *have* to call the paramedics to save him, or do I just smile into his face while he checks out? Can you tell I'm really *mad* about what he did to Kate?

Mr. Whitlock stared at me, trying his hardest to regain his composure—but he was failing.

I filled the silence.

"So, that's some of the reasons we know this was a murder, Mr. Whitlock, and you'll be glad to know that I seem to be making *real progress* toward solving Kate's murder."

He tried to nod and smile at my assurance, but it looked more like a guy who'd had a large burrito for lunch and was in real distress at the moment.

My work here was done.

"Well, listen—you've been great to take a few moments out of your busy schedule to talk with me—I really appreciate it. I know how busy you are, so I'll get out of your hair now."

I stood and extended my hand—he did the same. I noted with satisfaction that his hand was clammy with sweat. I walked toward the office door and then stopped and turned back toward him with my hand on the knob for one last "tweak."

"Hey. The guys down at the precinct tell me that you're planning to run for governor and maybe higher—good luck with that. Oh, and that thing at the Tucson Mall the other day where people see you and just want your autograph when you're out in public—that's just going to happen even more!"

He nodded weakly and tried to smile again—it ended up just being a grimace.

The message was delivered. That's right slime bag, I'm talking to the police and finding things out about *you*, and you gave yourself away at the mall and I saw it *all*!

Is it just me or was *that* a *very good* meeting?!

(Pause for effect.)

I'm guessing it was *just me*!

(Insert evil laugh here.)

CHAPTER

— 89 —

Nicholas sat alone in his darkened office. He had sent his executive assistant home—it was time anyway—and he was just sitting and thinking.

Freaking out was more like it.

This wasn't supposed to be happening! He had so carefully arranged his life and set it on a course that might even lead to the White House.

And now this—this—"Private Investigator"—comes and sticks his nose into all this and could ruin it all!

He fought down the rage—he just wanted to *break* something—but his executive assistant would probably notice something was gone and wonder about him after his last outburst.

There was no getting around it—this guy had *way* too much information to ignore. They had his DNA—thankfully, he wasn't in the system, but he couldn't chance that somehow, they might get it.

And a *witness*?! How had he missed that?!

He couldn't let this go on any longer. He didn't *think* this P.I. knew *he* had killed Kate, but there were a few points when he was talking, that it almost *felt* like he was baiting him.

Whether he was or not, this had to *end*.

And the only way for this to end, was for Mr. Blake Moran, P.I. to *end*.

He got up and immediately felt better. He was in action mode and that always energized him. He'd have to be careful, but it was time to put an end to the Kate investigation by putting an end to Mr. Moran.

CHAPTER — 90 —

I headed back to The Hermosillo. I was feeling good! There was such a rush in staring the perp right in the eye and making him freak out—while he works so hard to not let you *know* he's freaking out.

Mr. Nicholas Whitlock is a very successful man, but I'm guessing that he's new to being a criminal—and unless you're a *full out psychopath*—you can't conceal being a "newbie."

I knew I was taking a real chance here. There's a reason that cliché works: "*Don't poke the bull or you'll get the horns.*" I had just told the killer that he was in some *serious* danger of being discovered—and the fact that I was there talking to him could *not* have been lost on him.

So, game on!

I needed to let Trent and Cindy know what had just happened and make some plans moving forward as to how we were going to prepare for him to act.

I activated my "hands free" system and got Trent on the phone. I told him to hold on while I conferenced Cindy in too. Once they were both on, I told them step-by-step how it had gone.

I started with the waiting for Mr. Whitlock to see, by looking at the tracker, that I was on his property, and then catching him looking out at me.

Relaying the conversation—blow-by-blow—and "little Nicky's" reaction brought me great joy.

The parting shots about the police and the mall were just the cherry on top.

When I finished, they both thought it had gone well, but were quite concerned about me.

Trent started, "Blake, just know that you marched up into a murderer's lair and spit in his face—a very powerful murderer. Now while he doesn't know that we already know he's the murderer, you gave him *plenty* to decide that that particular revelation may well not be too far away."

"Yep, that was the goal."

Cindy weighed in.

"When you corner a wild animal, it's only instinct is to come out fighting. You just told him that everything—including his political plans and aspirations—are potentially about to come crashing down. His probable response will be to attack—you."

"That's what I'm counting on. As you so clearly noted Cindy, if he just does 'nothing,' he may well get away with this. So, I poked the bear—I can't let him do 'nothing.'"

"OK," said Trent, "but you watch your six. At any point that you start thinking you might need some backup or maybe a 'shadow,' let us know and we'll see what we can arrange."

"Alright. As freaked out as he seemed—under the surface—I'm guessing he won't wait long if he's going to act. Let's keep to the plan and I'll keep an eye out and let you know if something seems off."

"So, Cindy, are we still on for our *date* tomorrow night?"

"What is this, Blake?" Trent said, "I don't want to be a part of this."

"But Trent, we're going to *church* together!"

"What?!"

Cindy was laughing in the background.

"Calm down Trent," I said. "We thought we might benefit from seeing what Kate experienced at Desert Christian—getting into her head to try and understand what was happening with her—that's all. Walking in her shoes—you know. Cindy is even going to spring for dinner!"

"Well, you two kids have fun—but for the record, you're both *weird*!"

Cindy yelled into the phone, "You want to join us Trent—I'll buy you dinner too!"

"Good night," said Trent, and hung up.

"Well, that wasn't a 'no,'" said Cindy.

She was still laughing when she said goodnight.

CHAPTER — 91 —

I made some phone calls and got started on a few cases that had come in while I was away. A couple of them sounded pretty interesting, but I had to let them know that I was out on another case, so I would have to get back to them once I had completed this one.

Most of the day got away from me—but I did end up taking yet another nap! This was becoming a habit! By the time I woke up, I had to jump in the shower and get ready pretty quickly to get over to Desert Christian Church to meet Cindy, but I made it with ten whole minutes to spare.

Cindy's Camaro pulled into the parking lot just a few minutes after I did. She got out and once again, looked like a million bucks! I could really get used to this!

I told her how nice she looked—and she seemed to like that—and then she actually took my hand for us to walk in together. This was *really* going well!

As we walked up, there was a "Welcome/Information Center"—an open-air place—where some nice people said "hi" and pointed us to the auditorium for the service.

The guy at the door introduced himself—said his name was Larry—and when he realized we'd never been here, he told us that we were going to "love it."

Well, we'll see about that.

The auditorium was already about half-full and was filling quickly. They had what they called a "café" in the back, where you could sit at high bistro tables and either watch the stage, or the big screens, or the TVs around you. We decided to sit back there—it was less conspicuous, since we didn't have *any* idea what we were about to experience.

I was just hoping it wasn't going to get weird!

When the stage lights came on, the band was taking the stage—and I was surprised to see Pastor Brian standing up there with a guitar. Who knew?

The music was upbeat, and everybody started clapping along. Cindy looked at me, shrugged her shoulders and started clapping along. I'm not a big clapper, but I couldn't help but tap my foot and move back and forth a little—the Blakester has a little rhythm!

They had everybody sit down after a few songs and another Pastor came out and welcomed everyone. He talked for a while and then showed a hilarious clip that showed animals doing funny things—they said, "for no real reason," and they were right, but it was good for a laugh.

Pastor Brian then said that they wrote their own music and then explained where in the Bible he got the next song and what it was about. The title and gist was we could "Call on Him"—being God, when life wasn't going well.

They played the intro, then as they played the song, I have to admit—I felt a bit of a lump in my throat—it was moving. I wanted to hold it together, but then I glanced over at Cindy and there were tears rolling down her cheeks.

"Are you OK?" I asked.

She nodded "yes" and just kept listening.

After a few more songs, everyone got to sit down, and music and video animation hit the screen. A woman did some "here's all the stuff going on at Desert Christian," interspersed with some funny clips.

At that point, there was a countdown, where it said the satellite locations were joining us, and then there was Pastor Brian in the middle of the stage, starting his teaching.

The teaching was about thirty minutes and he had us laughing almost immediately, then all the sudden you found yourself really *thinking* about what he was saying.

By the time Pastor Brian had one of the other Pastors at each location come out and do the close, I was surprised it was already over.

All of a sudden, the cool music came back on, and everyone was talking and getting up. I looked over at Cindy, and she was just sitting there, taking it all in.

"So, what did you think?" I asked.

"I liked it—and I can see why Kate was drawn to this place."

"Yeah, I know what you mean."

"Were you OK during that first slow song? I was concerned when I saw the tears."

"They were good tears. I already told you about the rape and the impact it had on me—his introduction pointed to life falling apart—like mine did. The idea that we could "Call on Him," is an idea I would *love* to be true—I could've used that at that moment. It just got me emotional, thinking that just maybe it could be true."

"Hmmm."

I didn't know what else to say.

"Blake?" someone asked.

I turned, and there was Kristi—Pastor Brian's wife—with at least three little kids around her.

"Well, hi!" I said. "Kristi, this is my friend Cindy Rios—she's one of the Detectives that I've been working with from TPD on Kate's case. Cindy, this is Pastor Brian's wife."

"Cindy, it's so nice to meet you," Kristi said.

"You too. Are these your kids?"

"Oh, no—these are three of our grandkids—our kids are all grown up now."

"Really—you're a grandma?" I asked.

"I am—nine times over!" she said proudly.

"How many kids do you have?" asked Cindy.

"Five."

Dumbfounded would be the term.

Cindy rescued us, "Well, they are adorable."

"Most of the time," laughed Kristi.

"Any more progress on Kate's case?" she asked.

"*Big* progress," I said, "I think we're getting close."

Cindy kicked me under the table.

"Hey," I said with a smile, "*You* can't comment on an ongoing investigation—you're the police—not me!"

Cindy just shook her head.

"Well, I'll let you two do your thing—glad you could be here—I hope you liked it."

"We did," I said, and Cindy nodded.

"Good—I do too," Kristi said laughing. "Have a good night—nice to meet you, Cindy."

"Nice to meet you too," said Cindy.

Kristi waved and was gone.

CHAPTER

— 92 —

We walked out of the auditorium, and I took Cindy's hand this time.

Instead of heading for the parking lots, Cindy said, "What's up there?" There were a bunch of people up on an upper tier, passed a play fountain of water where kids were getting wet—it looked designed that way—and they were having fun.

We found a food court up there and Cindy said, "Well, I told you I'd buy dinner—how about this?"

There were a lot of people sitting around at the tables, the food smelled good, and it was an awesome setting—the sun just setting over the Tucson Mountains.

"That works for me."

So, we got in line and ordered our food and then found a table off to the side. There was a big play center by a pond, and both the fountain and the play center were full of kids.

We were just taking it all in and making small talk when someone plopped down in the chair next to us. We looked over and there was Pastor Brian.

"Hey," he said.

"Hey yourself," I said.

"Kris told me she saw you here—can you introduce me to your friend?"

"Sure—this is Cindy Rios, one of the Detectives that I'm working with from TPD on Kate's case."

Pastor Brian stood and leaned over the table to shake Cindy's hand. "It's a pleasure to meet you."

"You too," Cindy said.

"What brings you two here?"

"We wanted to get a feel for what Kate experienced here—it clearly had a huge impact on her," I said.

"Hmmm. I can see that—try to see it through her eyes—see if there are any clues that way. That's a good idea. Any progress?"

Cindy gave me the stink eye.

"Well, I'm not supposed to say, but yeah, *big* progress—we're getting it figured out."

"That's awesome—I really hope you two are able to provide some justice for Kate—from what you've told me, she sounds like a great lady. And I gotta like her since she liked Desert Christian so much!" he said laughing.

We laughed with him.

Cindy then cut in, "Can I ask you a question?"

"Sure."

"When you introed that song, 'Call on Him,' do you really believe that God is there for us?"

Smiling, Pastor Brian said, "Yes, I do—I actually wrote it looking back to when my first wife died in five days from a brain tumor."

"Oh my gosh, I'm so sorry," said Cindy.

"Thanks. Because of what I know about God, I can tell you that God was there with me every step of a very difficult time in my life."

"But honestly, I can also tell you that's *irrelevant*."

Confused, Cindy asked, "What do you mean?"

"Cindy, I'm just a person—just like you are just a person—what *difference* could it possibly make *if I believe* in something? Or even if I '*experienced'* something? If all I have is 'I think' or 'I believe'—it really doesn't mean very much."

"The reason that song is true—and I *know* God is really there for us if we 'call on Him'—is because God has provided us *proof.* God has always proven Himself—He has to, because *true 'faith'* is to be *based on real 'facts.'* So, you don't have to take my word for it—that would be weak proof—you can take *God's* word for it. Then you can have real confidence."

"I heard you say that in the service—is that really true?"

"Yeah, it is. If you're interested, our seminar called 'Facts Behind the Faith' shows you the facts."

I jumped in, "Kate actually had that seminar Cindy—I have it now back at the hotel."

"Well, there you go. If you want to know, you can—it's up to you. But the short answer to your question is 'yes,' I can honestly tell you that God is there for us—and that song is true."

Cindy looked choked up again.

Pastor Brian got up.

"I hope you two liked the service."

"We really did—a lot," Cindy said, and I nodded.

"Great. Just so you know, we're praying for you as you chase Kate's murderer. Be careful."

"We will be—thanks," I said.

We just sat there, holding hands, watching the night sky, and enjoying the moment.

CHAPTER
— 93 —

Cindy and I walked out to her car about an hour later and enjoyed kissing for a while. I'm not sure how that works—playing "kissy face" in a church parking lot—but it was fun!

Things turned serious when Cindy focused on my face and said, "Blake, you really need to be careful now—you've clearly '*poked the bear*' by going into Whitlock's office and saying what you did. If he was trying to lay low before—it's doubtful if he will now—and *you* are the danger. Are you ready for the 'eyes in the back of your head' living from here on out?"

"I am. I realize that this approach can be dangerous, but we've put everything in place that we can. I think our plan is good—and I honestly don't know any other way to get ol' Nicky boy to do something stupid so that we can get him. Without me as bait, I'm afraid he would get away with this—and I just can't let that happen."

"I respect that. However, as you know, I've dialed it up to '*I really like you*' and '*I would like to keep you around.*' So, allow me to tell you what the cops at TPD sometimes tell each other on the way out to a potentially dangerous scene . . . "

I waited and she gave me a stare.

"'Don't get dead.'"

"Wow—you 'professionals' are nothing, if not articulate!"

"Real funny—just *don't get dead*—OK?"

"OK."

And then she kissed me again and got into her car and left.

I stood there for a moment and looked around. I needed to hang out here for about twenty minutes—if I was to go by the plan—so I just leaned up against Black Beauty and replayed the evening in my head.

I decided that at least tonight—to my amazement—this was one of my best "dates" ever and "church" had been awesome! (Note the half-smile on my face as I thought about it.)

CHAPTER
— 94 —

After waiting the twenty minutes, I took one more look around—after all, that tracker was still "tracking"—took a deep breath and got into my truck and headed back to The Hermosillo.

It was now getting close to 9:00 and was as dark as night could be in the desert. I drove a bit of a circuitous route to get back to the hotel—I wasn't in a big hurry—I was still burning time.

One *clear* indication that I was just "*burning time,*" is that I took the time to use the word "*circuitous*". If that's not a word you use just to fill up time, I don't know what would be!

Once I got back in the vicinity, I was playing "eagle eye." My head was on a swivel, and I was trying to see anything out of the ordinary. There was lots of darkness out there—not particularly good for me, but a great place to hide for Mr. Whitlock or a hired lackey with nefarious plans—which you can read as simply trying to *kill* me!

"*Nefarious*"—another "*burning time*" word.

I took a moment to try and cite in the most dangerous areas—what would be the best "line of sight" areas that would result in the best "*kill zones.*" (Is my life exciting, or what?!) I tried to think like a killer, and where I would be and how I would do it if I needed to get rid of a threat as big as me in a hurry.

The closest area would be the trees off to the *west* of the parking lot that was next to where I parked my truck. Since Whitlock—or someone he hired—had already been to see where I parked when he placed the tracker—I was guessing that *if* he was going to try and take me out here, he'd plan around my parking spot.

I was figuring that close-up was less likely than a distance shot—if he used one of his many guns. For one thing, already putting some distance between yourself and the target meant that you had a better "head start" to getting away than if you were right there close. Since handguns are a lot harder to be accurate with at much of a distance, if I was the one shooting, it would be with a rifle.

That meant that the *south* was the premier location for a distance shot—lots of dark and lots of uncluttered "line of sight". The fact that the parking lot was so lit up would make for an ideal "from the dark" shot. Oh, goody!

So, trying to abide by Cindy's *"don't get dead"* admonition, I tried to alter the balance. I needed to throw him off a little. I decided to park *closer* to the hotel than my usual spot—I'd never done that before—which would have the added benefit of making the tree area to the west a tougher shot with a handgun. That was just in case I was wrong about the distance shot.

It also made the longer shot a little more off-kilter—and would require a quick readjustment from what he might have planned. Anything I could do to even slightly unnerve anyone trying to inflict harm on me would be a plus. *If* they had a plan to try and kill me tonight, and *if* that plan was based on me following my typical pattern, then this move could throw them off, I only needed a *little* unbalance to *greatly* change the outcome.

And I *greatly* wanted to change the "*outcome,*" being that the intended outcome was me dead on a slab.

I made sure to park under one of the lights—just not in my usual place—so that I would still be considered a good target in a different place. I didn't want to change so much that I inadvertently shut down what we needed to happen.

I turned off the truck and sat there for a moment, knowing that if anything was going to happen tonight, these next moments made the most sense before I got into my room. Whitlock would know I was on my way to the hotel by tracking me and he, or someone he paid, could be all set up—based on what he thought I would do.

If he was out there, I'd thrown a bit of a wrench in his plans by not parking where he thought I would, now I needed to unsettle him a little more.

So, I just *sat* there. There could be a variety of reasons someone would sit in their vehicle for a while before getting out—taking or making a phone call or writing down some notes about something or even just listening to a good song that was on the radio—so it wasn't suspicious. However, what it would do is *freak* someone *out* if they were waiting for the target to come into view.

So, I waited. I let it stretch past five minutes. A little before ten minutes, I figured that I was pressing my luck, so it was *time to make my move.*

I took my jacket and my shoulder gun holster off and tossed them in the back. I got Molly in my hand, *locked and loaded*, and I was ready to go to war. I took a deep breath and opened the door.

The interior light went on. I stayed as much behind solid parts of the truck as I could as I got out, but since the threat could come from the west or the south, I knew I would be vulnerable at moments—nothing I could do about that.

I had parked at an angle that shielded me somewhat from the trees—at least until I decided that maybe the threat would come from there—and then I'd have to walk more out in the open.

It occurred to me right then, that I could be doing all of this production for absolutely *no* reason—I could be all on my own out here—not a killer to be found. But I couldn't chance it.

Cindy had told me, "*Don't get dead.*"

I shut the door and the interior light went off. I stepped toward the front of the truck, and for the first time, my head and shoulders were *exposed*. I was guessing that target was a little too small—but I sure hoped I was guessing right!

I stepped forward and cleared Black Beauty and *immediately dropped my keys*. I quickly bent down to pick them up.

I actually *heard* the bullet go passed, right before I heard the "*crack*" of the shot—in my mind, it seemed like I *felt* the wind go by where my body had just been.

It is weird the things that happen at moments like that—things slow down, and as I was hitting the ground, I actually thought, "*Wow, he's a really good shot.*" Then my adrenaline was off the charts, and I was scurrying back to my truck to get some cover.

The shooter clearly freaked because he clipped off three more shots in succession—one that hit the ground where I just had been and two into the side of Black Beauty!

Now I was *mad*!

When the shooting ended, I quickly got my eyes above the bed of my truck to look. I only stared into the darkness for about seven seconds when off in the distance—probably close to 1,000 feet—I saw the interior lights pop on as someone scrambled to get into a vehicle. The interior light set-up showed it to be a big truck.

I steadied myself on the bed of the truck and aimed Molly carefully, trying to allow for the distance and some of the *"fall"* of the bullets. I had fourteen rounds in Molly, and I kept pulling until she was empty, alternating my position to try just to hit the vehicle one way or the other.

Now, for the record, a bullet from a handgun like mine will travel *over 2,400 yards*! That is *over eight football fields*! So, you can read that as *a long way*. However, it's just that accuracy is the issue. But I'm a pretty good shot, and there wasn't any wind to speak of, so I figured with fourteen chances, I had a chance to hit it.

I actually thought I heard a couple of hits before the big truck roared off, but I can't be sure I wasn't just doing the *"hoping" hearing.*

I quickly dropped Molly on the front seat and grabbed the walkie-talkie that Trent had given me.

"Trent—Cindy," I started, "Perpetrator engaged, fired four shots, almost hit me, but did *not* hit me. He is in a large truck, south of my hotel by about 1,000 feet. He just took off, heading east on unknown road. I shot fourteen times at him and may have hit the truck—please pursue—and alert forces."

"Blake, we are on it—Cindy is to your west, but I am to the east—we will both pursue. Please stay at your location, and wait for forensics to arrive to try and retrieve any evidence."

"Cindy, I'll call out the troops with the direction to specifically look for Nicholas Whitlock's truck by his tag number and I'll start by heading down I-10, since that would be his fastest escape route. You take Ina Road and get some of the other guys on the other major roads. Let them know that if they do end up pulling over Mr. Whitlock, he should be considered armed and dangerous—he will probably feel pretty backed into a corner."

"Copy that—Blake, you sure you're, OK?"

"I'm good—and as requested, *I didn't 'get dead.'*"

"Copy that. Rios out."

I heard both of their car's sirens in the distance as they went on the pursuit—and within minutes, I heard more.

About that time, I just went *weak* and sat down on the ground. The adrenaline was gone and the reality that I could have been *killed tonight* sank in. If I hadn't timed that key drop just right, he would have got me. I just sat there and enjoyed being able to still breathe and hoped they could catch that murderous perp!

CHAPTER
— 95 —

It only took about thirty minutes for the forensics team to get to The Hermosillo—and then things got a little crazy.

Everything was taped off as a crime scene and, as you would expect, people from all around came out to watch what was going on.

One of those people ended up being Jordan Smithe—with a hard "i" instead of "smith-e." Do you remember him? He's the manager of The Hermosillo—the one who had been so apologetic when we saw on the recordings that *my* truck had been vandalized in *his* parking lot.

For the record, that was just *after* I'd been "mirandized" by what is now my "girlfriend," and right *before* she and Trent had sheepishly had to take those metal cuffs off my wrist.

(Also for the record, he had also been *entirely too attentive* to my now girlfriend, Miss Rios.)

Well, you can imagine what Mr. Smithe—with a hard "i"—was feeling *now*! I had now been *shot at* in his parking lot?! (He had no idea that I'd basically worked to *coordinate* the attack—that will need to be our little secret.) I have to believe that he secretly was just wishing I would check out!

"Mr. Moran," he began, "I can't tell you how sorry I am. I assure you that nothing like this has ever happen at The Hermosillo—I just cannot apologize enough sir!"

Actually, he could—and that was enough. I admit it, I was feeling bad, knowing that I'd set all this into motion, and *he* was feeling responsible. Not bad enough to *admit* it to him, but enough to assure him that it was OK. If it was his *rating* on *Yelp* that he was worried about, it was safe.

I gave my report to forensics about what happened, how many shots were taken, where the perp's truck had been located and how many shots I took. They had to take Molly into custody, but they assured me that they would be good to her. They also sent part of the team off to try and find the location of the shooter's truck. They clearly did locate it, because when I looked far to the south, I saw them setting up lights around the area where the perp had been.

They had to dig the *two slugs out of Black Beauty*—one in the front right quarter panel and the other out of the passenger door. That *hurt*! They then set out to look for the other two, based on my description of where the bullet had gone past me. To do that, I had to reenact the assault—that was a little *unsettling*.

About an hour into all this—and less than two hours since the attack—I got a call from Trent.

"We got him Blake."

"Was it Mr. Whitlock himself?"

"Yep, it was. He was trying to get back home on some backroad surface streets—*which I'll admit was a clever approach*—but one of our uniforms happened to see the truck from one of the major roads and came up on it to check the tag."

"Did he try and run?"

"No, he tried the '*good citizen*' *routine* where he says, '*what can I do for you officer?*' Then, after asking to look at his license and registration—to make it seem like a normal stop—he asked him to step out of the vehicle. Mr. Whitlock played the '*do you know who I am?*' *card*—he even mentioned the Chief of Police by name and started to get agitated—even irate."

"Interesting."

Trent continued, "At that point, since they'd been given the '*armed and dangerous*' *declaration*, the officer pulled his firearm, pointed it at

Mr. Whitlock and told him to *get out of the vehicle.* And he did. He cuffed him and is waiting for another forensics team to get there. Other cars and officers are already on the scene."

"Did Mr. Whitlock say anything else?" I asked.

"Just, 'I want my lawyer.'"

"Time to '*lawyer up*,' huh?"

"Yep. You'll be happy to hear though that the officer peered into the back seat of the truck, and there is a rifle laying on the floor of the truck."

"Really?!"

"Yep—he must have tossed it in when he was trying to get out of there. Just hadn't had time to get rid of it yet—he was too busy trying to get away."

"That is awesome!"

"You said it, *Wyatt Earp*!"

"What?"

"Well, I found it interesting that the officer also took note that there appear to be *five bullet holes* in the driver's side of Mr. Whitlock's brand-new truck. As you can imagine, having a brand-new truck *worth well over $100,000* show up with bullet holes in one side causes police officers to think, '*Hmmm.*'"

"Are you serious? *FIVE*? I hit his truck *five times out of fourteen from over 1,000 feet away?!*"

"Now Blake, we're police officers, and must not make such assumptions—but yeah—unless some crazy guy just decided tonight to redecorate the side of a one-hundred K truck—you are in fact the infamous *WYATT EARP*! Good shootin' '*partner.*'"

"Thanks Trent."

"Are you OK? It sounded like it was a lot closer call than we hoped it would be."

"It was—if I hadn't timed that key drop just right, you'd either be coming to see me at the hospital or the morgue." Taking a deep breath. "Yeah, I'll admit I'm a little shook up."

"Well, I'm glad you're OK. I know we have a distance to still go, but you have really pulled it off Blake—we might just get this perp for Kate's murder."

"About that," I said, "I need you to do something a little extra when you test everything . . ."

CHAPTER

— 96 —

I ended up with forensics finishing up a little after midnight—I hadn't heard anything more from anyone—and I was ready to get some sleep.

Or so I thought.

That night, I ended up sleeping in fits—I woke up a few different times in a cold sweat—thinking I was being fired at again, only these times I got hit. I would actually be checking my body for the wound when I realized that I was in bed, and I had dreamed it all. It felt like the whole PTSD thing—not fun.

I finally gave up trying to sleep—cuz I just did *not* want to have that dream again—around 7:30. I got up and looked around on TV at the local news. The only thing that was mentioned on one channel was a late-night chase throughout town last night by a large contingency of the Tucson Police.

I got some pastries and some coffee from the lobby and went back to my room. After a little sugar and caffeine, I felt a little better and decided to jump in the shower.

I ended up missing a call from Detective Rios, (see how formal I'm being?), so I called her when I got out of the shower.

"Hey Cindy, how are you?"

"Tired, but OK. Did you sleep well?"

"Not really," I said, "I kept having the same unsettling dream over and over."

"Yeah, that's pretty common after a shooting—were you actually getting hit in the dream?"

"Yep, and it wasn't fun."

"I'm sorry about that."

"Thanks. Have you been up all night?"

"No, but most of it. I wanted to call you and let you know that they are going to be giving us a lot of the forensics mid-morning today—they did *not* get any sleep last night—they had lots to do."

"How did you get them to get it done that quickly?"

"Well, when you have a suspect that has lots of money, power, anger, and lawyers, you'd best move pretty quickly."

"So, *Mr. in-the-Public-Eye* is pitching a fit?"

"That he is—and just so you know, the governor's office has already called to ask what is going on. We haven't heard from the White House yet, but it wouldn't shock me."

"So, he's going on a power offensive—well allow me to say that that is very '*offensive*' to me—given what he already did and then tried to do last night. I'd like to say this isn't personal, but I'm petty, and when someone tries to blow my head off—well, let's just say I get a little '*miffed.*'"

Cindy chuckled tiredly. "Well, I wish you'd told me you were that shallow *before* we started dating."

I laughed. "So, what's the plan?"

"Dating or the case?"

I laughed again. "The case."

"We were hoping that you could meet us at the station later today. I know it's Sunday, and you'll probably want to watch football, but we'd really like to put our strategy together to nail the highly esteemed, 'Mr. Whitlock.' We have to get it right Blake, cuz his attorney is going to seize on anything to toss this out."

"I know that's a crazy thought, given what he's done, but I've watched attorneys pull a perp's butt out of the fire before. It's a horrifying thing to watch and has very little to do with the truth."

"They can do all kinds of bad stuff, so we better not miss even *one* thing, or they have us. So, despite the football thing, can you make it," asked Cindy.

"Just so you know, for future reference Cindy: one, I do watch football, and two, college and professional football isn't played in the summer—so there *is no* game today."

"Just let it go! Can you be here or not?"

Oops, apparently Cindy had reached the end of her "funny" this morning.

"Sure, what, about 10:00?"

"Make it 11:00 so we can get as much of the forensics back as possible. And I'm sorry for snapping at you Blake. I'm just tired and nervous this jerk might walk on some of this."

"No problem M'lady, and don't worry about Whitlock with all his power and money—*I have a plan*—we'll get him."

"Oh no, Blake has a plan—*we're doomed*."

OK, maybe Cindy still had a *little* funny left this morning.

CHAPTER
— 97 —

By the time I got to the station, Trent and Cindy had commandeered conference room "C"—the same one we were in when I did the big "reveal" of who the killer was. I'm guessing they wanted to make sure we were "*off the beaten path,*" so that our planning didn't become public knowledge.

After all, ol' Nicky boy was powerful and rich, *with way too many contacts*—gotta keep this on the "down low." (I'm not sure, but I think I just dropped a "*gang sign*" when I said that—I gotta get a grip.)

We all got seated around the large table and the forensic chief arranged his paperwork to tell us what they had found.

"As you probably know," he began, "each bullet gets marks from going through a gun barrel. If the bullet isn't destroyed by the impact, those marks can be matched to a particular gun barrel."

"As far as the rifle found in the accused truck, we were able to match the rifling impression on the bullets to the rifle—the bullets came from that rifle."

"Secondly, we found the shell casings—or '*brass*'—at the suspected shooting site, south of the location of the target."

I moved uncomfortably since I had just been reduced to "*the target.*"

"This means that the rounds were in fact, shot from that location."

"Thirdly, as you may know as well, small amounts of the rare element 'antimony' are found in most ammunition. When a gun goes off, a cloud of fine particles *covers the hands of the shooter*—leaving behind a bit of the telltale metal."

"The hands of the accused were tested for this on arrival—*at great objection by both the accused and his attorney*, I might add," he said, shaking this head, "and this metal *was* found on the hands of the accused."

"While this does not prove that he shot this particular rifle—it does prove that he shot a gun very recently and had not had opportunity to thoroughly wash his hands off yet."

"As you all undoubtedly know—the rifle was clearly evident, having been thrown into the back of the truck owned by the accused."

"So, we have a rifle that had recently been fired, at a specific location just south of the target, the rifle being found within the hour, inside the truck of the accused, with gunshot residue on the hands of the accused."

"Obviously, *the implications are clear*."

We all nodded.

"Fourthly, we were able to lift the clearest and most recent tire prints from the dirt at that site—they matched the make and model of the tires on the truck of the accused."

"Now to the *handgun* used by the *target*."

"*Molly* and *Blake*," I said.

Everyone looked over at me like I'd just farted in church—the guy just looked at me confused—I just wanted to get some names on the record.

"*Molly*?" the forensic guy asked.

"The name of my Glock."

"You *named* your firearm?" said the guy, clearly giving me "incredulous."

"Yeah—doesn't everybody?"

He just stared at me for a moment—like he was looking at a bug under a microscope. It is just me, or are you guessing that this guy is more of an "*indoor*" sort of guy?

I looked over at Trent and Cindy—they were both slowly shaking their heads.

Fine!

The guy took a deep breath and went back to his notes: "As far as the bullets from the Glock . . ." I muttered "Molly" under my breath—again, I never said I was mature. ". . . we recovered twelve of the fourteen-round capacity of the magazine."

He turned to me, "May I ask how many rounds you believe you had?"

"I had fourteen."

"And you discharged all fourteen?"

"Yes—I kept pulling the trigger until Molly locked open—she was empty by the time I was done."

He blanched at the name again.

"Well, I'm quite happy that we recovered twelve out of the fourteen bullets. We dug five out of the side of the accused truck and dug the other seven out of the berm where the truck was and the surrounding ground."

"We compared these slugs to the Glock 40," he glanced up sharply to see if I was going to call out her name again—I didn't—it's called personal growth, "and they were a match. They came from the Glock."

He turned to me, "I have to say, hitting that truck at over 1,000 feet—five out of fourteen times—is remarkably accurate shooting with a handgun."

I was taken aback—I didn't expect that—maybe this lab rat was cool after all! I tend to feel that way toward people who praise me.

I smiled at him and was in the process of trying to say, "why, thank you," when he moved on.

"Gunshot residue was detected on the target's hand as well when they were tested on site. This again places the truck of the accused at the suspected site, just south of the target."

I was getting tired of being called the "target," although it did occur to me that I didn't know this guy's name either.

"Finally, at the special request of Detective Trent Burgess," he nodded Trent's way, "we ran for DNA on the rifle itself and checked it against the accused. Once again, this was greatly objected to by both the accused and his attorney. The result was that the *only* DNA found on the rifle was in fact that of the accused."

Trent nodded at him. "Thanks for doing that," he said as he glanced over at me.

"Are there any questions at this time?" asked forensic man.

(I wonder if you could make a superhero out of that? *"He pulls prints from the smallest places! He gathers DNA from hair and toothbrushes! He analyzes blood splatter! He is 'FORENSIC MAN'!")*

I realized everyone was looking at me. Did I say all that out loud?!

Oh, they were just wanting to know if I had any questions—that was close!

"Nope, I'm good."

We did all the "thank yous" as the guy gathered all his papers and then *"FORENSIC MAN"* left . . . *"TO SAVE THE DAY!"*

Sorry. Couldn't resist.

CHAPTER

— 98 —

Trent got up and closed the door, then sat back down.

"Well, this is looking pretty good—I'm not sure how Whitlock could squirm out of this," said Trent.

"You can bet that he and his lawyers—oh, and the governor—are going to try," said Cindy.

I was thinking through what I just heard. They just looked at me while I did. I finally looked up, realizing it had gotten uncomfortably quiet.

"What?" I asked articulately.

"What are you thinking?" asked Trent.

"Well, first of all, with what are you going to charge him?"

Trent glanced over at Cindy, "I'm thinking 'aggravated assault' and 'attempted murder.'"

Cindy nodded.

"There could be others like 'discharging a weapon within city limits,' but those aren't the big deal."

"How are you going to approach him?" I asked.

Cindy weighed in, looking over at Trent. "How about we give him a little rope to hang himself by just telling him the charges and see what he and his attorney try and do with them?"

I liked the way she was thinking. Give him a chance to really step in it before showing our hand.

Trent was nodding. He glanced back over at me.

"You had me get that test—what are you thinking?"

My turn, "I have a concern that we will get him on these charges—which of course they will try and plead down once they hear all the evidence we have—and that in the process, Kate's murder will get lost in all the noise."

"I know he tried to kill me—and I want him to pay for that—but Kate's murder is why I'm here."

"What are you suggesting?" asked Cindy.

"Well, this is your case Detective Rios—you are the lead—but I think I know a way we can nail Whitlock for *both* of these crimes and have him *so* locked down that he can't squirm out of either one of them."

I had their attention.

"Enlighten us," said Trent.

So, I did.

CHAPTER
— 99 —

We were moving toward the limit of time we had of keeping ol' Nicky locked up without being charged—a fact that his attorney was yelling about to everyone, including the governor—so we scheduled to talk with Whitlock and his attorney at 5:00 p.m.

As you can imagine, having arrested a man of Mr. Whitlock's fame, power, and prestige, caused quite the stir around the station, and we all knew it wouldn't be much longer before some news organization got ahold of it and the onslaught would begin.

We needed to get this thing in the can before all that pressure came dropping down on our head—and it needed to be so ironclad that there wouldn't be anything anyone could say except, "Just throw away the key."

Trent and Cindy were in the interview room, along with Mr. Whitlock's high-powered attorney. I gotta say that his attorney was really embarrassing me—he just kept pointing out that he was "*from Phoenix*"—making the clear statement that he was from the "big city," and all you people from "the Old Pueblo" (Tucson), were a just a bunch of backwoods, hillbilly rednecks.

His $5,000 suit, $1,000 *Magnanni Viggo Cognac Crocodile* loafers, and his $10,000 *Rolex* watch did *not* endear him to anyone either. Dang, only a guy like Whitlock could even *afford* a guy like this!

Needless to say, he wasn't winning any popularity contests with anyone—and that included me! And I was from Phoenix!

Trent looked like he was ready to eat this lawyer whole—and he looked anxious to do so.

Since I am not "one of the boys in blue," I was sent into exile, to watch the proceedings on the screens. But Trent and Cindy were ready to execute our plan, so we were ready to go.

Mr. Whitlock was escorted in. It was weird to see him in his jail "attire"—"Property of TPD" emblazoned on his back. I gotta say, I don't think orange is his color.

Well, the clothes might be different, but this was a man incensed! He's had a night in "the clink," and a man of his stature must *never* have to endure such frivolity!

He was itchin' for a fight!

He stared spewing before they even got him seated.

"How dare you treat me like this! Why am I even *in* here?! Do you know *who* I am?! I could buy and sell every one of you!"

His attorney tried to quiet him.

"That goes for *you too*!" he roared. "Why do I even pay you all that money if this is all the service I get?!"

Whoa, Mr. fancy pants just got *told*!

"Have you heard from the governor? He is not going to allow a couple of petty functionaries to treat a man of my stature with such disrespect!"

Trent and Cindy were just staring at him, just like we planned—letting him crucify himself.

"Don't just sit there, you morons, why am I in here?!"

Trent cleared his throat.

"Mr. Whitlock, you are being charged with '*aggravated assault*' and '*attempted murder*' of one," he picked up a clipboard and acted like he was reading it—as though he didn't know my name, "Mr. Blake Moran, a Private Investigator from Phoenix, whom I'm led to understand, '*finds stuff*.'"

I about had a cow! Did Trent just tweak me on camera with my tagline?! I had to laugh. That was aimed right at me, and I didn't know Trent had it in him!

"Who is this Blake Moron?" Whitlock asked indignantly, purposely saying my last name as a derogatory.

"It's Blake Moran, and I believe you've met him at The Palms and most recently at your executive offices."

His attorney broke in, "You don't have to answer that sir."

Mr. Whitlock waved him off and pretended to think.

Cindy jumped in to jar his memory, "He saved a young woman in your employ at The Palms from being raped by one of your other employees."

Way to go Cindy. Remind everyone that I'm a superhero!

"Oh, that—yes, I remember briefly meeting him."

"And in your office on Friday?" Trent asked.

"Vaguely. He stopped by and we talked briefly before I had to leave for an appointment. Why on earth would you accuse me of trying to kill some loser that I don't even know?"

Hey! Now that was uncalled for!

Cindy stepped in, "Could you first of all explain sir why you had a rifle on the back floor of your truck when you were pulled over?"

"Has that become a crime in Arizona of which I was unaware?"

"No sir, but it would help if you could explain its presence."

"You don't have to say anything, Mr. Whitlock," his attorney reminded him.

"It's not a problem Theodore."

That figured that this pompous jerk would be named "Theodore." His poll numbers just kept on rising!

"I'm a wealthy man, and I always carry a firearm with me in case I would need it."

Trent weighed in, "But a rifle sir? A handgun would make sense—just about everybody in Arizona is carrying one of those—but a rifle? It's pretty cumbersome for quick protection, don't you think?"

Whitlock blanched, “Not for me.”

“OK. When is the last time you shot it sir?”

His attorney shook his head at ol’ Nicky.

“It’s been a month or two since I could get to the range.”

“Hmmm,” said Cindy, flipping through some pages, “it seems that when you came in, your hands tested positive for gunshot residue. That would typically mean that you had pulled a trigger in the last five to six hours.”

Silence.

“I think we’re done here,” said the attorney.

“Oh, come on Theo,” said Trent, “I’m sure Mr. Whitlock can explain it.”

Clearly “Theo” was not amused at Trent’s tweak. You could almost *hear* the gears grinding in Mr. Whitlock’s brain over getting caught in a lie.

“Oh, that’s right, I had been to the range earlier in the day to sharpen up—I forgot.”

“You forgot?” Trent asked, “You’d been shooting a high-powered weapon to ‘sharpen up’ and you ‘forgot’ you’d done that?”

“Yes,” he said, though even “Theodore” didn’t seem to buy that one.

“Can I ask where you were going when you were picked up last night?” asked Cindy.

“Home.”

“From where?”

“I made a trip up to Phoenix and was coming home.”

“Is that where you went to a target range?” asked Trent.

“What?”

“Well, gunshot residue only lasts so long on the body, so it would seem that you would have had to shoot your rifle up in Phoenix.”

“Uh, yeah, that’s where.”

“So, just to sum up,” said Cindy, “you took a trip to Phoenix, where you did some target practice at an unknown range and were on your way home when you were pulled over."

"Yes."

"Can you explain the slugs in the side of your truck?" asked Trent.

"You do not have to answer that Mr. Whitlock," said his attorney.

He waved off his attorney. "I ended up driving through a sketchy part of Phoenix and got lit up by some 'gangbangers.'"

"Really?" said Trent.

"Yeah."

"Why were they shooting at you?"

"I can only guess it was the nice, expensive truck—a little jealousy—a couple shots."

"Hmmm."

"Fascinating," added Cindy.

Trent nodded at her, and I thought how often really *smart* people made really *stupid* criminals!

CHAPTER
— 100 —

"Mr. Whitlock," Cindy said, "I think you're *lying* to us."

"How dare you!" fumed Whitlock.

"I have to agree Mr. Whitlock—let me tell you what we know," said Trent.

A little "deer in the headlights" from ol' Nicky.

"You fired four shots at Mr. Moran as he got out of his vehicle in the parking lot of The Hermosillo."

"I most certainly did *not*!" shouted Whitlock.

Trent put his hand out to quiet him.

"We recovered all four slugs—two of which were dug out of Mr. Moran's truck—and matched them to your weapon, found on the floorboard of your truck in the backseat just an hour later."

Whitlock just stared.

Cindy continued, "You took those shots from a dirt road just over 1,000 feet south of the parking lot."

"No," Whitlock muttered.

"We have the brass from your shots, found at that location—and matching your weapon. In addition to that, we pulled tracks from the road that matched your truck's model and make."

"Mr. Moran also shot," continued Trent, "using his Glock 40. He emptied his magazine toward you and was able to hit your truck with five out of the fourteen rounds he fired off. We were able to recover twelve of the bullets. The five slugs were dug out of your truck and were then matched to Mr. Moran's handgun."

"So, no 'gangbangers' in Phoenix," added Cindy.

"All of this places you conclusively at the site of the crime, firing your rifle at Mr. Moran," finished Trent.

A long pause.

"Maybe someone stole my rifle and shot it," Mr. Whitlock tried.

"Well," said Cindy, "first of all, that is *not* what you've said up to this point, and secondly, we had your gun checked for fingerprints and DNA—just in case you tried to say something like that—and yours were the only fingerprints and DNA found on the gun."

"We have you 'comin' and goin' Mr. Whitlock," said Trent.

"Can I have a moment to speak with my client please," asked Theodore.

"Sure."

CHAPTER
— 101 —

You could almost feel sorry for Theodore the attorney. How was he going to turn this cow patty into a breakfast pancake? I just was not seeing the path—but he was going to try.

Trent and Cindy and I talked during the break, and then they headed back in.

Theodore jumped in first.

"My client is seeking a reduction in sentence—perhaps pled down to just 'aggravated assault'—with the acknowledgment of my client's status in this community and far beyond."

Wow. The guy had some serious cajones to ask for this—especially asking it in that way.

Trent gave him the "Clint Squint" for a moment and then said, "Well, there's more. Detective Rios?"

"Thank you, Detective Burgess"

She looked up at the camera and said, "Mr. Moran, could you join us please?"

Mr. Whitlock went bug-eyed and Theodore the attorney erupted.

"This is highly irregular!" he sputtered.

I opened the door, walked in, and sat down, staring at Mr. Whitlock. It was not a nice stare.

"Mr. Whitlock," continued Cindy, "the question remains as to *why* you would try to kill Mr. Moran—a man whom you don't know and with whom you've had little contact? So, we began to look for the common denominator. That answer could only track back to one of my cases, the case that Mr. Moran has been here working on. That case had currently been considered a 'cold case'—of which I was the lead detective. This case was the Kate Walker murder."

She let that sink in.

"Mr. Moran has been here, working *only* on this case, for a little over a week. At your own admission, you do not know Mr. Moran, except that he rescued one of your employees from rape and from a short meeting on Friday—both of which you said you barely remembered."

"Now Mr. Moran asked my colleague specifically to make sure and check your rifle for *both* fingerprints and DNA."

"Unlawful search," tried his attorney.

"I'm afraid not, Theo," she tweaked him, "because this was to make sure that Mr. Whitlock didn't try and say that someone else had taken his weapon and fired it—which if you remember—he did."

We were looking at a deflated Theodore.

"Since the only reasonable explanation for your animosity toward Mr. Moran would be the case on which he was working—the Kate Walker murder—I did some cross checking."

"You may remember Mr. Whitlock," I chimed in, "that you emphatically stated to me that you *'didn't know Kate and had never been to the Casa Hacienda Resort.'*"

He just stared.

"So, you could imagine my surprise," continued Cindy, "that when I ran your DNA against the DNA found under Kate Walker's fingernails from fighting off her attacker—they were a *perfect match*."

You could have heard the proverbial "pin drop."

"So, Mr. Whitlock," concluded Cindy, her eyes growing hard, "not only will there *not* be 'a reduction in your sentence' for trying to kill Mr. Moran *or* an 'acknowledgment of your status in this community and far beyond'," saying that, glaring at both Whitlock and his attorney, "*but you are also being charged with the murder of Kate Walker*."

"And I hope you get the death penalty," I had to add.

CHAPTER

— 102 —

To say that Mr. Whitlock and his attorney had a distinctly different attitude when we returned to the interview room after their most recent "con-fab," would be an understatement. They both clearly knew that this was over, and if this ever went to trial, Mr. Whitlock was going to partake in a life-ending cocktail of lethal injection.

We sat and waited to hear their response.

"Mr. Whitlock," his attorney began, "would like to offer a confession in exchange for avoiding a public trial and taking the death penalty off the table."

"Does Mr. Whitlock understand that he would still get life without parole if we accepted this deal?" asked Trent.

He looked over at Mr. Whitlock, who nodded.

"Yes, he understands."

Trent looked over at Cindy, "It's your case. What do you want to do?"

"Excuse us for a moment," said Cindy, and the three of us got up and walked out.

We went over to the conference room.

Cindy turned and looked at me, "How do you feel about this?

"I'm torn," I admitted. "You have a slam dunk case here, but I know how hard it is to get the death penalty—at least to have them actually *do* it."

"Yeah," Cindy said, "in addition to that, the trial would stretch out for potentially years—even in a slam dunk case like this."

"I'm trying to think about her brothers—Greg and Johnnie. I'm guessing that for them to be able to know what happened and why, might bring them some closure—if there is such a thing in a situation like this."

"Do you want me to see if the Attorney General will make the deal, then? Given who Whitlock is *and* the fact that the Governor has been calling, he'll have to make the call."

"Sure—see if he will."

Cindy was off to find out.

CHAPTER
— 103 —

An hour later, the three of us walked back into the interview room where Whitlock and his attorney were waiting. Cindy handed the attorney a piece of paper and we all waited while he went over the offer from the Arizona Attorney General that took the death penalty off the table.

After he was satisfied that everything was in order, he conferred with Mr. Whitlock and had him sign the document. Cindy made sure all the recording equipment was working correctly and the murderer's confession began:

"The relationship with Kate began after I met her at one of my functions at The Palms. I noticed her as she was working—how could you not—she was so beautiful."

My gut clinched a little—I didn't want to hear this from him—but there was nothing I could do about it.

"After I ran into her again after one of the Board of Directors meetings, I asked her if she would like to go for a drink with me. She actually said 'no' that time, so I just used that to tease her into going out with me. About the fourth time I asked, she agreed to go out to dinner with me."

"Did you ever mention to her that you were married?" asked Cindy.

"No, I didn't—and I haven't worn a wedding ring in years."

Scumbag, I thought.

"We went out a number of times and our relationship became sexual, right before Kate discovered that I was married. She was very upset by this—she said she felt lied to (you think?!), but she simply ended us seeing each other—there was no 'scene.'"

"I would see her around The Palms and try to talk to her, but she would just politely tell me she had work to do, and she would walk away from me."

"I admit that I was somewhat consumed with her and just couldn't let her go."

"Right after she ended us seeing each other, she started going to that 'Desert Christian Church.' Apparently, that started her down some religious path, at least that seemed to be the case."

"Weeks went by and I finally cornered her and begged her to at least sit down and talk with me—I told her that I needed some closure. She reluctantly said she would for my benefit, but not at The Palms—not in her professional space."

"I suggested the Casa Hacienda Resort and Spa across town, since I was an investor there and was familiar with it."

"You told me you'd never been there and knew nothing about it," I said.

"Yeah."

"I had a runner from my business go over with cash and book one of their best rooms for Saturday night, January fourth. I was hoping a nice place like that might put her in a frame of mind to get her to reconsider."

"I got there early to get everything just so."

"But you knocked before you went in, didn't you?" I asked.

He looked at me, a little confused, then you could see the light go on and he said, "Yes, I did, just in case she got there before I did. How did you know that?"

"Remember Mr. Whitlock, I have a witness."

"Oh, right."

I said all that because I wanted to remind him to tell us the truth—he didn't know how much I knew, but he at least knew I knew some stuff. His "deal" was contingent on him telling us the truth.

"So, I knocked; no one answered, so I used the pass key and went in. I got some music playing, opened the wine, and poured two glasses. I also adjusted the drapes and lights for the best look. I was there for almost an hour before Kate got there."

"When Kate got there, we sat and talked and enjoyed the wine, and things began to get romantic."

CHAPTER

— 104 —

Trent stepped in, "Mr. Whitlock, allow me to remind you that your agreement is contingent on you telling us the *truth* about what happened. Should we catch you in a lie, that deal goes out the window and you may find yourself on the receiving end of a needle. It would seem that is a high price to pay just so you can lie now."

"I would also point out," continued Cindy, "that you have literally nothing to gain by lying to us—your sentence of life without parole is set, it will not be reduced—but a lot to be lost if you lie. Remember, we have a witness and all the hard facts, that have to be explained or we'll *know* that you're lying to us."

You could see the conflict in ol' Nicky's face—he wasn't used to being "handled" like this, and he wanted to tell the story in his best light—but his very *life* was on the line. He took a moment to compose himself and decide what to do.

"Fine. Kate didn't even want to sit down—I had to beg her to even do that. She had a little of the wine, but I drank most of it—I was already a glass and a half into it by the time she got there."

"That's better," said Cindy.

"I started to tell her how I felt about her and beg her to reconsider, but she stopped me immediately and told me that there would never be anything between us and that I should be faithful to my wife and stop chasing her."

"Probably got that stuff from that stupid church!" he said with real venom.

"Anyway, that set me off—I didn't like her moralizing to me, and I told her so. She told me that it was up to me what I wanted to do, but that her only reason in coming here was to make it clear that this was over with regards to her and that I needed to step back and leave her alone."

Pause—deep breath.

"That really set me off. I couldn't believe that she wouldn't listen to me and change her mind. I got belligerent and told her that, and she got up and said she was leaving."

"I jumped up and grabbed her and she fought back. I picked her up and took her over to the bed and threw her on it. She tried to get back up, but I got on top of her. When she tried to scream, I covered her mouth."

Pause.

"Then I held her down and raped her."

You could *feel* the anger toward him in the room. I'm not sure, but I think even "Theodore" was mad.

"After I began, she kept fighting so strongly and scratching at me, that I started slamming her on the bed. I ended up slamming her head against the headboard and knocking her out."

"As she lay there, I panicked. I thought I might have seriously hurt her, my marriage, and my empire, and that my future political future might be put in jeopardy by this."

"So, I tried to figure out something quickly. I ran into the bathroom and started to run the water in the tub, then I took off all of Kate's clothes and carried her into the bathroom."

"I guess the water was a little too cold—when I went to put her in the tub, she came around and stared right up at me. I think she quickly realized what I was going to do and started fighting and scratching me again."

Deep breath.

"So, I held her down under the water while she fought to get out. I held her there until she stopped."

He just sat there, slumped over.

"What did you do then?" asked Trent.

He startled, like out of a stupor.

"Oh. Well, the water had gone everywhere and was running over, so I turned off the water and got all the towels. I sopped up the mess and then wiped down all the surfaces in the bathroom."

"I then went out to the rest of the suite and wiped down everywhere I'd been. I piled all the towels in the corner of the bathroom, got all of my stuff, grabbed the wine glass I'd used, and quietly slipped out of the room, leaving the 'do not disturb' sign on the door."

It seemed that he was done.

"Is that all Mr. Whitlock?" Cindy asked.

"Yes, that's all."

She looked around the room to see if everyone was satisfied with what they heard, and then called in the officers to take Mr. Whitlock to jail.

Kate's murderer was found and would be punished—about as much "justice" as could be expected in this world.

CHAPTER

— 105 —

The three of us sat in the conference room and just stared off into space, thinking about what had just happened.

We got the perp. For all of his wealth and arrogance, he was now headed for temporary lockup and then, after the judge signed the final agreement, off to a maximum-security penitentiary. When this hit the news, it was going to blow up all around the country.

We could only hope that Mr. money, power, and prestige, would be treated with the upmost respect by all the "got nothing to live for" prisoners who will surround him.

Did that sound snarky? If it didn't, I meant for it to—maybe I'll need to work a little on my delivery.

Trent was the first to break the silence. "Well, my man, this is what we live for—this moment right here."

"It's sweet, isn't it?" I asked.

"That it is."

"I gotta thank you Trent. If you hadn't been willing to at least let me take a shot at this, none of this could have happened."

"You're right—I'm a good guy, aren't I?"

"Well, let's not get carried away."

Trent chuckled.

"You did good work Blake—*real good* work."

"Thanks Trent, I appreciate it." And I did.

"If you ever decide you want to get out of all this P.I. stuff, let us know, I wouldn't mind having you on our team."

"That's nice Trent, but I don't think I could handle having to follow all the rules you guys have to deal with."

"You make a good point—now that I think about it, I don't think you could either," he said, laughing.

"So, are you outta here?" he asked.

I stood up, spread my feet out in a stance with my hands on my waist, and said with a low voice, "Yes lad, my work here is done."

Think classic Superman moment—but from an Ironman perspective.

Trent just shook his head at me.

I think Cindy thought it was funny.

"Well, I'd better get out of here. It *is* Sunday after all, and I'm supposed to be hanging out with Trent II and Jess—maybe I can catch them for a little while before bed."

"Alright, I'll see you."

Then Trent did something that surprised me—he came over and gave me a hug! Now *that* was weird!

"Seriously man, you did good. And I'm glad that you *didn't get dead*."

Trent was getting a little emotional on me—and I was feeling it now. Be strong, man of steel, be strong!

"Thanks."

Trent lumbered out of the conference room, and it was just Cindy and me now.

"So, Mr. 'my work here is done,' now that you're heading back to 'the big city' soon, what do you think about 'us'?"

Whoa, Cindy does *not* mess around—get right to the point girl!

"Well ma'am," (imitating any number of cowboys from any number of old westerns), "I was hoping you'd see fit to join me in a late dinner tonight, before I have to be skedaddling outta this town."

Cindy just gave me dead eyes.

"Cut the cowboy schtick Blake and answer the question."

Whoa, somebody was wanting to talk serious!

"OK. I was hoping that since Phoenix is only about an hour and a half away, just maybe you'd be willing to continue to see me on a regular basis."

"I would," she said, after pausing and thinking.

"Awesome," I said immediately, realizing I had been holding my breath a little when she paused.

"In that case, I would love to take you up on your offer of dinner tonight," Cindy said.

"Well, Cindy Lou Who—it would be an honor."

That got me daggers. I just smiled back.

But we did just that. We had some great food and a great time and made some real plans to continue to see each other.

This trip had really turned out great. We got the bad guy, when the bad guy was *not* going to be "gotten" without our effort.

I got the girl—and she was something special.

I was going to get a good night's sleep tonight—one last time at The Hermosillo on Greg Walker's dime.

I was going to get to call Greg and Johnnie tomorrow and give them the full report about their sister. No one would call what I had to tell them "*good news*," but there was a certain justice and maybe a little closure in at least knowing what really happened. And especially knowing the perp didn't get away with murder—literally—and was going away for life without the possibility of parole.

At least I hoped that some "closure" would be in the cards for them.

More good news for Greg in that I hadn't spent his entire $5,000! However, I was going to see if I could deduct the cost of getting Black Beauty fixed—can't leave those bullet holes in her—and I'm pretty sure my insurance doesn't have a "weapons assault" clause. Even with that, this gig even paid pretty well.

I was even looking forward to getting back to my office. I was pretty sure that would only last until I got close enough to smell the stench of whatever concoction of animal pellets the cattle feed factory was creating this week! But you know what it's like—going "home" makes you forget certain things—even have fond thoughts—until your eyes start to water, the closer you get.

I might have to spend some time on my "thinking couch"—thinking about that—and while I'm at it, maybe a little about whether I keep *"we find stuff"* as my tagline or not.

RESOURCES

For free access to the seminar referenced in this book, "Facts Behind The Faith," please visit the author's website, www.daviemacbooks.com.

NOTE FROM THE AUTHOR:

If you loved this book, please tell everyone you know.
If you didn't, let's just keep that our little secret.

Davie Mac

Taken and Afraid

A Blake Moran Novel

A Preview

PROLOGUE

Where was she?!

Her head hurt and she was having trouble focusing.

And she was confused.

She had been with her mom and baby Abby in the store, and then her memory just got blurry.

But how did she get here?! And where was here?!

She was trying to clear her head when she heard a noise—a noise from above her. It was mostly dark where she was—the lights just showing enough to know that she had never been in this place before.

For some reason, she started to feel scared. What was going on? Where were her parents? What was this place?

Then the noise got louder—it was someone moving around above where she was. She wanted to scream for help, but something told her that would be a mistake.

Suddenly, there was the distinct noise of something being moved. Then, something was opening—it sounded like a door—but like a trap door in the ceiling above her.

She strained to see what was going on and suddenly, at the far end of the room, she saw some legs coming down a ladder. They paused as she heard the trap door being shut, and then down they came.

It was hard to see in the semi-dark, but a man turned toward her and stared at her. She had never seen him before.

He said, "Hi Skylar."

She screamed.

ABOUT THE AUTHOR

Davie Mac (aka David McAllister) is a resident of Tucson, Arizona, and has always been a big fan of the "whodunit" genre. David is currently working on the fifth book in this series and planning for a sixth. He is also a song writer, having written over 60 songs to date, he plays the drums in a band, and is an avid weightlifter. Professionally, David has been in Christian ministry for over 40 years, and founded and has pastored The Bridge Christian Church in Tucson for over 30 years. David and his wife Kimberly have seven children and fourteen grandchildren.

For more information about the author visit:
www.daviemacbooks.com

Other books by Davie Mac:

Printed in Dunstable, United Kingdom

75003189R00221